SHATTERED LANDS BOOK I

IN THE
SHADOW
OF LIONS

TRAVIS
STARNES

Maps available at
https://tstarnes.com/book-series/imperium/

Signup to get free previews of upcoming books before they're released at
http://tstarnes.com/preview-notification-newsletter/

Table of Contents

Chapter 1

Starhaven, Kingdom of Sidor

"The king is dead."

"What? When?" Aldric said, turning from the balcony, where he'd been lost in thought, watching the sprawling island city beneath him and the sparkling sea beyond.

"Not ten minutes ago. The sickness finally finished what the Lynesians started," his brother Edmund said, stepping onto the balcony.

Aldric sagged, leaning against the railing as the words hit home. For all of their eldest brother's faults, and they had been legion, he still loved the man. The Golden Lion had been a towering figure. It seemed impossible for him to be gone.

"Why didn't you send for me?" Aldric asked, getting ahold of himself.

"To do what? He's been hanging onto death for almost a month now. What would you have said that you haven't already? And what would it have mattered? He couldn't hear you. Grieving over our idiot brother and his recklessness won't bring him back."

"Mind your words," Aldric warned.

Edmund waved a hand dismissively and said, "I'll instruct the stewards to begin preparations for a receiving in the Grand Hall worthy of his station. Happy? Now, there are more important matters to be concerned about. Serwyn is destined for the throne, but he's barely out of childhood. He's going to need guidance, and we have a war to think about."

"What do you mean?" Aldric asked, eyes narrowing suspiciously.

"As the eldest, or at least eldest still living, I'll serve as regent and guardian for Serwyn until he comes of age."

"Serwyn *is* of age. He's fourteen, hardly a boy anymore. He doesn't need regency. Guidance, yes, but he's entitled to rule in his own name."

Edmund waved a hand, dismissing the thought.

"The law grants me regency until his coronation. We cannot afford to look weak now, not with men still in the field."

"I think the nobles will have something to say about your interpretation. Our brother is not even cold yet, and you're already plotting. You're only granted the right to maintain the kingdom, not a regency."

"The nobility will respect my decision. The boy is untested and needs guidance. Either way, you said yourself that I have the right to maintain the kingdom. We cannot hold Serwyn's coronation until after Gavric's receiving is done and the rites are finished. Until then, I have the responsibility, and the right, to ensure Sidor's strength. And I'll need your help."

"What kind of help?"

"I will stay in Starhaven with Serwyn, serving as his advisor. Since we can both agree that he is too inexperienced to lead men in war, you will go to Lynese and take command of our forces, finishing what Gavric started. They need a member of the family at their head and we've spent too much of the treasury on this foolishness already. We need to either defeat the Lynese or sue for peace. I don't care which, as long as this drain on the kingdom ends."

"I disagreed with him as much as anyone, but Gavric proved the war could be won. Maybe the scheme their emperor had with the Alchmara didn't warrant it, but he was right about needing to show Baudric he couldn't interfere with our lands. Walking away now will embolden the man."

"Fine, then win the war. I don't care. Just take care of it."

"But ..."

"No. As regent, this is my decision to make, and I've made it. One of us must go, and we both know who's better suited,"

Edmund said, pausing. "Unless you think it wise to let one of the other dukes lead the army?"

"Of course not," Aldric said.

Edmund had him in a box. He was correct when he said he had no mind for war. For every martial virtue Gavric had maintained, Edmund had focused on manipulation and politics. It had served him well, and during their brother's rule, he'd used it to strengthen their house, but it did not suit him to lead men into combat.

"Then it's settled," Edmund said, turning and leaving as abruptly as he'd come.

William brought up the wooden training sword, parrying the slash with a quick turn of the wrist, the clack of wood on wood echoing across the empty courtyard. It had been a spirited attack, but clumsy. He and his cousin Serwyn might be the same age, but William was the superior swordsman. That wasn't just his own ego speaking. The sword master had said as much several times, although tactfully enough to keep from being on the receiving end of his cousin's ire, which wasn't an easy feat.

William was far less tactful and couldn't repress a smile as he countered his cousin's attack, pushing him back on the defensive. Serwyn grew increasingly frustrated, his defense becoming wild and uncontrolled. William watched Serwyn carefully, reading his body language and predicting his next move. As Serwyn lunged, attempting to regain the momentum, he overextended his reach. William sidestepped it and landed a stinging blow to Serwyn's back.

His cousin stumbled forward, barely keeping his feet under him, whirling to face him, his cheeks reddened by exertion and anger.

"You got lucky," Serwyn spat, clutching his training sword tightly.

William said nothing. It had not been luck, and they both knew it. What really added insult to injury was that Serwyn trained for hours every day under the best weapon masters in the kingdom, while William had to make do with whatever guardsman might be available to work with him.

Any time he asked for better tutors, his stepfather had demurred, claiming other obligations came first. Not that William didn't train as hard or as often, but much of that was alone, against practice dummies, working things out on his own.

Which didn't sit well with his cousin any time they sparred and William won. Serwyn launched himself forward with a roar, swinging his wooden sword toward William's ribs. William pivoted deftly to the side, Serwyn's blade whizzing past him with inches to spare. The duel had been going on for some time now, and Serwyn's attacks were growing increasingly reckless as frustration took hold.

After a quick flurry of strikes and counters, William spotted an opening in Serwyn's defense. He feinted left, then as Serwyn moved to block, he ducked low and swept his leg out, knocking Serwyn's feet out from under him. His cousin hit the ground hard, his sword clattering away across the stones.

William reached down to offer his cousin a hand up, but Serwyn slapped it away, letting out a strangled cry of rage as he leaped to his feet. William had put his sword into his offhand, assuming the match was over. It wasn't until the last second that he noticed his cousin had taken a handful of dirt, and was unable to move as Serwyn flung it into his face.

William stumbled back, temporarily blinded as the grit stung his eyes. He scrubbed at them furiously, cursing under his breath. He barely managed to clear it in time to block Serwyn's attack.

"Not so good now, are you?" Serwyn snarled.

"If you think cheap tricks will help you win, you're more a fool than I thought," he shot back, blinking away the last of the dirt and gripping his sword tightly.

Serwyn let out a bellow and charged forward, but William was ready. He parried a wild swing and delivered three quick blows - one knocking the sword from Serwyn's hand, the next to his ribs, and the last squarely on his back, sending him sprawling once more.

Panting, William stood over his cousin with the tip of his sword hovering just above Serwyn's heaving chest.

"Do you yield?" he asked sharply.

Serwyn's face twisted in anger and humiliation. He spat in the dirt but said nothing.

William shook his head in disgust, stepping back and lowering his practice blade. "I'll take that as a 'yes.'"

"I don't yield to peasants, not even a jumped-up one like you. You're not even a real Whitton."

"Real enough to know your father would never take a cheap shot like that. If you want to be king one day, you need to figure that out. It's pathetic."

He knew he was baiting Serwyn, but the shot about not being a real Whitton cut deep. Even though his stepfather had officially named William his heir, he always felt like he wasn't a real member of the family. An insecurity Serwyn picked up on a long time ago and used when he wanted to hurt William.

The baiting worked. Serwyn's face darkened even further, and his fists tightened. Though he knew Serwyn was about to throw a punch, he also knew that he couldn't give the spoiled prince the beating he truly deserved. Not with his stepfather likely to take Serwyn's side if things escalated. The last thing William wanted was to be sent to the high tower, tasked with cleaning quills and binding pages under the watchful eye of the Disciples. He'd rather face an angry sand lizard than endure that tedium.

When Serwyn reared back, William deftly stepped out of reach. His cousin's wild swing met only air. Before he could regain his balance, William darted back in and grabbed Serwyn's wrist, twisting just enough to send him sinking to his knees with a grunt of pain.

"Don't," William said sharply.

Serwyn's face contorted, torn between rage and pain. Just as it seemed he might wrench free and renew his attack, or William would have to commit and really hurt him, a commanding voice cut through the courtyard.

"That's enough!"

Both young men turned to see William's stepfather, Edmund, striding toward them, annoyance etched across his face. Though not a warrior by nature, William's stepfather nevertheless cut an imposing figure in his rich doublet and cloak, a silver circlet resting upon his golden curls. His handsome face was creased into a deep frown as he looked between his nephew and stepson.

"Let him go, William," Edmund snapped. After a pause, he repeated the command more firmly. "Now!"

With a frustrated sigh, William released Serwyn and stepped back, shooting his cousin a warning look. Serwyn slowly climbed to his feet, embarrassment warring with resentment in his blue eyes as he clutched his sore wrist.

Edmund looked them over critically before speaking again, "You're not a child anymore, William. Brawling like this is beneath you."

William bit his tongue. Of course, he blamed him. It didn't matter that it took two people to fight, or that Serwyn had thrown the first punch. All that mattered was William was there, which meant he was at fault.

"I came here with serious news to discuss, so let's put this behind us for now. Although, if I see it again, there will be punishments. Clear?"

"Yes, Father," William said, looking down.

"Good. I'm sorry to be the one to tell you, nephew, but your father is dead. Even though we all knew this day was coming soon, ever since his ship landed and we saw his condition firsthand, I know it still comes as a shock. I'll understand if you need a moment," Edmund said in a gentle voice William had never heard directed at him.

For Serwyn's part, he seemed barely bothered by the news. There was no outpouring of grief or anguish from the prince over his father's passing. True, the news wasn't a complete shock, not with how long the great king had been lingering on the brink of death, but William had expected more. Who knows what was going on inside of Serwyn's head, but to William, it seemed he was more annoyed at the interruption to his sparring than sad to hear his father had just died.

For William, it was as if someone had punched him in the stomach. He'd always idolized his uncle, who regaled him with battles and adventures when he was younger. Gavric inspired him. Made him want to be better. And now he was gone.

"Take some time, and then we need to start discussing your coronation. You're going to be king, but there's much to do before you're crowned officially."

"I'm ready," Serwyn said.

"You will make a fine king. I have no doubt," Edmund said, clasping a hand to Serwyn's shoulder and steering him out of the courtyard without another glance at William.

Serwyn suddenly glanced back at William, his blue eyes cold. A slight, cruel smile curved his lips in an unmistakable threat. A promise to punish his cousin for past grievances, real or imagined.

William barely registered the glance, wiping away a tear that had started to form, fighting the grief that threatened to consume him.

Chapter 2

Though it had been several days since his father delivered the news, William was still unsettled by his uncle's passing. Once again secluded in his rooms, he grappled with the loss, trying to make sense of what it was going to be like now that the king was gone.

Gavric had been the closest thing to a real father William had had in his life. Edmund may have adopted William shortly after marrying his mother, but that had been a dynastic play. William's mother was young when they married, so Edmund expected to have trueborn children to supersede William, and only adopted William to help strengthen his place in the line of succession. Bastards, which children from previous marriages tended to be treated as, were never spoken of, leaving little tradition to guide how they should be dealt with in inheritance.

Fate had a will of its own, though. No one could have foreseen the fever that took her. Since then, Edmund kept his distance, choosing to ignore William whenever possible, and barely tolerating him when that wasn't an option.

Gavric, on the other hand, had taken a genuine interest in mentoring William, taking him to tournaments and even arranging the occasional training session for him. It was one of the reasons he and Serwyn never got along. Though William never intentionally slighted his cousin, Serwyn seemed to resent William for stealing his father's attention. William never knew why Gavric and his son were so distant, but he certainly had never done anything to slander his cousin.

Now Gavric was dead, Serwyn would be king, and William had lost the only ally he'd ever really had. His thoughts returned to his uncle. He recalled Gavric's booming laugh and the sparkle in his eye when the sword master would knock William down to show him an error. He remembered the amazing warrior on the jousting field, defeating knights ten years his junior. But most of all, he remembered the kindness beneath Gavric's gruff exterior.

A knock interrupted his melancholy train of thought. Before he could respond, Edmund entered, sweeping into the room. William rose to greet him properly, having learned a long time ago the penalty for not showing the proper deference.

"Still mourning, I see," Edmund said coolly, looking at William.

William clenched his fists but held his tongue. The words may have been benign, but the indifference in Edmund's tone betrayed his true feelings, or lack thereof, about his brother's death.

Edmund continued, oblivious to William's anger. "The vigil ends tonight. Tomorrow you will swear fealty to Serwyn, and then you will begin preparations to join your Uncle Aldric when he sails to reinforce our armies in Lynese."

"Yes, Father," William said, trying to keep his face neutral.

He failed, unable to hide his displeasure of being sent off or having to swear fealty to his cousin.

"Don't give me that look. If you are to succeed me, or even become a baron in your own right, you must learn to lead men. You're old enough to come out from hiding behind tutors and wet nurses and begin to learn like a real man. Hell, when I was your age, I'd already been a squire for two years."

While that all seemed reasonable, William wasn't fooled. Edmund had never made a secret of his desire for power, and he'd seen his adoptive father with Serwyn enough times to work out how he intended to get it. As much as he ignored and dismissed William, he coddled Serwyn, quick to find a reason to accompany his nephew on this or that errand. Always offering to help and advise him. Gavric, who'd always had a soft spot for his brother and seemed unable to notice his more power-hungry side, had always acted as if it was a favor and was glad for the help.

Now that Gavric was out of the way and he could become more overt in his courting of Serwyn, Edmund didn't need a little thing like an unwanted heir hanging around, mucking up the process. Maybe he even hoped the Lynesians would do him a favor and solve the problem of William for him.

"The ports should be clear of ice in about three weeks, and Aldric will be sailing at the first opportunity. Talk to your tutors, take what you need, but I want you on that ship when it leaves. If you have any questions, talk to Aldric."

Edmund turned and left as abruptly as he came, not waiting for a reply from William. Alone again, William sighed and sank back onto his bed. His uncle's funeral would be held tomorrow, the final farewell before he was burned on the pyre. William had no desire to see Gavric's body consumed by flames, even if it was tradition.

William had never given it much thought before as to why the ceremony around death happened like it did. When his mother passed, he'd been young and so sad that he hadn't been able to think about it beyond the agony of knowing she was gone. When Gavric had turned ill, however, his tutors had decried it as a good opportunity to teach him about their history and why the tradition was done in the way it was.

According to them, it all went back to the time of magic, before the great cataclysm that wiped that power from the world and split the land into three continents. They'd explained that people, especially kings, were burned so that their energy could become part of the bloodline, empowering their descendants with their knowledge and wisdom. While William was skeptical that had ever been true, let alone still held any meaning, traditions died hard. While most people would bury or scatter their loved ones' ashes, following the burning, the ashes of kings and great men were preserved in ornate urns in crypts and mausoleums. When William asked his tutors why, they didn't have a real answer, offering only maybes and ifs.

Now, William didn't care. Tomorrow, his uncle would be gone, reduced to ash, and William would be alone.

The great bell rang in the city square, sounding the beginning of the night watch. Families would be gathering for meals, offering up prayers to their ancestors to watch over them. William wasn't hungry and had no desire to sit at the table and watch his father dote over Serwyn. He decided instead to head to the Grand Hall to see Gavric one last time.

William chose to give the guards assigned to protect him, as was custom for all the royal family while in the capital, the slip. Maybe not the smartest thing, but most had been handpicked by Edmund while the king was off at war, and they were almost certainly instructed to inform on his activities to his stepfather. While it wasn't exactly wrong that he'd visit his uncle's body lying in state, it would be out of the norm at this time of the night, especially after the conversation he and his stepfather had just had.

Thankfully, the streets between the palace and the Grand Hall were only lightly filled with people, making his journey to the massive building quick and hassle-free. Although the market was not far from the main thoroughfare that ran between the palace and the Grand Hall, the merchants had all closed-up shop, and those patrons who didn't go to their families for dinner had moved off to the far eastern side of town, where the bulk of taverns and brothels could be found.

William entered the vast expanse of the Grand Hall, marveling as always at the unearthly pristine white floors, remnants and reminders of the amazing skills of the ancients. Despite having little interest in books or scholarly pursuits, he couldn't help but be awed by the sheer scale and grandeur of the ancient structure. Tall marble pillars lined the hallway, reaching up to support arched ceilings painted with intricate murals depicting scenes from a long-ago age.

Acolytes garbed in simple gray robes, many with arms full of crumbling leather tomes and cracked scrolls, were still wandering the halls, coming in and out of side passages. Their hushed voices and shuffling steps lent an air of solemnity to the space as they went about whatever their daily tasks were. While his tutors had covered the acolytes and their preservation of history, the only part William ever paid attention to was when the lectures turned to the seekers, who roamed the kingdoms in search of artifacts from the age of magic. It was impossible not to daydream about mystical swords and powerful amulets while his tutor droned on, even though that almost always ended in a rap on the knuckles for not paying adequate attention.

Finally, he reached the massive central chamber where the body of the king lay in state upon a raised marble dais. Kneeling on the cool white floor next to the catafalque, William bowed his head. This was why he was here, to pay his respects, and seeing the shroud-covered body was enough to focus William's thoughts. In the morning, Gavric would be taken to his final resting place, and William would only be able to visit his tomb, never able to see the man again.

"He would be pleased to see you keeping vigil by his side," came a quiet voice next to William, jolting him from his reverie.

He looked up to see his Uncle Aldric settling down on his knees beside him, golden hair falling across kind yet weary eyes. William just nodded. Being here, seeing his uncle's body, made the feelings of loss all the more real, and a lump had formed in William's throat.

"I'm surprised to see you here this late," Aldric said. "Isn't it time for your evening devotional?"

"I thought ... I could do it here just as well as at the sacellum," William said, referring to the small shrine most homes, even palaces and castles, kept for household members and guests to pay respects to the ancients.

"How are you holding up?" Aldric asked gently, placing a hand on William's shoulder.

"I'm not sure. Everything is changing, and ... I don't know. It feels like the world is crumbling around me. Did you know Father is sending me with you to Lynese? To the war?"

"Yes, he told me," Aldric said. "Are you worried?"

"No. Yes. I don't know. I know it won't be like the practice rings. And I've never been outside of Starhaven before, except on trips to visit Father's vassals. But then we had his retainers and guards. This is ... different."

"It's normal to feel fear when facing the unknown," Aldric said. "You know what the ancients taught. That courage isn't the absence of fear but pressing on in spite of it."

William only nodded again. He'd read the testaments, as every noble child was made to do, and he knew of the virtues. Reading about them and having to face them in real life, however, were not the same thing.

"Did you know Gavric hated battle? He always said it was a waste of resources and lives and saw it as proof that he'd failed in his duties to negotiate on behalf of his people."

"But ... the king was the greatest warrior I've ever seen," William said, surprised at the revelation. "He was winning the war. He won every fight he was in."

"Being good at something and thinking it right are not the same thing," Aldric pointed out. "It's much like bravery. You can exhibit qualities and have feelings that contradict those qualities. Everyone does. You can be brave and afraid at the same time, just as you can be a good general and hate the idea of war."

"Father is just trying to get rid of me," William said, finally putting his real fear into words.

"I'm not going to defend my brother's decisions or actions," Aldric said. "I know the two of you do not have the best relationship, and he has other things concerning him now that don't include you. I imagine that's hard on a young man, and there isn't anything I can say to ease what you must be feeling. I will say that your best choice is to focus on what's in front of you. Whatever his motivations, he's done you a favor."

"How?" William asked incredulously.

"Did you know I went on my first campaign when I was about your age? Gavric was leading one of our father's armies. He was just shy of twenty at that time, but already he'd shown his genius on the battlefield. The storm over the maw had been huge that year, and our father sent us to help deal with the Chaosborn that had escaped it and were plaguing the western reaches of the Shadowhold. I wasn't just worried, as you are now. I was terrified. But Gavric took me under his wing and taught me to control my fear. He taught me the nature of war and how to do what must be done while not losing myself and what I believed in."

"And that's what you're supposed to do for me?"

"Well, it's what I'll try to do. I don't think I could live up to the example that Gavric set for me, but I will do my best. Ignore your issues with your father for now and just focus on learning the lessons you need to learn. This is a great opportunity, and I think you're smart enough to take advantage of it."

William fell silent, gnawing on his lip as he thought.

"I miss him so much," William finally confessed in a small voice. "I ... I always wished he'd been my father instead."

"I understand, and I miss him too. It's good that we keep him in our thoughts, but dwelling on our grief achieves nothing. We must look to the future now."

"What future?" William burst out bitterly. "Serwyn's taking the throne? You haven't lived with him, spending every day with him like I have. He's cruel and petty. His favorite game is to see how miserable he can make the servants, always trying to get them beaten for doing things he made up. And he hates me the most, more than I think he's ever hated anyone. As soon as he's crowned, he's going to get even for all the times I beat him on the practice fields or made him look foolish."

"I don't think it will be that easy," Aldric said, holding up a placating hand. "No matter how Edmund feels about you, you are still heir to King's Heart and the only son of the regent. You have a lot of power in your own right, or you will one day. You'll also be leagues away on the other side of the Straight of Terrors, and he'll have other things on his mind."

"But imagine what he's going to be like for the kingdom," William argued.

"We don't know what kind of king Serwyn will become. He's young and still finding himself, just as you are. He has people advising him, steering him on how to be a leader. We should give him the chance to show how he will adapt and change with that guidance," Aldric said, although William thought he didn't sound as convinced of that as he had of the other things he said.

"He has my stepfather as a mentor," William pointed out. "And I'm not sure power won't just make him worse."

"Perhaps. Perhaps not. As his vassal, I am bound to follow him, as you will be one day. That can't be helped. Besides, history has a way of dealing with kings who treat their people badly," Aldric said, before shaking off the moment and looking back to William. "What you can do is ensure that when you take your place, you do the best you can. You do the best for your people when you become a ruler in your own right."

"How? How can I do right by anyone if my king is evil?"

"A king has a lot of power, true, but he doesn't control the daily fate of the average Sidorian. The dukes and barons are who the people deal with on a daily basis. They protect their people, ensure their communities are safe and run well, and maintain the peace. Now is the time for you to learn how to best do that. This could be an opportunity for you, a chance to learn leadership away from the toxic politics of the palace."

William scowled, "I long to fight as much as the next man, but how can war teach me to govern?"

"War is more than just killing," Aldric said. "It's strategy, planning, logistics, and organization. It's leadership. Qualities that every good leader needs, king or not. And you won't just be with lords and nobles on the battlefield. You'll get to know the soldiers. Soldiers that come from all walks of life and are more like the people you will lead than anyone you might meet in the palace. That experience will serve you well in the future."

"I guess I never considered that."

Aldric smiled, "A smart leader draws wisdom from many wells. Book learning is important, but practical experience is just as important. This campaign will give you that, which is a rare gift. Make the most of it."

William just nodded, thinking about what Aldric had said, only looking back up when Aldric broke the silence.

"Did you know Gavric spoke of you often?"

"He did?"

"Oh, yes," Aldric said, smiling sadly. "He was so proud of you. 'That boy has the makings of greatness,' he'd say. He regretted leaving you behind when he went to war and thought you'd do well on the campaign when you got older. I think he was even contemplating bringing you with him after this winter ended, before he was injured, of course."

"I didn't know that."

"No. My brother was many things, but he wasn't good at telling people what he was thinking. He had a bad habit of surprising people, be it good or bad news. It had its uses, playing things so close to his chest, but it caused him problems too."

"I won't fail him," William vowed solemnly. "Or you."

"I know you won't," Aldric said, patting him on the shoulder and standing, giving his brother one last look.

William looked at the king's shroud-covered form as well, thinking about what Aldric had said. He could do it. If Gavric had thought to take him on a campaign this year, and Aldric was right about what he needed to learn, then William would do whatever it took to learn the lessons his uncle would teach him.

He'd learn how to do right by both of them.

The Shimmering Palace, Valemonde, Empire of Lynese

In the opulent heart a majestic lake side palace, Baudric Montbore the eight, Emperor of Lynese, sat at the head of the ornate dining table, savoring thin slices of venison. His rotund form overflowed the intricately carved chair, its detailed etchings narrating the conquests and betrayals of his forebears.

To his right sat Baudric the Ninth, his eleven-year-old heir, fidgeting slightly, bored as his eldest sister, Viviane, recited her latest poetry for anyone who cared to listen, which notably didn't include her father, who'd tuned her out almost immediately. Next to Baudric sat his sister Isolde, who was leaning over, whispering to her brother, trying to cajole him into eating instead of playing with his food. Although she was only sixteen and the youngest of the emperor's daughters, she had always been the most serious, taking on the parenting role of her deceased mother.

Their other sisters also ignored Viviane's poetry. They all found the eldest sibling equally pompous, preferring equally vapid discussions of fashion and boys at court. Not that it ever stopped Viviane from attempting to share whatever her newest work might be.

The emperor ignored all of this, of course. Although he'd known part of his duty was to sire an heir, he'd never imagined it would result in so many daughters before he finally got the male he'd actually wanted. Worse than being women, they were worthless. Well, that wasn't entirely fair. Isolde had potential. Of all his children, she had the most potential. Clever, curious, and ambitious, she would have made a fitting heir if she'd been born a man.

Unfortunately, she wasn't. Worse, since he hadn't seen her as being valuable, he'd left her in the charge of his wife and her tutors, who'd taken the girl's curiosity and wit and warped it with notions of charity and weakness. It wasn't until later, when he'd realized her potential, that Baudric had stepped in and attempted to right their wrongs. She'd never be able to rule, but if she could be disabused of her weaker notions, she might be useful to her brother. It was still too soon to tell what kind of man the boy would be, but it was clear he'd never be as strong as his sister, but he wasn't hopeless either.

The emperor was still considering his children in between mouthfuls of the highly spiced meat when the heavy doors to the dining room groaned open, admitting Lord Agravaine, his first minister and head of his Imperial's Council, who hurried across the large room, clearly agitated.

"Your Imperial Majesty," Agravaine said, bowing deeply before his emperor. "A wyvern just arrived with an urgent message from one of our agents in Starhaven."

"Yes," the emperor said when Agravaine didn't say anything else.

"The Golden Lion is dead."

"Are you sure?"

"He is our most reliable agent, Exalted One, and we've known of the king's illness for some time. Yes. I believe it's true."

"Gods," the emperor whispered.

He'd been ready to chastise his minister for interrupting him during dinner. This, however, was news worthy of an interruption. Gavric, the Golden Lion, had been a thorn in his side since he'd risen to power not long after Baudric's own ascension. Unlike Gavric's own father, who'd been a weak man, Gavric had been strong, decisive, and worst of all, diplomatic. The Sidorians' greatest weakness was their barons, nobles given too much power, in Baudric's own estimation, constantly infighting among each other.

Gavric had shown the rare ability to corral all of their avarice and greed, directing them as he saw fit. If it wasn't for Gavric, their current war probably would never have happened. His father, certainly, wouldn't have been able to get all of the barons to contribute knights and yeomen to make up the army that currently sat on the eastern coast of Lynese, threatening his entire empire.

His death signaled a chance for him to finally end this war, and perhaps even extract victory from it.

"Your Imperial Majesty," Agravaine said, "we should seize this opportunity and strike the Sidorian armies now, while they are leaderless. Drive them back through the Narrows before they can regain their footing."

Baudric leaned back and stroked his fat neck with one hand, thoughtfully. It would be nice to push their armies into the cursed waters separating their two continents. Nice, but impractical.

"I appreciate your bold approach, but that would be an idiotic choice. The Sidorian army still outnumbers ours, at least until Nicolas returns from Thay. If he's successful in securing their assistance, or at the very least their mercenaries, then maybe. Until then, we would be throwing our men to slaughter. The king may be dead, but their generals are not. Every report we've received suggests both Alistar Everwood and Rowan Pembroke earned their reputations through skill, not mere chance."

After stopping to swirl his wine, taking a large drink, the emperor continued, "No, we must be smart. You're right that their king's death presents an opportunity, but we must determine how best to use it. While we still cannot face them in open battle, we can apply pressure. Perhaps enough to force them to negotiate on our terms."

To Baudric's surprise, Isolde, who he'd all but forgotten about once the news was delivered, spoke up, interrupting his thoughts.

"Father, why not try to negotiate with their new king, once one has been crowned? Save lives through diplomacy rather than more bloodshed?"

Baudric scowled, "Because that would give them time to stabilize. For their new king, or more likely his advisors, since the child Serwyn is next in line to the throne, to rein in the barons and reestablish control. Even if we tried to negotiate now, they would stall us until they ended up on better footing. No, that would be foolish indeed."

"But, they're already fighting because they believe you were attempting to get the Alchmara to raid their villages from the north. If we attempt to take advantage of this and apply pressure like you said, wouldn't it breed more resentment? Make them more determined to continue fighting rather than negotiate for peace?"

"You fail to grasp the intricacies of ruling, child. War is not so simple as you imagine," the emperor said, frowning at her before turning to his advisor. "Send word to our allies in the north. Tell them the time has come to increase pressure on Sidor's barons. Sow seeds of unrest; turn them against this fledgling king. Either their petty squabbles will tear the kingdom apart or, at the very least, force them to accept concessions."

"Yes, sire," Agravaine said with a bow before rushing out as quickly as he had come in.

"Please, reconsider," Isolde pleaded, her voice rising in frustration. "This is just going to further stoke unrest, ultimately leading to more bloodshed for our people."

Baudric's scowl deepened at his daughter's continued protestations. "You're being naïve. This is why women should never rule. You're weak-willed and soft, unable to understand the sacrifices that must be made for the sake of our empire."

"The empire, or your ambition," Isolde shot back.

"You go too far, girl," he growled, his face going purple with rage. "Remove yourself before you sour my appetite further."

Biting back angry tears, Isolde rose and hurried from the hall, the swish of her skirts punctuating her undignified exit. He watched her with pitiless eyes. He knew she might hate him now, but it was for her own good. Her compassion was a weakness he must purge, if she was ever going to be of use to the empire. She would learn in time the harsh necessities of power.

Or perhaps not. Either way, it mattered little. If she didn't get in line, she still had value. He could ensure a vassal's loyalty by bargaining her as a wife.

One way or another, she would serve the empire.

Chapter 3

Starhaven, Kingdom of Sidor

William stood among the gathered nobility in the Grand Hall of Starhaven, waiting for Serwyn's coronation to begin. The cavernous hall had changed since William's last visit, when he paid his final respects to Serwyn's father. It was, if anything, more grandiose than it had been for Gavric's lying in state, lavishly decorated for the occasion. Banners emblazoned with the royal crest hung from the vaulted ceiling, and braziers etched with intricate scrollwork stood at attention along the perimeter, bathing the coronation dais in a bright, warm light.

Normally, these halls would be arranged for the winter solstice, as people gathered to mark the middle of the long winter, halfway to the end of the Mawseason, when the great rent in the world released so much of its evil spawn, causing havoc up and down the coast of the three great continents; Sidor, Lynese and Thay. Which made it no surprise that Serwyn would have chose this for his coronation day. He couldn't stand anyone, or anything, but himself being the center of attention. William wouldn't have been surprised if he turned Blessing's Day into Serwyn's day.

The crowd of noblemen, court favorites, and lords and ladies mingled in the expanse in front of the dais, their low conversations melding into a single murmuring hum that echoed off the stone walls and high arched ceilings.

There were no commoners present at the coronation, judged as unfit to see the man who would guide their futures given the crown. William hadn't been born when Gavric was crowned, but he knew the coronation always happened in the Grand Hall, under the watchful eye of the Acolytes, who trotted out every piece of the remaining magic they'd been able to put their hands on for the occasion.

Part of William wondered why this didn't happen in front of the Grand Hall, where some commoners might get a chance to see it, although it was no surprise to him that Serwyn wouldn't want that. While Serwyn thought everyone was beneath him, he definitely had a prejudice against the 'mob' as he and William's father called the average citizen of Sidor.

For their part, the high-born that were allowed to attend were in high spirits. A new king meant new opportunities. Gavric had been a great king, at least in William's eyes, but not all the lords felt the same way. William figured every ruler made their fair share of enemies, as was the inevitable result of politics, but Gavric had seemed to go out of his way to make them. Or maybe the assembled throng was excited because Serwyn was so young. Gavric had been on the throne a long time and had cemented his authority early in his reign. Perhaps they felt Serwyn would be more malleable to their machinations or, at the very least, their bribes.

William scoffed at that idea. If they thought that was the case, they were mistaken. Not because Serwyn wasn't for sale, but because he was already bought. William's father already had his claws sunk deep into his nephew, and William doubted any of the barons or even the other dukes would have enough strength to pull those talons free. And it would only get worse the more time Edmund spent with Serwyn.

William was pulled out of his thoughts when the constant murmur began to die off. It didn't happen all at once. Even the rich and powerful had a pecking order, and some members were further to the sides of the grand hall, with less visibility to see what was happening than those along the aisle or up front. William, at least, didn't have to worry about that. As a member of the royal family, he was up on the lowest level of the dais, on the far-right side, standing next to his uncle Aldric.

From his vantage point, he had a clear view as the crowd turned to look toward the entrance of the Grand Hall as Serwyn made his way through the towering stone archway, his pace measured and deliberate, shoulders pulled back in practiced regality. His blond hair was perfectly coiffed, and the ermine mantle of state rested across his shoulders, the pure white fur standing out starkly against his black tunic. Behind him marched a procession of guards and advisors, the sound of their metal armor and boots absorbed by the miraculous mystical flooring of the Grand Hall.

William watched as Serwyn ascended the dais. He was a little impressed that his cousin, whom William knew to be a coward deep in his heart, showed no trace of nervousness. His blue eyes were cold as they swept over the family. Even William had to admit he fit the kingly mold, at least outwardly.

As he took his place in front of the throne, the seemingly ancient Elder of Sidor, draped in the grey robes of his order, shuffled slowly from his position on the left side of the dais, with the crown of Sidor cradled reverently in his hands. Stopping in front of Serwyn, he lifted the crown high into the air as Serwyn knelt.

"I beseech the wisdom of the Ancients. Test your servant, Serwyn Whitton. Judge his soul and anoint him rightful ruler of Sidor," he said in a reedy voice, lowering the glittering crown onto Serwyn's golden head.

As he took a shuffling step back, just to the edge of the dais, the elder stretched out his hand, taking a knotted, wooden staff from an aide in the same grey cloak of the Acolytes, who rushed forward to hand it to him before disappearing again back behind the dais. The staff was covered in arcane symbols and glowed a deep blue. Lifting the staff high in the air, the elder brought it down, gently tapping the crown where it rested on Serwyn's bowed head.

A visible ripple of energy passed through Serwyn as the staff made contact, like the surface of a pond disturbed by a falling pebble, before spreading out across the entirety of the Grand Hall. As if in response, the white floors glowed a brilliant light, forcing everyone present to squint momentarily as the light flared, and then passed.

William watched, awestruck. It was the first real magic he had ever witnessed. The power of the Ancients, channeled through the Elder, validating Serwyn's right to rule. A king ordained and blessed with the mystical forces of old. It was a powerful ritual.

The Elder stepped back and proclaimed, "The Ancients proclaim you His Majesty King Serwyn Whitton, twenty-first of his line, Ruler of Shadowhold, Kingsheart, River Mark, Iron Keep and The Icelands, chosen of the Acolytes and defender of the Ancients, and true-born king of Sidor, it's land's and people! Glory to the Crown."

The gathered assembly bowed their heads and repeated the words.

"Glory to the Crown," William said, the words bitter on his tongue.

Serwyn lifted himself up, his back straight and chin held high, trying to keep his face stoic. William knew him well enough to see the expression under that stoic facade. He was loving the adulation.

"My loyal subjects," Serwyn began, his voice laden with practiced gravitas. "Together, we embark on a new era for the realm of Sidor. My father's war with Lynese will be brought to a swift and glorious end under my leadership. Even now, our armies prepare to leave their winter encampments to teach them once and for all the cost of meddling in Sidorian affairs."

The crowd erupted into raucous cheers and applause as his cousin paused for dramatic effect.

"But victory abroad is not enough," Serwyn continued. "Prosperity must also reign within our borders. We will usher in a new golden age for Sidor. Sidor will become the envy of nations, a beacon of culture, learning, and advancement that all will look upon with awe."

Murmurs of agreement rippled through the crowd. Serwyn allowed himself a small smile. He had them hooked, and he knew it.

"I pledge to you that under my reign, our kingdom shall rise to heights never before seen. We shall not merely be a powerful nation; we shall be an empire, a beacon of light in a world of darkness, bringing justice and prosperity."

"But this prosperity will not come easily. Sacrifices must be made. As your king, I will require your loyalty and support," his tone hardening ever so slightly. "Those who seek to undermine the Crown will suffer the consequences."

"Wise governance requires order," Serwyn went on. "Dissent will not be tolerated. The laws of Sidor have served us well for generations. Under my rule, they will be upheld without compromise. Justice will be swift, and those found guilty will face the King's judgment."

A slight unease rippled through the assembly. Justice under Gavric had been stern but fair. Serwyn's words hinted at a more draconian brand of rule.

Sensing the shift in mood, Serwyn adopted a more conciliatory tone, "In return, I promise prosperity only ever dreamt of. The rivers will teem with trade, united under the banner of Sidor. On the heels of our victory in Lynese, we will stand ready to claim our rightful place in this world. Our future shines bright with promise and glory!"

He lifted his hands skyward, eyes blazing with zealous fervor. Caught up in the moment, the crowd erupted into thunderous applause, the hesitation of a moment ago forgotten.

William did not join them. He knew Serwyn. His cousin didn't care for Sidor or its people. The only person Serwyn ever cared for was himself. He was vain, selfish, and cruel. Nothing he was saying sounded like anything he'd ever heard Serwyn say before, except for the part about 'Dissent will not be tolerated.' That sounded exactly like Serwyn.

Leaning over to speak low into his uncle Aldric's ear, William muttered, "My father's work, no doubt."

Aldric nodded almost imperceptibly, "Yes. He felt it best if Serwyn's first speech had the right tone."

"By tone, are you also including the stuff about loyalty, dissent, and swift justice?"

"That wasn't Edmund."

"I thought not. Demanding everyone do exactly what he says is Serwyn's hallmark."

"Careful, William," Aldric cautioned, his tone serious but not unkind. "Walls have ears, even here."

William opened his mouth to say something back, but seeing the look in his uncle's eyes, he just shut it again and nodded. Turning his attention back to his cousin, William joined in the polite applause as Serwyn's speech came to an end. He had to look away when his cousin gave his trademark smug, self-satisfied smile.

As much as he'd complained about being shipped off to Lynese, now he looked forward to it. Anything to get away from what was sure to become a cesspool as all the worst sorts courted Serwyn for favor or patronage.

Two days later, Serwyn watched as Edmund paced the length of the his private study, continuing to recite from a list of boring topics. As a place for lectures goes, the private study was a comfortable one, Serwyn guessed, though he'd still prefer to be anywhere else at the moment. Gone were the decorations of his father, the tapestries and the leather bound books. Serwyn had never thought the style befitted a warrior-king, which his father most certainly had been. He'd had them removed and replaced with a collection of weapons and armor his father had kept as trophies from his various victories. They weren't ceremonial, either. These were weapons taken from dead men's hands. Proper decoration for a true king, Serwyn thought.

"When holding court, you must greet each petitioner by their full title, no matter how lowly. Give each matter your full attention, but do not commit to any request outright. Tell them you will take their words under advisement," Edmund said.

Serwyn stifled a yawn.

"I know how to hold court, Uncle," Serwyn said with a hint of annoyance. "Father let me sit in on his councils since I was ten."

"There is a difference between observing and leading," Edmund replied, pacing again. "You are king now. Every word, every gesture carries consequences."

"I'm supposed to be down in the training pit, working with the master-at-arms. As the king, I'm going to be leading armies into battle. Shouldn't I be preparing for that instead of listening to the complaints of people who don't matter? My father wouldn't have wasted his time on this."

"Your father did this every time he was in court, as did your grandfather and your father's grandfather. I know it's tedious, but it's how ruling is done. A kingdom is not held together by the strength of its king's sword arm alone, your majesty. Yes, it's sometimes necessary, but more important is keeping your vassals not only in line but loyal. Hearing the commoners' petitions is for appearances, but hearing your dukes' and even their barons' concerns is key to maintaining the strength of the kingdom."

Serwyn scowled, "They should be loyal out of fear and respect for their rightful king!"

"That's true. Our house, between my duchy and your uncle Aldrich's, has the largest armies in the kingdom, and the crown has forces of its own, but we are not the totality of our empire's might. The other duchies still provide a large number of men currently called to your banner, and are a key source of revenue for paying the armies. Without them, we would find ourselves in a much weaker position."

"They grow too bold," Serwyn complained. "I should remind them of their duty. They swore oaths to our house, swore on the Ancients. I will not tolerate disloyalty. My father may have been tolerant of that, but I will not be."

Edmund paused his pacing and turned to face Serwyn directly, his expression growing serious.

"A sword can be an effective tool when wielded judiciously," Edmund replied, "but brute force alone risks turning those you seek to control into bitter enemies. There are other paths to power than outright domination."

Serwyn fell back in his seat. Everything he said, his uncle had a counter. He was king now, but it seemed like he had even less power than he did before. Everyone was always telling him what he needed to do, where he needed to be, what he should say, and what he couldn't do. He was sick of it.

"It won't be like that forever," Edmund continued. "The barons spend more time at each other's throats than complaining to the crown. They live for their petty squabbles. We just have to bide our time, find out who is loyal and who must be dealt with while they break their own bonds with each other. When they're fragmented and alone, we can remove those who refuse to submit to your will. If you prefer another tactic, then I, of course, serve at your pleasure. You've grown into a clever man, Serwyn, and I have no doubt you'll find a way to deal with their disloyalty that leaves the crown stronger than before."

Serwyn frowned. Maybe his uncle was right. His father had told him many times that a general leads more with his head than his sword. Of course, he would then go right out and fight on the front lines, covering himself in glory, but maybe his father hadn't meant that he was needed for the battlefield. Maybe he was trying to tell Serwyn how to deal with the barons. His father knew, after all, that Serwyn would follow him to the throne one day.

"Fine. We should handle the barons carefully. I agree with you, but what about the commoners? Surely what they think doesn't matter."

"It's less a matter of what they think than what we can convince them of, my king," Edmund said. "The peasants are easily led, but there are many of them and most of your soldiers come from peasant stock. Think of it less as caring what they think and more as finding the best way to use them. The mob is a tool and a powerful weapon, and if wielded properly, they can be a valuable tool against the barons. A good king knows the sword isn't the only weapon, and is often not even the strongest weapon."

Serwyn sat up, thinking about this. He liked training, but this ... His father, and even Uncle Edmund before his father died, never talked to him about these things. About how to control people, make them do what he wanted them to do.

"But how do you do that? How do you turn them against their barons?"

"That's the easy part. The mob's wants are simple. A little bread, a little coin, and they will forget their former allegiances. The mob's favor is fickle."

"Fine, I will listen to them, but there are things I need. I've tried to talk to several of the advisors you've given me, and everyone always tells me why we can't do this or why that isn't practical."

"Such as?" Edmund asked, raising an eyebrow.

"Expanding the royal armory, for one," Serwyn said firmly. "Everyone knows the finest weapons come from Lynese. Why is that? We control a third of their lands, so why are their artisans still there? We should have the greatest armors, the greatest craftsmen. People should want to come here, and not Lynese, if they want the best."

Edmund nodded slowly, "A reasonable request, though not cheap. Still, your reasoning is sound. You did promise a golden age, and what better way for people to see that? I'm certain funds could be arranged, and instructions could be sent to the army to find us the right artisans and convince them to adjust their loyalties. Excellent Serwyn. You're thinking like a true king, looking beyond the simple things lesser men notice, to the real truths."

Serwyn sat up a bit straighter. It had been an offhand comment, just the first thing he thought of, but as his uncle talked, Serwyn realized it actually wasn't a bad idea. He had, in fact, promised a golden age. True, his uncle had written that part, but that didn't make the sentiment bad.

"Very well," Serwyn conceded.

"Don't look so down. We'll keep the audiences short today and I'm sure we can find time for you to still get down to the training field. You're King after all, and you should be able to do what you want."

"It's about time someone realized that. I'd started to think I served all of you instead of the other way around."

"We're always happy to see to your wishes, sire. As your advisors, though, we'd be remiss if we didn't try to give you the best advice we could. I, for one, want your reign to be a long and powerful one."

"Okay, let's get this over with," Serwyn said.

Chapter 4

Starhaven, Kingdom of Sidor

Three weeks after the coronation, William found himself walking up the gangplank of a massive ship, hugging himself tight against the chill winter air. William had thought he'd have more time before his step-father shipped him off to Lynese, what with ice still floating in the harbor, but as soon as the Blessings day ceremonies ended, Edmund had declared that, now that the Maw was closed, it was time for him and his Uncle Aldric to get started.

"The *Lion's Pride* is the most powerful ship we have," Aldric said as they ascended the gangplank onto the deck, seeing William looking up at the massive ship. "It was Gavric's ship. There isn't anything afloat that can touch us in this."

"I'm not worried about that," William said as confidently as he could.

"Ever since we left the palace, you've had a look like someone just took the last wyvern out of the coop," Aldric said, stopping as they reached the deck of the ship and turning William to face him. "If it's not the journey, what's troubling you?"

William hesitated, looking down at the deck, "It's nothing, Uncle. Just nervous about my first time sailing."

Aldric studied him for a moment before speaking, "Come now, Will. We may not have spent a lot of time together as you grew up, but I know you well enough to know that isn't what's bothering you. Something's weighing on you more than just that."

With a sigh, William relented, "It's my father and the way he's just sending me off. I know he's wanted me gone for years, and

29

with King Gavric gone, he finally has his chance to get rid of me. I know you said to make the best of it, but it still makes me so mad."

"I know, and I'm sorry I can't say anything that will make that feeling go away. The best I can do is try to convince you that this is an opportunity, and suggest you at least try your hardest to pretend that that's the truth. You'll be surprised to find that, sometimes, just believing something hard enough will end up making it true."

"How can I just pretend like he doesn't hate me, or that this will make any difference? I don't think, no matter how hard I try, that I can forget how he treats me."

"I didn't say forget; that would be asking too much. I guess I'm trying to say you shouldn't let it rule you. Focusing on your anger toward him only gives him more power over you. Ignore it and focus on what you need to do and do your best at it. I've always found the best way to deal with people like your father is to just ignore their games and petty jealousies and try to excel at whatever's put in front of you. Make him bitter because of your success, instead of you being bitter at his neglect."

Before William could think of a reply, he was distracted by a tall, broad-shouldered man with blond curly hair and vivid blue eyes walking up to them. William just stared in surprise. Everything about the man, from his stature to his blond hair and blue eyes, to the curving tattoos on his neck identified him as being from Thay. Considering how most people from Sidor, and Lynese for that matter, felt about Thayans and that Thayans tended to return the feelings in equal measure, it was completely baffling why one would be on the Sidorian flagship.

William had never actually met anyone from Thay before, although he had caught glimpses of their delegations during audiences with his Uncle Gavric. Thay was a land of pirates and heretics, and they had little to do with the people of the two other major continents. What he did know about them had mostly come from his tutors.

When the Ancients had fallen in the Cataclysm, their great continent had cracked and ripped apart, forming the three nations of Sidor, Lynese, and Thay, all centered around the Maw. But while Sidor and Lynese had recovered to an extent, Thay had become a barren desert, wrecked by the wild magics unleashed during the sundering of the world. Its people eked out a living on specialized drought-resistant crops and piracy, but mostly piracy.

More worrying, at least to most non-sailors, was their predominant religion. Unlike Sidor and Lynese, who followed the Acolytes in their worship of the Ancients, revering the magical artifacts and history of the past, the Thayans had embraced the Purifiers. This shadowy faith taught that magic had corrupted the world and its remnants must be destroyed to cleanse the land. Considering what magic had done to their homeland, perhaps it was understandable that many Thayans would adopt this belief. But their destruction of some of the most powerful of the artifacts left behind after the fall of magic was seen as a treachery so deep that its sin passed down to later generations of believers. It was a grudge that most people, at least on Sidor, held.

So much so that, three hundred years ago, tensions had erupted into a religious war, one of the only times Sidor and Lynese had allied against a common foe. Ostensibly, it had been over Thayan piracy, but most knew the Purifiers' agenda had been the real cause. The fact that his ancestor had led the Sidorian armies in that fight was one of the main reasons his family didn't get more flak for the apparent Thay blood somewhere far back in their line, evident in their blond hair. It made all Whittons stand out from the rest of Sidorians, who mostly had hair in shades of brown and black. The fact that William had light brown hair had always made him stand out from the rest of the family, forever marking him as an outsider in the family.

"William, I'd like you to meet Sergeant Eskild Alsufi," Aldric said. "He's been my right-hand man for years and will be assisting us on this campaign."

Eskild inclined his head respectfully. "It's a pleasure to meet you. Your uncle has told me great things about you, including how good a swordsman you are becoming."

His accent was thick, like there were too many letters in his mouth and he wasn't able to get them all out. On top of the surprise that his uncle's right-hand man was a Thayan, was the fact that Aldric had talked to him about William. Other than the last month or so since Gavric's death, he and his Uncle Aldric spoke maybe once or twice a year and didn't have much in the way of a relationship. Which made it surprising that he would tell his right-hand man anything about William, let alone say good things about him.

"I ... I hope I can live up to his praise," he stammered.

"While we're on campaign, during times when we're not engaged with the enemy, you'll be assisting Eskild with his duties. Consider it a chance to learn the intricacies of war firsthand," he said before lowering his voice conspiratorially. "And if you're lucky, Eskild may even give you some pointers or spar with you. He's the finest fighter I've ever seen."

William just looked at the Thayan, still trying to wrap his head around everything that had just happened.

"If you'll excuse me, I need to discuss our route with the captain," Aldric said. "The northern seas will still be choked with ice, so we'll have to plot a careful course. William, use this time to learn a little about what you'll be doing on the campaign from Eskild. We have at least two weeks until we land in Lynese, so this will be a good time to prepare you for what's to come."

"We could always sail around to the Eastern side of Sidor and cut past Thay to the south," Eskild suggested wryly.

"I think not," Aldric chuckled, clasping William's shoulder warmly before heading towards the front of the ship.

William glanced back at the docks of Starhaven, watching the bustling activity as the last supplies were loaded onto the other ships in their fleet and the gangplanks were pulled up in preparation for making sail. Beyond the docks, the white towers and steepled roofs of the capital city rose up, the palace prominently visible on its hilltop perch overlooking the harbor.

"So, how does a Thayan warrior become the right hand of one of Sidor's dukes?" William asked, turning back to Eskild.

The sergeant smiled, his blond beard crinkling around his mouth, "Your uncle bested me in battle and I became his captive. Aldric can tell a good fighter when he sees one."

"He captured you? During a raid?"

"I was part of a war band, trying to pillage along Sidor's eastern coast. We thought the lands north of Shadowhold, where we normally raided, would be easy pickings. But your uncle set a trap and ambushed us in the dead of night. A large number of us were killed, and a dozen or so, including me, ended up in chains."

"And you were left as a prisoner?"

The Thayan shrugged, "My family didn't have the means to ransom me back, even if they had wanted to, which they didn't. I rotted in a dungeon for over a year. But eventually, Aldric realized he could make better use of me, and I was given a choice. Keep wasting away in chains, or pledge my service to him."

"That must have been difficult, going from captive to this."

"I don't think either of us intended for it to happen. I thought it would be an easy way to escape the dungeon and get back home, and join a new war band. I don't know exactly what he expected, but I don't think it was this. Over time, though, I saw what kind of man he was; how he treated others, friend and enemy alike. It's hard not to follow someone like that."

William glanced back at Starhaven again, watching the waves crash against the sea wall as the *Lion's Pride* pushed away from the docks.

"You don't seem excited," Eskild observed, watching William. "Most men your age would relish a chance for adventure and glory on the battlefield."

"It's not that. I'm not being sent off to war; I'm just being sent away. This has been my father Edmund's goal for years. Now that my Uncle Gavric is gone, Edmund finally has his chance to get rid of me."

Eskild cocked his head, frowning, "If your father is so cruel, surely being away from him is not so bad?"

"It's complicated," William said. "Part of me is thrilled to escape Edmund's presence. But it still hurts, knowing how little he cares. I want to prove myself, to show I'm more than he believes."

Eskild clasped his shoulder, "Your uncle sees potential in you. Focus on that, not your father's judgments. Use this opportunity to learn from Aldric. He is a good man."

William shook his head. "That's what Uncle Aldric said, but I barely know him. He rarely visited court or our duchy when I was growing up. And now, suddenly, he wants to mentor me?"

"Aldric's absence in your youth was not about you, I don't think," Eskild said gently. "Aldric and his brother do not get along, and the few times I was around when both were present, it was clear the hatred went both ways."

"Why?"

Eskild looked back in Aldric's direction and then to William, "It's not really my place to say ..."

"Please," William said, "I promise I won't tell Aldric you told me. I just want to understand him a little better, now that my future has been put in his hands."

"Well, as I understand it, many years ago Aldric was courting a woman named Alyssa, who he was deeply in love with. The problem was that Alyssa was the daughter of a very wealthy merchant, and Edmund fancied her as well, although more for her substantial inheritance than her beauty."

Eskild paused, looked back to Aldric on the other side of the ship a second time, and said, "Edmund apparently pulled many tricks to try and separate them, including paying people to lie and spread rumors to sow distrust. Once, he even tried openly to convince Alyssa to break off with Aldric and marry him instead. But Alyssa stayed true to Aldric, and they were eventually married, despite Edmund's interference. At the wedding celebration, Edmund said some horrible things to Aldric in his bitterness and jealousy. Things I don't care to repeat."

"I had no idea," William said, thinking of his aunt, who'd always seemed friendly and caring the few times they'd met.

"After that, I heard that Edmund found another woman to marry, presumably your mother. But Aldric never forgave his brother for what he did. I think Alyssa is the only person who hates Edmund more than your uncle."

William just stared at the deck, deep in thought as he processed this new information. He had completely misjudged his Uncle Aldric. William had thought him distant and uninterested in him, when it turned out he was only estranged from Edmund. He had just been collateral damage from Edmund's own actions.

"I ... I never knew. Aldric never told me any of that."

"It's not something he likes to talk about," Eskild replied. "Understandably so. But know that despite past grievances, I think he cares a great deal for you."

William glanced back in Aldric's direction. His uncle stood near the helm of the ship, one foot up on the railing as he conferred with the captain and watched the receding coastline of Sidor.

"Thank you for telling me this," William said sincerely to Eskild. "It helps me to make sense of things."

"Of course. Just remember, some wounds run deep. Aldric has his reasons for maintaining distance from court and his brother. Don't take it personally."

William nodded. "I won't. And this stays between us."

"Good man," Eskild said, clapping William on the back. "Now, we have a long journey ahead of us. Why don't I show you around the ship so you can get your bearings? And then maybe you can demonstrate some of this famous swordsmanship I've heard about."

"That would be great," William said, blushing a little at the clearly unearned compliment.

Rooksberry, Ducy of Iron Keep, Kingdom of Sidor

As with any small fishing village, Rooksberry was quiet in the evening. Peaceful. The people there worked hard from sun up to sun down. The men were out in boats catching the fish that both fed the town and brought in what small gold they received, while the wives, children, and elderly worked to prepare the fish for sale further inland. They all repaired nets and boats, and did all of the work needed for a small, fairly isolated little village.

The last days of winter were ending, but this edge of the empire, the northernmost tip of the Duchy of Iron Keep, saw snow and ice late into the season. Most people didn't think of Iron Keep as a northern duchy, but part of it extended further north than almost half of the Duchy of the Ice Lands, and only a little south of the island nation of Alchmara.

The chilly sea breeze carried the scent of salt and fish, which mingled with the damp odor of decaying wood and seaweed as the flotsam frozen over the winter thawed. For the few villagers still awake at this hour, the rhythmic lull of the waves was the only thing they could hear, the sound broken only by the occasional creak of a hut or a beached fishing boat from the occasional gust of wind.

Even if there had been more than a sliver of moon to light the waters, there wouldn't have been anyone looking out into the darkened waves to see the small band of longboats appearing out of the darkness, their hulls sliding almost silently onto the rocky beach. Nor was there anyone there to see the large men in their thick padded fur tunics, typical of the Isle of Alchmara, as they hurtled over the sides of their ships, swords and axes in hand.

They broke into small bands of five as they ran towards the huts of the village, each raider carrying an unlit torch wrapped in wax-coated cloth to prevent errant sparks. At the front of the main group, Igoran waved his men forward, his bald head and bushy black beard identifying him even in the darkness. His weathered face was set in hard lines, scarred knuckles gripping the haft of his broad axe.

Without a word, the raiding party fanned out through the village's narrow streets. The calm of the night was broken as Igoran kicked in the door of the first hut he came to, the crash jolting the elderly couple inside awake. Before they could react, Igoran's great axe silenced them, blood spraying the rough woolen blankets on their bed.

All around, the raiders set upon the defenseless villagers. Screams pierced the night as doors were smashed in and people were dragged from their homes. Raiders lit torches and set fire to the thatched rooftops, the flames quickly spreading to engulf the simple wooden structures.

Bearded raiders pulled young women from their families, and children cried out for their parents, only to be cut down mercilessly.

A young father charged through a broken door, a simple j-hook used for catching fish turned into a makeshift weapon in his hand. He bellowed with rage and sunk its curved, sharp end into the large man dragging his wife from their home. The raider went down with a gurgled shriek, the metal hook still embedded deep in his back, but the man's victory was short-lived as two more raiders set upon him, blades opening his belly to the night air.

As he collapsed, his entrails spilling onto the dirt, his wife was dragged kicking and screaming toward the longboats. After what seemed like an eternity to the villagers not killed outright, a piercing whistle sounded from one of the raiders, the shrill sound cutting through the cries and screams of the ravaged village. At the signal, the raiders began dragging their captives toward the beach, the light from their burning homes revealing tear-streaked faces and blood-spattered clothes.

The burly raiders handled the villagers roughly, not bothering to bind them until they got to the boats. One young woman kicked and thrashed as her captor dragged her by the hair, only to be cuffed across the face, stunning her into submission.

Other raiders emerged from the huts, their arms laden with blankets, tools, bags of grain, anything they could grab of value. A few raiders lingered to shatter furniture and overturn pots, spilling stew and porridge across the wooden floors in an act of wanton destruction.

Looking back at them, Igoran bellowed, "Enough! Back to the boats!"

At his command, the last raiders sprinted from the village, loaded down with their spoils. They dumped their burdens into the longboats and began shoving the small vessels back into the frigid surf.

Fifteen minutes after they arrived, the longboats slipped back into the darkened waters, melding into the night. Behind them, the fires raged on.

Chapter 5

Sidorian Army Camp, Doree River, Empire of Lynese

The sounds of men and beasts could be heard well before William, his uncle, and the small force that traveled with him crested a hill to see the sprawling encampment of the Sidorian army. Situated on a vast plain surrounded by gentle hills, thousands of tents and pavilions formed an orderly grid, with larger elaborate pavilions at the center marking the locations of the nobles and commanders. Flags and banners bearing the sigils of Sidorian houses fluttered in the crisp morning breeze.

As they passed through the outer perimeter marked by sharpened wooden palisades, the sentries saluted sharply, fists to chests in salute to the royal party. Aldric nodded in return, his manner easy and familiar, even though this was his first time joining the army that Gavric had led onto the Lynesian shores. For his part, William struggled to take in the huge force and its organized chaos.

He'd accompanied his father to several baronies across the duchy of King's Heart and his Uncle Gavric to a tournament he had thought, at the time, was the largest assembly of men and armor the world had ever known. Both were dwarfed by the military might displayed in this camp.

At the center of the camp, grooms rushed to take their mounts as they dismounted in front of the commanders' pavilion. The heavy canvas structure was hung with banners of gold and white, emblazoned with the royal lion of the House Whitton. Inside were a dozen men dressed in the gambesons and padding they would wear under their armor, when the time came to don it.

As William followed behind his uncle, Eskild caught William's arm, pulling him aside.

"Best you take a place over there," he said, pointing to a far side of the tent with a clear view of the map and wooden markers that filled the central table. "Listen, but stay silent. It's a rare thing to be present at something like this, and a good opportunity to learn."

William just nodded, moving to take his place. In truth, he had no plans to speak at all. These were seasoned warriors who made William feel just how few his sixteen years were. He knew they paid him no mind, focusing on their new commander, but William couldn't help but feel there were eyes watching him, evaluating him for weakness.

"Lord Aldric," said a powerfully built knight with a neat brown beard. "We did not expect you so soon."

Aldric clasped the man's hand warmly. "I made haste, Sir Alistair. Our new king has declared the end of the war to be his highest priority, and winter is ending. Had my brother not passed, I imagine you would have already marched for the spring campaign."

"We would have at that, but ... the crowning of a new king takes precedence. However, now that you're here, we can make up for lost time. You know Baron Pembroke and Sir Halwyn," he said, pointing at one of Aldric's barons and a man William didn't know, but presumably his uncle did. "These are commanders Baldwin and Haverhill."

The grizzled older men inclined their heads respectfully.

Aldric moved to stand before the table, surveying the markers and maps intently, "Tell me of our progress. The dispatches sent to Starhaven have been vague regarding the war's status."

Sir Alistair cleared his throat, "Truth be told, we've made little headway since taking the coastal cities and northeastern peninsula last season. Baudric has bolstered the smaller forts on the central river crossing over the Dorée, cutting us off from the main part of the Lynesian plains and the central part of the continent. Worse, most of the other side of the Dorée is covered by the Dead Man's Hills, which I understand are a nightmare as far as scouting goes. Cave systems, little water, some pretty spectacular cliffs, and false valleys, it would be easy pickings for bandits or locals on our supply lines if we went that way, which leaves us only the northern pass between the hills and the ocean. They know this and have concentrated their strength there, mostly along the central crossing over the Dorée, here. The next nearest crossing is twenty miles northwest and is not only a lot smaller, limiting how quickly our men can get across at a time, but the bay on this side of the peninsula is still in the hands of Baudric's navy."

"From the reports, I had thought we'd made it further inland than this. He still has all of these northern ports open, giving him easy access to Werna and its markets. Holding only one peninsula, no matter how big it is, and the mouth of the straits doesn't do us any good."

"Did you try pushing across here? I understood you outnumbered the enemy?"

"We did, and still do, although they have heavily reinforced over the winter. The issue is, besides a small blocking force at the crossing, they hold the forts here and here, two miles north and south of the crossing, and they've divided their army almost equally between the two forts. We can push through the blocking force without much problem, but from there, things become complicated. We can't keep charging straight through because our supply line will be open to their men in the forts, and if we attack either of the forts, the other one will sally and assault our rear. Gavric tried splitting our forces and attacking both simultaneously last fall, just before the first snows, but we got bogged down in sieges when we didn't quickly take the forts. It was in an attempt to take the forts that Gavric was injured."

"I see," Aldric said, cupping his chin in one hand, staring hard at the map. "And what is this northern fort like? What are the defenses?"

"It's at a small curve of the river, which makes it difficult to assail from that side. The southern approach is on a fairly steep rise, giving their catapults and archers a fair view of the fields in front of it. It does flatten at the rear, but with the way the land lays and how the fort is situated, you have to come in almost completely from the north to get the advantage of that more shallow side, with the men in the fort watching you the whole time you circle it. There are also two small defensive fortifications behind it, guarding the northern approach. Not forts, really, more redoubts protected by thin trenches facing north against a wooden barricade."

"You've gotten men around to see it?"

"No, but we have a woman in the town between the fort and the river that hikes up to the redoubts and forts each day to sell bread," Sir Cedrick said.

"And you trust her information?" Aldric asked.

"She has no love for Baudric's men. It's a small town, and some of the soldiers are less disciplined than they should be. She also has a baby to feed and needs the coin."

"I see," Aldric said again, and then fell quiet for several minutes, studying the map. "We will hold the bulk of our infantry, archers, and artillery here, to be used in the crossing, along with one-third of our knights."

He tapped a location farther upriver, "The other two-thirds of the knights will ride north under your command, Baron Pembroke. You'll circle around to this smaller crossing here. You'll then swing south and attack the northern of the two forts. I will take the remaining force here, force the bridge crossing, and attack it from the southern face. Between us, it should collapse fast, giving us time to wheel around before the southern fort rallies. Facing our then combined force, with half the power they had before we crossed, they'll have to retreat or we'll destroy them. Either way, the crossing will be done and we can continue our march toward Valemonde."

Pembroke raised an eyebrow, "That's easily twenty leagues, through rough country, and they'll certainly be watching that crossing. We'll lose the element of surprise."

"Not if we do it right," Aldric countered. "We'll give you a portion of the scouts to take with you. Half of them were cutthroats and bandits before they were pressed into the levies. The tree line goes right to this crossing, and there's a rise here, limiting their line of sight if you bring your men in this way. It's a bad position to hold watch from, but they don't have much choice but to watch the crossing. According to the star watchers, we should have a moonless night three days from now. You need to get your men in position, covered by the trees, and send your ... most talented scouts across in the dark. They must take out *every one* of the Lynesian scouts. If they miss *any*, word will get out and this whole plan will turn into a fiasco. Take only the lightest of provisions, to speed your march."

Pembroke looked at the region around the crossing, nodding slowly as he saw what Aldric was saying.

"If you push hard, it will take you the better part of the day to reach the fort, but it should still give us several hours to take the fort. We will attack at noon watch, to draw their attention as you get close. With their eyes focused on us, you should have a clear shot to the walls."

"It's risky," Pembroke said slowly. "If they should look north; if your attack is early; if our attack is late; if a scout escapes. There are a lot of chances, any one of which will turn this into a tragedy."

Aldric nodded. "War is ever a gamble, my friend. But I believe this offers us our best chance to take the fort quickly and with minimal loss of life. Assuming our success, of course."

Pembroke nodded solemnly, "I'll need to select the lightest armored knights and fastest horses. They'll be tired when we arrive, but if we have surprised the enemy, the battle should be short. It can be done."

"Excellent." Aldric clapped the baron on the shoulder. "I know I entrust this task to capable hands. I have one more command. You are to take my nephew with you."

"My Grace, we're going to be moving fast and with minimal support forces. I'm not sure we'll have time to act as mentor or tour guide."

"Don't worry, I won't be sending him with you alone. Sergeant Eskild will go with you and will take responsibility for the boy."

"Then take him we will," Pembroke said, giving a nod to Eskild, who returned it.

Eskild placed a hand on William's shoulder, leaning in to speak softly. "Come, it's time we take our leave. Your uncle and his commanders have much planning to do, and we have to get you ready to travel."

William nodded, allowing himself to be steered towards the tent entrance. As they stepped outside into the bustling camp, he glanced back over his shoulder, watching his uncle gesturing animatedly over the map table, deep in discussion with his advisors. He felt his stomach twist. He'd just arrived at the army, and he was already being sent off. Not to safety or to be out of the way, like his father would probably have done, but to join a force on a real attack, doing something useful. Sure, he'd be kept at the back of the line, and mostly have to just watch, but he'd still be there. With them. It was a chance to prove himself.

Sensing William's disquiet, Eskild guided him away from the tent towards the supply tents, "You know, this could be a fine opportunity for you. Observing a battle firsthand, seeing how the commanders plan and lead. It's a rare education."

"I know. I'm excited, not worried. Well ... not very worried," William said, and then turned to look at Eskild directly. "Maybe I'm a little nervous. I've never been in a real battle before."

Eskild smiled reassuringly. "No one escapes nerves before their first taste of combat. But this is a good opportunity. We'll be with Baron Pembroke; he's one of your uncle's most trusted men. He's got a good head for strategy and doesn't throw his men away needlessly."

"You make it sound so simple," William muttered. "Just stay close and keep my head down, I suppose?"

Eskild laughed heartily, clapping William on the back, "Now you've got it! Though it wouldn't hurt to keep those eyes open, observe how the other knights handle themselves. Courage and faith in your own abilities will carry you through, so long as you keep your wits."

William just nodded, not trusting himself to say anything else that might show his nerves. Eskild seemed to read his thoughts and just put a hand on his shoulder, continuing to guide him toward the supply tents. The supply area was a maze of tents, some holding crates and sacks of supplies, others with entire smitheries set up inside them. It was into one of those tents Eskild took William, where they found a squat, barrel-chested man inspecting the mail hauberks hanging from a wooden rack.

"Otto, I've brought you some work," Eskild called.

The man turned, bushy eyebrows rising as he looked William up and down. William was large for his age and could be mistaken for a very thin young man, if you saw him at enough of a distance. Close up, it was hard not to see how few years he had on him.

"Let's have a look then," Otto said gruffly, gesturing William forward.

He spun William around, lifted an arm and dropped it, then spun William the other way, the entire time making small grumbling noises. Eskild stood back, infinitely amused by the whole thing.

"Plate or mail?" he said, looking at William, but clearly addressing Eskild.

"For a young lordling? Plate, of course. Wouldn't want him getting any of that fine Whitton blood scratched."

"I see," he said, looking back at William, seemingly with new appraisal. "Have you had much experience in armor? It takes some work, getting used to the weight."

"I competed in a few squire jousts, for my uncle. They had sets of plate. And I … Some of the weapons trainers allowed me to practice wearing it."

He was a little embarrassed to admit he'd gotten the weapons master to allow him to dress up in the armor Gavric had gotten him for the joust. Those had been wasted days, since he hadn't really gotten used to doing much more than sitting on a horse in it, but he didn't want to give the armorer reason to believe he couldn't wear it.

"I see," he said, then repeated himself. "I see. Well, I think I have something that might work. A knight of shorter stature ordered a set. He's a little broader than you, but I can adjust it. Perhaps we might do a half-suit. Breastplate and pauldrons, then mail for the rest, to give you time to adjust."

"That would work fine, Master Smith," William said as formally as he could.

In reality, he wanted to run around in circles whooping for joy. His own armor, which he'd wear into a real battle. This was everything that he could have hoped for and more.

The man let out a booming laugh and said, "While I appreciate the courtesy, I'm afraid 'Master Smith' might be a bit too much hubris for my blood to take. Please, just Otto is fine."

"Yes," William said, dipping his head slightly in a casual sort of bow, "Otto. Thank you."

"It's my pleasure. How much time do I have," he said, again looking to Eskild.

"A day. Two maybe, but it's possible we ride early to make sure everything's in place."

"A day? You blond-headed demon, I should curse you here and now."

William held his breath. Calling someone a blond demon was tantamount to calling them a Purifier. A heretic. He'd seen boys fight over lesser words.

Eskild, didn't seem to mind, just laughing along with Otto, "I have faith you'll manage."

"Fine, fine. I'll do my best, but you will remember this," he said, shaking a finger at Eskild.

"Of course I will. I always remember my friends, even the short, bald ones."

"Always the sweet talker," Otto said, as they both continued laughing. "Out, out. I have much work to do.

Starhaven, Kingdom of Sidor

Courtiers and petitioners crowded the massive audience hall of the royal palace. High arched windows let in large amounts of sunlight, which fell across gold and white banners draped from the ceiling. Seated in the intricately carved oaken throne, embossed with golden lions and wheat sheaves on a raised platform, was King Serwyn Whitton. Scribes and messengers waited a few steps down, ready for his slightest command, with a wall of guards creating an open space between the assembled mass and the great throne. Edmund had arranged everything to make sure that Serwyn was projected in the right light, putting all of the weight and power of the kingdom behind him.

This was all made harder by how obvious it was that Serwyn didn't want to be there. Lounging on the throne, one leg kicked over its arm, his elbow resting on the other arm of the throne, his hand supporting his head. It was obvious to anyone who looked at him how bored the young king was.

"An envoy from Baron Garris Sinclair of Stormhaven, Your Grace!" one of the royal heralds standing at the perimeter of the ring of guards said, a slightly disheveled and dirty man in riding leathers standing behind him.

"Send him forward," Edmund said.

All eyes turned to watch the travel-stained man walk through the ring of guards, stopping on the gold and white carpet that ran down from the throne all the way to the far door of the audience chamber. Reaching the appointed spot, the man dropped to one knee, bowing his head.

"Your Grace, I come bearing urgent news from my lord, Baron Sinclair of Stormhaven."

Serwyn shifted in his seat, regarding the messenger with a bored expression, "Out with it then."

"Your Grace, my lord Baron Sinclair sends his regards and requests the Crown's aid in a matter of the utmost importance. Over the past month, a dozen villages and hamlets across the Iron Keep and Ice Lands have been sacked and burned by raiders from Alchmara. Houses burned, livestock stolen, people killed or carried off. The scale of the destruction and loss is catastrophic."

He paused, taking a breath, "Two-thirds of the Stormhaven's knights and near half our levies have sailed to Lynese with the Royal Army, and we know most of the other baronies are in the same state. We lack the men to patrol the entirety of the northern shores, much less meet this threat head-on. Our remaining men are overstretched, leaving our villages vulnerable."

"And what does that have to do with the crown?" Serwyn asked, bringing his leg down from the arm of the chair and sitting up straight.

The question came out aggressive, almost as a challenge.

"With respect, Your Grace, the recent ... increases in taxes to support the war have left many baronies without resources to expand patrols or rebuild defenses, and without the men already pressed into service, we are left with few options. My lord humbly requests men and arms from the Crown to reinforce the coastal garrisons and bolster our defenses. Else, at least return some number of our marched levies and knights, that we might better protect our people."

As the messenger spoke, Serwyn's face darkened more and more as he became increasingly agitated.

"If your lord is a loyal baron, then he will deal with this matter himself and understand the needs of both his men and his taxes to the Crown. And if he cannot maintain his lands with his remaining forces, then perhaps he should not be a baron at all."

The messenger paled at the harsh tone. Before he could respond, Lord Edmund smoothly interjected.

"What His Grace means," Edmund said diplomatically, "is that there are limits to what the Crown can provide at this time. Much of our strength is committed to the war in Lynese, as I'm sure your lord understands."

"He does, my lord. But without assistance or some of our men back ..."

"However," Edmund continued, holding up a hand. "We will, of course, investigate options on how we may assist Baron Sinclair and the other threatened coastal holdings. The defense of the realm is paramount, of course. But until such measures can be enacted, it remains beholden upon all the barons to maintain their obligations. That includes adequately garrisoning and defending the lands tithed to them."

The messenger gave a low, sweeping bow, and said, "Thank you, Your Grace. I will deliver your words to my lord baron."

There wasn't much else he could do. He was a messenger and not one to argue his baron's position for him. Edmund was surprised the man had gone as far as he had, since men of his station had paid dearly for such impertinence in the past. It did speak to how bad things must be on the eastern shores of the kingdom.

The man turned and hustled through the ring of soldiers and the crowd, leaving the audience chamber. Edmund lifted a hand, halting the herald from calling forth the next petitioner.

"Your Grace, a word," he said quietly, kneeling next to the king's throne.

In contrast, Serwyn made no effort to keep his voice down, "Do not presume to tell your king what he means, Uncle. My words were clear. If Sinclair and the rest cannot defend their lands, I shall find barons who can."

Edmund nodded, speaking softly. "Of course, Your Grace. In fact, I agree with you. I just ... think we should be careful not to move with undue haste. The time is fast approaching when we shall be able to deal with these disloyal barons as is their due, but we are not there yet. Your rule is still young and there is much groundwork to be laid before we can ... make changes."

"I will not coddle these wretches!" he snapped. "They should be grateful I allow them to kneel before me at all!"

Edmund bowed his head contritely, "Forgive me, Nephew. You are right, of course. But men like Sinclair are well entrenched in their baronies and hold long claims to their titles. The Duke of Iron Keep grows old, with no heirs of his own. Soon, the time will come when a new duke will be selected. We will need the support of many of Iron Keep's barons to install the right man in Windermere's place. Once our ally holds the duchy, we can reshape the landscape there as we see fit."

"I do not want to wait," Serwyn said petulantly, then sagged. "Fine. I will follow your counsel for a little longer, but my patience is not infinite. I grow weary of diplomacy, of always coddling them."

"I understand completely, Your Grace."

Chapter 6

Sidorian Army Camp, Doree River, Empire of Lynese

William lifted his foot into the stirrup and swung himself up onto the horse's back. The bay gelding shifted nervously beneath him, picking up on his rider's unease. There really wasn't a reason to be nervous, yet. Unless the scouts his uncle had sent with Pembroke were less skilled than advertised, William wouldn't see his first taste of battle for a day or more, depending on how quickly they made the ride back south after crossing the northern ford.

And yet, now that he was on his horse, wearing his armor, with a sword next to him, it felt real for the very first time. The screeching cry of a wyvern overhead made William glance up. The camp was bustling with activity as the army prepared to march. The wyvern was probably headed back to the small force left to guard their supply lines leading back to their ships, or maybe even all the way back to Starhaven with news of the upcoming battle. William took a deep breath, steadying his nerves.

A sudden, low hiss behind him to his left caused William to jerk the horse to the side, worried a snake or some other creature might have made its way underfoot. While it was unlikely that such would affect the horses, the animals were still wary of creatures and could panic and buck when startled by their appearance.

It wasn't, however, a snake. Turning, he saw a giant war lizard. Fifteen hands tall, nearly ten feet long, with mottled green and brown scales that blended into camouflage patterns along its back and a pair of spiny protrusions running down the length of its neck. William had heard of, and even seen pictures of, war lizards, but he'd never seen one before. Most Sidorians, or even Lynesians, had never seen one. As far as he knew, they only lived on Thay, which made them their predominant mount, instead of horses, because of their hardy nature and the ability to go longer without water than a horse could ... a vital adaptation in their dry, hot climate.

Eskild sat atop this giant animal, his massive size amplified by that of his mount. Seeing the giant Thayan, William turned the horse toward the lizard, so he could talk to the man without shouting, only to jerk the horse almost immediately back as the war lizard snapped its jaws, baring several rows of serrated teeth.

"Keep your distance from Ghormbaan," Eskild warned. "He's good during battle, but if left idle, he becomes a little unpredictable. Best give him space lest you lose a hand ... or your head."

William reined his horse back a few more steps, eyeing the war lizard warily. Its yellow, slit-pupiled eyes stared back unblinkingly. He could just imagine what those crushing jaws could do to a man.

"Just keep focused on the task at hand, and you'll be fine," Eskild said, repeating the mantra he'd been giving William for the last two days.

Before William could respond with the denial of nerves, as he did every time, horns blared, and men on horseback began to move.

"Here we go," Eskild said, giving William a bright smile.

It was dark ... so dark William couldn't see his hand in front of him, let alone the other men around him. They were still a distance away from the river, the sounds of its waters muffled by distance and the forest. No one spoke, and even the horses seemed to be holding their breath.

And then the thundering of hooves of horses returning at speed could be heard, followed by a piercing whistle.

Everyone had been prepared for the signal. Torches were lit here and there along the column, to keep the horses from running into a tree or otherwise killing their rider, and the entire column moved out. Five minutes later, the entire column exploded from the tree line and across the ford they'd been listening to for several hours while they waited for the scouts to complete their tasks. Near a copse of trees, a handful of scouts sat on horseback, lit torches in their hands, human signposts of where to go in the moonless night.

Crossing the river, William sucked in a breath, surprised by the grim sight that greeted him. Bodies lay strewn haphazardly across the ground; limp forms sprawled in awkward angles. He could almost feel more bodies beyond the torchlight. There had been dozens of Lynesian scouts, none of whom remained alive to contest their crossing.

William paused his horse, looking down at the bodies. The glassy stares of lifeless eyes seemed to follow his progress, reflecting the torchlight. A cluster of six scouts sat mounted behind the bodies, grins on their faces telling any who saw them who was responsible for the recent dead.

These were the first dead men that William had ever seen, not counting men lying in state, like his Uncle Gavric. That had been different. Gavric, and the few others he'd seen before, had been cleaned up, made to look as if they were simply sleeping. This was different. Raw.

"Keep up, lad!" Eskild called as he rode past, stirring William out of his thoughts.

William gave the bodies, then the scouts, one last glance and urged his horse on, following the column that began its hard ride south.

They rode on through the night and into the following morning, not at top speed but still pushing their horses hard. Finally, from his position at the rear of the column, William could make out the defenses arrayed around the rear of the fort, protecting the sloping ground behind it. While formidably built up with wood and earth, these bulwarks lacked the height and stone strength of the fort's own walls.

Spurring his lathered horse forward, William advanced with the others toward the defenses. Ditches and sharpened stakes offered obstacles before the ramparts, but the column poured relentlessly onward. Arrows flew from the walls, thudding into the earth around them, taking some men off their horses, injured or dead.

Following the rest of the men, William spurred his horse on as he reached the first defense, a long trench filled with sharpened stakes. The land was against the defenders. They'd tried to narrow the approaches as best they could, laying out pits and trenches, but there's a reason forts have high walls.

William clung tightly to the reins as his horse surged forward, powerful muscles bunching beneath him as it launched itself over the ditch. He landed hard, gritting his teeth against the jarring impact. All around, men were pouring across the obstacles, some thrown as their horses were struck by arrow or spear.

Arrows and spears continued to rain down, though the walls remained tantalizingly out of reach of their weapons. William hunched low, shield raised over his head. Ahead, the first ranks were over the final trench, inside the string of defensive works around the base of the fort.

The charge carried William forward as the Sidorian knights crashed against the Lynesian defenses around the base of the fort. All around William, men and horses screamed as they were cut down by spear and arrow. But momentum was on the Sidorians' side as their heavy horses tore through the lightly armored men guarding the supporting breastworks around the fort.

A man stood in William's path. A Lynesian, spear in his hand, his back turned to William as he tried to impale a Sidorian knight in front of him. William slashed out with his sword, cutting the Lynesian down from behind. His blade sliced through boiled leather and bit deep into the man's back. With a gurgling cry, the spearman collapsed to the ground.

It was the first time he'd ever drawn blood in anger. The first time he'd cut a man. The first time he'd killed. But there was no time to dwell on it as another Lynesian soldier charged at William, sword raised high.

William spurred his horse forward to meet the attack. His sword swung up to parry the overhand strike. The blades rang out as they met. William's arm jarred from the force of the blow. Gritting his teeth, he riposted quickly, driving his foe back.

The Lynesian recovered and came at him again, hard. His sword whirred through the air, nearly slipping past William's defenses. William gave ground, backing his horse, trying to redirect the man's desperate, wild attacks. Suddenly, the Lynesian's chest exploded in a spray of gore. Eskild's war lizard had struck without warning, appearing from somewhere in William's periphery, as if out of thin air, with its terrible jaws clamping down over the swordsman's shoulder and upper torso.

The Lynesian's dying screams mixed with the rending sounds of crunching bone and tearing flesh as the war lizard thrashed its prey. Blood spattered across William as he stared in horror at the carnage in front of him. Eskild, on the lizard's back, met William's stunned gaze and gave a fierce nod, breaking his momentary shock.

All around, the Sidorian knights were smashing through the final obstacles around the fort's base.

The last of the palisades blocking access to the fort's walls cleared, knights began dismounting and clambering up the rise near a low point in the wall, which the palisades had been defending. William threw himself from the saddle, landing in a crouch, and ran to join them. Above them, on the walls, Lynesian defenders threw spears and rocks to try and dissuade the attackers, but there were too few of them. His uncle's assault on the opposite side of the fort was in full swing, and there weren't enough defenders to repulse attacks from both sides simultaneously. Men threw hooks on the end of ropes up and over the edge of the parapet above; while others brought up the handful of ladders they'd brought with them, now assembled and ready to be climbed.

All along the barricade, grapnels flew into the air, the iron hooks of some finding purchase while others fell back down. Ladders were hauled up and leaned against the wall, held steady by a knight at the bottom. Men swarmed up the ropes, only to meet a grisly fate at the hands of the defenders. Spears impaled the first climbers, their bodies crashing lifelessly back down. Another rope party gained a brief foothold atop the wall before being slaughtered, hacked apart by axes and billhooks.

The ladders fared little better. As two men mounted the initial rungs, arrows rained down, killing the first man, sending him crashing into the men below him. The defense was still formidable, but it couldn't hold out for long.

Finally, one of the knights on the ladder to the far right made it to the top, killing two men who stood there. It was enough for the man behind him to join him. There were just too many places for the defenders to protect, and Pembroke had his men spread out as far as they could across this section, using the rise and the very short distance they needed to ascend to their advantage.

On the left, two of the men pulling themselves up with hooks managed to get over the top, then two more near the center. The foothold grew as more knights reached the top. Teams swept left and right along the parapets, pushing back the exhausted defenders through force of sheer numbers. The Lynesians retreated, ceding control of this section of wall inch by bloody inch.

William had waited for his chance to ascend, held back by Eskild when he'd tried to rush in with the initial group. Finally, the knight at the base of the ladder in front of William stepped aside and waved him forward. William dashed forward and scrambled up the wooden rungs. He climbed as fast as he could, fully exposed on the ladder's side.

He reached the top, relatively safe now that this section of the wall had been cleared, although arrows began to come up in ones and twos from the fort's interior below. Bodies littered the walkway, some dressed in Lynesian colors, others in Sidorian. William drew his sword and rushed to join the attack.

The crush of Sidorian knights surged down the stone steps, pushing through the knot of Lynesian defenders trying to bar their advance. Jammed shoulder to shoulder, the knights hacked and slashed their way down. Screams echoed off the enclosing walls as men were shoved over the edge to tumble to their deaths.

The defenders thrust out with spears and swords, desperately trying to hold back the tide. Blood slicked the steps as bodies fell, only to be trampled underfoot. Still, the Sidorians kept coming, their numbers carrying them on despite the brutal toll.

Step by step, the knights forced their way down over the dead and dying. The stairway was choked with bodies in crimson-spattered steel. Exhausted from the brutal press, the defenders fell back, unable to hold against the ferocity of the Sidorian onslaught.

William rushed down behind them into the courtyard below with the last group of knights. All around him, the clashes and cries of battle echoed off the enclosing walls. He emerged into madness. The confined space was choked with men locked in desperate, bloody combat.

He'd chosen the closest set of stairs, which the Sidorians hadn't cleared yet. At the base of the stairs, a knot of defenders barred the way, determined to halt the advance from the wall. William joined the tidal push of knights trying to force their way through. The defenders stood firm, spears and swords taking a brutal toll on the attackers. Bodies tumbled back down the stairs, only to be replaced by more.

Finally, the defenders' line broke beneath the relentless assault. William found himself carried along into the seething melee in the courtyard. A Lynesian swordsman charged at him, eyes wide with fury. William barely got his blade up in time to parry the overhand cut. The force of the blow rang through his arms. William fell back, desperately trying to redirect and deflect the raw power behind each hacking swing. Sweat stung his eyes as he gave ground, step by step.

A sudden opening presented itself. As his foe recovered from an off-balance swing, William lunged. His sword tip pierced an opening in the side of the man's chain shirt, sinking deep into his side. With a choked cry, the swordsman collapsed. William wrenched his blade free in a spray of crimson before the body hit the ground.

There was no time to catch his breath. A spear thrust at William's face, forcing him to knock it aside. He riposted quickly, driving his pommel into the spearman's face. Cartilage crunched wetly as the man's nose shattered. Howling, the spearman clutched at his spurting nose. William silenced his cries with a quick slash across the throat.

All across the courtyard, the Sidorian knights wore their enemy down through dogged ferocity. Step by step, they pushed the defending Lynesians back, carving a path toward the inner keep.

A sudden cry of warning made William spin. A Lynesian axeman charged straight at his unguarded back, heavy blade raised high. William threw himself desperately to the side, but the dodge came too late. The axe cut the air where William's neck had been a heartbeat before. Instead, the heavy blade slammed into William's shoulder, denting the metal pauldron, pressing steel into his flesh, sending a shock of pain down his shoulder.

Agony exploded through William's body. His sword dropped from suddenly numb fingers. He crashed hard against the blood-slick cobblestones. The axeman loomed above him, weapon raised for a killing blow, when a Sidorian knight barreled into the axeman from the side, sword piercing through the man's armor and into his chest.

The Lynesian died with a bubbling gasp, his axe falling harmlessly to the ground.

"On your feet, lad!" the knight roared, already turning to rejoin the fight. "It's not over yet!"

Gritting his teeth as he pulled the pauldron a little looser, so it no longer pressed painfully into his shoulder, William scooped up his fallen sword and rejoined the battle.

William spotted a young knight beset by two Lynesians, giving ground beneath their assault, desperately parrying their thrusts. William charged forward and slammed his blade down onto one spearman's wrist. The hand severed, sending the spear tumbling as the maimed man screamed.

Another knight appeared at the same moment, slashing the other attacker before he could turn and react to William's sudden appearance. Just as the man fell, a cheer rose up from the far side of the large courtyard. William turned to look just as the large main doors of the fort burst open, a tide of Sidorian troops pouring through the sundered doorway, crashing against the rear of the defenders like a hammer blow. Trapped between converging forces, the remaining Lynesian garrison stood little chance.

As the remaining Lynesians threw down their arms, William raised his, joining the cheer of the other victorious Sidorians.

He'd done it. Fought, and survived, his first battle.

Chapter 7

Valemonde, Empire of Lynese

Princess Isolde slipped through the doors, the hem of her gown whispering across the marble floor as she entered her father's chambers. It was late, but she knew he liked to retire one last time to his chambers after meeting with his advisors, to read over reports from his less public advisors.

She had spent the last several days working on plans of her own, but the planning was over, and the time had come to actually talk to him about them. Which is what she had been trying to do for the last twenty minutes, pacing back and forth in front of the ornate doors to his private study, working up her confidence.

The last time they argued about the state of their people, he had told her that if she wanted to do something she should do it instead of "whining to him." She knew he'd said it mostly to get her to leave him alone, but she'd decided to take him at his words, and not his meaning.

"Father, do you have a moment?" she said, stopping inside the large front parlor of his expansive chambers, shifting her weight from one foot to the other and back again.

He was behind his desk, reading papers, just as she'd known he would be. He looked up, annoyed at her interruption, but smoothed his features after a moment.

"What is it, Isolde?" he said, setting the letter he had been reading down.

"Last week, when we were discussing the injured coming back from the front, and you told me I should do something about it,

I began working on a plan. The winter was very hard on them, and there have been reports of outbreaks of illness, malnutrition, and the Disciples have not received enough medicine for the men put in their care. As you said, the empire is stretched thin as it is, fighting the invaders, so I've coordinated with some of the noble houses to gather supplies; food, medicine, and clothing to help with some of those shortfalls. It's taken weeks to organize discreetly, but we've amassed enough to make a real difference for our men," she said, the words tumbling out, without the steady rhythm she'd practiced over and over in her head.

It was hard to stay calm. This was her chance to actually do something good. Something that mattered. It had been difficult convincing the merchants and nobles to give up anything, but she'd persisted. She'd managed to convince enough to give donations of material and a little money that she finally pulled together a large enough shipment of supplies, especially once she convinced the Order of Aid to add to what was donated. Considering all of the Orders' stance on avoiding anything political, funds for supporting soldiers had been difficult, but she'd made enough assurances and had the backing of the Disciples from the Order of Aid, who had seen firsthand the deplorable state of their wounded.

"Fine," he said, waving her off again, reaching to pick the letter back up.

"The Disciples also told me we have men being held by the Sidorians. The Order has set up treatment there, but as you can imagine, the invaders have provided little in the way of supplies for them. The Order has tried the best they can, but they have never had much in the way of funds. When I get to the front, I plan on, under a flag of truce, delivering supplies to the men caring for our wounded prisoners as well."

As she spoke, she saw his eyes narrow and the letter fall once again to the desk, this time fully ignored. She knew what that meant, not that she was going to let that stop her.

"Absolutely not," he said as soon as she finished speaking. "It is far too dangerous for you to travel to the front lines yourself."

"I will take guards with me, as well as some of the Disciples."

"With the army occupied, the roads are less safe than they once were, and the Sidorians are nearly at the Chansol River. If they make it to that, it's onto the Lynesian Plains. It's much too dangerous for you to be traveling."

"But, Father ..."

"*I told you 'no,*'" he said, harshly, and then softened, holding a hand out to his daughter. "I'm sorry. I didn't mean to yell."

She gave him a suspicious look, since this was far from the first time he'd yelled at her, but she went to him anyway, taking his hand.

"I know your heart's in the right place and how much you care about our people, and I commend you for the amazing success you've had. If you could get the nobles to unclench their fists long enough to let one coin slip through, then you've done something truly spectacular. I think next time I need to haggle with the Viceroys, I should send you in my place."

"Father, I'm serious."

"And so am I, child. Still, I know you have a good heart and this means something to you, so I will not let your efforts be for nothing. I will send Sir Gilberton with the supplies and instruct him to request, under a flag of truce, that the supplies be delivered to the Disciples tending to our injured captives. Is that fair?"

For a moment, Isolde wanted to argue with her father. She'd done all this work and didn't want to see it finished by someone else. This had been an opportunity for her to really see her country. She hardly ever got out of the capital, and when she did, it was to visit the stuffy libraries and shrines of the Acolytes, where she only studied and worshiped. Of course, that reasoning was sure to convince her father not to let her go. As much as she longed to see the world, he wanted to keep her locked away from it.

"Yes, Father," she said finally, casting her eyes down so he couldn't see what she was thinking.

Not that it would help. Her father was incredibly clever and seemed to always know what everyone around him was thinking even before they thought it. If he knew her thoughts, though, he said nothing.

Patting her hand, he said, "Good. On your way out, tell the guards to send for Sir Gilberton. I will give him instructions tonight, and have him ride out with the supplies by midday."

"Thank you, Father," she said, trying to sound like a dutiful daughter.

He gave her a small smile, one of the crooked ones that meant he knew more than she did, which suggested that he did indeed read her true wishes as he waved her away. At least she'd succeeded in getting the supplies, and they were going to be delivered.

That's what was actually important.

Starhaven, Kingdom of Sidor, Duchy of King's Heart

Edmund sat behind the massive wood desk, quill in hand, as he reviewed ledgers detailing the kingdom's finances. Across the room, Serwyn slouched in an oversized chair, idly flipping a dagger end over end, catching it by the handle as it fell each time.

"I don't see why I have to be here. This is work for clerks and scribes, or the Exchequer. It's not my job to read these reports," Serwyn complained, tossing the knife again.

Edmund resisted the urge to point out he wasn't actually going over anything, only playing with a knife.

"The Exchequer is who gave us these reports. While clerks, scribes, and even your own nobles are valuable assets, and make the running of the kingdom feasible, delegating all of it to them is a recipe for corruption. It is the king's job to at least be aware of the state of his kingdom."

"And what is the state of my kingdom?" Serwyn asked, clearly sounding like he did not care what the answer was.

Edmund set down the quill and leaned back in his chair, steepling his fingers as he regarded his nephew.

"From a financial viewpoint, not good. Not good at all. The war has strained our resources considerably."

"So? Wars cost money. We'll just take what we need from Lynese after we crush them."

"It's not that simple," Edmund said, rising and pacing slowly, his hands clasped behind his back. "The campaign against Lynese has already dragged on far longer than your father expected. Our coffers are nearly empty. Tax revenues have fallen sharply, hampered by poor harvests two years running in the northern baronies."

He ticked the points off on his fingers. "We've had to take out substantial loans from lenders in Inos and will almost certainly have to go to them again this year, at the very least. Our debt to them grows to the point that, even the riches of Lynese might not be enough to pay it back. And they aren't the only ones we owe money to. We've borrowed from the merchant cartels here as well, just to keep paying the troops. Half the Crown's ships are committed to maintaining supply lines across the Sea of Kings. And the coastal raids from Alchmara have only made matters worse. We can almost certainly expect the Iron Keep baronies, at least those along the coast, to return less than we've projected. Potentially far less. And some of the other baronies there might decide to do the same, since Windermere doesn't have the fortitude to force the issue as he once did."

"Then we loan him the fortitude and take what the barons owe us. Why are we even having to pay their men in Lynese? Those are their men. They should pay them."

"Yes, but we called their men to service. While tradition states that we pay for our subjects' forces when in our service, there's a good reason for it beyond tradition. The men in those armies, especially the conscripts and yeomen pressed into service, aren't able to generate revenue while they're in the field for us. If we make the barons pay for them on top of losing the revenue those men generate, they might be inclined to hold back the next time we ask."

"Then we just increase taxes on the barons to make up the difference. They're the ones causing these problems by not paying what they owe. We just don't tell them it's needed to pay their men."

"They will see through that, nephew. Many of the coastal barons are already strained to their limits by the Alchmaran raids. Demanding higher payments from them now could push some to outright rebellion. I know it's tiring to hear, but we must handle this delicately, without provoking those barons already chafing under their obligations."

"It is tiring to hear. The only thing you seem to know how to say is 'let them get away with defying us.' I made it clear at my crowning that I would not accept defiance from anyone in the realm. Including them."

"I'm sorry if it seems that way, Serwyn. My only goal is to give you the best advice I can to ensure your rule is both long and prosperous. Politics is not an easy game, but it is one you must learn. Besides, there are other ways to deal with this. Ones that allow us to collect the revenues we require without unduly burdening the nobility or further straining their loyalty."

"Like what?" Serwyn asked, finally stopping the knife's incessant motion.

"We increase taxes on the peasants," Edmund said, stopping his pacing and looking almost pleased with himself.

"On the peasants? How? Surely, the barons would take any additional tax on them and still claim poverty."

"There are ways around that. Ways we can better track. For instance, a tax on salt, which all need and which we control the production and distribution of through the royal saltworks. Perhaps an extra copper on each bushel of grain sold or traded, all of which the baronies keep records of. Perhaps even a head tax on every family, which sheriffs can easily collect."

"But would it even be enough? How much could one family pay?"

"That's the beauty of this, my grace. We don't need to tax each family much. A little here or there, added up over the thousands of peasants in the kingdom, can become a large sum very quickly. Better yet, as long as this doesn't come out of their own coffers, most of the barons won't care, as long as they don't feel the pinch themselves."

"Fine. Do that then. So, are we done? Have we solved the kingdom's burdens?" Serwyn asked, pulling himself out of the chair and sliding the knife back into its sheath.

Edmund nodded agreeably, maintaining his polite smile until Serwyn turned on his heel and strode from the room. As soon as the door closed behind him, Edmund let out a slow breath and allowed his shoulders to slump.

Dealing with his nephew was proving more difficult than anticipated. Serwyn seemed to have little interest in anything beyond his own pleasures, leaving the tedious business of actually governing the realm to others. In some ways, Edmund mused, that made things simpler. With the boy diverted by his hobbies, it gave Edmund an easier time arranging everything else as it needed to be, without having to cajole or convince his nephew to do it instead.

Still, there were risks to doing it this way. His nephew had always been ... capricious. Should some crisis arise that engaged the young king's interest, there was no telling how he might overreact. Serwyn's pride and arrogance could easily turn him tyrannical, if challenged.

Edmund moved to gaze out the window, clasping his hands behind his back as he pondered the conundrum his nephew presented. Some way must be found to make the tedious business of governing appealing, even exciting, to the youth. To engage his competitive nature and pride in a positive direction that motivated him to take his duties seriously. Then, as long as he let the king be the one to make the decisions, managing the flow of information to him instead of making them for the boy in his own right, any difficulties could be more easily passed on to someone more ... expendable.

Sidorian Army Camp, Chansol River, Lynese

William was again standing silently in the corner of the command tent, watching as his uncle Aldric and the other commanders pored over campaign maps as they discussed the army's next strategy. The pieces representing the two armies were separated by a winding blue ribbon that denoted the Chansol River, a major waterway that formed a barrier between the Black Hills and Rendalia Bay. There had once been a bridge spanning the center of that river, old and solidly built of stone. The Lynesians, in their retreat, destroyed it to ensure no one followed across behind them and onto the Lynesian plains.

"They've learned. After their mad retreat from the Dorée, instead of clever force placement to keep us from crossing, they simply smashed the bridges behind them," he said, gesturing at the wide expanse of blue curving across the heavy parchment map. "Worse, the Chansol is wider and swifter than the Dorée, so there won't be any fords like we found there to bring men across."

"And the inlet is still contested enough that taking ships around won't work," Baron Pembroke said, pointing at the outline of Rendalia Bay that stretched in from the Sea of Kings. "We could try to push them back long enough to ferry men across to the other side of the river, but we're about evenly matched, and even if we were successful, we don't have enough boats. They'd be able to easily counter the small waves of men we could send across at a time."

"What about going through the Black Hills?" Sir Alistair asked. "I understand it was a problem when we were further east, by the Dorée, but the hills only end a few miles beyond the Chansol. It couldn't be more than a day's ride to cut across and come out onto the plains of Lynese."

"It's still enough to spread our men out and force our horsemen to dismount and go on foot. And they'll have men waiting on the other side just as we have men guarding the hills to our south, in case anyone attempts to cross them and gain the upper hand," Aldric said. "Our men would come out scattered and be easy prey for the heavy infantry the Lynesians gravitate toward."

"Then it's back to bridging the river under fire from their archers and larger weapons," Baron Pembroke said.

"Perhaps, but not yet. We don't have enough men to throw at building a bridge that they will be trying to light on fire. I've attempted a bridging like this once before, when Baron Ironstock attempted his ill-planned insurrection. He only had the smallest fraction of men I had, and still the casualties were horrendous. No, we are not so blessed in soldiers that we can afford to do that unless it's the other way around."

"It might b..." Sir Cedrick was saying when the heavy canvas flap was suddenly brushed aside and a dusty scout entered.

"Enter," Aldric said, waving the young man, not much older than William himself, forward.

"Yes, Your Excellency," the scout said quickly. "A group of Lynese have come out of the Black Hills by the old smuggler's trail. They've got a line of carts with them, pulled by mules and oxen, loaded up with supplies."

"An ambush?" Pembroke asked, although sounding a little confused.

The scout shook his head. "Doesn't seem so, milord. Sir Drummond checked the wagons himself. It's medicine, food, things like that. The Disciples with them claim its relief supplies donated by nobles in Lynese. Collected by the emperor's daughter, they say, and meant for the Disciples tending to the wounded here and at the Order of Healing chantry in Rendalia City."

William had grown up hearing stories about Rendalia City, the birthplace of the Whittons, before they conquered King's Heart and started the Whitton dynasty. In the stories, it had always seemed like a wonderous place, foreign, yet still somehow part of their legacy. The reality was somewhat different.

The first city conquered by Gavric during the war, it was still the primary port for Sidorian ships, and where the *Lions Pride* had docked when they'd arrived. The city was still in ruins from the fight to take it, but the level of poverty William had witnessed could not have been solely caused by collateral damage. He had no doubt the Order's chantry there was busy, and in need of supplies.

"The knights escorting them. How many are there?" Aldric asked.

"No more than ten, armored and armed, but letting the Disciples do the talking. The Disciples said the knights are just guarding the supplies on account of the bandits in the hills."

William watched Aldric considering. He knew his uncle to be a good man, but he was also a pragmatist. While the Disciples were generally considered non-state actors and granted passage between lines, it was rare that it was allowed, owing to the jumpy nature of most armies. William had read a lot of tales of war and famous battles, and he'd never heard of an offer like this, and he was pretty sure his uncle hadn't either, from the expression on his face.

After a long moment of consideration, Aldric shook his head. "As much as the Disciples could use these supplies, and caring for the enemy's wounded might free up our own resources, I cannot risk letting any of them behind our lines. The hills are a warren; who knows what else lies within?"

William was surprised at his disappointment for his uncle. While he was sure it made military sense not to let men from an enemy country behind their lines, the laws of the Acolytes commanded that all Disciples doing the work for their order be allowed free passage. That each was a nation unto themselves and in service of the Ancients. He'd heard it preached often by the elders. Surely, this was covered by that commandment.

William knew Aldric to be a true follower of the Acolytes, and hadn't even considered that his uncle might say no.

"Perhaps there is still some way we could turn this to our advantage," Sir Cedrick said. "The Disciples clearly found a path to bring wagons through the hills; might we follow their route back and find a way around? It would solve our current dilemma and allow us to break free onto the plains of Lynese."

Baron Pembroke shook his head. "There is a reason the enemy has not attacked from the hills themselves. Any force we sent would come out scattered and easy prey. It is too great a risk."

"But we learned in the Great Temple it is our duty to assist the Orders when able. This seems one such chance," William pleaded when it became clear none of the men were going to speak up for doing the right thing. "Shouldn't we allow the Disciples and their supplies through, if only this once? Besides, they have *our* men held prisoner as well. It would give the Lynesians reason to treat our own people better in return."

Aldric turned to look at his nephew, his expression unreadable as he stared hard at William, making the younger man take a step back from the stare alone.

William was so focused on his uncle's attention that Baron Pembroke's voice almost made him jump when the older man spoke.

"I must object, Your Excellency. Allowing any number of the enemy behind our lines is too great a risk, especially with …"

"Perhaps my nephew is right," Aldric interrupted, raising a hand to quiet Pembroke's protest. "While military caution must rule our actions, we also have a duty to the Orders decreed by the Ancients themselves."

Aldric paused, glancing back at the map pensively before looking at William.

"Very well. If he thinks this is a good idea, I will allow this aid through, albeit with precautions. William, consider this your first test of leadership. Take a contingent and inspect the shipment thoroughly to make sure this isn't a trick. If all is in order, ask Sir Drummond to provide an escort through our lines to the chantry. The Disciples only. No Lynesian knight may cross our lines."

"Thank you, Uncle," William said.

"Eskild," Aldric said, turning his attention to the Sergeant. "Help him pick out a detachment to take and then go with him, in case he has any questions. Also, make it clear to Sir Drummond that the final decisions are Lord William's."

"As you command," Eskild said, slapping his fist to his chest.

With a respectful bow, William turned and strode from the tent, Eskild on his heels. His first command and his chance to show everyone he was ready for this.

Chapter 8

Starhaven, Kingdom of Sidor

Edict of Travel

By Order of His Grace, King Serwyn Whitton the First, King of Sidor, on this day, let it be known that for the preservation of order and the safety of its people, the following restrictions on non-landed people living within the boundaries of the Kingdom of Sidor and its manor lands are hereby imposed:

Part One: Non-landed citizens shall not be permitted to travel outside their manor lord's lands and purview without obtaining written permission from their baron or the baron's appointed official. Permission shall only be granted for short durations when absolutely necessary for business or family reasons, and at the discretion of their baron or the baron's appointed official.

Part Two: Until such time as the raids and unrest along the coast of Iron Keep have abated, travel to and from the Barony of Stormhaven is hereby prohibited without exception for any non-landed citizens not currently residing in that barony, for their own safety. Any non-landed citizen found to have traveled to or from the Barony of Stormhaven shall be considered a fugitive and face punishment.

Part Three: Non-landed citizens are forbidden from conducting business outside their home villages without obtaining a trade permit from their King or the King's appointed official. Permits shall impose fees and only be issued when the King deems the business essential.

Part Four: Non-landed citizens must obtain all goods and services from approved village merchants and artisans as designated by their baron. Trade with outsiders is forbidden without baronial permission.

To enforce these restrictions, barons shall implement documentation checks on roads, increased patrols, and inspections of non-landed citizens' homes and property. Violators shall face imprisonment, forced labor, fines, or other such penalties as seen fit by local authorities.

Additional restrictions may be announced as deemed necessary for preserving order and stability within the kingdom. All non-landed citizens shall comply fully and without delay.

"Uncle," Serwyn said, letting the parchment fall onto the desk as he looked up. "I've read this over several times now. While I understand the intent, limiting the movement of peasants seems … pointless?"

"On the contrary, Your Grace, there is sound reasoning behind these restrictions. While, of course, the public reason is safety and security of the kingdom, in response to Baron Sinclair's request for action on the part of the Crown, there are real reasons for enacting this. For one, we have started seeing some … disquiet among your non-landed subjects that, if not accounted for, could lead to wider unrest or even revolt. Since unfettered movement allows for the spread of dissent and sedition, limiting it will limit the danger of a wider problem, should tensions boil over. It also prevents certain … elements, in the kingdom from gaining more power and becoming a potential problem. This early in your reign, there are those who will try and use the transition as an opportunity to gain power for themselves."

"Elements? You mean Baron Sinclair, I assume," Serwyn said, holding up the decree.

"I do," Edmund nodded. "Garris has always been too sympathetic to the complaints of the masses. And it is no secret his barony has become a hotbed of peasant agitation and whispered schemes against the Crown."

"You keep telling me how dangerous Baron Sinclair is, and yet, every time I suggest the surest way to protect ourselves from him, you tell me executing the man for treason isn't an option."

"I understand it's frustrating, but it is the reality of ruling. As I've said, while Sinclair has undoubtedly overstepped, he remains well-respected by many of the barons. Openly moving against him risks dividing the kingdom, perhaps even sparking civil war."

Serwyn still seemed unsure, mostly because he found sorting through the politics of rule frustrating. He knew his uncle meant well and was doing the best he could to guide Serwyn, but … being faced with all the things he didn't know, that he should have, caused him to have unpleasant thoughts. In spite of himself, Serwyn frowned and began tapping out a rhythm against the arm of his chair, a habit he had when he was feeling frustrated or angry.

"It goes beyond just boxing Sinclair in, though, Serwyn. Limiting the ability for new peasants to come into his lands, or his dissatisfied peasants to leave is one strategy, and will cause unrest that he will have to deal with, but it isn't the only one. Sinclair's barony is one of the more prosperous ones in Iron Keep. Not so well off as the baronies of Delaney Heights or Everwood, but still, it's prosperous, which is why he's been able to amass the power that he has. The new taxes will limit trade between the baronies, except for those who get permits from the Crown, which will weaken our enemies and strengthen our allies, since we decide who has to pay the new travel tax."

"Seeding distrust between them, pulling the barons apart."

"Correct, and giving incentives to those barons to curry favor with the Crown, in order to get their own permits. The barons are not fools, either. They will understand who our target is. They will not want to have any of Sinclair's disfavor rub off onto them, further driving them apart."

"And it puts more money into our coffers," Serwyn said, picking up the paper again, reading it over once more.

"Exactly. I believe you'll find that, sometimes, there is more to be gained by careful maneuvering and subtlety, than by brute force, Your Grace."

Setting the paper on the desk in front of him, Serwyn picked up his quill, dipped it in ink, and signed his flowing signature at the bottom with a flourish.

"There. It is done," Serwyn said, and then frowned again, the tapping returning.

Edmund took the letter and, sprinkling fine sand across it to help the ink dry, busied himself with affixing Serwyn's seal to it while Serwyn thought.

Just as his uncle turned to leave, Serwyn said, "I know you wish me to handle matters more delicately, Uncle. I understand your point, that direct action is not always the best way to do things, and I am trying to learn. It's just ... thinking three steps ahead here, two steps left there, it feels unnatural. I ... I just wanted you to know that I *am* trying."

Edmund placed a hand on his nephew's shoulder, giving it an affectionate squeeze, "I know you are. I can see it, as can any who've seen the effort and time you've put into your new role. Ruling is … it's not like being a warrior, which I know is disappointing. But when you succeed, when you leave your opponent guessing, when you cause them to play into your hand … well, it's a unique feeling you won't soon forget. You're doing well, Serwyn. I knew you were a bright young man and ready for leadership, but even I didn't predict how quickly you would grow into your role. Have patience with yourself. This all takes time to master, but you are already well ahead of where I was when I was your age. In time, I have no doubt you will outshine us all."

Serwyn smiled, one of his rare, genuine smiles.

"Thank you, Uncle. In time, perhaps it will be I instructing you, instead of the reverse."

Edmund laughed, "I've no doubt of that, Your Grace. You've your father's strength and your mother's intellect. Fate has granted you the makings of a great king."

Edmund collected the documents and was halfway to the threshold when Serwyn spoke again.

"You know I cannot let the matter of Sinclair lie forever. Once we've cut him off from his allies, I will demand his head. There is a time for discretion, and a time for action. When the moment comes, I will not hesitate to strike."

"As is right and wise, Your Grace," Edmund said, looking back with an approving look. "Patience now, action later, once the ground is properly prepared. You see, you understand statecraft better than you know."

Serwyn smiled to himself again. He was learning. In time, he wouldn't need to heed anyone's advice or counsel but his own. When he was ready, he'd show everyone what it really meant to be King.

Dead Man's Hills, Rendalia Province, Lynese

William felt powerful, important at the head of his small column of mounted men-at-arms. While Baron Pembroke hadn't seen fit to send any knighted men with William, maybe because it would be beneath a knight to take orders from a young man, even one from the Whitton family, William didn't mind. Ten strong, seasoned soldiers under his command was more than he could have hoped for when he stepped aboard the *Lion's Pride* with his uncle several months ago.

He'd always hoped for a command, but he never imagined getting one this early. It was all he could do to keep the smile off his face as he attempted to emulate the stern, stoic expression Eskild always wore. The Thane Sergeant seemed to William to be the pinnacle of what a soldier should be. Strong, disciplined, and obviously respected by his comrades.

As they approached the camp, sentries called out a challenge, then waved them through once recognizing William's armor and insignia. Riding between the handful of tents that made up this small command post, William made for the pavilion flying the standard of the Barony of Cloud Harbor; a simple keep, clouds on either side.

Dismounting, William stepped beneath the faded canopy of the pavilion, his helmet under one arm. Sir Drummond stood in the center, conferring with a grizzled captain but looked up at William's approach.

"Sir Drummond, I bring orders from Baron Pembroke." William extended the letter, the wax seal imprinted with the sigil of a wyvern in front of two small hills.

The knight took the letter, broke the seal with a gnarled thumb, and quickly read the contents, his brow creasing as he did. Wordlessly, he handed the letter to the man beside him.

"It seems you're in charge of this little situation we have, My Lord," he said.

William thought he could detect the hint of a smirk in the way the man said 'my lord,' but let it pass.

"Show us to the wagons," he said, in as official a tone as he could muster.

Sir Drummond exchanged a silent look with the other man, gave a near imperceptible nod, and then gestured for William to lead the way. This was a border encampment, mostly in place as a central point for patrols riding up and down this section of the Sidorian line. The small wagon train lay a few dozen yards beyond, watchful soldiers standing guard over it.

There were nine wagons in total, each painted with the sign of the Order of Healing: twin hand palms holding an open flame. William had seen their robed brethren before on the streets of Starhaven, administering to the sick and needy in the city, but standing next to the Disciples were men wearing the gold and red wyvern of the House of Montbore. Maybe it shouldn't be surprising; after all, the Acolytes served everyone, no matter their nationality. But, William had always felt the Ancients were with them, aiding them in battle, hearing their offerings, so to see the same symbols with those they were fighting against was ... jarring.

The brown-robed men, and it seemed to be all men, busied themselves about their wagons. While all of the orders contained men and women, it made sense that they would send only men into a war zone like this, especially on a mission through the Dead Man's Hills. Most bandits sold their honor a long time ago and had no problem with harming anyone, regardless of how untouchable they should be. There were stories of seekers, those that the Acolytes tasked with searching the world for newly unearthed or hidden mystic objects from the time of magic, who had disappeared while on their journey, only for their possessions to reappear in the hands of captured bandits.

Turning to Sir Drummond, William said, "Keep your knights here and keep an eye on them and the hills beyond, just in case. I'll take my men to inspect the wagons."

Sir Drummond gave him another look that suggested he might not think that was the best idea but only said, "As you command, My Lord."

"You, with me," he said to the men-at-arms he'd brought with him. "We're going to search these wagons. There should only be medicine and foodstuffs. Anything that you find, no matter

75

how innocuous, that isn't either medicine or foodstuffs, report it immediately. We all know what the Lynesians are like. I don't put it beyond any of them to sneak something in with the Order's supplies. Sergeant Eskild will lead the search while I speak to the knights."

Giving what he hoped was a commanding nod to Eskild, William turned his back on them, trying to seem confident that they'd follow his orders without question, and walked toward the still-mounted knights.

"I want to commend you on doing your duty and upholding your sworn oaths by escorting these Disciples through the hills. However, I cannot allow you to pass through these lines. You have it on my word as a Whitton and member of the Sidorian Royal Family that I will see them delivered safely to their brothers, so they may continue their good work. Please return to your master and convey my thanks for his kind gesture in ensuring that these supplies arrived safely."

William tried to remember every tale he'd ever heard of knights, every protocol he'd heard from both tutor and weapons master about the duties and responsibilities of nobility, and how those duties were to be handled. While these were his enemy, he had a responsibility, and he wanted to make sure that it was carried out to its fullest.

The knight at the forefront of the group gave a nod and backed his men up, but did not return to the hills. For a moment, William wanted to turn and look at Sir Drummond, to see how he should handle that, but he resisted the urge, instead turning to the wagons to help with the search. Eskild was directing the men-at-arms to check this, then that wagon, telling them to look here, then there, going over each wagon inch by stubborn inch.

So far, they had searched two wagons and found nothing other than what was expected, just as Sir Drummond had predicted. It wasn't until he noticed Eskild watching the Disciples and not the wagons, that he had any sense that things might not be going as smoothly as it seemed.

William looked to the men Eskild had been watching, although William was aware he was being more obvious about it than the sergeant had been. It took a minute for him to see what Eskild was clearly seeing. It was subtle at first: a nervous glance shared between two Disciples as the third wagon was inspected, one man shifting his weight and adjusting his robe, another whose eyes darted about too quickly. If William had only noticed that himself, he might not have thought anything of it, but the look on Eskild's face said he should be concerned.

William opened his mouth to voice his suspicions to Eskild, but the sergeant was already moving. In two swift strides he closed the gap to the nearest Disciple, seizing the man by the front of his robe. The Disciple cried out in surprise as Eskild yanked him forward, ripping open the front of his robe to reveal chain and gambeson underneath bearing the red and gold wyvern of Lynese.

"Armor!" Eskild bellowed. "These are no Disciples!"

Around him, men cast off their robes and swords rang from scabbards as the false Disciples drew their weapons. William spun, pulling his own sword from its sheath. All about him there were shouts of warning and the clash of steel.

The knights he had just sent away wheeled their mounts, brandishing their swords as they thundered toward the ranks of William's footmen. William barely had time to brace himself before they smashed into his line.

Men cursed and screamed, blades slashing ruthlessly. William parried a swipe from a false Disciple, then cut the man down with a backswing. He managed to jump back just as a mounted knight rode past, the blade meant for his head only grazing his scalp. He could feel the sharp sting on his scalp, but there was no time to do anything about it.

All was chaos. His men grappled desperately with the ambushers, fending off the pounding hooves and slashing swords of the knights. They were cut off from Sir Drummond and the rest of the Sidorians and in real danger of being annihilated. Through the madness, he caught sight of Eskild.

The sergeant waded through the fight, sword and dagger reaping lives with ruthless efficiency, a whirlwind of death. Even with Eskild's ability, his men were falling fast, surrounded and outnumbered. There had been dozens of false knights, not to mention the mounted knights. William had only brought ten men, half of whom fell when the deception was revealed, unprepared to protect themselves. Drummond had perhaps two dozen on hand, but half of those were archers whose job it would be to dispatch anyone coming from the hills in the distance, not repel an assault that appeared before them as if by the magic of old.

"Regroup on me!" William yelled.

He slashed desperately at the press of bodies. His sword turned aside another thrust before finding its mark, stabbing the man through. Risking a glance behind him, he saw Sir Drummond leading a knot of men into the fight, trying to break through to William and his surrounded detachment, bellowing like a giant. His hands swung a massive sword that William most certainly wouldn't have even been able to lift, smashing through metal and man. The turn to look back had been too risky. One of the false Disciples saw the distraction and charged. If not for the man-at-arms who stepped in front of William, taking the sword meant for him, William would have been dead.

Instead, the man he'd commanded, the man he was supposed to have been leading, dropped dead at his feet. William slashed out with his sword, screaming with rage, his blade ripping the man's cheek and mouth open, spinning him away and into the dirt.

William swung his sword in a desperate arc as more enemies attacked and more of his men died, trying to keep the press of enemies at bay. Blood ran down his forehead from the earlier sword cut, half-blinding him. He blinked it away just in time to see a sword thrust coming for his belly. Twisting aside, the blade only grazed his side before Eskild's dagger found the man's throat.

"Back to back!" Eskild bellowed, an arm going around William and pulling him forcefully backward. "Form up!"

The remaining three men clustered around William and Eskild, presenting a ring of steel to their attackers. William parried and stabbed, struggling to keep up with all the attackers coming at them. A knight's sword caught his pauldron, denting the metal into his shoulder. He gasped at the burst of pain.

Across the melee, Sir Drummond crashed into the fight like a battering ram, two knights falling before him, skulls crushed by the giant blade.

"Break through!" Drummond roared. "To the Viscount!"

Step by bloody step, his knot of men battled toward William. So close now. William redoubled his efforts, trying to fight his way to meet them. A sword gashed his thigh, and he stumbled, nearly falling. Eskild held him up, his dagger finding the man's heart.

"Whitton!" Sir Drummond yelled, his voice cutting above the noise.

"Fight through," William yelled, turning and attacking toward Sir Drummond.

They had to get out of this and to the rest of their men, only a handful of steps away now. He stabbed one man, smashed a mailed elbow into the face of another, and then they were through. The fighting of Sir Drummond's men was intense, but they no longer had men on all sides.

"Sir Drummond," one of the men yelled.

William twisted to look. The knight sprawled on the ground, blood pouring from a deep gash along his ribs. Two men struggled to lift him. William shoved through to help, ducking as a sword whistled past his head. Together, they hauled the huge knight up. William wrapped Drummond's arm across his shoulders, bearing up under his weight. Drummond's men closed ranks around them. The big knight was barely conscious, feet dragging.

"Hold on, Sir Drummond," William urged. "Just a little farther."

William looked to the battle. More Sidorians came charging in on horseback, drawn by the sounds of the fight. The tide had turned, and the immediate danger was over. As he dragged the large knight, Eskild and the remaining men laid into the last of their enemies. Knights and false Disciples fell before them until none were left standing.

As William lowered Drummond gently to the ground by the command tent, the sergeant strode up, his blade red with blood.

"We've carried the day," Eskild said grimly, "but only just."

"It's not over yet," William replied. Turning, he scanned the milling Sidorian soldiers until he spotted one wearing the sash of a mounted scout.

"You there, runner!" William called out with as much authority as he could muster through his exhaustion. The scout hurried over.

"My Lord?"

"Ride as fast as your mount will take you back to Baron Pembroke and the main force. Tell him Sir Drummond is down, and we expect to be attacked shortly by forces coming through the Dead Man's Hills. Tell him I'm gathering in patrols and preparing to repel them, but that this assault will most likely be spread out, and our number is depleted."

The runner just stood there for a moment, staring at him and then at the distant hills.

"Go. Now!" William said, his tone commanding, and for once not forced or false.

William watched as the man vaulted into the saddle of a fresh horse held by another soldier, then galloped off toward the Sidorian encampment upstream along the river as Eskild asked, "Are you sure?"

"I am. This ambush was to break our line, allow them to gather scattered forces coming out of the hills and be prepared before our reinforcements could arrive. Pull in the wounded and form up every man you can. We need to attack as soon as they appear out of the hills. If they consolidate their forces, they will roll over us and we will lose in our rear line before Pembroke can arrive."

Eskild looked at him, judging, then with a nod, turned and started barking orders.

Chapter 9

William walked slowly across the blood-soaked field, carefully stepping over the bodies of the dead and wounded. The fighting had ended hours ago, but the moans and cries of injured men still filled the air as Disciples moved among them, doing their best to treat gruesome wounds. The real Disciples who arrived shortly after Baron Pembroke, the ones who'd been traveling with the Sidorian army, not the fake Disciples brought by the Lynesians.

Eskild walked silently at William's side, his face an impassive mask. For William, it was all still painfully fresh: the ambush, and his failure in detecting it. He had led good men into battle and paid the price in lives lost or ruined bodies. The only reason any of them had been there, and allowed the Lynesians to get that close, was because of decisions he'd made. The weight of that responsibility felt crushingly heavy on his shoulders.

They came upon a wounded soldier lying on his back, clutching at a deep stab wound in his belly as he whimpered in agony. The man's eyes were glassy with pain and fear—he knew the wound was mortal. One look and William could see the guts spilling from the wide gash were already going black.

"We need a healer over here!" William called, but he knew it was likely too late to save the man. He crouched down beside him, putting a steadying hand on his shoulder. "Be still, friend. Help is coming."

"Am I dying?" the man, not much older than William, asked in a whisper.

William glanced helplessly at Eskild, unsure of what to say. Of how to tell a man he's about to die. Eskild gave a subtle shake of his head, telling William to go on.

"I fear so," William said gently. "But we will stay with you until the end."

The young soldier closed his eyes, tears leaking from the corners. His breath came in short, pained gasps for several long minutes until, with a final ragged exhalation, he lay still.

"All any commander can do is give his men the chance for an honorable death in battle. Many meet worse fates in this world."

"And what fate will I meet when called to account for those I led into slaughter?" William yelled at Eskild. "How many more will I throw away without even considering the effect of my commands?"

Eskild didn't flinch or even acknowledge the anger William turned on him. "Until your last breath or the war's end, whichever comes first. This is what war is."

William stood and wiped his face, looking away so Eskild wouldn't see his tears. A Disciple finally arrived, kneeling next to the man and closing his eyes. William and Eskild moved on, leaving the Disciple to usher the man's soul to the Ancients in peace. As they walked away, Eskild looked back as the Disciple knelt over the dead soldier. His face hardened.

"There will be consequences for the Lynese disguising themselves as Disciples," he said. "I've seen men killed for less."

"I'm surprised it bothers you so much. I would have thought, being from Thay, you were a ... not a follower of the Acolytes."

"You can say Purifier; it will not cause me to be flayed alive," Eskild said. "And yes, I am, but that doesn't mean I take issue with the Disciples. I have seen them heal and tend to too many dying men in too many battles. Besides, we aren't as different as you'd like to think. We believe in the Ancients, just not your veneration of them."

"Oh," William said.

It was like hearing someone tell you they could fly like a wyvern and land on the moon. Instead, he asked, "What of Sir Drummond? Does he still live?"

"Yes. They took him to the field hospital, half-dead and leaking, but he was alive the last time I saw him."

"I should ... when we're done here, I should go see him. Do you think he'd want me to?"

"Why wouldn't he? I understand your people take visits by members of the royal family as some sign of good deeds."

"Because I'm the reason he's there. My uncle and Baron Pembroke both said letting this group in was a mistake, that they couldn't be trusted. I spoke up and convinced my uncle to let them through. Because of my words, good men now lie dead or dying on this field."

"Do you know for a fact that they wouldn't have died otherwise?" Eskild asked. "They were waiting, under guard, yes, but still close to our lines. Are you certain that, if their bait was not taken, they would have remained at a distance, not tried to attack anyway?"

"No, Sir Drummond was watching them, and he had his men ready to deal with them. My bringing new soldiers to reinspect the wagons, allowing us to become surrounded, forced Sir Drummond to respond, charge in to rescue us, thereby weakening our position. Had I not demanded the Disciples be let through, he would have been better prepared. Yes, some may have died still, but far fewer. And almost certainly not the majority of the men we brought with us."

"Or, they could have convinced Sir Drummond to give them another look, this time surrounding the men without someone like Sir Drummond on the outside, ready to charge in and keep the ambush from turning into a slaughter. Perhaps they kill Sir Drummond and all his men and run into the countryside. Or, the ambush doesn't work, but Sir Drummond's forces are still weakened, except this time, there isn't someone to call for reinforcements, realizing the full scope of the enemy's plan. It is impossible to know what would have happened differently," Eskild said, and then stopped, placing a hand on William's shoulder. "Difficult decisions are inherent to command. Evaluating your decisions is wise. Learning from them to keep you from making the same mistakes again is wise. Second-guessing yourself, using information you have now that you didn't have then, is an exercise in futility. It's foolish."

"My uncle had the same information, but he would have made a different decision if not for me."

"So is he foolish for letting you convince him against his better judgment, or is he so in your thrall that he has no will of his own, save yours?"

"I don't ... It's not like that," William protested.

"It's not? Then how is his judgment to let you come here and reinspect the wagons blameless, while you asking him to allow you to do it makes you a fool?"

"I ... that's not the same thing."

"I'm just telling you how it is; it's your choice to believe me. What you can't do, is let the weight of your orders overwhelm you. Leadership is the art of bearing that crushing weight of responsibility you're feeling without faltering. Of considering each life with equal gravity, and being willing to put those lives at risk if it is needed."

"Maybe my father was right, and I'm not ready."

"I'm not sure there's such a thing as being ready to lead men into war. You only really know once you're there and see how you hold up under pressure."

"And we can see how I'm holding up."

"I'd say you did well. Are you judging yourself unfairly now? Yes. But in the moment, you didn't stop to chastise yourself or feel sorry for yourself. You gave the orders that needed to be given and put more men's lives to the test, because that's what was needed. That's the man I'd judge, not the one seeing the battle's aftermath now."

"But will the men trust me next time?"

"If you show them what you did today ... yes. The men do not expect perfection. Anyone who's fought in war knows how unpredictable and unforgiving it can be. What they expect is that you weigh decisions well, and that when you spend their lives, you do it consciously, with reason. If you do that, you will have their trust. Speaking as one of those soldiers myself, what I saw today from you was a good start. You kept your head in battle, made the right decisions in a moment of chaos, and gave us a victory. No small feat."

"Thank you," William said.

"I was not offering you a compliment, only an honest appraisal."

William was interrupted before he could think of a response.

"Lord Whitton," a runner called, jogging over to them. "With Baron Pembroke's compliments, My Lord, he requests you join him and the other commanders at the assembly area at once to discuss the situation."

"Tell him we'll be right there," William said, sending the man back the way he came.

As the man ran off, Eskild said, "They don't normally call failures to go over post-battle strategy." With a pat on his shoulder, Eskild turned and followed the runner toward the gathered commanders. William gave one last look around the battlefield, before he, too, followed, leaving the dying and dead behind.

Starhaven, Kingdom of Sidor

Edmund Whitton stood on the balcony overlooking the palace square, his hands clenching the railing tightly enough to turn his knuckles white. The sound of hundreds of people shouting and screaming floated up to him, each shout for Serwyn's abdication and each jeer causing his hands to grip even tighter.

A cordon of knights stood fast, blocking the wide entrance into the palace square, but the mob was pushing against them hard. Edmund was no knight, but seeing the numbers of peasants continue to grow, he imagined it only a matter of time before there were enough of them to make it impossible to hold the tide back.

He couldn't see actual weapons, but here and there peasants were holding lit torches, in spite of the midday hour, which boded ill.

Things had spiraled out of control too quickly, much faster than he'd expected. Yesterday, there had been only fifteen or twenty peasants. Edmund had sent them away, ordering the palace gates barred to all petitioners, thinking they would calm if given time. It had been a non-event, so much so that he hadn't even told Serwyn about it.

When the boy did finally notice there were people outside, gathered by the courtyard entrance, Edmund had told him he'd handle it. It would not do to fail at such a public, and local, problem. Serwyn was still malleable, and Edmund had yet to remove all the people in the palace who might try to challenge his role with the boy.

"Send for Captain Bramwell," Edmund yelled over his shoulder to one of his stewards, not bothering to look back at him.

It took almost ten minutes for the captain to appear, Edmund's fury growing with each minute as he watched the crowd below.

"Your Excellency," Bramwell said, stopping just outside the doorway to the balcony.

Edmund whirled on him, moving close to the captain, "Explain to me what is happening out there. Why have you done nothing about it?"

Captain Bramwell straightened to attention, keeping his gaze fixed steadily ahead, and said, "Your Excellency, the crowd started gathering before dawn, enlarging on the group that was here yesterday. At first, just a trickle of peasants drifted in through the city gates. My men kept watch but did not intervene as the numbers were small. However, over the last few hours, more and more have flooded into the square. I attempted to speak with some of the ringleaders, to convince them to disperse peacefully, but they are too angry to give up yet. By my estimate, there are close to a thousand peasants crowded into the square now, with more arriving by the minute. My guards are heavily outnumbered. Any attempt to remove them now will come with bloodshed."

"Then why have you waited so long? Why have you done nothing?" he repeated. "When I brought you here from the countryside, your orders were to keep the peace in Starhaven. I gave you wide authority to use the city guard to stamp out any threat of unrest."

"You did, Your Excellency," Bramwell nodded. "But you also instructed me to keep the peace and ensure no scandal tarnishes the crown during the King's transition. I have done my best to follow that directive by negotiating with the leaders in the crowd, attempting to get them to disperse peacefully. I had hoped, that by not pressing them and giving them time to calm, they would see the danger in the situation and clear the square without bloodshed. I was trying to follow your standing order, Your Excellency."

"You thought my order was to allow rabble to insult the King? To throw things at the palace? Are you a fool? I don't care what it takes, Captain. I want them out of that square immediately, by force if necessary."

"As you command, Your Excellency," Bramwell said. "I will have them removed at once."

"See that you do," Edmund said, and turned his back dismissively on the captain.

After several long minutes, Edmund spotted Bramwell emerging from the main palace gates, flanked by ranks of armored city guards. The crowd pressed together as the guards marched on them, perhaps in some vain hope that the guards were a show of force and not an actual threat. The guards stopped a few paces away from the rabble, their shields up.

"Disperse now, by order of the King, or we will remove you by force!" Bramwell shouted, pulling his sword.

The response was a hail of stones, rotten vegetables, and crude insults. Finally, Bramwell proved he wasn't a complete incompetent, by giving the order again, before bringing his sword arm down and signaling the guards, who began their charge, smashing into the packed mob, proving his threat was more than a bluff.The screams could be heard all the way to the grand hall.

Sidorian Army Camp, Chansol River, Lynese

William ducked his head as he entered the healers' pavilion. Rows upon rows of ragged cots lined the interior, some shielded by thin partitions, others open to the central aisle. The tang of herbs and ointments mingled with the iron scent of blood, creating an unsettling atmosphere.

Brown-robed Disciples moved among the wounded soldiers, changing soiled dressings, administering elixirs, and offering reassuring words. Some briefly glanced in his direction as William passed, but otherwise ignored him, used to his frequent visits of late.

William threaded past the dying and the injured, pausing occasionally to greet a man here or there, offering words of encouragement. Most were sons of tenant farmers and small landholders, not career soldiers. Men called up by the levy to fight in the war far from their homes. He finally stopped by the patient he'd come to see. The one he'd visited each day for the past week.

Sir Drummond lay unmoving under a thin blanket, his skin pale and damp with sweat. Bandages swathed his chest and shoulder, marking where he'd suffered the grievous blow coming to William's defense. Guilt gnawed at William as he looked down at the loyal knight. If not for William's mistakes, Drummond would still be whole and healthy.

A Disciple in brown robes paused next to William. "He still clings to life, my lord, though his condition is unchanged. We have cleaned and bound his wounds, but the rest lies with the Ancients now."

It was the same as every other day, the Disciples apologetic they could do no more than they had, and a report that his condition remained unchanged.

"Thank you for everything you've done."

"Of course. Let me know if you need anything." The Disciple bowed and continued on his way, leaving William alone with his thoughts.

A dance repeated, day after day. William pulled over a three-legged stool and sat heavily, weariness seeping into his bones. While his guilt brought him here each evening, he still had his own duties to attend to. Mostly sitting in on councils of war as his uncle and the commanders worked to find a way out of their stalemate.

The new bridge over the Chansol River was progressing slowly. It was a costly project, with Lynesian archers firing continually at them as they worked. His uncle had ordered barricades built, great hulks of blackened branches roped together to shelter the builders, but that had only helped to some extent. The Lynesians would fire arrows with lit cloth on the end, setting the barriers on fire, until the Sidorians threw them into the water, leaving the workers unprotected.

The activity repeated much the same way every day, as his uncle spent men's lives to complete the bridge that would get them through this region and onto the open Lynesian plains. When he'd first heard the plan, a week ago, before his ill-fated first command, William had thought it genius. Yes, the predicted death toll had been on the high side, but that seemed a fitting exchange for getting their army into the open and ending the war. He'd even thought it the more humane option, since the sooner the war ended, the sooner their men could return home and leave this damnable place.

Now, he wasn't as confident. He knew his uncle wasn't callous or throwing men's lives away without purpose. He also knew he'd been right, that it was better to end the war sooner, rather than drag it on endlessly. And yet, he'd learned the cost of ordering men into action knowing they would die, and couldn't imagine how his uncle handled it.

But handle it Aldric did. While it wouldn't be true to say he was happy to do it, he seemed unbothered each time they talked about it, and William was having trouble wrapping his mind around that fact.

He stared down at Sir Drummond. Just one of the many he'd cost in his short battle. Twelve had died where they stood, including half of his original ten men he'd been given charge over. Three more had died of their wounds since then, and William had been powerless to do anything about it.

William sat in silence for some time when a quiet voice spoke. "Beggin' yer pardon, m'lord. I don't mean to intrude."

He looked over to see a soldier with one arm bound across his chest reclining on a nearby cot.

"It's no trouble. How are you?" William asked, indicating the man's injury.

"Well as can be with this hole in my shoulder," the soldier said, raising his slung arm slightly. "But the healers say I'll keep the arm, so there's that."

"I'm glad to hear it."

The soldier eyed Sir Drummond lying still on the cot. "I seen you here every day sitting with Sir Drummond. With him not being awake and all, I wondered what's the point of a lord like you visiting an unconscious man?"

William studied the older man's face before answering.

"You're right that he can't hear me speak, but then that's not why I come here. I come here because it's my duty, both as his lord and as the one who ordered the action that sent him here. He saved my life in the recent fighting by the Dead Man's Hills, the least I can do in return is to be with him while he recovers. Watch over him."

The soldier frowned slightly but said nothing. William could see he didn't get what he was trying to say.

"The lives of every man there were placed in my hands," William continued, trying a slightly different tack. "As was the decision of when and how to risk those lives to achieve our ends. Such choices come with a great burden of responsibility, especially when the cost is borne in blood. My orders and my mistakes are the reason this man lies here now. So I will sit here, and though he cannot hear my words, I hope in some way Sir Drummond knows that I am here."

The soldier regarded William thoughtfully. "Can't say as I ever heard of a lord acting as you do, visiting his wounded men every day. Most highborns I've known don't spare a thought for the common soldiers bleeding for 'em."

William shrugged. "I can't speak to what other lords may or may not do. I only know my own mind in this. When men pledge their service to you, you owe them your care and protection in return."

"That's fair," the soldier replied. "And more than most would say these days."

"What's your name?"

"Garr, m'lord. Garr of Eliston."

"I am William," he said, extending a hand.

Garr stared at his outstretched hand for a moment, as if it were some foreign thing, before reaching out and shaking it.

"Where were you injured?" William asked.

"By the Chansol River, fighting against the Lynesian rear guard, trying to take the bridge before they could destroy it," the soldier replied. "We got damned near it too. Had those knights not come charging across, we would have had it. Still, being what it is, we held together as they hit us. Took an arrow to the shoulder for my trouble."

"You were with Sir Alistair's men then?" William asked, his mind going to the maps he'd looked over at his uncle's councils, trying to remember who led the charge to take the river during the first advance, before the bridges were burned.

"Aye."

"A difficult business, from what I heard."

Garr didn't respond right away, only shifted on his cot, wincing slightly at the movement.

"Begging your pardon again, but might I ask a question?" he said, finally.

"Of course."

"I was just wondering. Seeing as how Sir Drummond is an ordained knight and all, it makes some sense a lord would come see to him. And it has me wondering: would you have done the same for a common man-at-arms as you do for a knight?"

William was a little surprised, more than he should have been after spending time with Eskild. He'd assumed the ... informal nature of the Thay sergeant had been due to either his close relationship with Aldric or his upbringing in Thay, but this man had similar attitudes. William hadn't spent much time outside of Starhaven, and there, the weapons masters and tutors had always been exceedingly deferential. He wondered now if that had been why they'd been picked, beyond their actual skill.

"I would, and have been, in fact. The other wounded men were all simple soldiers, men-at-arms, and not knights. I visited them just as I have Sir Drummond, until the last one was released yesterday. Of the men I fought with, only Sir Drummond remains."

"Oh," Garr said, looking past William to Sir Drummond.

"I haven't ever traveled there," William said. "Tell me about life in Everwood. Tell me about Eliston."

Chapter 10

Starhaven, Kingdom of Sidor

Captain Bramwell stood outside the heavy oaken door leading to King Serwyn's personal study, taking a moment to prepare himself before raising a gloved fist to knock firmly three times. The sound echoed down the stone corridor, almost like a warning. One of the commanders he'd brought with him flinched slightly at the sound.

Instead of being bidden to enter, as he had the other times he'd been forced to interrupt the king, the door was flung open, surprising Bramwell. Standing in front of him was a tall, broad-shouldered man with a cruel smile. Bramwell didn't hide the sneer on his face at the sight of the man. Colm Thranton was the jumped-up thug that the duke used as his personal bagman and guard. Bramwell had never understood why the duke would trust someone like Thranton, who'd just as easily stab you in your sleep as do your bidding. And yet, he did.

The last Bramwell heard, Thranton wasn't in the capital. He'd remained in Silverhall when the duke had come to care for his injured brother, before his death. As far as Bramwell was concerned, Thranton should have stayed there. He hated Thranton, and knew the feeling was mutual. The two men stared each other down for a moment before Edmund called from within the room.

"Colm, let the Captain in."

Thranton stepped aside with a mocking little bow. Bramwell signaled his commanders to wait in the hallway and entered, back straight and jaw tight, edging away from Thranton, who shut the door and moved to stand in the back corner of the room. Part of him wanted to turn, to keep the man in sight. He didn't enjoy having the duke's pet attack dog behind him.

Even without Thranton, it was an intimidating room to enter, designed to show the opulence and power of the king with tall arched windows along one wall overlooking the city below, framed by heavy velvet drapes in the white and gold of the House of Whitton. A few bookshelves laden with leather-bound tomes sat against one wall, dwarfed by a large collection of weapons lining the paneled walls. The weapons weren't ornamental or ceremonial. These were worn pieces, used in battle. Weapons that had tasted blood. Not the king's trophies, though. If Bramwell had to guess, they were relics from the king's late father. Thoughts Bramwell would never let cross his face, knowing his fate if he did.

The young king himself sat at a ornate desk inlaid with gold filigree, the richly carved legs depicting snarling lions. His normal petulant scowl had turned to one of annoyance as he shuffled through papers in front of him, absently slipping one off onto a separate pile as Bramwell approached the desk. Duke Edmund loomed over Serwyn's shoulder, one of his finely manicured hands resting on the back of the king's chair almost possessively as he reached over and straightened the document the king had just thrust aside.

He didn't envy the duke his task. Tutoring a king had to be perilous work, since all tutoring involved some kind of discipline, and who could discipline the most powerful person in the kingdom?

"What do you need, Captain?" the duke asked, not even bothering to look up from the documents the king was reading or mask the annoyance in his voice.

Bramwell stopped a few feet in front of the king's desk, posture straight, arms behind his back, and said, "I'm afraid there are more reports of unrest throughout the city, Your Grace. After the riot in the Royal Courtyard and the subsequent one in Peddler's Square were put down, there has been a significant increase in ... disloyal talk among the lower classes."

The king dropped the papers he was holding and looked up, pale eyes fixing the captain in an intense, unnerving stare. The boy might have been young, but he had his father's legendary intensity. Bramwell had only ever met King Gavric once, while traveling in the duke's service, but the brief meeting had left an impression. The former king had a way of holding anyone he spoke to spellbound, making them feel as if they were the center of his world. He'd found the experience both intimidating and exciting at the same time. Serwyn, on the other hand, made the focus of his attention feel like they were about to be executed at any moment for the crime of annoying His Grace.

Bramwell withered slightly under the king's glare as he said, "They ... I am sorry to have to repeat the words, My Lord, but they call for an end to the edict of travel and ... some have suggested, perhaps a change in ... leadership."

Starhaven, at least these days, was a place where the messenger often paid the price for the message they carried, sometimes excruciatingly. Had it not been a dishonor to him or a disservice to his men, Bramwell would have sent anyone other than himself to deliver this news. Telling the king that peasants were demanding his head, not to mention some of the things they called him, could have been almost certainly fatal. He'd originally tried to find Duke Edmund, so he could give His Excellency the news and let him break it to his nephew. Unfortunately, the duke had been with the king as he often was, and this was not something that could wait.

After the riot in the Royal Courtyard, the duke had ordered him to report on any other disturbances. The duke might not have been as vicious as his nephew; he was cleverer, but punishments, while not generally fatal, could be unpleasant enough all the same, leaving Captain Bramwell in an unfortunate position.

"And you let them do this?" Serwyn demanded. "Isn't dealing with such matters precisely your role as captain of the city guard?"

"It is, Your Grace. My men have instituted curfews in the most problematic areas and arrested dozens who were spreading seditious claims against Your Grace's rule. But the dungeons are overflowing, and the tide of resentment has yet to turn. I have concerns ..."

"Damn your concerns. You should have heads on pikes. Of course you have seen no change. Letting treason go unchecked is asking for more treason."

"I'm sure the captain is doing his best to ensure the traitors are dealt with," the duke said, moving his hand from the chair to the king's shoulder. "I have every confidence he will correct this issue and is only notifying us of the situation. We appreciate your report, Captain. Please use all means at your disposal to keep the peace, prevent any more uprisings, and remove the traitors from our streets."

Captain Bramwell paused, considering his next words carefully. "I appreciate Your Excellency's confidence in me, but I fear the situation may be escalating beyond containment through arrests alone. No matter how many we detain, the seditious attitudes only seem to spread. There are concerns ..."

"You idiot," the king said, interrupting his second attempt to get the warning across. "If arrests aren't working, then start executing the traitors. That's the only thing to do with their like. After a few heads end up on pikes, the rest will fall in line."

Captain Bramwell clenched his jaw, holding back a response that would be sure to, at the least, get him removed from his post and, more likely, have his head put in the same place the king wanted to put the traitors'. Thankfully, he was saved from having to say anything by the duke.

"What His Grace means, Captain, is that more forceful measures may be required. We know the people love their king, and these malcontents and traitors are surely a small, vocal minority."

Bramwell bit his tongue again. Whoever told them the king was loved was either lying or a fool. The riots proved that. The people, at best, feared their king. Lately, that fear had begun to turn to resentment and anger, which is why they were in this very situation.

"They have friends, though, Your Excellency. Supporters. Executing people able to convince so many of their neighbors to take treasonous actions would surely make them martyrs if put on the block."

The king opened his mouth, most likely for another tirade about executions and heads on pikes, but stopped as the duke gave his shoulder a squeeze. The words cut off, the king chose to glower at Bramwell instead.

"A point," Edmund said instead. "Perhaps, instead of making an example of the leaders, we could remove them from the board. Maybe we could arrest the ringleaders and ship them off to join the army in Lynese. I'm sure my brother could find use for them in the war effort, and communication is very limited between the soldiers there and the people here."

That was the duke, always thinking in layers. Where Bramwell would have arrested the men and left them in chains, and the king would have executed them, both solutions that were sure to cause a backlash, the duke's solution would remove the troublemakers in a way that caused the least, or at least less, resentment.

"A clever solution, Your Excellency," Bramwell said after considering the idea for a moment. "Perhaps it would be best to make the notifications public. It's possible that if we pull men off the streets, or from the dungeons, and send them off to Lynese in the middle of the night, it would be no different than if we had them killed. Men disappearing suddenly has a tendency to cause … unnervings among the populace."

In truth, he doubted simply disappearing some of the more vocal troublemakers would solve the problem. This rot had spread deep already, and there were more than enough left to pick up what those men had started, as the policies they were protesting remained the law of the land. It also wasn't a captain's duty to tell dukes and kings how to run their kingdom. All he could do was carry out the orders given to him and hope the results were successful since undoubtedly failure would still fall on him, regardless of whose idea it was.

The king, clearly, also had his doubts.

"No!" he said, slamming his fists down on his desk. "They should be afraid of us, not us of them. They should be executed. Dead traitors cause no more trouble."

"Your Grace," the duke said, almost gently. "I understand the desire for decisiveness, but we must consider the wider implications. These men have families who would take poorly to such harsh action. We risk turning disaffection into outright revolt."

"They should accept their king's judgment without question. Anything less is treason."

"Perhaps, Your Grace," Edmund replied carefully. "But we must be pragmatic as well as decisive. Removed from the city, yet kept alive, these men cease to be a threat here while their fate serves as a warning. Allow the captain to arrange transport of the ringleaders to Lynese as conscripts. Untrained, as they are, they will end up dead at the Lynesians' hands, solving our problem without the complexities of doing it ourselves."

For a moment, the king looked up at his uncle, and Bramwell wasn't sure which way the young monarch would land. Finally, though, he gave a small nod, picking up his discarded papers and going back to his previous task.

"By your leave," the captain said, assuming that the decision was made. "I will begin organizing the transfer immediately. The next troop ship departs in a week, and I believe you would prefer if they were on it."

Although the king didn't look up from his work, the duke said, "Good. If you have any trouble, let Colm know. He's been assigned as the king's personal guard during these trying times, but he's available should you need additional assistance."

Bramwell looked back at the man, whose lips turned up in his version of a smile. He'd swim across the Maw before he ever asked Colm for assistance, but it didn't do to publicly insult the duke's right-hand man.

Instead, bowing, he said, "As you wish, Your Grace. Your Excellency."

The duke had already turned his attention back to the king, effectively dismissing Bramwell. The captain turned on his heel and made a retreat, ignoring the following eyes of Thornton as he left the room, closing the heavy door behind him.

"Assemble the watch commanders. I want them in the barracks in twenty minutes," he said to his lieutenants as they fell in step with him.

"Yes, sir, right away!" the men said, the pair veering off down a side passage.

Bramwell gave a glance back at the closed door, frowning. This was going to end badly. He could feel it.

Sidorian Army Camp, Chansol River, Lynese

William picked his way through the rows of ordered campaign tents, dodging soldiers and laborers as he made his way toward the center of the camp where his and the other commanders' tents were located.

He wasn't heading to his own tent, which he wasn't sure should be with the leaders of the army anyway. Instead, he was heading to one closer to the central command tent. Not the largest, which would have been Baron Pembroke's, or the flashiest, which would have been Sir Alistair's. Although larger than the common soldier's tent, it wasn't ostentatiously so. If it weren't for the golden lion on white above blue lines of water on the banner outside, he might not have even known it was his Uncle Aldric's tent the first time he came here.

No guards were stationed outside, although there were enough armed men around that it would be foolish to try to attack their leader, so one wasn't needed.

Stopping by the entrance flap, William called out, "Uncle, it's William."

At the muffled invitation from within, William swept aside the heavy canvas and ducked inside. He found Aldric seated on a folding camp stool at a small portable desk of rough-hewn planks balanced precariously across two supply crates. Not exactly the ornate writing desk Baron Pembroke carted around with him on the campaign.

He was holding a small, curled piece of paper, the tell-tale sign of a wyvern's message, which he rolled up and slid into a battered leather satchel hanging from the corner of the desk as William entered.

"Have a seat," Aldric said, pointing to another camp stool next to the makeshift desk. "Is everything alright? You look troubled."

"I'm not sure," William said after a long pause.

"Eskild mentioned you were troubled after your fight on the line, and I know you've been spending a lot of time in the healers' tents."

It made sense that Eskild would talk to his uncle. The sergeant seemed like a good man, but he was also his uncle's man. William trusted his uncle implicitly, but it was something to keep in mind in the future.

"My first command ... it was a disaster. If Sir Drummond hadn't been able to push through, we'd have been slaughtered. As it was, only two-thirds of my men were slaughtered. I know Eskild said it was a victory, but ... with victories like that, the Lynesians don't need to win to chase us home."

"You feel responsible for the lives lost under your command." It was not a question.

William nodded miserably. "I just came from seeing Sir Drummond. The healers say his recovery is going well, thank the Ancients, but he took that wound saving me. How can I call myself a leader when my men pay the price for my mistakes?"

"The burden of command is a heavy one," Aldric replied. "Every decision carries risk, and, even with the best intentions, lives will be lost. What matters is how you bear that burden and whether you have the courage to keep leading despite the cost."

That wasn't far off from what Eskild had said, and William didn't have a response to it, other than nodding slightly. It made sense, but it also felt like a platitude.

Aldric leaned forward and, almost conspiratorially, said, "I felt much the same after my first command. Worse, even."

William looked up at his uncle, who fell silent; a shadow seemed to pass over his face at that moment. William waited, almost holding his breath, watching his uncle as emotions played across the older man's face.

Finally, he looked up into William's eyes and said, "It was many years ago, during the Winterfang Rebellion. My father was growing old by then, and Gavric had taken over leading most military campaigns. We were tasked with putting down the rebellion.

Normally just a training ground for green recruits, a group of disgruntled veterans had seized the old fort there and proclaimed themselves 'The Freed People of Winterfang Isle.' Foolishness, but no less dangerous for it. Gavric was certain that agents from Alchmara had ... never mind. It's not important to the story. What matters is these men had a few thousand villagers and rejects from the Ice Lands at their command and had threatened to throw any king's man they saw back into the sea."

When he paused, gathering his thoughts, William didn't dare interrupt the story. Gavric had told William stories about past military adventures, but Aldric never talked about his past. William had actually heard about this campaign from Gavric. There had been a sudden sneak attack on their rear that had almost cost him his position. He managed to defeat the rebels and finally take the fort in a climactic battle that required them to breach the front gate with battering rams. Gavric had been one of the first through, cutting men down with his massive sword. William had thought about that battle often in his youth, but he hadn't realized Aldric was there as well.

"They didn't just hole up in their fort, though," Aldric continued the story. "They had too many bandits in their number for that. No. The island itself is basically one big mountain, and the fort is right at the center of it. They had men in the few main passes to the fort, ambushing and setting traps. It would have been a brutal fight to get through to their base, but your uncle Gavric was clever. He had a plan to take a small command, leaving most of the army behind, and force a march through the mountains, using smugglers' paths he'd learned of from deserters."

Aldric's eyes had a faraway look now as he recalled the events. "A blizzard was blowing in off the Frozen Sea, and our scouts reported the enemy still far forward, in the passes, trying to harass our main army. Gavric thought if we could take their fort and leave them out in the open during the storm, it would weaken them considerably. The problem was, although our main force was well supplied and dug in, the men Gavric would need to take through the pass wouldn't be. Even after he first proposed the plan to his commanders, he'd been unsure if it was a wise move. We would suddenly have a smaller force, exposed, and caught between the rebels left in the fort and their army in the passes. He thought about it all through the night, unsure if he should try for the quick victory, or continue to grind the enemy down, day by day, losing valuable men along the way."

Aldric fell silent, looking at his rough hands, lost in thought. For a long time, William just sat there, waiting, as his uncle relived whatever that night had been, and the shame he clearly still carried from it.

When he could take the silence no longer, William quietly asked, "What happened?"

His uncle didn't answer right away, and when he did, he didn't look at William. Instead, he maintained that faraway expression as he looked past the tent and the army camp around them and into the past.

"It was an unmitigated disaster. We had the rebels contained, their fort under siege. My brother was right, if we pressed hard with a smaller force along the mountain paths, we could have taken them unawares, and we did. But he was still worried. We had placed ourselves between the forces in the mountains and their fort and given up both our prepared positions and numerical superiority to do it. He wanted to break our small force again, split it in half. One part would continue to besiege the fort, which only had the smallest token force, and the other would block the pass leading into the small valley where they'd built their fort."

"That was the genius of the rebels' position and why we hadn't been able to win the direct assault," he said. "While the pass on the other side, where we had been attacking, was full of cutbacks and carve-outs where ambushing forces could hide, on this side, it was solid, unpassable mountains except for this pass, and the smaller trails the deserters had told us about. I guess they thought no one would know about the small trails on the far side of the range, so they left those unguarded. The main pass was small, but it narrowed even more, just as it crossed into the valley. Any force that tried to come through it could get maybe twenty men across before the terrain became unworkable for a good hundred-yard stretch. Gavric figured we could do to them what they had been doing to us. Bottle up that pass, clear the fort, and send a wyvern to the main body. With the enemy trapped in the mountains between our forces and with no refuge, we could let them starve or dig them out. Either way, we'd end the rebellion and he'd be a hero."

"I was young and proud, desperate to prove myself. I told him to send me. When our scouts reported the passes seemingly clear and we didn't think they'd be coming back, I told him I could lead the men and hold it while he took the fort," he said, shaking his head ruefully. "By the Ancients, he must have loved me. It's the only reason I can think of that he'd do it. He must have seen the look on my face, how much I wanted it, and decided it was worth the risk."

"He sent you?" William asked when Aldric fell silent again.

"Yes," he said, finally looking at William again. "He gave me fifty footmen and twenty knights. Told us to dig in, hold the pass. I was to send a runner if they showed back up and hold fast behind whatever defensive position I could dig in."

"Did they come for you?" William gently prodded again, after the silence had stretched on.

"Yes. We marched to the entrance of the pass. It was just as Gavric predicted - the perfect spot to block the only way through the mountains back to the rebel fort. I set my men to digging trenches and hauling stones to make our position harder to assail. They didn't have much in the way of horses, so a concentrated charge wasn't a worry. We sat there all through the night, listening to the sounds of the mountains. I swear, I thought every tumbling rock and gust of wind was the enemy plunging in on us out of the darkness."

His voice had grown raspy. Pausing, he leaned back and reached over, taking his cup and drinking deeply.

"They came the next morning," he said, setting the cup back down. "Our lookouts spotted movement in the pass. The bulk of the rebel force was returning, just as anticipated. And there we sat, bottling up the only route through to safety. We had them. I knew Gavric would take the fort that day; we just had to hold them long enough. But I had a plan. I assembled my men, telling them that today was the day we would end the Winterfang Rebellion and be heroes."

He gave William a sad half-smile. "What a fool I was. The rebels charged down through the winding pass, but our barricades held them up as intended. They were packed in, unable to effectively maneuver or bring their numbers to bear. It wasn't a slaughter, but we hurt them. Which is why, when they started to fall back, I was so certain they were routing. All we had to do was charge after them, scoop up the remaining enemy. Gavric would arrive and see I'd defeated them. Which is why I ordered a charge, to smash them while they routed. I had good men. They all followed me, screaming as they charged. All but one knight. He mounted and rode away, hell-bent for leather. I cursed him for a coward. He was the smart one though."

"It was a catastrophic mistake," he said, shaking his head. "We slammed into them alright, pushing them straight out of the narrows. Right where they were waiting. It had been only a diversionary force, sent to take a beating and retreat. As soon as we were through the narrows, the rest came pouring down from the hills, sweeping in behind us, completely boxing us in. In what seemed like seconds, the tide had turned completely. The retreating rebels turned and joined in the fight. We were completely enveloped. I watched my men being cut down all around me as I struggled to rally a defense."

"But Gavric came for you, right?" William asked, not waiting for his uncle to continue.

"Yes. The man I cursed hadn't been running in fear. He'd seen the disaster I was riding into and went for help, knowing what was about to happen. He rode all the way to Gavric, told him I was in grave peril. Gavric had to abandon the siege and bring all his men to our rescue. He arrived right as an axe caught me from behind, slamming through pauldron and muscle. As I went down, I saw his men riding into the enemy, a desperate charge to try and rescue the few of us who remained."

"He saved you?" William asked.

"He did, although I didn't know about it at the time. The Disciples had to put me to sleep while they tried to get blood in me and mend my shoulder. I woke two days later in the healers' tent, bandaged and splinted. Gavric sat at my bedside looking more haggard than I'd ever seen him. The enemy had rallied from the fort behind him, leaving him no option but to fight through to our main encampment, harassed the entire way. We lost two-thirds of the men we'd taken into that valley, with nothing to show for it."

"But you defeated them in the end?" William asked tentatively.

Winterfang Isle was still part of the Duchy of Icelands; William knew that much.

"Yes. Gavric sent a wyvern to Father, telling him of the failure. We were forced to ask Lord Windermere for support. He lived off that glory for a long time, using it to press Father, constantly reminding him why he was needed. Why he could disobey the will of the king. And the worst part of all of it … Gavric took the blame for everything. He ordered the men with me that day, the few still living, to never speak of what I did. All he told Father was that his plan failed. It took a long time for Gavric to regain Father's confidence after that."

William sat quietly as his uncle finished the story, thinking. While it was exciting, hearing about his uncles at war, it brought his own fights to his mind. Was Aldric warning him against being brash? Acting before he thought?

"Did it affect you, after?" William finally asked. "Knowing you'd gotten so many men killed?"

"Yes," he said, gazing down at the floor of the tent. "And no. In that particular case, yes, it affected me deeply. I acted rashly because I wanted glory, and good men paid the price. I carry that always."

"That's my fear. That I'll always remember convincing you to send men out there, putting men in danger. I don't know if I can recover from my mistake the way you recovered from yours."

"You can. All men make mistakes, and you have the heart of a Whitton. But you've misunderstood me. What do you think my mistake was?"

William didn't answer, uncomfortable at pointing out his uncle's flaws, but the man's eyes bore into him, demanding it.

"Convincing Gavric to split his forces and then leading that charge."

"Only one of those was my mistake. When I requested Gavric to send men to the narrows, even when I requested he send me, that was all it was. A request. I didn't force him to make the decision. Had I held my position, even if my command had fallen, that would have been on Gavric. My mistake was not following my orders, of taking my men into danger."

"But, if you're the one to ask ..."

"Do you think Gavric was a fool when he allowed me to go? Do you consider me a fool for allowing you to go? There's risk in commanding men. There always will be. The job of a commander is weighing that risk and making the best decision you can. Even when you make the right decision, the best decision, you will still have men die. That's the nature of war."

"In my case, Gavric knew there was a good chance they'd send for reinforcements. They probably had already, in fact, considering how quickly the enemy got back to us and set up that trap. And I weighed my decision to allow you to go. I'd like to say your words about our duty to the Ancients played a part, but it was more practical considerations. Something felt off about the wagon train coming through the mountains, about the Disciples having Lynesian escorts. Pembroke can often be too dismissive of things outside his experience. We'd been in an argument for several days already, each having different opinions of how to cross the river."

"He's your vassal," William said, shocked.

"He is, and he's a good one. Which is why I not only want him to speak his mind, I demand it. I find different points of view give me more options, make me a better leader. Yes, at times, it's tiresome, but it's worth it in the long run. Coming down on him makes it harder to get that kind of pushback when I need it, so your offering was an excellent excuse to do what I wanted without the repercussions. I knew Sir Drummond was there, and he's a good man, and I sent Eskild. We also instructed Sir Alistair to get a command ready, just in case. If we didn't need them, we'd send them on patrol, but as it turned out, we did. It's how Pembroke got to you so fast."

"Oh, I didn't know that."

"No, because you didn't need to. You did exactly what you were commanded to do, and when the moment came and you did face a choice, you made the right decisions. You've done significantly better on your first command than I did on mine."

William stood, his mind awash with thoughts about everything Aldric had told him, "Thank you, Uncle. This talk ... it has helped."

"Good," Aldric said. "And don't think you won't ever make mistakes. You will. All commanders do. When it happens, learn from it, become better, and move on. While I appreciate what a good heart you have, this kind of self-pitying, navel-gazing does you and the men who serve you no good. They need a decisive commander. One who learns from his mistakes but doesn't dwell on them. When the time comes, remember that."

"I'll try," William said.

Chapter 11

Aleor's Mill, Barony of Stonehill, Duchy of Kingsheart, Sidor

Gareth Bevan looked up from the row of cabbage seedlings he was carefully thinning as the trio of unwanted guests approached on their horses. As the village elder, Gareth had served as leader and advocate for Aleor's Mill for thirty years, and it was always his duty to deal with the baron's men on the community's behalf. In his youth, the duty had been unpleasant, as most duties a lord requires of a commoner are, but reasonable, as such things go. The lord taking his toll, but never more than the village could handle. He had even let the village skip one year after the blight took half the harvest.

But those days were long gone. Each passing year, the baron's men grew more demanding, entitled, and corrupt, taking more and giving less in return. And that was before the new 'edict of travel,' which the bailiff had brought word of on his visit the previous month. Gareth felt weary in his bones as he pushed himself from the dark soil, brushing the dirt from his trousers. Another visit so soon could only mean trouble, he thought.

The portly man wearing a fine velvet tunic at the head of the group drew his horse to a stop in front of Gareth, looking down imperiously.

"Elder, I am Reeve Myrick. We are here on behalf of His Lordship, Baron Harald, to collect your spring taxes."

Gareth bristled inwardly at the man's tone but kept his face neutral, "Greetings, Reeve Myrick. You all must be weary from your journey. Please rest yourselves while I gather the necessary records."

Without waiting for a response, he turned and began shuffling toward his small hut, where he kept the records their lord commanded them to keep, detailing a counting of every bundle of wheat and every sow in the village.

Returning to the group, he found the three riders had dismounted and were milling around the village center impatiently. Reeve Myrick's doublet strained to contain his ample belly, giving him a puffed-up look that matched his imperious manner. His two bailiffs flanked him - tall, stern men with weathered faces and perpetual scowls. Not the knights or bureaucrats the previous Baron Stonehill had sent, but jumped-up cutthroats given title. The perfect men to take from simple folk.

One nudged the other and muttered something as Gareth approached. Their sneering grins made Gareth's stomach sink even further.

"My Lord, our records as requested," Gareth extended the scrolls with both hands. "I must inform you the past season's yields were quite meager. The winter crops set in poorly, and a harsher-than-normal freeze killed much that did grow. With the poor harvest, I fear it will be difficult for my people to pay what the baron demands."

Reeve Myrick snatched the records without a glance or word to Gareth. Leafing through the pages, his eyes tracked back and forth over the numbers Gareth had recorded over the long winter.

"You're right; these figures are too low. I couldn't help but notice when I looked over the records for your village, Elder, that you have had many such years. The baron, in his graciousness, has allowed you leniency, but that time is ending. Your duty to your lord is clear, as are the minimum taxes he requires. Those minimums have also gone up since the last season. You will just have to do without until your next harvests."

The reeve paused, withdrew another page from his cloak, and cleared his throat officiously. "For this season's tithe, the village of Aleor's Mill owes a minimum of twenty-five bushels of winter wheat, thirty head of ..."

He droned on while Gareth's heart sank. There had been mention in the notice last month of a higher tax rate as well, but it had been unspecific. He'd hoped for only small increases, but this was far more than their meager harvests could support. And then came the next insult on top of the taxes.

"In addition," Myrick commanded after finishing his list of minimum payments required by the baron. "We have been informed that six villagers journeyed from here to a village within the Barony of Harrowdale last week to sell goods, in violation of the Edict of Travel. For this violation, each man must pay a fifteen silver fine, due today."

"Fifteen silver?" Gareth blurted out, unable to contain himself.

A trip to another village to sell goods would, on a good trip, net at most five silver. Fifteen was more than double the annual earnings of any man in the village. It was an outrage.

Reeve Myrick's face hardened at the outburst.

"The edict is clear. Any unauthorized travel between villages warrants punishment," he said, motioning curtly to his bailiffs. "See what stores they have and take what is required. Check every hut. These people like to hide valuables in their little hovels like animals."

The bailiffs, hands on swords, pushed roughly past Gareth, sending him crashing to the ground, a sharp pain shooting up from his hip.

"Please, I beg your mercy," he pleaded. "We will pay the tax, but the fine is too steep."

"It is not your place to question the baron's justice," Myrick snapped.

Gareth stared helplessly as the bailiffs stomped toward the nearest huts, roughly shoving aside any of his people who got in their way. Cries of alarm and outrage erupted as mothers pulled children back and men stepped forward to block the intruders' path.

"You can't just barge into our homes!" shouted Eadmund, the barrel-chested man whose hut sat nearest the village center.

Behind him, his wife, Orla, covered her mouth in dismay while their young son peeked wide-eyed from behind her skirt.

"Out of the way," one bailiff growled, thrusting out a meaty arm, pushing Eadmund.

The shouts drew other men from the surrounding fields, men carrying scythes, picks, and shovels. The bailiffs ignored them, focusing on Eadmund.

"You dare interfere with the baron's men performing their duty," Myrick shrieked. "Torin, seize that man."

The bailiff reached out and put a hand on Eadmund's shoulder, while his other hand rested threateningly on the hilt of his sword. Orla's eyes went wide with panic and desperation as she tried to step between them, words of pleading pouring from her as she begged Torin to stop. Sneering, he reached out and roughly gripped a fistful of Orla's hair. With a swift, violent motion, he swung her into the nearby hut, smashing her into the thick timber. She cried out and collapsed to the ground, unmoving. Little Aled let out a terrified shriek and darted past the men to his mother's side.

A cry of rage exploded from the gathering villagers. Eadmund's face twisted in fury, and without hesitation, he grabbed Torin's outstretched arm and pulled him in, delivering a powerful blow with his free hand that crunched into the man's nose. Blood erupted from Torin's nose as he stumbled back, hand going to his shattered face.

"Stop this madness!" Gareth shouted, holding up his hands pleadingly from where he still lay on the ground.

The words fell on deaf ears, the crowd having given themselves over to the anger built up over a lifetime of hard labor and poor treatment. More villagers rushed forward, makeshift weapons in hand. Shovels, rakes, axes - anything they could grab in their fury. The bailiffs drew their swords in response.

Eadmund grabbed a nearby pole, the haft of an unrepaired axe, and, with a roar, charged the injured Torin, who barely managed to raise his sword in time. The axe handle smashed into the sword, sending Torin staggering back under the force of the blow. Eadmund pressed his advantage, swinging wildly.

The stalemate was broken the moment Orla fell, the other villagers reacted. A few feet away, one of them swung his shovel two-handed, aiming for the other bailiff's head. It was a clumsy attack by a man not trained in combat, and the bailiff lashed out indiscriminately with his sword, slicing across the man's chest. Enraged, two more peasants rushed in. One caught a glancing blow to the arm even as his companion smashed the bailiff's knee with a mattock. With a howl of pain, the bailiff dropped to the ground. More peasants converged, pummeling him mercilessly with fists and clubs.

Eadmund ignored them, his fury focused only on Torin, hammering again and again at the man. Chunks of wood were gouged out of the axe handle with each blow, until it finally splintered, sending half of it cartwheeling onto the roof of the hut. Torin saw the opportunity and finally took the offensive, smashing the butt of his sword into Eadmund's face. He staggered and Torin pressed forward with a series of swift cuts and slashes. Eadmund scrambled back, avoiding the first two strikes, but not the third which opened a deep gash across his arm. With a cry of pain, he clutched the bleeding wound and stumbled backward, tripping over Orla's ...

The bailiff raised his blade for a killing stroke, but suddenly convulsed as a long hay fork burst through his chest from behind. He sank to his knees, revealing Gnith, the young man the village used for handy work and odd jobs, holding the now bloodied farm tool. Gnith yanked it free and the bailiff slumped face-first into the dirt.

Even with the immediate threat gone, the villagers' anger was not satiated. Turning, they saw Myrick still on his horse near the prone body of their village headman and charged, two of the men grabbing onto the reins of his horse. Panicked, the reeve fumbled with the reins of his skittish horse.

"Unhand me!" he shrieked, kicking out one finely crafted boot, catching one of the villagers across the cheek, causing him to lose his grip.

Taking advantage of the momentary distraction, Reeve Myrick yanked hard on the reins, pulling the horse's head up. As the horse reared in protest, the other villager was forced to release his hold to avoid getting trampled.

Wheeling the animal around, Myrick drove his heels into its flanks. The horse bolted, charging through the gathering crowd of villagers, scattering them. Leaning low over the horse's neck, he pushed the animal hard, away from the village, his fine velvet tunic flapping behind him, chased by the shouts of the futilely pursuing villagers.

Watching his people slowly come back as they abandoned their chase, Gareth pushed himself up from the dirt, gritting his teeth against the sharp pain in his hip. The chaos around him was dissipating as the adrenaline faded from the villagers. Men milled about in shock, makeshift weapons now loosely held, forgotten. Women clustered around Orla's still form, little Aled clinging to her motionless body as he wailed piteously.

Gareth hobbled over to where the village men stood over the bloodied corpses of the two bailiffs. Torin's dead eyes stared blankly upward, a broken tine of the hayfork jutting grotesquely from his chest. Gareth felt only numbness looking at the gruesome scene. He had failed his people. This would bring the weight of the baron down on them and might even be the end of his village.

"What have we done?" Eadmund said, his voice hollow as he cradled his bleeding arm.

The other men shuffled their feet uneasily, exchanging uncertain looks.

"It doesn't matter," Gareth said heavily. "What's done is done. What matters now is what comes next. Once word of this reaches the baron, he will demand vengeance."

The men's faces paled. They knew as well as he did the types of punishment that would rain down upon the village from the baron's men.

"Quickly now, take what food remains and distribute it among those with the greatest need," Gareth commanded. "Hide any surplus where it won't be found. They will demand more taxation now, most likely taking everything we have. If we are to make it until the harvest, we must be smart."

As the men moved to obey, Gareth put a hand on Eadmund's shoulder. "Take your son and flee into the hills. You and any who drew arms must get away from here before more of the baron's men arrive. Their families, too, in case the reprisals go further."

Eadmund nodded grimly. He still had a child to look after, a duty to do as a father. Gareth looked around at the faces of his people, etched with fear and uncertainty.

"Shouldn't we bury their bodies? If they don't find them here ..." someone started to say.

"No. The reeve will tell them what happened. Hiding the bodies will do no good and might convince the baron and his men this was planned on our part, bringing greater reprisals," Gareth said, interrupting the man. "I will remain when the baron's men return. I will tell them I alone am responsible for this. With luck, they will be satisfied with only my head."

Cries of protest erupted from the villagers. Gareth raised a hand to quiet them. "We each have our part to play. Yours is not to throw away your lives needlessly. Now go, prepare yourselves as best you can."

The villagers dispersed to follow Gareth's instructions. Gareth stayed a moment, looking down at the bodies of the bailiffs. He mourned what was about to happen to his people, and that he would almost certainly not survive long enough to see them through the reckoning that was coming.

Valemonde Palace, Valemonde, Empire of Lynese

Princess Isolde stormed through the opulent halls of Valemonde Palace, the heels of her satin shoes clicking sharply against the polished marble floors and the sound echoing off the gilded walls.

Reaching her destination, the elegantly engraved doors depicting scenes of their ancestors' legendary victory against the Gharnatá Sovereignty seven hundred years ago, which had established their house and control over Lynese, she normally would pause to admire the intricate carvings, tracing her fingers over the finely wrought ridges and grooves, feeling pride in her family's history.

Today, she didn't even notice, shoving the door open without preamble, not bothering to announce herself to the guard stationed outside. Baudric looked up in evident surprise from behind his large desk as she stormed into the room. She knew his feelings on the importance of proper manners and decorum, even when it came to his children, but today she didn't care.

"You seem upset," he said, recovering quickly and folding his hands in front of him on the desk.

"You know very well what's wrong," she said, marching straight to his desk, palms slapping down on its polished surface as she leaned toward him. "I just received word about what you did with the aid shipment I arranged for our injured soldiers being held captive in Sidor. You substituted the Disciples with soldiers, and used my mercy mission as a chance to ambush the Sidorians!"

Her father regarded her coolly. "I did what any good leader would do. Why does that surprise you?"

Isolde gaped at him. "You sabotaged my efforts to provide comfort to our country's soldiers; soldiers wounded fighting in your war! And after I specifically asked you not to interfere. Who knows if any of those supplies will reach them now, or if the Sidorians will ever allow me to minister to captives in their territory again?"

"Spare me your naive outrage," Baudric said dismissively. "No guarantee existed whatsoever that the Sidorians would have given any portion of those medical provisions to our men, captive or not. More likely, they'd have kept every measure for themselves. I simply ensured that if anyone was to benefit, it would be us."

Isolde gaped at her father in disbelief.

"The Disciples would have told me if the supplies weren't reaching our men. They would have no reason to lie to me. They serve no king or country, only the tenets of their faith."

"Which doesn't change the reality of the situation. The supplies would still be gone, taken by the Sidorians, for no gain on our part. I simply turned a disadvantage into an advantage."

"And you think nothing of what your violation will cost us in the long run. The Acolytes are protective of their rights and traditions, and this might be the greatest betrayal of those since the great alliance. The Gray Isles are bound to retaliate."

"A necessary risk for the greater good," Baudric replied dismissively. "I'm not concerned with mystical politics. My duty is to our people here and now."

Isolde threw her hands up in exasperation. "But your actions betrayed our people! Our injured soldiers will suffer without those medical supplies."

"I want to help our people too, my daughter. But the only way to truly do that is to defeat these invaders and get them off our land. If you haven't noticed, the war goes poorly for us. The bridge the Sidorians are constructing to cross the Chansol grows longer by the day. Soon, they'll be over the river and loose in our heartland, raiding and pillaging."

Pushing his bulky frame out of his chair, he began to pace behind his desk, something he did often when he lectured her.

"It's my duty as Emperor to protect our people from such devastation, and the only sure way is to defeat the Sidorians before they gain that chance. If I have to deceive them once to save thousands of Lynese from their violence, so be it."

"What about brokering for peace?" she interjected, cutting him off mid-sentence.

Baudric stopped pacing and turned to face her, scowling.

"Peace? With the Sidorians?" he let out a derisive laugh. "There can be no peace with those savages."

"But isn't it worth trying?" Isolde pleaded. "This war has raged for over a year, with tremendous loss of life on both sides. Wouldn't it be better to at least attempt negotiations before sacrificing more soldiers?"

"You speak of things you do not understand, but I can forgive you your youthful innocence. The Sidorians cannot be trusted. The moment we show weakness and agree to talks, they will see it as an opportunity to press for more concessions while giving up nothing themselves."

He came around the desk, standing before Isolde with his hands clasped behind his back. Though she stood taller than him by several inches, he had a way of making her feel small.

"I'm proud you wish to involve yourself in the art of ruling," he continued, his tone softening. "But you still have much to learn about the reality of power. There is no room for naiveté or weakness on the throne. A leader must be shrewd, cunning, always prepared for others' self-interest, even if it means being self-serving himself. Honor and morality are luxuries of the powerless. For those with authority, the only true duty is to accumulate and hold power by any means. That is the Great Game all rulers play, though few have the courage to admit it."

"That's ... barbaric."

"So is the world. I know these words seem cold to you now, but in time you'll understand it's the only way to secure our people's wellbeing. I look forward to the day you're ready to lead our people. But clearly, today is not that day."

As he lowered himself back into his chair, ignoring her once more, her eyes blazed with fury. She longed to unleash a torrent of curses at him, to slam her fists upon his desk, to tell him exactly the sort of cold, heartless ruler he was. She also knew it would be pointless. With one last smoldering glare, she whirled around and stormed out of the study as angrily as she had entered it.

Starhaven, Kingdom of Sidor

Serwyn paced the council chamber, crumpling the message in his fist until his knuckles were white with rage.

"This is outrageous!" Serwyn seethed.

Edmund remained calmly seated, steepling his fingers on the table before him, watching his nephew stomp back and forth across the chamber.

"I understand your outrage, Your Grace, but we knew some pushback was to be expected. The smart thing for us to do now is let Baron Stonehill deal with this."

Serwyn whirled to face his uncle. "I will not tolerate those peasants defying my authority! I will raze their pathetic village to the ground, kill every last one of them! Let it serve as an example to any who would dare oppose me."

Edmund held up a placating hand. "A show of strength is often necessary, I agree, but ..."

"You think I should let their treason go unpunished?" Serwyn interrupted, his lip curled in a sneer.

"Not at all," Edmund replied smoothly. "The perpetrators should face justice, without question. But it would be best to let Baron Stonehill dispense it. He rules that land. Those are his people. Allowing him to handle the matter puts the responsibility for it on him, and not you."

"I thought Stonehill was loyal. Why would he allow such blatant disobedience?"

"He is loyal, Your Grace. But even loyal vassals can have unruly subjects from time to time. If you intervene directly, it allows the situation to be used against you, painting you as a tyrant, even if you're only doing what must be done. Part of the reason we put these laws into place, and the onus for enforcing them on the barons, was to lessen the popularity of the barons. It is important that the crown is seen as a refuge to the people and the barons as the source of their troubles."

"Don't they know the edicts came from the crown? And the new taxes?"

"Some do, maybe intellectually, but it isn't your men taking the taxes and enforcing penalties, it's the barons. People put blame on whoever enforces the rules, not on who made them. In fact, we could play this to our benefit," Edmund said, leaning back, looking at the arched ceiling as he considered. "Perhaps we instruct Baron Stonehill to raze the village, but at the same time we dispatch our own men, someone with enough authority to stop the reprisals. Give the village a reprieve, settling for only the heads of the instigators. You will be their savior, the baron their tormentor."

"Wouldn't that turn Stonehill against us?"

"No," Edmund said, waving the idea off dismissively. "He understands what's happening. I'll send him a message privately, explaining it. He won't like the plan, but he won't go against us either. We must remember that the other barons will be watching. They will see our actions for what they are and take them as a warning. It will make them less likely to allow this kind of thing to happen in their own lands, for fear of reprisals."

"Fine. I still want someone to pay, but if you think your games will have an effect, Uncle, then you can play them. I still would prefer a more direct course of action," Serwyn said, throwing himself down into a chair, his anger somewhat faded.

"I know you would, and I appreciate that you still heed my counsel. Besides, we have greater concerns as well."

"What greater concerns?"

"This uprising may be more than just disgruntled peasants," Edmund said. "I worry there is more to this."

"What do you mean? Speak plainly, Uncle."

Edmund was quiet for a long moment, considering.

"It's possible ... not certain, but possible that this was not a natural reaction, but one orchestrated by outside forces to push back against the crown," he finally said. "I have received reports of increased wyvern traffic between certain barons in the last few weeks."

Serwyn's eyes narrowed. "Between which barons? We should march on them at once for this treason!"

"Patience, Your Grace. The wyvern traffic alone is only an indication that something might be occurring, not proof of treason. And it is not the only concerning matter of late."

"There's more?"

"Yes. The barons here in Sidor are not the only ones with increased wyvern traffic. There have also been an unusual number of messages from some of these same barons to our forces in Lynese. Now, messages to and from the front are expected, of course, and all of the barons in question have sent their men with the armies. But the timing and frequency here are ... suspicious," Edmund waited another moment, letting that sink in before continuing. "I worry that some of the unrest here may be spurred on not only by local barons, but by those serving under your uncle in Lynese. Some of those men are very ambitious and have given the throne a covetous eye for years. Fear of your father kept them in place, but now ..."

Edmund spread his hands out suggestively, as if to say, 'Things have changed.'

Serwyn looked almost wounded. "But Uncle Aldric has always been loyal. He supported my father his whole reign."

Edmund nodded. "Aldric is loyal, although that loyalty is because of his love for your father more than any duty, which has never been something your uncle has held in high regard. However, I think it more likely that other barons in his command, Baron Pembroke for example, might be the issue. They are loyal to my brother, and they were loyal to your father, but they have always craved more power than their titles and family station have allowed them. I know Pembroke has hoped this war would elevate his status, but ... if things are not going as he'd like them to, there is a chance he might see a faster road to the power he craves."

"I assume we can't do anything about them either," Serwyn said sullenly.

"Not directly. But that does not mean we are powerless," Edmund said. "We must send a message; let these treasonous barons know that we are watching their actions closely."

"Which means what? Since you said we can't do anything about them directly."

"Which means we do something indirect. My first thought would be to cut funding and support for our armies in Lynese. If they cannot adequately feed and supply their men, the generals will have no choice but to slow down operations and turn their focus inward. They will be too preoccupied with managing their forces to continue stirring up unrest here at home."

He paused, considering his next words. "I believe the prudent course is to cut off support to the armies in Lynese. Reduce the supplies and gold we send."

"What?" Serwyn blurted out. "We can't win the war that way!"

"If it truly affects the war effort, we can restore the funding," Edmund said smoothly. "But this will put pressure on those barons supporting the unrest. Force them to turn their attention away from fomenting chaos here and towards supplying their own men."

Seeing the king still looking unconvinced, Edmund said, "You must remember, Your Grace, this war has already been extremely costly for Sidor in both gold and men. Even if we win, we cannot realistically conquer and hold the entire continent of Lynese. There are simply too many people over too vast a territory. The civil unrest from such an occupation would bankrupt us, and the amount of manpower required would bleed this kingdom dry."

"But they have to be taught a lesson."

"They are being taught a lesson. We entered this war to teach the Lynese a stern lesson, to stop their meddling and supply of arms to the Alchmaran raiders who plague our coasts. In that regard, we have already succeeded. The Alchmarans' attacks have lessened considerably thanks to your father's decisive action and we've shown Baudric that we can take his land from him when we want. He will think twice about interfering a second time."

"But the Alchmara are still raiding our coasts?" Serwyn said. "We get near weekly wyverns from Baron Sinclair complaining about it."

"Only because so many of our soldiers are committed to the war in Lynese, leaving our coasts vulnerable. Once we bring our men home, the coast barons will be more than able to defend themselves. The Alchmara only test us because they know our armies are away and the cost to them is low. Once we have our men back, they will rethink their actions. Yet another reason to end this war sooner rather than later."

Serwyn didn't answer right away. Instead, he pushed himself out of his chair and began pacing again, like a caged animal. Although the cage, in this instance, was the one not allowing him to just do what he wanted. Edmund felt for the boy, but he needed to learn sooner, rather than later, that in politics, the quick emotional response was rarely the right one.

"I understand your hesitation, Your Grace," Edmund said gently. "But we must think of the long game here. Sacrifices are sometimes required for the greater good."

"Fine, you win again, Uncle. Cut the funding as you see best."

"Serwyn, it isn't about winning or losing. I am not against you in this. If you truly wish to march our men onto the barons' lands and start a war with your vassals while the majority of our people fight overseas, of course we can do that. As my king, I am yours to command. I simply offer alternatives for you to consider."

"Don't do that, Uncle. I appreciate your loyalty, but don't treat me like a child. If I ordered our loyal vassals to turn on the traitorous ones, you would send wyverns before my men ever left, suggesting caution and promising to deal with it yourself. I can feel your hands on my strings."

"Serwyn, if I ever gave you the impression ..."

"I'm not chastising you, Uncle. I know I have a lot to learn, so I put up with it, because, of course, you're right. An all-out civil war is not the answer, and that would almost certainly be the result if I had my way. Just know that one day I will not need your guidance, and when I truly ask it, your machinations must end."

Edmund resisted a frown, but only just. Serwyn's sudden self-awareness was a surprise. In other times, it would be a welcome one, but Edmund would have preferred it directed at someone other than himself.

"Of course. As I said, I only want to see your rule be long and prosperous. We are blood, you and I. You will always have my loyalty."

"Thank you, Uncle. Back to the matter at hand. If we do this, I don't want to just guess. We need men in these people's houses. You said the increased wyverns were not proof of treason, so get me proof. I'm tired of waiting and reacting to whatever the barons may do next."

"As you command, Your Grace," Edmund said, bowing.

Chapter 12

Ebbwater, Barony of Dunwics Reach, Duchy of Kingsheart, Sidor

Tom Fletcher stood atop a wagon, looking out at the assembly of men gathered in Geoffrey's barn. Local farmers and craftsmen mostly, though he noted more than a few road-weary travelers among them, faces etched with hardship from weeks' worth of travel to get here. At a glance, Tom counted seventy men at least, so many that the great barn seemed full to bursting, even with both large doors thrown open to let in the late spring air.

The noise washed over him as the people, angry and frustrated, vented their rage. He'd seen firsthand how angry the people were getting, but even he didn't realize it had gotten to this level. When he'd sent out word to friends and friends of friends that there would be a meeting to discuss how to deal with all of the new insults made by the crown, he'd made it clear he was looking to talk to some of them, hear their stories, and not to tell them how they would fix it or offer solutions right away.

None of that seemed to matter to the people who'd shown up. They wanted relief, and even the hint of someone able to offer it was enough to light a fire under each of them, demanding answers.

"These new taxes will ruin us!" a farmer cried out, his face flushed with anger. "My family already goes hungry. We'll not last the winter at this rate!"

He shook his fists in the air as others shouted their agreement.

"At least you can still till your land and grow crops," another man retorted, this one a little better dressed in a woolen tunic. "My business is trade, carrying goods from one barony to the other. How can I work if I'm not even allowed to leave The Reach?"

More shouts started piling on top of others, men shouting at the same time.

"Half my crop wasted, rotting, unable to sell it two towns over."

"The tax collector took my only milk cow for back taxes!"

"My son was arrested for simply asking why the taxes were so high this year. Who tills my fields now?" an older farmer lamented.

"Enough is enough! We should drive out the next collector that comes round!" A large, barrel-chested man bellowed, shaking his fist.

"Fighting the king's men is madness. I heard of a village up north that tried. Burned to the ground, every last one," another yelled in reply.

The noise rose as more and more shouted, until it became a cacophony, words spilling on top of each other; it was all unintelligible shouting. He wanted to see how much fire they had in them, if they were ready to do what they must. Now he knew.

"Friends! Friends! Hear me!" Tom said, raising his hands.

He waited as the din slowly died down, heads turning in his direction, faces still angry. Some continued shouting and shaking their fists until their neighbors nudged them to silence.

"Friends, I share your outrage. The new restrictions and taxes are unjust, no argument there."

Murmurs of agreement rippled through the crowd.

"And you've got fire in your bellies, I like that. Shows you've got heart. But we've got to be smart about this." Tom paused, holding his hands up for quiet again as angry shouts threatened to drown him out. "What you heard about the village up north is true, and it's a harsh lesson. They dragged a dozen men off in chains, fathers and husbands just trying to put food on the table. And what they did to the village headman ... no, that is not how you want your story to end. None of you."

The crowd was silent now, taking in Tom's warning.

"Well then, what do you suggest?" challenged the barrel-chested man who'd called for vindication against the king's tax collectors.

"I'm not saying we do nothing. We need to act, that is for sure, but we need to be smart about it. They've shown they're willing to take this out on our families and kill anyone they have to, if it means upholding their tyranny. If the crown can blame one village for an act of vengeance, they'll bring their wrath down on every man, woman, and child everywhere."

Murmurs of agreement spread through the crowd.

"And we can't fight their knights in the field," he continued. "Yes, there are more of us than them, but they can bring armored men, archers, and all the tools of war. We'd never be able to stand up against them."

"Those all sound like reasons for us to do nothing," the trader said.

"No, they're reasons why we can't do something impulsive. Foolish," Tom said. "That isn't the same as doing nothing. The king's men are spread out, trying to collect taxes from everywhere at once and there are more of us than them. We know these lands, these people. They don't."

"So we become bandits?" someone else said.

"No. Not bandits. Anything we liberate, we give to the villages hit the hardest. We keep none of it. Our goal is to make the cost of collecting these taxes so high that they can't afford it anymore."

"What about the baron's men?" someone asked. "Most of the tax collectors work for the barons, not the king."

"True," Tom said. "We have to be careful. Our fight is with the crown, mostly, and not the barons. Some of the barons are in bed with the crown, but many are as unhappy with the new taxes and edicts as we are. They can't openly defy the crown, not without an army at their gates."

"How will we know which is which?"

"Because they will be supporting us quietly, in their own way. Food for those who need it. Weapons for those with the courage and skill to use them. We can coordinate with them, after a fashion. If we plan to strike the king's men, their soldiers might just happen to be in the wrong place at the right time, keeping their men from becoming involved. When they're forced to collect the crown's taxes, we will find it easier to relieve them of those unjust burdens without any bloodshed, so the coin can find its way back to the people."

"How does a woodcutter know so much about barons and their plans?" someone in the crowd called out, eliciting good-natured chuckles.

"Does it matter?" Old Neil asked. "Known Tom since he was a boy! Good head on those shoulders, and eyes open to more than chopping wood. Fine man and there's no better to lead our cause."

There were nods of agreement from men around the room who knew him. The problem was that that was only a small portion of the gathered men. This was a diverse crowd from all over, most of whom didn't know Tom, or even who might be talking to them. All they knew was there had been word that someone might have a solution to the sudden outrages coming from the crown ... and that they were desperate. They were also suspicious. The king's men were about, and what was being said here could be taken as treason.

"I have been fortunate enough to have made many friends over the years, some who know people beyond the type someone like myself might encounter. And these are good people. People who want to help. They searched around for someone they could talk to, asking friends and then friends of friends, until they landed on me. I didn't ask to be put in this position, but I can't shrink from it either. Not with what I've seen happen recently. So I agreed."

"Why do any of the highborn even care?" another called out.

"A fair question, and one I don't have answers for. Their reasons are their own. Some do it because they have a love for their people; others because they see the way things are going and believe they are bad for the kingdom, which would ultimately be bad for them and their own fortunes. Some probably see profit in it and look to use us. Honestly, when pressed, I can only ask, do we care? If they come through with what they promise, we should take it, and use these tools to lessen our burdens. They have used us for long enough; I say it's about time to return the favor."

"What if it's a trap, to catch anyone disloyal?"

"That's why we will be careful about this, and why nothing will happen right away. We make sure each step of the way that they can deliver what is offered, and only put a few of us in danger each time, so that if it is a trap, we cannot name others when pressed."

More murmurs this time. They were coming around, and only needed a push to go the rest of the way.

"In the end, I don't care about any baron or duke or any other lord who seeks to rule us. I care about the people. Our people. We just want to live our lives and support our families. For that, I stand ready to spend blood and limb. I'm ready to take a stand and to do what must be done to rid ourselves of this tyranny. Who stands with me?"

The murmurs died down as they came to the moment of decision. Up until now, it had been complaining, men grousing about the actions of those above them. Now was the time to commit, and it was up to each man to do that on his own.

"I'm with you," the barrel-chested man said, taking a symbolic step forward.

"And me," said another, joining him.

By twos and threes, men stepped forward, until it became a rush of men offering their oaths to fight the king's men. Tom jumped down and stepped up to the large man who'd spoken with such fire and been the first to step forward.

A good first step.

Sidorian Army Camp, Chansol River, Lynese

William shifted uneasily, adjusting his weight from side to side in the saddle as he watched the ragged band of 'recruits' being led into the encampment by Starhaven Guardsmen. Even from a distance, he could see the hopeless, defeated postures of the recruits, their shoulders slumped and heads bowed low as they trudged along. It was clear they weren't there by choice or free will.

The guardsmen, who'd been a constant presence in the capital when he was younger, now seemed out of place marching next to the army. Their ornate armor, which had always impressed William with its intricate decorations, now appeared almost fanciful compared to the solid, well-used armor of the soldiers.

As the procession drew nearer, William noted the recruits' tattered clothing, smudged skin, unkempt hair and beards, all showing signs of long-term neglect: skin stretched thin over jutting bones, eyes sunken in gaunt faces. Seeing them, it didn't feel right to William. These men had no reason to be in Lynese, let alone joining the army.

Aldric's face was flushed with anger as he watched the recruits being herded into the camp like so many head of livestock.

"Get them situated and see to it that they have adequate food, water, and bedding," he snapped at Pembroke, a rare edge of anger in his tone, not taking his eyes off the poor devils.

"I'll see to it, Your Grace," Pembroke said, looking equally disgusted.

As the baron rode off, Aldric cursed under his breath. "Damned fool's idea of justice, this."

William's head whipped around toward his uncle, surprised at the vehemence in his normally calm voice. The older man's composure had always amazed William. Even on the battlefield, Aldric never rushed, never panicked, always maintaining rigid self-discipline no matter the circumstance.

Still not looking at William, he said, "Mark my words, Edmund's behind this, sending these men here against their will. It's foolishness, pure and simple."

William shifted uncomfortably, not sure how to respond. He wasn't about to defend his stepfather, although he didn't understand how, or why, Edmund would have sent these poor wretches to war.

"But why send peasants and tradesmen to fight?" he asked, genuinely curious. "What purpose does it serve?"

"It has to do with the new edict the king signed, placing restrictions on travel by the common people between baronies and increasing taxes on those same people in an attempt to extend the crown's control over the barons, some of whom might see a young king as an opportunity to expand their power. Edmund pushed Gavric for years over what he called 'the baron problem,' and it seems now that he has a more ... active role in the decisions made by the crown, he plans on focusing on that 'problem,'" Aldric said bitterly. "In what should have been a shock to no one, it generated quite a bit of outrage and dissent among the people. And when people are outraged and desperate, they act rashly. The king, or more likely your stepfather, decided the best way to deal with this problem, without creating martyrs for more peasants to rally behind, was to round up the troublemakers and ship them here, to fight in the king's armies. It allowed him to remove a problem from himself and shift it to me."

"Why would he want to create problems for you?" William asked. "I know there's been ... issues in your relationship, but you're still commanding the king's soldiers in a war. Doesn't he know this could affect the outcome?"

Aldric finally turned his horse to face William, away from the camp and commotion.

"Edmund doesn't believe in this war. He just wants it to end, not caring how that happens," he said in a calmer voice.

"Why? I thought my stepfather supported the war effort."

"Publicly he does, but privately, he sees it as a waste of resources that distracts from consolidating power at home. I should admit that I was also against this war when Gavric first proposed it. I tried to convince him that invading Lynese was not worth the manpower or cost, but he refused to listen. My brother could be stubborn as an old mule when he set his mind on something," he said, before pausing, looking off past William to the army, again in thought. After several moments, he seemed to shake himself out of his thoughts and back to the moment. "Now that we have men in the field, however, the only thing that makes sense is to finish it. Or at least push far enough that we can sue for reasonable terms from their emperor, which was Gavric's original objective, anyway."

"But if he thinks it's a waste of resources and effort, why would he do something that's bound to cost more, even if he doesn't care about winning the war? I know for a fact he cares a great deal about wasting money. Does he hate you that much?"

"It's not about hate," Aldric said, and then frowned. "It's hard to explain and isn't important right now. What's important now is that these people are not only useless as soldiers and additional mouths to feed, but they're going to be angry, causing disruptions among the real soldiers, many of whom will have started hearing the news about what is happening to their families back home. It's bad for morale."

"But how do you know all this?" William asked. "I see almost nothing from home distributed among the army."

"I get dispatches from home," Aldric replied simply, his expression softening slightly as he saw the confusion in William's eyes. "While not going so far as to intercept news from home, Pembroke felt it better to let the news trickle in slowly, rather than unbalancing our army as a whole all at once. I'm not sure I agree with him, but since I have no better solution to the problem, I acquiesced. We have bigger problems anyway."

William waited, but when his uncle didn't elaborate, he asked, "What problems?"

"The supplies we've been getting from home will be decreasing soon, by a significant amount, it seems. The news hasn't been made official, but a friend at court sent a wyvern that arrived this morning, letting me know that it's coming."

"Not wanting the war or caring if we just ended it now isn't the same as starving out half the sworn men in the kingdom. How does he expect us to feed everyone if our supplies are cut off?"

"That's a good question," Aldric said, before turning his horse and riding away.

William watched him go, frustrated by the entire conversation. He knew there was more going on here than his uncle was saying, more at play, but he didn't have enough context to know what.

All he did know was that life was going to become very difficult soon. For all of them.

Starhaven, Kingdom of Sidor

Edmund's quarters were an odd blend of lavish opulence and Spartan austerity, all at once. Each item had been deliberately chosen for the impression it would make on the rare few invited into the space. On days when Edmund's mood was contemplative, he enjoyed looking over the carefully curated surroundings, taking satisfaction in their precision.

This was not one of those days. Edmund barely noticed the quarters around him as he paced back and forth over the plush fur rug, his footsteps etching a track delineating his repeated path.

Instead, his attention was focused on the pockmarked man standing indifferently in front of him. Edmund had to repress the urge to yell at the man, berate him for his lack of proper deference. Besides being counterproductive, he knew the man well enough to know it was pointless.

"We need you to start hiring more men, Colm," Edmund said, stopping his pacing and turning to face Colm. "Men not assigned to the city guard or even the duchy forces. Men specifically under your direct command, outside of the normal bounds."

"I can make that happen. What kind of men, exactly, are you wanting?" Colm asked, a slight smirk on his face.

"You know exactly what kind of men I want, Colm," he said, his lips tightened into a thin line. "Men who can ensure loyalty, men who will follow orders without question. Men who are willing to do the kind of work more ... civilized people might find difficult."

"That shouldn't be a problem," Colm said. "I know where to find such men, although loyalty costs extra."

"I'll pay it. And I need them soon. The situation is more delicate than I anticipated, and I need to be able to act quickly if necessary."

"Begging his lordship's pardon," Colm said, his tone belying the words he spoke. "But the king's got all these noble men guarding him with their fancy armor and finery. What does he need with more unsavory men like myself?"

"Because the unrest is growing worse, and I fear it will continue until we can stamp out the malcontents. The city guard and even the duchy's forces are valuable, but with what is coming, we will need men willing to do what must be done. Men whose loyalty I can be more assured of, outside of the traditional obligations."

"If it's so bad, why not have your brother killed?" Colm asked.

Edmund froze, his head cocking to one side as he looked at the 'captain,' "What do you mean?"

"I heard what you said to the whelp king a few days back. Something about a baron from River Mark's army being behind the trouble here. I know you told the prince your brother was loyal, but what you meant behind the words was pretty clear. Even the boy heard it."

"It's of no consequence," he said, waving the question away dismissively. "My nephew is still new to the game of politics. He doesn't yet understand the subtleties of it all. I need a way to weaken the barons overall, but more specifically, the barons of the River Mark. Men like Pembroke can possibly upset my future plans, and I need to deal with them while they're still distracted by the war. The problem is that Aldric swears by his liegemen, and Serwyn holds my brother in an unfortunately high level of esteem. As long as Aldric stands by them, Serwyn won't listen or do what needs to be done. I need to create distance between my brother and nephew, to get him pointed in the right direction. Which has been the point of nearly everything we've done since my nephew became king."

"Whatever, it's none of my business anyway." Colm shrugged, clearly losing interest before Edmund even finished speaking.

That is one of the things Edmund liked best about the captain. He cared little for politics. As long as he got paid and had opportunities to indulge in his more violent predilections, the man was happy to go where he was sent.

"How long will it take you to get the men?"

"I'll need to be away from the capital for a few days to start collecting them," Colm replied. "Maybe two weeks to get enough. What do you want done with them once I have them?"

"House them in the city proper, not in the palace or any of the official grounds," Edmund said, his voice firm. "I'm not sure yet what role they'll play exactly, but I want them available when I've figured it out. I'll pay them all the same."

Colm smirked and gave a mockery of a salute, "As you wish, My Lord."

Without being dismissed, he turned and walked out of the room, slamming the door shut behind him. Edmund couldn't help but shake his head in disgust. The man had no subtlety to him at all. While that was useful, it did make him stand out here at the palace.

Edmund gave one last look at the closed door, thinking further through his plans, moving the pieces on the great board around in his head, before returning to his desk against the far wall, overlooking the city below.

While not exactly going as planned, things were still advancing in the right direction. But it was a delicate thing, and needed proper tending if he was going to achieve his goals.

Chapter 13

Cresswell Hills, Barony of Langmere, Duchy of Kingsheart

Tom Fletcher lay on his stomach, peering through the tall grass at the narrow, winding pathway that sloped and curved between the steep grassy hillsides. The Cresswell Hills were notorious for their rugged terrain, with sharp, rocky cliffs interspaced among the grassy slopes, creating dips and valleys all along the chain of hills, making them the perfect place to hide.

A man named Ivor, who'd joined their group a few days before, whispered, "How can you be so certain they'll come through here? There must be other ways for them to go."

Nodding toward a man a few meters down, Tom said, "Godric there told us this was the only pass through these hills that wouldn't add miles to their journey. We know where they're heading, and we left a big enough trail of gossip that a blind man should be able to follow us in this direction. They think the 'escapees' are a half-day's ride down this trail. They haven't shown a lot of imagination so far, so I don't expect we'll see a lot now."

"But this is dangerous, right? This isn't like scattering one or two bailiffs and stealing wagons. I heard there was a fair number of them," Ivor said, looking nervously at the other men scattered along the hillside with them.

"Yes, of course it's dangerous, but these men have been hunting people who did nothing but travel to the closest market to their village to sell their wares. Now, they're being hunted like animals for sport. There's a justice beyond the king's justice, and these men who are hunting our people deserve it. You don't have to fight with us if you don't want to. I don't ask any man to fight against their will. I, however, am going to show these men what happens when you harass and kill people who are just trying to live free."

"No, no. I'm not saying ..." Ivor started to say, until Tom held up a hand, silencing him.

Cocking his head, Fletcher listened hard to the wind and the rustling grass until he heard it again, the faint but unmistakable sound of hoofbeats and voices of men not trying to be silent. Another moment passed before he saw them, a small force of two knights and around twenty bailiffs, all on horseback rounding the bend in the path below. The two knights rode at the head of the column in what looked like well-used armor.

Behind rode some twenty bailiffs, their gambesons and surcoats marked with the watchtower and hills of Langmere. The bailiffs were deadly, but not outside of his men's ability to deal with. The knights, however, would be a bigger problem, especially if their trap failed.

Tom waited, watching the men ride closer, before raising his hand in a silent signal to his men waiting on the opposite hill. A few of the men on the far ridge raised their hands in return, a silent acknowledgment of the message.

"Get everyone ready. As soon as those knights hit the trap, we move in," he said to the man next to him, one of the first to join their band. "They're so confident in their own superiority that they don't even have scouts out."

As if almost on cue, the lead horse stepped into a pit concealed beneath a layer of leaves that covered this entire stretch of the pathway. The animal's dappled front legs plunged through the camouflaging leaves and branches, sending its front half into a hole. It wasn't deep enough for the whole animal to disappear into, but it had just enough depth that its momentum sent the armored knight tumbling forward over the horse's head into the pit.

The wounded animal's front legs kicked and thrashed in confusion and pain, its hooves almost certainly further injuring the helpless knight trapped beneath it. From within the pit came the sounds of snapping branches and crushing leaves as the horse

135

continued to struggle, interspersed with the cries of the trapped knight.

The second knight had better reactions, quickly reining in his nervous mount before it could stumble into the same trap.

"Now! Attack!" Tom yelled, rising swiftly to his feet.

At his command, fifty peasants sprang from their hiding places, raining a deadly barrage of arrows and stones upon the unsuspecting men below. The volley descended with deadly accuracy, piercing the lightly armored bailiffs or smashing against their unhelmeted heads with sickening cracks. Cries of panic and pain rose up from the men as they scrambled for cover, many toppling clumsily from their terrified mounts that whinnied and bucked wildly to escape the attack.

Attempting to form a protective line, the surviving bailiffs raised their shields against the unrelenting incoming fire. The remaining knight bellowed commands, urgently trying to rally his men, one of whom turned his horse to flee before being cut down a few steps away from the rest.

Tom's men poured fire down the rocky slopes, loosing arrow after arrow from behind the sparse cover of boulders and stubborn bushes clinging to the hillside. Each volley drove deeper into their confused ranks.

The remaining bailiffs were falling quickly, but the knight still posed a serious threat. Their simple weapons were useless against his heavy plate armor, which rebuffed every shot sent his way.

"Concentrate your fire on the men nearest the knight! Separate him from the others!" Tom shouted at the men closest to him.

At his command, a concentrated rain of arrows slammed into the panicking horses and men near the knight. The massive warhorses, trained for battle yet terrified by the onslaught, reared up and kicked out with iron-shod hooves, crushing one unfortunate man. Amidst the chaos, a single lucky arrow found its mark in the knight's mount, sending it toppling to the ground, spilling its mail-clad rider onto his back in a crash of steel.

"Now, while he's down. Swarm them, now!" Tom shouted, his voice barely audible over the din of battle, waving his sword in a signal for the men on the opposite hill.

At his command, the peasants poured down the hillside, spilling into the narrow pathway. Tom let the bulk of his men finish off the few remaining bailiffs while he held back his best men—those who had seen real combat when pressed into their lords' armies. He had ordered them to stay near him for precisely this moment.

"With me!" he commanded.

Tom and the five men charged the knight, who was struggling to get off his back, his foot stuck under the heavy, lifeless body of his warhorse. Tom, who led the charge, arrived first and lunged with his sword, but it was deflected by the knight's sword as he slashed wildly while he continued to try to pull his leg free.

One of Tom's men stepped too close, missing his thrust, and paid dearly for his mistake as the knight's sword slashed across the poor boy's stomach, spilling his insides. The boy fell back with a gurgling scream, his hands clutching desperately at the bloody mess of his abdomen. Seizing the opportunity afforded by the boy's sacrifice, a large farmer named Wilum swung with all his might at the distracted knight's helm, his massive club smashing into the man's head, the thick wood splintering as it connected. Though strongly delivered, the crushing blow only slightly dented the finely worked steel of the helm, but the force of the impact was enough to momentarily rattle the man within. The knight's swings slowed as he struggled to regain his senses.

Tom seized the opportunity, lunging forward with his sword aimed straight at the gap between the knight's helm and breastplate. The blade sliced cleanly into the exposed flesh of the man's neck, releasing a crimson torrent as the knight's body went limp and collapsed to the blood-soaked ground.

Pulling his weapon free, Tom could see the bailiffs' bodies scattered around the path. Sadly, among the fallen were some of his own men. They had all known the dangers that came with this uprising, but it still pained him deeply to see men who'd entrusted their lives to him fall.

A frantic noise from the pit drew Tom's attention. The knight's horse was still desperately struggling to break free, its coat now lathered with sweat from the exertion, its dark eyes wide with panic. Tom could also hear the injured knight groaning faintly from the bottom of the pit beneath the distressed animal.

Tom signaled to his men to finish the job. They quickly gathered heavy stones and dropped them onto the helpless knight, crushing him beneath their weight until all noise from the man ceased. While they were dealing with that grim task, Tom swiftly dispatched the suffering horse, sliding his sword across its throat in one clean motion to grant it a merciful end. Better to put it out of its misery than to let it continue to suffer.

The battle over, Tom surveyed his losses. Three of his men lay dead and another handful had various injuries, although none life-threatening. Two would be laid up for a time but should recover. In return, the king and his baron had lost twenty-two of their own men, including two battle-hardened, experienced knights. A costly victory, but a victory nonetheless.

"Search the bodies," Tom ordered. "Take anything of value and give it to the families of the fallen. We'll make sure they're well compensated for their loss. Collect all the armor and weapons! We'll need them for the coming fight. And gather up any living horses as well. Each dead man's family gets a horse. We'll take the rest with us."

The men worked quickly, stripping the bodies of their armor and weapons, and leading the surviving horses away. The men were in high spirits, laughing and slapping each other on the back as they worked, flushed with pride. He didn't fault them for their joy. If someone had told him a year ago that a group of poorly armed peasants could do this, he would have scoffed at them. They had a right to their celebration, but he couldn't share in it.

This would provoke a swift and brutal response from the king, probably against other peasants who had taken no part in the ambush. This was a necessary step to break the cycle of suffering, but he couldn't feel joy knowing the price they were bound to pay for it.

The Chansol River, Lynese

The late spring had already begun to turn hot, the sun beating down on William and his patrol as they rode north, roughly following the path of the Chansol River as it flowed away from the main Sidorian army toward Rendalia Bay. They had been on horseback since before dawn, and William could already feel the knots and cramps forming in his lower back after so many hours in the saddle.

Ostensibly, they were there to patrol for bandits, which had started to become a problem after the local lords and officials retreated with their army across the river, in many cases, stripping villages dry as they'd done so. In need of food and seeing an opportunity, many locals had turned to banditry, plundering their neighbors to make up for their lack of supplies.

While important work, William knew that wasn't the only reason his uncle had given him this assignment. The fact that he'd been sent alone, in charge of twenty seasoned men, was a sure sign this was another test by Aldric, a means to gauge his readiness for greater command. At sixteen, he was young for the position. However, he knew his Uncle Gavric had commanded a significantly larger force when he was just a year older, so it wasn't unreasonable.

William also couldn't help but note that his uncle had not sent Eskild with him this time. The Thay sergeant might have been his uncle's right-hand man, but since William had been assigned to his uncle, the seasoned warrior had been his more or less constant companion. William had started to take comfort in knowing the seasoned warrior was always there to help him and offer advice when he was unsure of what to do. Which was probably the exact reason his uncle had kept the man back.

There was an even bigger reason for the patrol than to just test William's mettle, however. One William himself was proud of. For the last several weeks, ever since the fake Disciples convoy, William had been working on a plan that, although unlikely to turn the tide of the current conflict, would greatly increase the chances of the Sidorian forces successfully crossing the river when the bridge was finally finished and the assault to cross it began.

What's more, his uncle had approved the plan, although conditionally. While searching for bandits and proving he could lead seasoned men, William was to scout the land still further north, looking for an area of the river free from Lynesian eyes. His uncle had even given William two of his better scouts, men who knew how to find the enemy, even when they didn't want to be found.

William realized his mind had started to wander and pulled himself back into focus, reaching up under his helm he wiped away a bead of sweat from his forehead. As he settled the metal back in place, one of his scouts whistled, pointing at the horizon. There, above the tree line, was a thin wisp of smoke, the exact thing his patrol was supposed to inspect. Waving his men in that direction, he turned his horse to investigate.

Ten minutes later, they found the source of the smoke nestled against the edge of the dense forest, a settlement barely large enough to even be called a village. No more than a dozen thatch-roofed cottages clustered around a dusty central square, with a few small fields on the outskirts. The most notable thing about it was that it was populated—a far cry from the last two villages they'd encountered, both of which had been deserted by their inhabitants when the Lynesian army had fled across the river.

It wasn't until they got nearer to the village that he realized the smoke he was seeing was too thick and dark to be from simple chimneys or cooking fires—some of the huts themselves were on fire. Quickening his horse's pace, he closed the rest of the distance rapidly, his party forced to speed up to stay with him as he passed the first few cottages on the outskirts and entered the village proper.

What he found in its center shocked him. Instead of the Lynesian bandits he'd been expecting, William saw Sidorian soldiers ransacking the village, arms laden with pilfered goods, driving terrorized villagers at sword point as their huts burned behind them.

One soldier was using an axe to hack apart a wooden door, splintering the planks as he forced his way inside. Another carried a large sack overflowing with grain and foodstuffs, the contents spilling out over the top as he lugged it along. Three more soldiers were in front of a small cottage, shouting threats as they used the pommels of their swords to smash the clay pots and woven baskets sitting outside.

In the village square, a group of five soldiers had gathered around one of their fellows, who knelt in the dirt pinning a whimpering peasant woman beneath him, tearing at her clothing. Her face was twisted in fear and disgust, tears streaming down her cheeks as she struggled helplessly. His comrades stood nearby, shouting encouragement and crude jokes.

William dug his heels into the sides of his horse, urging it forward, anger surging through him.

"Halt!" he shouted, his voice ringing out across the square. "In the name of the Duke, stop this at once!"

The soldier on top of the woman looked up in surprise, then scowled in annoyance at the interruption.

"Piss off, boy," he spat. "We're taking what's owed us. These Lynesian scum have food while we starve on wormy biscuits and moldy cheese."

William hopped off his horse, charging at the man, whose expression changed to one of surprise as William's heavy leather boot slammed into his ribcage, knocking him off the crying young woman onto the dusty ground. The man let out a pained, guttural growl as he clutched his side, and began to push himself up from the dirt only to freeze as William's sword pressed against his throat.

Behind him, William could hear several of his men dismounting and coming to back him up, the sound of steel sliding out of leather scabbards audible even above the noise of burning huts and whimpering peasants.

"There is a standing order from the Duke himself that no Lynesian villages are to be pillaged or raided behind our lines. If you're not getting enough to eat, we will see to that; but we will not do it this way. We are not barbarians," William said, his sword still pressed against the man's throat.

The soldier glared up at him defiantly in spite of the cold steel. "Easy for you to say! You get to ride about on your fancy horse, sleeping safe and warm in plush tents while we toil in the mud on empty bellies. We've had naught but moldy bread and bean stew for weeks! We deserve what's ours."

Murmurs of discontent rippled through the group of soldiers, and they began to close ranks around William's patrol, hands drifting to axes and swords. There were about thirty in total, armed about as well as his own men. William noted several moving to cut off his patrol's only exit route, the situation poised to turn bloody at any moment.

Just as it seemed everyone would attack, a voice called out from the back, "Wait! Hold!"

A man stepped forward, pushing his way urgently through the throng of soldiers. He was tall and lean, with a rough weathered face and a scar above one eyebrow. William recognized him immediately as the man from the medical tent, the one he'd talked to while checking on Sir Drummond.

"Garr!" William exclaimed, unable to keep the disappointment out of his voice. "What are *you* doing here?"

The man looked at him, his face apologetic, his eyes downcast. "It's true, what he said. We haven't been getting enough supplies from Sir Alistair, and our commanders haven't been listening when we've complained. We're hungry, My Lord. We're all desperately hungry."

As Garr spoke, the men around him relaxed, ever so slightly, hands coming off weapons, the tension dissipating a little. William took a cautious step back, removing his sword from the throat of the man sprawled on the ground, willing to let things deescalate now that they'd moved away from the precipice of violence. The man on the ground reached a hand to his neck where fresh blood was trickling from the thin cut there.

"You have my word as a Whitton, I will see to it that your situation is rectified, for you and any others I can find. But I cannot let this devastation stand. I have to place you under arrest in the name of Aldric Whitton, Duke of Rivermark, for theft, arson, and assault. You will accompany us back to the main encampment, where your fate will be decided."

Angry shouts arose from some of the men, hands flying back to weapons. William raised a placating hand.

"However, if you come along willingly, without struggle or complaint; I will personally vouch for your character and petition the Duke for leniency. At most, you may have to make reparations to these villagers, but I'm confident I can persuade him to show mercy."

The men looked uncertain, torn between defiance and self-preservation. Men looked from one to another, edging toward violence.

Finally, Garr stepped forward, again pushing his people back from the brink, his hands in the air. "I surrender, My Lord. I'm sorry for what we've done. We were just trying to survive."

One by one, the other soldiers followed suit, laying down their weapons and submitting to William and his men. William let out a sigh of relief, grateful that the situation had not escalated further.

"Take them into custody and see that they are treated fairly," he ordered his men. "We will deal with them once we return to camp."

As his men rounded up the soldiers, William couldn't help but feel a sense of sadness and frustration. He'd met Sir Alistair and knew him to be an honorable man who wouldn't starve his own soldiers. This had to track back to his father cutting funding for the army, driving their own soldiers to desperation.

He wasn't sure if his uncle could do anything to change their situation, but he should be able to help mitigate their circumstances. If only he had the ability to talk to his father as easily and convince him to change his foolish policy.

Chapter 14

Valemonde, Lynese

Isolde pushed through the bustling crowd that filled the streets of Valemonde's Traders' District. The people parted in surprise at the sight of the princess in her deep blue silk gown, adorned with intricate silver embroidery. She made her way through them, ignoring the hawkers shouting their wares and the smells of roasting meats and baking bread mixed with the musky odor of filth.

Normally, the trip was a heartbreaking experience as she exposed herself to this side of the city, feeling pangs of regret and shame that so many of her people lived like this. Not today.

Today, she barely noticed the cramped shopfronts and apartments stacked haphazardly atop one another, leaning precariously over the street. She paid no mind to the ragged children with dirty faces who laughed and played tag, darting between carts piled high with goods.

Instead, her rage boiled over as she stomped toward her destination, clouding everything around her. Behind her trailed a burly man with a thick beard and a stern expression, unable to hide his clear anxiety. His eyes darted from person to person as he struggled to keep pace with the princess through the press of bodies. His uniform, emblazoned with the royal crest of House Montborne, marked him as a member of the Royal Guard, drawing even more attention.

"Princess," he said as he caught up to her. "Your father has ordered that you remain at the palace. It is not safe for you to be out here."

Isolde paused, her gaze fixed on the imposing structure looming before her. The Order of Healing Hospital, a massive stone building with high arched windows and a soaring spire, the banner of the Order, two hands, palms up, a flame in between them, fluttered in the breeze above the entrance.

"I don't care what my father ordered," she said, whirling on her guard, finger stabbing at him like a sword. "If you want to take me back to the palace, you're going to have to tackle me and carry me back over your shoulder. But I warn you now, I will kick and bite you the whole way."

"Princess, please," the man said, holding up his hands, looking uneasy, "You promised your father. We just care about your safety. This is a dangerous area of the city."

"My safety?" Isolde scoffed. "What about the safety of the men who are lying in there, wounded and dying, because my father saw fit to use them as pawns in his political games? I know what he did with my supply shipment, and if he can lie to my face, then I can lie to his."

With that, she turned on her heel and marched towards the hospital, her skirts swishing around her ankles. The guard hesitated for a moment, then followed her, his face a mask of resignation.

The Disciples of Healing looked surprised to see her but pleased as well. This wasn't her first visit to the hospital, and she had a reputation for being kind and compassionate to the soldiers in their care. They were also some of the few who didn't fear her father's wrath, their order placing them outside any worldly cares. Which might be why she liked coming here so much, as opposed to visiting the army directly, where her father very well might have had her tied up and returned to him.

She took a moment to shake off her anger. She might be furious at her father, but these men didn't deserve that. They had fought and were wounded in her family's name, and they deserved every bit of her focus and compassion. Putting a smile on her face, she paused beside a young man whose leg was swathed in blood-spotted bandages.

"How are you feeling, Tristan?" she asked, taking his hand in between hers, remembering his name from a previous visit.

"Better, My Lady," he said, smiling weakly as she said his name. "My leg doesn't hurt so bad anymore."

"Good. I've prayed to the Ancients for you. I'm glad they heard my prayers."

"They would have listened to you, My Lady."

She gave him a small smile. He was a good man, not much older than her. The idea that he'd been forced to see some of the things he had at his age, with an equally young wife and child back at home, made her heart ache.

"The Disciples tell me you'll be able to walk again soon. Next time I come by, I expect to see you ready to stand, even if it is with a cane. I know your wife wants you home to help with the baby, not lying about in here, talking to girls and being lazy."

He smiled and gave a weak laugh. In truth, the Disciples had also told her he would probably never walk without a limp. They exchanged a few more words before she excused herself to continue her rounds.

At the next cot, she found a soldier staring vacantly at the ceiling, his face pale and eyes hollow.

"Alric? Can you hear me?" she asked.

He was a fairly recent arrival, one of the many to be brought back, injured from the fighting near the Chansol River. On her last visit, he had been very weak, but awake. She looked around, worried that his condition had deteriorated so badly.

A Disciple, seeing her look around, approached, his voice low. "I'm afraid the infection has spread, Your Highness. We've done all we can, but I fear he may not last the night."

Isolde nodded, excusing the Disciple, blinking back tears as she looked down at the man's ashen face. Gently, she brushed the hair back from his forehead and leaned close.

"May the Ancients guide your soul on its journey and welcome you into their eternal embrace," she whispered. "Your service and sacrifice shall not be forgotten."

Straightening, Isolde had to steady herself for a moment as grief threatened to overwhelm her composure. With effort, she regained control and continued down the row of cots, knowing there were many more soldiers who needed her now. She could mourn later, in private.

Some cots she stopped at to say a few words, others she knew the person either didn't like to speak to people or knew she made them feel uncomfortable. Those she would give a smile or a nod and pass them by, although she'd still talk to the Disciples about their condition.

Seeing a face she didn't recognize, which wasn't unusual with the newly wounded men being brought in every day, she stopped. He was older than her, but not that much older, maybe in his mid-twenties. His side was wrapped up in bandages, a light pink coloring on them as it already began to bleed through. His leg was also wrapped up tightly, boards on either side immobilizing it.

It wasn't his injury that immediately caught her attention, however. He had an odd expression on his face, one of almost resignation. She'd seen enough dying here over the last year to know that was as big of a danger to their recovery as their physical condition, and keeping their spirits up was as important as any medicine the Disciples might give them.

"How are you feeling?" she asked kindly.

The man looked up at her uncertainly. "All right, I suppose, M'Lady. This leg pains me something awful, though."

Isolde nodded sympathetically. "Have they given you something for the pain?"

"Yes, M'Lady, but it hasn't started helping yet."

"It will. I know it's hard, but you have to be patient, let the Disciples work the Ancients' will upon you," she said, and then paused, unsure how to ask what she wanted to ask. "When I first came over, you looked troubled. Is something else weighing on your mind?"

"No, M'Lady," he said, hesitantly. "I'm ... it's fine."

"It's okay," she said, putting a hand gently on his shoulder. "I'm here to listen to you, all of you. If there's ever anything I can do to help, I want to do it. Please, it would make me feel awful if there was something I could do and you didn't tell me."

She gave him a pleading look. She usually preferred compassion or sympathy to get through to reticent patients, rather than guilt, which tended to add to their troubles instead of easing them, but she could recognize the signs in him that neither of those would work. He was afraid to complain to someone high above his station, unsure of what would happen. It wasn't uncommon, especially among men who'd come from more rural areas, where they had less contact with those of a higher station.

In those cases, guilt was the only way she knew to get them to speak up.

"I'm sorry. I ... uhh ... Begging your pardon, M'Lady, but speaking true, I'm awful worried about my home. The Viceroy's men came and took me from my land near a year ago now. My wife and boys did their best to get the planting in, but with this bum leg, I'll be no use come harvest time, even if they don't make me go back to the army instead of sending me home. We've scrimped and saved, but I fear my family will go hungry this winter without my help in the fields."

Reaching into the embroidered purse at her waist, Isolde withdrew several gold coins and pressed them into the farmer's hand.

"Please, take this and send it to your wife. It isn't much, but hopefully, it will help her hire day laborers to bring in your crops."

The man's eyes grew to the size of saucers as he looked at the riches in his hand. That was probably more than his farm made in a whole year, and she'd just given it to him.

"My Lady! I can't ..."

"What's your name?" she asked, interrupting him.

He started to protest again, probably expecting her to say anything else other than what she did.

"M... Malteo, M'Lady."

"It's a pleasure to meet you, Malteo. I am Isolde. Now, this," she said, taking his hand and folding his fingers over the coins again, "is a gift freely given. To turn your back on the hospitality of another is an affront to the Ancients. You wouldn't want to do that, would you, Malteo?"

"N... No, M'Lady."

"You seem like such a good man, I didn't think so. Which means you're just going to have to send this home to your wife, so she can take care of your family. You see, this isn't even for you; it's for her, and I know she would be shocked if you turned down a gift in her name. I may not have worked as hard as your wife, tending a field and children at the same time, but I know a little of what it's like to be a woman. Trust me, I believe she has done everything and more to deserve this."

"Thank you, M'Lady. Thank you. Thank you," he repeated, relief washing over him as tears started to form in his eyes. "I will pray for you and your father, for helping us so."

"This is not from my father," she said, her tone much harsher than she intended. "Consider it a gift from me alone."

Her guard made a small noise of protest behind her, but Isolde silenced him with a look before turning back to a confused-looking Malteo, "Never mind that. You just promise me you'll look after your wife. Okay?"

"Yes, M'Lady," he said, nodding earnestly.

"Good. I have to go see some of the other men, but I'm here regularly and the Disciples have permission to contact me at any time. Please let them know if there's anything I can do for you."

"Yes, M'Lady. Bless you again."

She patted him on the hand and rose, moving on, stopping at various cots to offer words of comfort and more coins when needed from her dwindling purse. Though she tried to be discreet, word of her generosity spread swiftly through the hospital, eliciting murmurs of gratitude. By the time she reached the end of that row of cots, her purse was empty. She cursed herself for not planning ahead sufficiently. She'd been in such a fit of rage, she hadn't properly prepared for her visit.

She finished her rounds and started to make her way back to the front of the hospital for her return trip home. Seeing her go, several of the men still able to walk started to converge on her, wishing her well, thanking her for her words and her visit, or seemingly wanting to just receive a touch on the hand or shoulder, almost as if they simply wanted to be near her.

Her guard looked worried, but she could see it in these men's eyes they meant her no harm and she waved him away. Isolde felt a mix of emotions wash over her. On one hand, she was touched by their genuine affection and admiration. On the other, she couldn't help but feel the burden of their expectations.

"My Lady ..." her guard pleaded with her again.

"Yes, all right," she said with a sigh before turning her attention to the men gathered around her. "My brave soldiers, I'm sorry I must leave now, but I will come back. I want to thank you for your sacrifice and I will pray to the Ancients every day that you all recover and return to your homes and families. Your families should be proud of how valiant you all are, and how well you honored your country. Please know I will forever be grateful for you."

A cheer rose up among them, filling Isolde's heart.

Sidorian Army Camp, Chansol River, Lynese

After a day and a night in the saddle, with the added burden of escorting prisoners, William was more than relieved to be back at the main army camp. He'd longed for, begged for the responsibility to lead men in his own right, but the actual work of doing that was a greater burden than he'd imagined. Or at least a different kind of burden, one that he hadn't yet learned to deal with properly.

Pushing aside the heavy canvas flap, he discovered his uncle, as was so often the case, seated at his makeshift writing desk, a quill in hand, scribbling out a message on a piece of rolled parchment just small enough to fit in a wyvern's message case. That was one of the starker surprises William had found since joining his uncle's military campaign. A leader's job was more organization and logistics than leading men into battle. Worse, that difference seemed to widen the higher in leadership one got.

A very different picture than the stories his nurse had told him as a child.

Aldric looked up as he entered, a gust of wind catching the tent flap, fluttering it loudly against the outside of the tent until a guard could capture it and tie it off again.

Seeing William, Aldric rolled up the message and tucked it away before turning to face him directly.

"How did it go?" he asked, smiling at William.

"Good. It's not ideal, but I think it will still work. It will be difficult, to be sure. The river is wide there, and the current swift. We'll need many trips back and forth by small rafts to get everyone across. Still, the location is secluded and unpopulated, and the water slow-moving enough that a strong swimmer could make it across if they had to, which solves the problem of the lead line."

"And the trip back?"

"Exactly as I said. I know it's a long march back on foot, but it's doable, especially since everyone knows what would happen if we failed, both to us and the assault. I still believe it's our best bet to ensure the crossing happens and to finally get us moving again.

Aldric nodded thoughtfully, not really looking at him. William was used to this by now, and even marveled at his uncle's ability to hold the battlefield in his head, playing out scenarios as he considered possible movements, without the need for maps and markers.

Finally, Aldric smiled and said, "You've done well, William. You've really shown me something, both with the plan and how well you've prepared for it. When the time comes, I'm going to want you to lead it."

"Are you sure?" William asked excitedly, the stress and worry from minutes before fading into the back of his mind.

This was exactly the kind of opportunity he'd been wanting, although now that it was here he could scarcely believe it.

"Yes. When the time comes, I'll need to be with the main body of the army. Besides, this is your plan and you should see it through. Don't worry, this time I'll make sure to lend you Eskild again."

"Thank you, uncle," William said, trying not to sound too relieved.

He didn't want his uncle to think he'd become dependent on the Thay warrior, even though having him along on something like this would ease William's nerves. Planning a military operation and leading it in the field were very different things. Having someone he could turn to for advice or even just encouragement would go a long way.

"Go and get some rest now," Aldric continued, turning back to shuffle through some papers on his desk. "I'll meet with Pembroke to finalize our plans for the crossing. If all goes well these next few days, we should have a better idea of the timetable soon."

Instead of leaving as his uncle commanded, William hesitated, his hand hovering above the tent flap, glancing back.

"Is something wrong, William?" Aldric asked, setting his work down again.

"Yes. As we were scouting the crossing, we spotted smoke not far away. Since that was ostensibly our mission and we'd heard about bandits raiding villages in the area, we went to check on it. Instead of Lynesian bandits, we found some of Sir Alistair's men sacking the village for food and supplies."

Aldric's face darkened. "Desertion is a serious offense. What did you do?"

"That's just it; they weren't deserters, not fully. They left to find food but then were going to return to continue to fight. I even recognized one of them from the healers' tent when I was visiting Sir Drummond. He was injured but returned to his command to keep fighting. I confronted them and they surrendered without a fight. They said they were starving and had to find something to eat. They seemed desperate."

Sighing, Aldric passed a hand over his face. "This is becoming a bigger problem than I realized. I've asked for more support, but so far the 'king' has been unable to provide any assurances. I told Pembroke and the rest to do what they can to keep the men fed, but apparently, that isn't enough."

William could hear the quotes his uncle put around king and knew he meant his stepfather. Although he'd shied away from saying it directly, he knew Aldric believed Edmund was more or less controlling Serwyn at this point, directing the orders he gave. Or at least, that is where he put the blame for the decisions being made.

"This is why we need to get across the river now," Aldric continued. "If we can take Lynesian stores, we can lessen the strain on our own resources. It won't be enough to make up for our lack, but it will lessen the strain of it. We can't afford to stay in one place any longer."

"About the men I arrested, the ones raiding the village because they were starving. I made some promises, in order to get them to come quietly and keep the situation from escalating into violence. Well, and because it was the right thing to do, considering how we are treating the men we're responsible for."

"What kind of promises," his uncle asked, his tone businesslike and professional rather than accusatory.

"I told them that if they cooperated and caused no further trouble, I would speak to you about leniency. Those who only took food and supplies, and did not harm any villagers, I said I would argue for their release after paying restitution to the village. The ones who committed violence or arson, I promised I would ask that they only be put in chains rather than hanged."

William hesitated. Now that he said it out loud, he realized how that sounded. Something his stepfather had always pressed home was how important it was to never take on burdens of others and never give them to those of a higher station. That it was his job, as a noble, to avoid the pitfalls of obligation, ensuring he delegated difficulties in the correct direction. In this, he'd done the exact opposite, taking on the troubles of men with no station and making promises for his uncle, a duke of high station.

"I apologize for stepping out of my place. I know I spoke rashly, committing you without your knowledge. I only did so because I felt it was the only way to avoid further bloodshed and bring them in without a fight. And because I knew some of the men, knew them to be good men driven by desperation."

"Actually, if it was nearing bloodshed and their situation was as you described, you might have made the right decision. It is still my responsibility to review each case to determine what justice is appropriate. However, if things are as you say, for those who stole out of true desperation, and harmed no one, and have a good report from their commanders, I will follow your lead, likely demand restitution but then release them back to their units. For those who are deemed by their commanders to be troublemakers and problem cases, I will probably use this as an opportunity to make an example of them. I know you made promises and that might seem unfair, but there are opportunities that you have to take as a commander, for the army as a whole."

"You're saying sometimes duty comes before honor?"

"Yes. Honor is important. Having honor tells the world what kind of man you are and maintaining your honor will ensure you hold true to being that man. Duty is about what you owe to others, but especially those who have pledged themselves to you. Duty and honor often come together, but there will be times when you have to choose between your word and your duty to your people. Your people always come first. Always. As your uncle and now mentor, my honor is tied to yours, and my honor obligates me to uphold the word you gave these men. My duty is to the army as a whole, both in the service it renders to Sidor, and to protect the lives of as many of the sworn men under my service as possible."

"I understand," William said, repeating the words in his head.

"Good. Very good. I want you to know you did the right thing. You've shown compassion and understanding towards your men, and that's an important quality in a leader. That compassion will serve you well, if tempered by hard lessons like this. I'm very proud of you."

"And about the supplies?" William prompted.

"That is a bigger issue, one I'm not sure I will be able to solve right away. Soon, we'll cross the river and hopefully take some of the enemy's stores. In the meantime, I'll send a wyvern to the capital; hopefully, they'll recognize our problems and make the right call. Now, you've had a long couple of days. Go see to the rest of your men and get some rest. In the morning, we'll have one last council of war, to make sure everything is in place. You have a big job ahead of you."

"Thank you, Uncle. I won't let you down."

"I know you won't," Aldric said.

Chapter 15

Starhaven, Duchy of Kingsheart, Sidor

"How could this happen?" Serwyn demanded, his voice shaking with barely controlled anger. "How could a bunch of peasants defeat trained knights? I thought you told me the disruption would be minimal. Bailiffs and knights murdered. Supply shipments ransacked. Ever since I listened to you, Uncle, my kingdom has been in chaos. How could you let this happen?"

Every noble and courtier in the throne room tried to find somewhere else to look other than at Edmund or the king. That in itself was unusual. Many of the men who'd gravitated toward the throne over the last several months were exactly the type who usually glorified in this kind of display. It's why half of the men in this room came here, to see the misfortune of others and, occasionally, get an opportunity to enhance their own station from it.

This was not one of those displays. Both the king and the duke were notorious for their ability to hold grudges, and everyone knew who the real danger in that room right now was. Edmund might be keeping his entire focus on his nephew, but that did not mean he wouldn't be making a list of every man who took pleasure in this moment. And everyone knew retribution would be swift.

"Well? What do you have to say for yourself?" Serwyn continued when Edmund did not answer right away.

"Your Grace, I share your anger at this tragic loss, but we must keep perspective-"

"Perspective?" Serwyn interrupted him, half-rising from his seat. "I'm losing my kingdom, listening to your advice and counsel. What other perspective do you think I should have?"

Edmund took a slow, calming breath before continuing, his eyes never leaving his nephew, "You are right to be angry, Your Grace. I understand your frustration. These ... events are indeed troubling. Are the peasants displeased with the law? Of course. It's only natural for them to be unhappy with limitations, much like a child is displeased when a parent takes away a plaything or refuses a request. Does that make the parent's decision to limit them, for their own protection, bad? Of course not. The real problem here lies with the barons, who are failing in their duty to you. It is their job, as your vassals, given power by your hand, to enforce your laws and edicts. You have, as the kings before you, given them the decision of how to best enforce those laws, as they know their own people. While that has worked in the past, it is clear now that the current crop of barons and lords are unable, or unwilling, to do their duty in the manner their fathers did. They have failed to maintain order in their lands, and now, we are all paying the price."

"I thought that was the point," Serwyn grumbled.

Edmund frowned. The boy lacked any subtlety or understanding of the game. That was, indeed, the point, but to say it out loud, in court, was an error. The barons would already know, of course, that these new laws and edicts were ultimately to rein in the power they'd wrested from the crown over the last hundred years, but that was a different thing than having it put into words so directly.

The king all but saying the laws were passed in order to hurt the barons was tantamount to justification for further disobedience, as it broke the traditions that made up the foundation of the liege-lord relationship.

"My goal, and advice, has always been solely to deal with unrest in your lands. Unrest that is common when the crown changes hands. I promise you, however, that this will not stand. I will not stand idly by while this rebellion spreads. I will see to it that something is done about these people, and the barons who have allowed them to flourish."

"You better," Serwyn said, glaring at his uncle. "I won't tolerate any more of this."

Edmund nodded solemnly, bowing his head slightly, as he worked to school his face. Serwyn might be young and inexperienced, but he wasn't a fool. Worse, he had Gavric's temper, which would often be short and targeted at the first person he saw. Gavric had moderated his anger with a sense of duty to the kingdom that did not get passed on to his son. While Serwyn's more ... inward-looking nature made a useful tool in directing him, it also made the boy less able to be assuaged when his anger did fly out of control.

"I understand, Your Grace. You have my word," Edmund said as he started to back away from the throne before turning and taking his leave.

As soon as he was out of the throne room and the massive doors were pulled shut behind him, Edmund quickened his pace, rapidly walking toward the east wing of the palace where the family's rooms and work areas were located.

He schooled his features to remain calm, but inside he was simmering with anger. Things were getting out of hand. How that fool Blout could have let his men get waylaid like that, Edmund would never know. Bailiffs he could understand, since most weren't much more than jumped up peasants themselves, but twenty seasoned men-at-arms and two experienced knights?

It should have been impossible. Worse, he had to put the blame on Blout for this, since it happened in his Barony. Langmere had remained one of the more loyal of the barons, in spite of everything. He'd have to send a wyvern to him, let Quentin know this time he had to be the sacrificial lamb, and make promises of paying his service back in the future, when things were more settled.

Edmund found the man he was looking for in one of the courtyards, watching five men train with swords while he leaned on a column, looking bored.

"Captain, a word," Edmund called.

Colm looked up and then back to his men, as always going at his own speed, never in any great hurry, before pushing himself off of the column and joining Edmund.

"Your Grace?"

"Walk with me," Edmund said, setting off deeper into the palace, toward his rooms, Colm falling into step with him. "Were you able to gather the men I asked for?"

"I did. They aren't cheap, but I have seventy-five good men, ready to do whatever you require."

"I don't care about the price. Things have escalated, and I need the situation along the border of River Mark handled. I'd hoped the barons themselves could take care of it, but they are proving inept."

"I always said knights were all talk."

"Yes, well, the situation is outside of their expertise. The peasants have become guerrillas, operating in hills and forests, ambushing smaller groups and fading away before the full weight of the kingdom can be brought down on them. Regular forces just aren't trained to deal with that."

"My men won't have the same problems."

"Good. I want you to do whatever you have to do to chase these people down. Draw on any men you need to in my name as duke, or in the king's name, if you have to, but I want them dealt with brutally, execute any man found in defiance of the king. I will give you letters of marque to that effect."

"Consider it done."

"Good. I know how you hate giving reports, so I'm sending Orlan with you to give me updates and keep me informed on your progress. He is there as an observer and will not interfere with you, but you are to see to it that he is not harmed in any way. If he dies, you will bear the blame for it."

Colm made a grumbling noise but nodded before he walked away.

He knew Colm would hate having a minder, but he needed to be able to tell Serwyn something, and he knew if he sent Colm off on his own, the man would be a ghost for weeks or even months until he reappeared, his task finished. He just had to hope Colm, or one of his thugs, didn't kill Orlan in the process. It would take forever to train another assistant properly.

Chansol River, Lynese

William crouched behind the thick underbrush watching the opposing bank, his men lined up behind him, waiting silently in the dark. It was only three days after Pride's Fall, and the moon was still high in the sky. He would have preferred to do this when the moon was dark, or even on a less clear day, but their supply situation was getting worse. If they were going to take the river and push forward, it had to happen now.

In the distance, the sound of hooves and jangling tack grew louder as a Lynesian patrol came into view, right on schedule. William held his breath, which wasn't really needed considering the rushing of the river and distance between them. They were well concealed, and it seemed unlikely that they'd be discovered at this point, but the entire plan was his idea, and relied on stealth as much as anything else.

Not that the Lynesians were paying much attention to his side of the river. The current here might be slower, but it was much too deep to be forded, and armored men swimming across a river was never a good idea.

At least, he hoped that's what they assumed. He'd watched them on his last scouting pass and left men to watch this spot for the past several weeks, and they'd held to the same schedule every time. He waited until after they passed, listening for the sounds of the horses to fade north into the distance. After a few more minutes, for safety, William waved Dominic forward. A fisherman who lived on the Kingshold River, the man spent his life in waters similar to this, and everyone attested to him being a strong swimmer.

"Be safe. Tie it off and get into your hiding spot until we get across. May the Ancients watch over you," William said as one of the sergeants handed Dominic, who was wearing only simple trousers, a thick rope line and a knife.

"Thank you, Ser," the man said, his crooked smile showing badly rotted teeth, as he tied the rope around his midsection.

William slapped him on the shoulder and then he was off, wading into the water and disappearing from view. Even with the moonlight, it was hard to pick him out, but the rope began unraveling, slowly turning south, downstream as it went. For several minutes, they watched the rope travel, meter after meter, across the beach, further and further downstream. William started to worry that something happened to the swimmer.

"Look," one of his men whispered, pointing past William toward the opposite beach.

He was well south of them, but he'd made it, dashing across the beach and up the tree line until he was roughly parallel to their position, where he tied the rope off to a tree before dipping out of sight into a large piece of foliage.

William waved and half a dozen men came forward, dragging small boats out of the tree line. As soon as one got into the water, men piled into it, every one of them holding onto the rope, pulling their boat through the water toward the other side, fighting the current.

William got into the second boat, and joined the men with him, pulling with all his might. The current might have been weak enough to swim against, but he could feel it pulling hard against the boat. Every moment, it felt like they were going to be pulled away from the rope and swept downstream, toward the bridge under construction and the enemy.

And then they were across, the boat scraping onto the sand.

The five boats all made it across, and then the harder part began, as three men in each boat pulled them back to the opposite shore, where they would be filled with even more soldiers for the next trip. If even only one of the boats failed and went downstream, the entire mission would almost certainly be a failure.

William didn't have time to wait and watch their progress. The men in the first group had been chosen for their ability to move swiftly and silently, and their ability in a fight. They all knew their assignments and were ready when William signaled. At William's command, they followed the road north, after the Lynesian patrol. The enemy had a decent head start, but they hadn't seemed to be in a big hurry. William set a brisk pace, worried that the patrol might turn off the road or stop to rest before he could catch them. The last thing he wanted was to lose them and have an enemy force running around at his rear.

After fifteen minutes of jogging through the woods, William spotted the bobbing lights of the patrol's lanterns ahead. He raised a clenched fist, bringing his men to a halt, and waved them into the trees, out of sight. They crept forward, finding that the patrol had stopped and was talking in loud voices, drinking from flasks, taking a break. Reaching as far as they could go without exposing themselves prematurely, William pulled his sword, his men following suit.

Looking back to ensure they were all ready, he raised his sword and his men charged forward, out of the trees with a savage cry.

The Lynesian whirled in shock, scrambling to draw their weapons as the Sidorians slammed into them. Caught by surprise, they managed little resistance. William impaled the first man through the back before he could turn his horse. The rider toppled from the saddle, dead before he hit the ground.

William's men made swift work of the rest while they floundered in confusion. In half a minute, the six Lynesian soldiers lay dead or dying.

"Strip and release the horses, hide the bodies and tack in the bush. Hurry, we need to get back to the rest of the force."

The men moved to follow his commands, quickly removing any trace of their fight beyond the blood soaked into the dry roadbed. In a few hours, any sign of the ambush would be gone.

Five hours later, William was crouched behind a thick wall of foliage, shrouded in the dark blue of early dawn. His men were half exhausted, scattered out behind him, recovering from hours of running through the darkness as they retraced their steps on this side of the river. They'd run into two more patrols along the way, wiping both out in the process.

The string of bodies they were leaving behind them worried William some. Each one was more opportunity for someone to discover them and sound the alarm. His uncle's attack wasn't to start for another hour at least, which gave time for word of the patrols' death to reach the main Lynesian army. If they started investigating, there was a good chance his small force would be discovered. They were good men, but a hundred Sidorians stood no chance against the weight of Lynesians gathered on this side of the river.

He couldn't see the enemy from here, holding his men back far enough to be able to hide in the forest, but he could see the smoke from their cooking fires drifting up on the other side of the small rise ahead of them, blocking the army from sight.

For thirty minutes, they sat there, waiting, watching the river as the Sidorian army gathered on the other side.

"Ser," one of the men next to William whispered.

William pulled his attention from the Sidorians and the bridge to the rise between them and the Lynesian army. Two men were ambling down the rise toward them. William turned to the man who alerted him, thrusting his head toward the rest of the men. The sergeant nodded and moved slowly, at a crouch, making gestures and leaning in to whisper to the closest men, spreading the warning of the approaching Lynesians.

Watching them, William began to worry as they got closer and closer to where he and his men were hiding. If they'd been sent to retrieve firewood or something else that would send them into the trees, things would get very bad very quickly.

Thankfully, they stopped a handful of paces away, turning and leaning out to get a better view of the Sidorian forces on the other side of the river. They were so close William could hear them breathing. The trees were thick, and worked well for them to remain hidden from people looking from a distance, but if these two turned and started looking into the forest for more than a few seconds, there was a good chance of them seeing someone.

They stood there for ten minutes, speaking in Lynesian, while William and his men held their breath. Finally, they finished whatever inspection they were making of the Sidorian movements and ambled away, back toward the Lynesian forces.

William let out a long breath, feeling his men relax around him. That had been close.

For the next hour and a half, he and his men hid at the tree line, watching the drama of the final sections of the Sidorian bridge being put into place. Archers on both banks continued to exchange volleys, many of the Lynesian arrows embedding themselves into the wooden barricades which were now only a few handspans away from the opposite bank, still protecting most of the bridge builders.

A few times the Lynesians tried to use polearms and lances to catch the barricade, but his uncle's engineers had done their jobs well, calculating how far from the end they could get before bringing in the section that would extend to the final section of bridge.

On the opposite bank, also protected by portable wooden barricades, his uncle's forces were assembled and ready, hunched low to avoid the arrows. Finally, the last span was brought forward. William felt a moment of pity for the men in that detail, knowing what was going to happen next.

As they reached the end of the bridge, the barricade was cast into the rushing water below, men dashed forward and dropped the last bridge section into place, fastening it as quickly as possible. It didn't need much in the way of fastening, the engineers knowing what kind of assault the crew would be under as soon as the barricade dropped. Even so, the death toll among the final crew was brutal. Dozens of replacements stood ready to run in and take up the tools of the fallen men, all motivated by not only the victory so near their grasps, but also the supplies on the other side of the river held by the Lynesian forces.

Aldric had done his best to spread out their supplies, reducing everyone's rations, foot soldier and knight alike, but the pain was still being felt. That hunger motivated each man who dashed out under the rain of arrows to help attach the final bridge span.

From his angle, William could also see what his uncle had said about the bridge being higher than the opposite bank. Knowing they couldn't actually connect it to the bank, the bridge they built had sloped up ever so slightly, ending a few meters higher than the other bank, allowing the soldiers who crossed an easier leap as they made their assault.

Another trumpet blew as the bridge crew, what few survived, made the run back to safety. They were passed mid-way by the first wave of Sidorian foot soldiers, who let loose a screaming battle cry as they stormed across the bridge, the shields raised in front of them already peppered with arrows.

Reaching the end of the bridge, the men began to leap across and down into the Lynesians who'd gathered at the other end, closer than William would have placed his men in their place. It allowed the Sidorians to drop into the midst of the first and second ranks of men, causing instant chaos. If it had been him, he would have set his men several paces back, allowing a solid wall to push against the men jumping across. Once the Sidorians were mixed in with the Lynesians, it kept their rear ranks from easily pushing the attackers back and into the river.

The sound of clashing steel and screams of the wounded carried over the churning water as the men fought and slashed, working to clear a bridgehead for the Sidorians following behind them. Even with the chaos, at first the Sidorians made little headway, each man making the leap across finding himself completely surrounded, stabbed at from all sides.

The second Sidorian wave surged forward to reinforce their faltering comrades. The constant flow of soldiers tumbling off the bridge into the Lynesians started to have an effect. For a moment, there was a gap around the bridge as the Sidorians began to connect with each other, protecting and fighting with their comrades, forming a curving wall around their landing point.

The Lynesians could see it, too. Now that the enemy wasn't dropping in the midst of their front rank, they began pushing, threatening to force the second wave of attackers under the bridge and over the edge, down into the river. The ground around the edge of the bridge was choked with bodies, causing both sides trouble.

"Now, Ser?" the sergeant asked.

"Not yet," William said. "We need enough of the Lynesians engaged that they can't turn half their line to face us and still have enough to push the bridgehead back. Our men are making progress. A little further and we'll have a bridgehead well established. Then they'll have to choose between fighting us or the main army, and whichever they choose will cause the other side to fail."

The sergeant didn't look particularly sure of that but didn't argue back. He felt for the older man, who probably couldn't help but second-guess the youth he'd been commanded to follow. In this case, though, William knew he was right. He'd like to say it was because of some innate tactical ability, but truthfully, it was because Pembroke and his uncle had made sure to cover the topic very thoroughly, knowing that the timing of his attack would be critical to the success of the battle.

As the wall of Lynesians began to be pushed back, the third wave dropped in their midst, beginning to turn the tide around the bridge. The cost was still very high, and William shuddered to think about the death toll when this was all done, but this new wave of men was having an effect. Step by step, they pushed the Lynesians back, absorbing the losses as more and more men piled in behind them, able to land unhindered now that a bridgehead had been established, before charging in to join the fight. Each man that fell was instantly replaced by a new soldier, the bubble around the Sidorian bridge growing by the minute.

"It's time. Remember your assignments, and no war cries until we're over the ridge and the enemy sees us. Keep together and hit them hard. On my command."

The sergeant nodded and began to pass the word back. His men, who'd been waiting, pretending to be relaxed but really on edge as William himself was, began to form up behind him.

They'd practiced this several times in the woods near the Sidorian army camp, to prepare for this moment. They'd scouted the area thoroughly ahead of time. They'd gone over the plan again and again.

Now, it was time for all that planning to become reality. William pushed himself up, his legs protesting after hours of crouching, and raised his sword above his head as he began a slow trot out of the woods, conserving his men's energy until they were on top of the enemy.

William broke from the tree line, his men streaming out behind him as he led the charge up the gentle slope. Reaching the crest, he caught his first glimpse of the vast Lynesian force arrayed below. Row upon row of armored men stretched out before them, attention focused on the raging battle at the bridge.

"For Sidor!" William bellowed, his battle cry echoed by over a hundred voices.

Swords held high, they thundered down the hillside like an avalanche. The Lynesians whirled in shock at the war cries and the sudden appearance of a hundred Sidorians coming out of what must have seemed like nowhere. Few had even turned all the way to face this new threat when the new force of Sidorians slammed into the flank of the enemy forces like a tempest.

Fueled by adrenaline and after hours of watching the enemy, his men assaulted the Lynesians with a fury that seemed to catch them off guard.

And then they were in the thick of it. All around, his men smashed into the confused enemy, steel ringing against steel. Dozens of the enemy died in those first moments, unprepared for the sudden attack. William knew it wouldn't last, but they pressed their advantage while they could, carving deep into the side of the Lynesian line. William's sword cleaved through the neck of the first soldier he met, nearly decapitating him and creating a spray of crimson. All around him, his men were cutting down soldiers, some of whom tried to turn and run, only to find themselves stuck in the mass of fighting men.

As he predicted, their disorganization was short-lived and a few minutes later the Lynesian resolve stiffened. They began to coalesce into a more organized line, their greater weight of men threatening to envelop and surround William's small group.

"Back," William commanded, taking a step to the rear as he parried a sword thrust from a burly soldier, then dispatched his attacker with a riposte through the armpit.

They had seen this result coming enough to have prepared for this moment as well, his men taking practiced steps backward as they continued to fight. Slowly, his force was pushed back to the rise they had just come over, their numbers diminishing as they went. William fought hard, trying to keep his men alive and organized as they retreated, as an axe split the helmet of the man beside him, dropping the lifeless soldier to the ground.

The Lynesian line surged, threatening to break William's depleted force. He knew they couldn't hold much longer against such overwhelming odds. He also knew he didn't have to. The Lynesian force had reacted as any army would have, turning to meet a new, and at the time, more dangerous threat. But they'd taken their eye off the real threat, and as William started up the rise in reverse, a Sidorian war horn blared, reminding everyone where the real battle had been all along.

As soon as William's force had charged and the Lynesians had wheeled to meet them, the Sidorian waves across the bridge became a constant flood, pouring onto the bridgehead. Now that flood increased again as armored knights joined the men at arms and the balance of numbers began to shift back to the Sidorian side.

"Forward," William called as the pressure on his own men eased, the Lynesians turning to take on this new danger.

It was too late for them. Step by bloody step, the two Sidorian forces pressed inward, toward each other, a third of the Lynesian host trapped between them like a vice.

Split, outnumbered, and in shock, their defenses began to buckle.

It took time, and the losses had begun to stack up frightfully, but William's men and the men coming from the bridgehead began to near each other, cutting off of a third of the Lynesian army. He could see the Sidorian soldiers in front of him as he smashed the pommel of his sword into a soldier's face with a satisfyingly wet thunk.

Victory was so close William could taste it.

Cries of panic spread through the Lynesian ranks as the Sidorian knights, not mounted, but full-armored and well-seasoned, penetrated deep into the enemy host. Some Lynesians threw down their weapons and turned to flee, only to find themselves hemmed in on all sides while others fought on desperately, knowing retreat was impossible. They sold their lives dearly as the tide had turned decisively against them.

And then he was through, only a single Lynesian soldier between him and his comrades, standing over the fallen form of a Sidorian soldier who'd tripped in the mass of bodies and blood, dazed as the Lynesian began to bring his sword down to end the man's life.

William felt no pity for the Lynesian as he ran his sword through the man, the steel appearing on the other side, the stunned soldier gurgling once before William pushed the man's body off his blade, sending him crashing off to the side.

Looking down at the Sidorian on the ground, William was surprised to realize he recognized the man. He was one of the men William arrested along with Garr and the other Sidorians. The man laid there, on his back, staring up at William, a shocked look on his face.

"Don't lie there all day," William said, reaching a gloved hand down toward the man. "We have Lynesians to kill."

Grabbing the man's hand, he hauled him up and then stabbed past him, dispatching another enemy who had just started to come in from the side.

The soldier smiled and said, "Yes, My Lord."

Turning, they fought next to each other, side-by-side. William was honestly impressed by how well the man fought, killing several enemies who attempted to come in from the left. William was happy his uncle had decided to pardon some of the men. Seeing the man fight, William felt vindicated in his defense of them to Aldric.

The Sidorian line was now complete, a solid wall facing the Lynesians, the bridgehead firmly established. With a large section of their army cut off and being cut down mercilessly, the enemy line began to waver, and then crumbled completely. Panic spread like wildfire as soldiers threw down their weapons and turned to flee.

Just as with the battle at the fort, William was again amazed by how quickly the battle ended. One minute he was fighting all out, his life in danger every second, and the next, the enemy line all but vanished as the trickle of retreating men became a flood, none wanting to be the last soldier fighting, all on his own.

William finally lowered his sword, smiling at the soldier who'd stayed by his side since he rescued him. The rest of his small force, maybe thirty left that he could see, looked to him, as if asking if it was really over, if they'd won.

William raised his sword and bellowed, "For Sidor!"

His men, with the adrenaline and terror of battle turned into elation, raised their weapons in return, and matched his energy. And then surpassed it.

"For Sidor!" they yelled. "For Lord William!"

The sound crashed over him, the cries being picked up by men who hadn't been with him, who'd been with the forces that came over the bridge. Even the soldier he'd arrested, standing next to him, joined in, his sword held high in the air, yelling with all his might.

William kept his sword held high as his men crowded around him. This was a moment he'd never forget.

Chapter 16

Barony of Lindenwood, Duchy of Kingsheart

Tom Fletcher made his way through the small clearing where his men were camped, stopping to talk to this group or that, offering words of encouragement or just a sympathetic ear. These weren't soft men. They were farmers and woodsmen, hunters and craftsmen. Men used to long days of backbreaking work.

They all now had a new appreciation for the endurance of soldiers, after two days of marching, pushing from sunup to sundown across the Barony of Ambleton on their way to Lindenwood. Ambleton, like Langmere, was a puppet of the duke, and almost certainly had what men he had available looking for them, which meant they weren't able to use the major roads, making the journey even harder.

They made it, though. His entire band had breathed a sigh of relief when they finally left the fields of Ambleton. Besides the thick forests which sat at the western edge of the Shatterstone Mountain's foothills being an excellent place to hide, it was widely known that Baron Thurston was a man of the people and had been shielding his from the king's new laws. While he might not be in open rebellion against the king, it was unlikely they would be hounded in Thurston's barony the way they had been in Langmere.

Despite their exhaustion, his men were in good spirits. After their victory in the Cresswell Hills, they'd had two more battles against men from the king and his lackeys, both of which they'd won handily. That had been enough for Baron Blout to turn up the heat on them, which had ultimately been what drove them northeast out of the hills and toward Lindenwood.

Now they were here, and by tomorrow, they'd be deep in the forest, more or less safe from the king's men. From that point, he'd have to talk to the men and figure out where their next target should be. He also needed to make his way to Lindvale, the capital of the barony that shared the name with the forest they were in, and send a wyvern to their benefactor, whom he hadn't been in contact with since just before the battle of Cresswell Pass, as their glorious victory was already starting to be known.

Tom had almost made it back to where he'd been planning to settle down for the night when a shout suddenly rose from one of the groups closest to the tree line to the west, followed quickly by more cries. Tom's head jerked up just in time to see riders bursting out of the woods, surrounding their camp. His men reacted quickly, jumping to their feet and scrambling for weapons, as soon as the warning was given, but the enemy's surprise had been complete. Even as he pulled his own sword, the enemy was already pushing everyone toward the center of the clearing, the horsemen quickly moving around their edges, encircling them.

"Back. Back," Fletcher yelled, waving his sword over his head. "Form up."

His men reacted well. They weren't soldiers, but they'd been in enough fights to learn a little and had started to listen even more to the men in their ranks with actual time in service to the previous king and his armies. A few tried to make a run for it, cut down before they could get out of the clearing, but the vast majority followed his orders, picking up spears, swords, and bows, forming their own circle, as the attackers now came at them from all sides.

Just in time, too, as a wave of horsemen smashed into their flank. His men managed to push them back, spears and swords injuring animals and men that got close enough, but not without cost. Screams of pain and rage filled the air.

One of the supply wagons toppled, spilling bags of grain across the grass. Three of his men near it fell beneath the swords of the attackers as they tried to get into his lines. The few bowmen they had begun to notch and loose arrows as quickly as they could, taking down a number of the horses and men assaulting them. Not enough, though.

The ambushers kept coming, not losing any momentum. They weren't like some of the bailiffs they'd encountered, cowards who backed off as soon as they realized the people they were terrorizing weren't going to back down. No, these men pressed in mercilessly, herding the outnumbered defenders together. Tom could see what they were doing. If his men got backed together tight enough, it wouldn't take much for them to crush his force entirely and ensure that none escaped.

Even with his men fighting back in all directions, one thing was clear. They were going to be overrun soon.

"Everyone. Concentrate everything to the east," Tom bellowed, to the men in the center of the camp, closest to him, before turning to Godric, one of the men who'd been with him the longest. "I need you to take that group and hold tight around the rest while they break out. You have to fight hard, keep them looking in that direction, so they don't see their weak point until it's too late."

"What will happen to us when you break out?" Godric said, looking to the west where the largest group of the enemy were attacking.

He was a good man. He'd been a soldier for a short while and read the field better than Tom ever had. It's why he was the one to lead the rear guard as Tom got the rest out. He'd see where they needed to push to keep the enemy from reinforcing the breach, if it happened, in time.

Unfortunately, he was also smart enough to know what that would mean for him personally.

"I'm sorry," Tom said, putting his hand on his friend's shoulder. "We need to get as many men as we can out if we are going to continue the fight."

Godric frowned, misery playing across his face, before he pulled his mouth into a tight line and nodded.

"I understand," he said, his voice a little shaky. "We'll do what we can."

Time was critical, but Tom spared a moment to squeeze his friend's shoulder, looking him in the eye, trying to say everything he wanted to, but didn't have the time to say, with a look, instead of words.

Godric nodded, understanding, and said, "Go."

He didn't wait to see what Tom did, turning and yelling at his men, getting them to fan out, absorbing as much of the assault as possible, keeping the enemy busy while the rest attempted a breakout.

"With me," Tom bellowed, pointing at the spot he'd indicated earlier, a portion of the men already attacking the half dozen riders on that side that stood between them and freedom. "Cut through! Pull them down!"

The cost was high, but one by one, the riders were surrounded by angry commoners, pulled off their mounts or stabbed with spear or sword while they sat atop them. Some of the horses were taken with the riders, others sent running as their rider suddenly disappeared.

His men were desperate, the attack brutal. He joined them, stabbing up from the side of a rider who was wildly swinging his sword around his mount, trying to keep the swarm of attackers away, panic in his eyes.

Tom came through on a blind side, his sword sliding easily into an exposed spot where greave met leather chest piece when the man leaned over to attack someone on the opposite side. With a gurgle, the man slid from the saddle and collapsed. Tom pulled his blood-slicked blade free and pointed it at the tree line.

"Run. Into the trees and through," he yelled.

They would become scattered, and most did not know the destination. He'd try and pick up stragglers as he went, but his number was certain to diminish more than by just what was lost in the battle.

Still, there was nothing for it as Tom sprinted with his group, sparing a look back at Godric, who had spread his line out dangerously thin as the rest made a break for it, the enemy finally realizing what was happening and trying to get through or around them to chase down their escaping prey.

They crashed into the trees and through the underbrush, all of his men pushing hard, knowing it wouldn't be long until the riders were after them. Godric was still fighting, though. Tom could hear the sounds of clashing steel and dying men, fading but still audible, behind them as they drove deeper into the woods.

He'd gotten maybe two or three dozen men out, from what he could see around him. Perhaps there would be another dozen or so lagging behind or further out running in other directions. Some of those, the stragglers or the ones who'd cut too far north or south, would be caught and captured. If he was very lucky, he'd manage to save fifty of the over one hundred men he'd settled down in the clearing with. In ten minutes, he'd lost half his number, just when they'd thought they'd be safe.

Worse, something had changed. Those weren't men of the Lindenwood. He didn't see the branching tree on a field of green, the standard of the Barony of Lindenwood. In fact, he didn't see any kind of sigil on them at all.

These men were something new. He needed to talk to his friends and find out what was happening.

Valemonde, Lynese

Isolde sat quietly next to the soldier as he fell asleep, holding his hand, trying to offer comfort in what was surely one of his final days. Her father had refused to budge, since their argument weeks before, and she'd begun spending more and more time here, where it felt like at least she was doing something that mattered.

Now, more than ever. The hospital had swelled in recent days, ever since the Sidorians forced a crossing of the Chansol River, shattering her father's army and pushing toward Lysmir Lake, where the Dead Man's Hills finally narrowed and ended, opening up into the plains of Lynese. She knew these men were only the first, worst cases, sent here by the Disciples, from their field aid stations, where they had a better chance of recovery. Worse, even more of these men, the prime of Lynesian society, would have been beyond all hope, and had passed away without coming south.

She couldn't help but see the cost of her father's policies and decisions in every man's face.

Seeing the young man slip into a sleep, the pain finally leaving his face, Isolde placed his hand back on his chest, patting his shoulder before rising to move on to the next.

She was tired in her heart, but she also couldn't bring herself to leave. She'd only finished two wards, and there were still three more to go before she saw all of the areas assigned to the soldiers. She'd made a promise to herself not to leave until she'd seen all of the men each time she'd visited, and she intended to stick to that.

Checking on the last three cots she had not stopped at yet, she found each of the men asleep. It was early still, but many of the medicines the Disciples gave were specifically designed to force the patients to sleep, stemming from their belief that, more than any medicine or procedure they could perform, the best chance for men to heal was through rest.

Moving into the next ward, she instantly noticed something different about the setup, something she hadn't seen here on her last visit three days ago. Normally this room was packed with cots, row upon row, the full length of the room, stretching from one wall to the next. That was still true of the last two wards, but in this one the far corner was cordoned off, a barricade and screens erected and then another barricade past that, with no cots placed anywhere near that section, leaving a large, mostly unused space. Through a gap in the boards, Isolde caught a glimpse of a man thrashing against his restraints. She frowned, perturbed by the sight.

Isolde flagged down one of the Disciples moving amongst the patients. "What is all this? Why is that man bound and separated from the rest?"

The Disciple's face turned grim, his eyes downcast. "I am afraid he has contracted the Elder Curse, My Lady."

Isolde gasped, taking an instinctive step back, away from the evil. The Elder Curse? She had heard tales of the deadly affliction since childhood and again in her history lessons. How could her lessons not cover it? The curse had ravaged the entire world several centuries ago, wiping out a huge part of the population of not only Lynese but every kingdom in the Shattered Lands before it finally ended. It was quite possibly the most deadly event since the fall of magic itself, claiming more victims than any mortal conflict, even the wars of the great alliance.

To even know of someone afflicted with it now, let alone see a patient in its grips, was exceedingly rare. Following the sacrifice that had ended the curse, it had become less contagious, allowing the Disciples to quickly isolate and quarantine the afflicted, allowing them to die alone, without taking anyone with them. Isolde had only ever heard third-hand accounts of the few outbreaks that had happened in her and her father's lifetime from tutors and advisors, and wasn't aware of any occurring since she was old enough to track major events.

"How is this possible? Was he with the army?"

It wouldn't make sense for a civilian to be in this section. Aside from the fact that they had their own separate area of the hospital, putting him with soldiers who could potentially recover and rejoin their forces would be against everything she knew about how the Disciples worked.

The Disciple shook his head. "We do not know how it happened. The man arrived just yesterday, brought by a group of soldiers, already gripped by the curse's advanced stages. We had to restrain and isolate him immediately before the contagion could spread. Thankfully, it seems the other soldiers with him were spared catching the affliction, although we still have them sequestered in another area of the hospital. If they make it through the month without the spot, we will release them."

"Did you ask them what happened?"

"Of course, Your Highness. It is one of our order's highest commandments. If any of the great curses appear, we are to find the source through every means possible to ensure its containment. The Elder Curse rarely starts with someone so young, so we assume he contracted it elsewhere, but he would not say, no matter how much we pleaded. The other soldiers said they do not know him, and only know they were ordered to escort him here, for healing, and to ensure that he nor they came in contact with anyone on the journey south from Lake Lysmir. They said they did not recognize him, but it's possible he contracted it in that region, since your father's army is large. However, that area is well-traveled and highly populated, not even considering the armies in the field there. If it was contracted up north, near Lake Lysmir, we would have expected to see additional cases by now."

Isolde took a hesitant step toward the barricade, peering through the gap at the thrashing man.

"How long has he been like this?" she asked softly.

"The grip took him a few hours ago, which means he's begun the aging. Already, we can see lines appearing on his skin along with a few age spots, in addition to the mark of the curse, of course. By this time tomorrow, I expect his heart or lungs to give out."

"When was the last time there was an outbreak?"

"That I know of, ten years ago. A group of settlers, three families, I think, was foolish enough to begin a settlement between the Wyvern's Backbone and the Peaks of Oblivion, a few kilometers north of the shoreline. I didn't see it myself, but I understand they were in a hard-to-reach area, which is how your father's men missed them. It was only discovered when a member of their family, who was still healthy enough to travel, tried to go for help and was picked up by a patrol. As far as I'm aware, every member of the settlement died, along with a handful of members of that first patrol."

"And none since?"

"Not that I know of, but there have been instances of small parties being stricken and found months or even years afterward. We can tell from the bones, as the aging process deforms them in unnatural ways. The existence of these cases suggests there are perhaps there are others we've never found."

"I see. So where did he contract this? He's a soldier, so presumably he ran into someone with it and contracted it from them, since I doubt any of my father's men are left to just wander the wilderness. Not with the war on."

"We assume as much, but he wouldn't say. Before the grip began, all he would say was that he couldn't tell us. Now, his jaw is locked so tight, I doubt he can say anything."

Just then, there was a creaking sound followed by a man exhaling loudly. She peaked through the opening again to see the man had collapsed and stopped thrashing.

"It's passed. I need to consult with my brothers about the next stages of treatment."

"I want to talk to him. This is important. If there are afflicted people out there, we should find out and set up a quarantine right away."

"Please, My Lady, do not go beyond the second set of barricades. This is to keep people from getting too close, and none but the selected Disciples are allowed beyond the second barrier. We aren't completely sure how close you have to be to get it, but the proscriptions have set that as the minimum safe distance. Do not even lean over it. If you can't hear him, we will send in one of the brothers who have been administering to him to help with communication."

"Thank you," she said, slipping past the first barricade.

In that interim space in between, she felt a strange sense of foreboding. She knew it was in her mind, since she'd walked this area just days before, when there had been cots and injured men here, but she felt it all the same. She found herself stopping a few steps from the second barricade, her legs unwilling to carry her further.

She was afraid. She wouldn't say that out loud, not where the man could hear her, but in her heart, she knew how terrified she was. She'd seen drawings done during the great dying, of people who'd become more skeleton than human overnight. Not everyone who came in contact with a sick person, even physical contact, contracted the curse, but everyone who contracted it died. All of them.

"Can you hear me?" she said, her voice more wobbly than she would have liked. "I am Princess Isolde. Is there anything you need?"

The man's head lulled to the side, facing her, giving her the first full look at him. He must have been a young man, although it was hard to tell now. His cheeks were sunken in slightly, and age lines had begun to appear across his face, his skin sagging, giving him an appearance almost of melted wax.

He didn't look right at her, and she could see some kind of film building over his eyes.

"Water," he croaked weakly.

She began to take a step forward when an arm grabbed her from behind.

"My Lady, you mustn't go beyond this line," a different Disciple than before said. "The risk is too great."

"He wants water."

"I will go get his attendant," the man said. "Please do not step any closer."

"I'm sorry. I won't. I promise."

The man looked at her for another moment, clearly unsure if he should leave her on her own for a moment or not, before nodding and dashing away. A few minutes later, a man in a full gown, almost like a beekeeper, but with a thick leather apron over the garb, came into the ward. He had a strange mask over his face with no nose or mouth holes and only two tiny dots where the eyes should be. His hood was pulled tight over his head, cinched under his chin, which was itself covered in the same kind of cloth the mask was made of and then fitted over, not a trace of skin showing anywhere.

The costume would be terrifying if she hadn't seen them before. Disciples often wore them during other disease outbreaks more mundane than the curse. She supposed it kept them somewhat safe, although she knew that more than a few Disciples had fallen to the curse after tending a patient, no matter the precautions.

As she watched, the man went to a bucket on one side of the cot, pulling out what looked like a long handle with a small cup on the end. It wasn't quite a ladle, and she doubted it would hold more than a mouthful of water. What it did do was let the Disciple give the man water from several steps away. Another precaution. As she watched, he extended it to the patient, who opened his mouth. As much of the water ended up on his chin as in his mouth, but the man gave a satisfied sigh anyway, clearly feeling some relief.

"I must know, can you tell me how did you come by the curse? Please, if you can speak of it, tell me. It's very important."

The soldier turned his head toward her again, his filmed eyes unfocused. He worked his jaw, lips parting with effort. Several times he opened and closed his mouth, trying to speak, but not sound coming out.

Finally he croaked, "There's … a village … south of Varencia … near the backbone."

He paused, chest heaving with labored breaths. Isolde waited patiently for him to gather his strength.

"We were ordered there. Several were sick … the Elder Curse had broken out," he rasped, before stopping for another agonizing pause. "We were to take some of the afflicted … bring them north … to a village near the lake … where the Sidorians will arrive soon."

Isolde's eyes widened in shock.

Oblivious to her reaction, the soldier went on. "We tried to protest … but the count forced us. He offered assistance for our families … things we couldn't refuse. So we were as careful as we could be … never touched the afflicted directly … forced them into wagons with promises of a cure."

His breaths came harder now, each word a struggle. "We brought them to the village as ordered … left them in a vacant house. Never told anyone who we'd brought. We lied."

A tear leaked from his filmy eye.

"The Ancients cursed us for it. We broke their sacred commands. Now we're going to die."

Isolde stared in horror as the soldier's words sank in. Transporting the afflicted to secretly spread the plague among their enemies went against everything the Acolytes taught. She knew her father was ruthless in war, but never imagined he would stoop to such depths.

It wouldn't only kill the enemy. If any of the villagers stumbled on the vacant house, found them, it would spread. Her own people were in as much jeopardy as the enemy.

"I'll never see my wife and son again. I'm going to die wretched and alone. Please, Your Highness, promise me you'll make sure the empire cares for my family as they swore."

Isolde stared at the dying soldier, her mind reeling. Her father had ordered his own men to transport plague victims to secretly infect their enemies. It went against everything she believed was right. Not only would it lead to the horrific deaths of countless

Sidorian soldiers, but her own people were at risk, too, if it spread unchecked near the front lines.

"I promise, the empire will do right by them," she finally said. "You have my word."

The man's body sagged in relief, as if a great weight had been lifted from him. "Thank you, Your Highness. You are truly merciful and just."

His gratitude made her heart ache. She should have been furious with him for his role in her father's vile plan, but looking at this young man — who didn't look young at all anymore — she felt only pity. He was a pawn following orders, sacrificing himself for his family's wellbeing. How could she judge him when her own father had orchestrated such evil?

The soldier's eyes began to drift closed, his strained breaths slowing. Isolde backed away, maintaining a cautious distance as she'd been warned to. His admission weighed heavy on her soul. Her father's tactics endangered countless innocents, especially so close to the front where magistrates, marshals, and all the administrative apparatus of the state would have fled ahead of the Sidorians, leaving the civilians alone and unprotected.

Isolde glanced back at the barricaded corner where the young soldier now slept, his life fading away with each ragged breath. Looking at his gaunt, prematurely aged face, she could still hear his words, 'The Ancients cursed us for it. We broke their sacred commands.'

Something had to be done before the plague took root and spread. Even if it saved enemy lives, she couldn't let this happen.

Chapter 17

Starhaven, Kingdom of Sidor

Edmund stood beside the king's ornate throne, his expression sour as he watched the doors to the audience chamber swing open. The throne room of the Grand Hall in Starhaven was filled to capacity, the crowds of ornately dressed nobles and courtiers packed shoulder to shoulder along the sides of the long gold and white carpeted central walkway.

All heads turned as the great doors at the end of the hall swung open. Colm Thranton walked in confidently, making his way down the center aisle, head held high. The crowds murmured amongst themselves at the appearance, for good reason. Colm's scarred, devilish face was a far cry from the normal men and women who made their way into the king's presence. Some nobles shrank back unconsciously, as if to give him space as he passed.

Reaching the end of the carpet, Colm, who must have been instructed on proper etiquette for such a setting, dropped to one knee, head bowed in supplication to the king.

Edmund scowled as he watched Colm kneel before the throne. A stark contrast to everyone around him, still in his leather armor and weathered cloak, which had at least been cleaned before he'd been allowed to step foot in the chambers. He'd always done his best to keep Thranton out of the public eye, knowing how ill-suited he was for more polite company. And yet, here he was, adding a level of potential trouble Edmund had wanted to avoid.

"Rise," Serwyn said.

Colm stood, clasping his hands behind him in a manner much more casual than was considered correct. Edmund eyed Serwyn, ready for his nephew, so easily offended by the smallest slight, to say something, ending this charade.

Instead, Serwyn smiled and said, "Well done, Captain. Word has reached us of your swift justice against the peasants currently in rebellion in Kingsheart. You have shown the entire kingdom what fate awaits those who dare defy their rightful king, and corrected an error my uncle has allowed to fester uncontested."

"I am but a humble servant to Your Grace," replied Colm, inclining his head respectfully. "It was my duty to uphold the king's justice and protect the realm from the spread of treason."

Edmund's scowl deepened. More and more lately, his nephew had added small, biting remarks in their conversations and in public, still holding him to blame for the actions of the rabble. Now Colm, whom Edmund had brought in to correct the situation, was getting the recognition for solving the problem. Worse, the mercenary was playing into the role, acting very differently than he normally did. This was a man who would readily sever his own nephew's head from his shoulders for a few gold coins. Simpering and bowing before the throne was so utterly beyond Colm's nature, that it instantly made Edmund suspicious.

"You have done far more than your duty," Serwyn said. "By crushing this rebellion before it could grow, you have earned the favor and gratitude of the crown. The kingdom shall long remember your loyal service."

Edmund's scowl deepened further as Colm glanced in his direction, giving a knowing look and a slight smile before saying, "Your Grace, I must confess, since I was a boy, I have dreamed of being a knight. But due to the low nature of my birth, that honor has always been denied me."

It was laughable on its face. Not only was the man the farthest thing from a knight that had ever existed, in all of their conversations he'd never given any indication of interest in that direct, whatsoever.

Serwyn, however, seemed to miss the entire byplay.

"Since ascending the throne, I have learned that a man's worth has little to do with the circumstances of his birth. There are many who call themselves my loyal subjects, barons who trace their lineage back centuries, yet are lax in their duty to uphold the law. Sidor needs more men like you, Captain."

To Edmund's shock and outrage, his nephew stood and reached over to the Steward of the Sword, who held the boy's sword of state, taking the sword by the hilt and pulling the blade free from the scabbard before descending the steps.

"Kneel," he commanded, stopping in front of the mercenary.

Colm dropped to one knee, head bowed, again following the correct protocol, although where the man would have learned this, Edmund had no clue.

"What is your full name?" Serwyn asked.

"Colm Thranton, Your Grace."

"In the name of my forbearers and in the eyes of the Ancients, I name you Sir Colm Thranton, Knight of Sidor, duty sworn to uphold the kingdom with your body, soul and being. Rise, Sir Colm."

Colm stood, an uncharacteristically genuine smile on his face. "You honor me beyond words, Your Grace. I shall strive to be worthy of this honor and to serve you and the realm faithfully all my days."

Edmund seethed as he watched his nephew remount the stairs and casually hand the ceremonial sword to him instead of back to the Steward, as if he were some kind of a lackey. Serwyn settled himself on the throne once more, an amused grin on his face as he addressed the newly minted knight.

"Sir Colm, it is now your duty to see to it that the remainder of the rebels are rounded up and dealt with. I trust you will not fail me in this task."

"It would be my utmost pleasure, Your Grace. I shall not rest until every last rebel has faced the king's justice."

The mercenary bowed low, his eyes flicking up to meet Edmund's for a brief moment. The sly smile that played at the corners of his mouth was almost imperceptible, but Edmund caught it and felt his anger boil over. It took every ounce of Edmund's self-control to refrain from charging down the dais and throttling the man.

He watched as Colm walked confidently out of the throne room, the heavy doors closing behind him with a resounding thud. The room was silent for a moment before the whispers and murmurs of the gathered nobles and courtiers began to build once more.

When he'd heard Colm's initial report, Edmund had thought he'd finally regained at least some measure of control. He reported back to his nephew that the majority of the rebels had been slain or captured, with the prisoners being marched back to the Starhaven for a very public execution. Of course, he knew that really wasn't the majority of the rebels, but he'd needed to do damage control with his nephew, who'd become increasingly uncontrollable the longer the peasants were in revolt.

He still did not know how Serwyn had even learned of Colm's involvement. It seemed unlikely the mercenary would have been able to weasel his way into the king's good graces directly since, as far as he knew, he was the only connection between the two. The entire audience had been announced suddenly, and had blindsided him completely, with Colm taking the accolades that he'd counted on getting himself to set things right with his nephew.

Now, things were notably worse. He needed a way to restore his control over Serwyn and get the kingdom back in line. And he needed to do it soon.

Port Belmar, East of Lysmir Lake, Northern Lynese

William knelt on the floor of his tent, reading passages from his small copy of the *Tome of Remembrance*, one of the revered books of the acolytes. Occasionally, he would stop at a section and close his eyes, repeating the passage to himself, focusing on the words and their deeper meanings, as his tutors had taught him to do.

The air in his tent was thick with burning sage, the soot of which he had rubbed under his eyes to help him symbolically see through the veil to the time of magic. William considered himself a true believer, faithful to the Ancients and the acolytes, but he couldn't help but let his mind wander during these ceremonies.

This time last year, he'd been at the Grand Hall in Starhaven, surrounded by scores of Sidor's highest nobles as the high priest led the solemn rituals to commemorate the Fall. The pillars holding up the hall's massive ceiling were wreathed in burning sage, clouds of smoke filling the top of the room but not leaving a trace of soot across the wondrous ceiling. Another gift from the Ancients.

They'd recited the rituals, led by the elder of Starhaven, and listened to sermons about the Ancients, what they had left behind as their world fell, the ideals they had maintained, and what all believers should be doing to uphold those ideals.

Now, camped on foreign soil far from the Grand Halls, or really any of the halls of antiquity except those in Lynesian hands, William performed the rituals on his own. Cleansing his mind and body for the coming year, ridding himself of the evils he'd collected over that time, and recommitting himself in the sight of the Ancients.

He refocused, whispering the names of the fallen, whom he'd pledge to remember each year, building his list. His list of ancestors was still small and growing, but he'd heard some of the older nobles had hundreds of names, taking the entire day of remembrance to recite them from memory. Each name was someone they had committed to remembering and holding close, keeping their flame alive among the Ancients.

William remembered his mother first, as he did every year. Her face was shadowy, hard to recall accurately as the years passed, shrouded in his memory of her when he'd been a young child. He lit the first candle, whispering her name, pledging her memory. He lit another for the father he never knew, and one for a nanny who'd cared for him when he was little, when his mother had first been courted by Edmund. She'd been taken by the flux. He remembered crying so hard for her, the first person he'd known personally who

186

passed. This year, he added a new candle for his Uncle Gavric. The greatest man he'd ever known.

Part of him had wanted to light a candle for the men who'd fallen under his command, but William hadn't been close to any of them, not enough to add them to his list of the remembered. He was glad he didn't have to add one for Sir Drummond who, while not ready to take to the field yet, was walking around, still keeping up with the army.

Putting the wick out in a small bowl of sand, William reached to pick his tome back up, to recite the next passage, when a voice at the entrance to his tent nearly made him jump out of his skin.

"William?" his Uncle Aldric said. "Sorry if I startled you. I know you're in the middle of your remembrance, but I need to talk to you for a moment, and I don't have time to wait."

William set the book on the small altar below the flickering candles and pushed himself up, saying, "Come in, Uncle."

The tent flap parted, and Aldric entered, ducking his head slightly under the low canvas. Instead of armor or the under gambeson he wore most of the time in camp, Aldric was dressed in more comfortable clothes with a heavy cloak fastened around his shoulders.

"You're not performing the rituals?" William asked, surprised to see Aldric there.

Nearly every man in both armies would spend the day in worship, meaning the front, as it was at the moment, would be quiet for the time being.

"Not yet. Now that we've taken Port Belmar and cleared out most of the Lynesian shipping, I'll be sailing back to Sidor within the hour. I'll do my remembrances on the ship. Which is why I'm here. I'm sorry to interrupt your worship, but I don't have much time before I leave, and it's important that we talk."

"I understand," William said, grabbing one of the camp stools near his cot and handing it over to his uncle while he sat on the other. "What's happening? I didn't know you were leaving."

"I know. I hadn't thought we'd take a major port this quickly, so I haven't prepared for this as well as I wanted to. The main reason I need to talk to you is because of what's going to happen while

I'm gone," Aldric said, and then paused for a moment. "While I'm away, I'm leaving you in command of the army."

"What?" William blurted out in shock. "That can't be right. Surely Baron Pembroke or Sir Alistair would be better choices to lead in your absence."

"It's true both men have more experience, both in battle and in positions of command, than you have, but they are *not Whittons*. As much as some may wish differently, our family and Sidor are one, and our men expect a Whitton to lead them. It is vitally important for morale. Pembroke and Alistair are good men, and both will be keys to your success; but they can't hold the army together indefinitely on their own, not out here in the field. That requires a Whitton. It's why I agreed to come here when Edmund asked me in the first place. Once Gavric was struck down, the army foundered, in want of a Whitton."

Aldric reached out and put a hand on William's shoulder. "I have faith in you, William. Over the past few months, you've shown bravery, clear thinking, and, most importantly, a care for the men in your command. These are all important traits for a leader to have. You are inexperienced, but not incapable, and you're not going to be alone. Pembroke, Alistair, and Eskild will all be here to advise you and help guide you to the correct decisions. Okay?"

"Yeah," William said, still overwhelmed by the pronouncement, but mollified somewhat by the faith his uncle had in him. And the fact that he wouldn't be alone.

"Good. Now, listen to your advisors, take their suggestions to heart, but remember, you're in command. They may guide you, but the final decision rests with you. You may be young, but you are a Whitton ... serving in the name of the king and your father, the duke. These men are duty-sworn to follow your orders. Trust in that, and trust in yourself. Follow your heart and do what you believe is right. You've already proven you have the instincts and temperament for command. This is your chance to show the rest of the world what you're capable of."

"But why do you have to go at all? We finally got across the river and are making progress again."

"I know, and I wish, more than anything, that I could stay, but our supply situation has not improved. If anything, it has worsened. We've stemmed the shortage a little by seizing the stockpiled provisions we've taken from the Lynesians, but they will only sustain us for a short while. Once winter sets in, keeping the men fed and equipped will become much more difficult. I need to talk to your father and the king about securing more support for the army. In addition, I've received disturbing news about some of the soldiers' families back in Sidor. It won't be long until word reaches the men and begins to cause unrest. I'd like to have answers for them before that happens."

"Ohh!" William said.

He was aware of the supply situation, as he'd continued to look into it after the incident at the Lynesian village. And he received the same reports as his uncle. He'd sent three wyverns to his step-father and one to Serwyn himself, trying to explain the situation. He hadn't received a response yet, but he'd hoped that if they knew the true extent of the problem, they might do something.

"It's also mid-summer, and we have most of the levied men from the Rivermark here with us. By the time I arrive back in Sidor, the harvesting season will have begun. I think it likely that I will need to raise additional men and head for Shadowhold to reinforce our ranks before the Maw opens, which means it's unlikely I will return until after it closes again. I don't expect to sail until after Blessings Day, which means you will remain in command until early spring."

William nodded again. He hadn't considered that either, but it made sense. Every winter, the Maw opened and spewed forth the Chaosborn, foul creatures born in whatever demon realm existed through the Maw, sending them into the Straits of Terror and onto the closest shores of all three major continents. It happened on an almost regular schedule, and every year, the three closest kingdoms, Sidor, Lynese, and Thay, prepared for the onslaught. This year, things would be different. The largest contingent of forces in the army had come from Rivermark, and it would be short on soldiers. While not as close as the Duchy of Shadowhold, it still bore a large part of the defense. He knew Aldric sent many of his retainers south into Shadowhold to assist in keeping the creatures from breaking out of the nearly uninhabited swamps that extended from the Wyvern's Spine and into the duchy proper.

This year there would be far fewer men to stop the creatures.

"That being said, I expect the campaigning over the winter and even late fall to be minimal. The Lynesians will face a similar problem and I expect that they will have to shift a large number of men south to protect their heartland. Especially since they don't have the geographic protection that we receive from the Narrows or the Dying Lands. Use that downtime. Feel free to take any opportunities fate presents but otherwise keep the army buttoned up until I return. We will resume our offensive in the spring."

"If you don't return until the spring, how should we prepare for next year's offensive?"

"Work with Baron Pembroke to prepare for our campaign. He knows the goals and would be the one to design it, regardless of my presence. With things as they are, I expect you'll probably be over the Lysmir River and on the western side of the continent before the ground freezes, so I'm sure he'll have some notion for a push straight to their capital. Do not wait on me; you have good counsel here. Use your best judgment."

"I won't let you down, Uncle."

"I know you won't," Aldric said, patting him on the shoulder again. "Everyone knows we can rely on the 'Warrior Cub.'"

William rolled his eyes as his uncle laughed at him. After the battle, some of the men had pegged him with his new nickname. He appreciated their confidence in him, or whatever this was, but as names go, he could have hoped for better.

Seeing him blush at the name, Aldric only laughed harder.

Chapter 18

Village of Haxby, Barony of Lindenwood, Sidor

The barn was dank, smelling of dirty men and animals, reminding Tom of another barn he'd hidden in, not that many months ago, with many of these same men, plotting their defiance of the king.

The people and the location were where the similarities ended, however. For one, while many of the faces here had been present at that first meeting, many faces were missing, either captured or dead. The mood was very different from what it had been back then. Gone was the angry fire that drove them to stand up to the king, replaced by a malaise that threatened to end the entire rebellion here and now.

He and his men had run for days, dodging the pursuers who'd killed so many of them. Even when they'd shaken their pursuers, they'd kept running east, until they'd reached the very foothills of the Shatterstone Mountains yesterday, only stopping because one of the men had a distant relative here who'd been able to hide them while they reconsidered their options.

Since then, his men had done little more than feel sorry for themselves. He didn't blame them for it, but they needed to figure something out soon. They couldn't stay in one place for too long. Not with the king's men looking for them.

For now, though, Tom let the men vent their frustrations. They were weary, both physically and emotionally, from days of running and grieving those they'd lost, and they needed to lash out.

"It's over, Tom," Evan, whose relative owned this land, said. "We've lost too many. Half our number are dead or captured and more men slip away every night, returning home to their families."

Murmurs of agreement passed through the group.

"This was a fool's errand from the start," Fulk, a hunter from near the Thunderhorn, said. "We should never have stood against the king's men. What could a band of farmers and woodsmen do against trained soldiers? Godric had more experience than the rest of us, and he died covering our escape. What hope do we have?"

"He's right. It's over," Connal said. "I've a wife and babes at home. They need me there, not dead out in some field."

"We're out of our depth," added another. "The harvest will be in soon, and our families need us if they're going to make it through the winter."

"I'm from near King's Hold," a man named Aelfric said. "It's almost Maw season, and I don't want to leave my family unprotected. Especially not with so many of the baron's men off fighting in Lynese. What use is standing up to the king if everything I love is destroyed behind me?"

Tom let them go on for several more minutes, venting out their fears and anger. Only moving when the volume started to crescendo, raising his hand to call for silence.

"I know how difficult this is," he said, meeting each man's eyes in turn. "We've suffered losses that cut deeply. Losing Godric and the others hurts more than I can say. But we can't let grief and weariness defeat us. The king hopes we'll give up and slip away quietly into the night, back to our villages with our heads hung low. He wants us to feel this is hopeless. But it's not."

Tom paused, letting that sink in. The thing he'd gotten from most of their complaints and worries was how little control they felt they had over their lives. It was common among their class. Tom felt it himself. But breaking from that had been the main impetus that brought them all together. A belief that they could stand against their 'betters' and the unjust rules placed upon them. Their losses were making all of them forget that.

"We're also not alone. I've already sent word by wyvern to our benefactor, explaining our plight and requesting aid. Help will come, though I can't say how soon. We just need to hang on a little longer."

"You keep talking about this benefactor, but you haven't told us who he is," Aelfric said, frustrated. "We're risking our lives here - we deserve to know who we're fighting for."

He could see several of the men nodding in agreement.

"I understand your frustration," Tom said. "There are ... a lot of complications that come from that. They are risking a lot by helping us. More than just their and our lives are at risk."

"How can more be at risk?" someone else demanded.

"The future of the kingdom, your homes, your children's futures. It's all at risk. Sidor sits at a precipice. If the king, and the people advising him, continue the way they are, they're going to bring the entire kingdom down. Every barony will be on their own, fighting among each other, their people dying."

"I thought we were trying to bring down the kingdom."

"No. We need to replace those in charge or force them to stop these insane laws, but Sidor itself can be a good place, as it was under the last king."

Hushed murmuring passed among the men. Most had been angry when they joined up, only wanting to lash out. They were past that phase now and needed to have an actual goal, or at least a realistic goal, if they were going to continue. Something the last message he'd received from their supporter had mentioned.

"I know it's a lot to ask, and if some of you decide this isn't what you signed up for and you want to return home, I'll understand. I'll be sorry to see you go, as we desperately need you, but I won't try to stop you."

A few grumbled and walked out, but most fell silent or talked in small groups. Tom hoped the ones that left were just going out to think, but he expected to lose a few, at least. Rebellions were easy when they were winning. It was after losses that people became disillusioned.

Tom spoke to a few men here or there, but there was not much else he could tell anyone. They didn't have the men or supplies to do anything other than sit and wait. Even if they wanted to hit any of the king's forces, his men weren't in a place to take anyone on.

He slowly made his way through the back of the barn until he made it outside into the cool night air. Away from prying eyes, he allowed his confident facade to slip. They desperately needed a victory to revive morale before more men deserted. He hoped his friend came through because if help didn't arrive soon, they were doomed.

Sidorian Army Camp, Lysmir Woods, Northern Lynese

William planted his hands on the edge of the map table and leaned over it, as if getting closer to the markings would somehow make the situation laid out in front of him clearer. Across from him, Pembroke stood rigid as always, his normal sour expression somehow even less approving than normal.

"... they're stalled as badly as the center," Sir Alistair said, concluding his report on his survey of the left wing of the spread-out Sidorian forces.

"Damn it," Pembroke cursed.

"There are too many small villages where their armies can hole up. We're having to dig them out of each one like rats," Alistair added, eliciting an even deeper frown from Pembroke. "These forests are too thick. Without open ground, our cavalry is almost completely ineffective, putting the enemy on a more equal footing. Until we either break out of it, through this narrow gap between Lake Lysmir and the Dead Man's Hills, we're going to be moving very slowly, fighting for every centimeter of soil. We could cross the river here, north of the lake, and swing down through this more open section here, going straight south for the capital."

"I've said it before. Without the protection of these hills for our supply lines, we'll be open to forces coming out of the mountains to the west. If we could ..." Pembroke started to say, before the tent flap opened and a dusty and harried-looking messenger was ushered through by the guards outside.

"Speak," Pembroke commanded when the man froze, looking from Pembroke to Alistair to William, clearly unsure of who to report to.

The messenger cleared his throat and said, "Message from Commander Haverhill, my lord. During a scouting mission this morning, they found the village opposite them … abandoned."

Alistair's eyes widened, and he exchanged a worried glance with William. Haverhill was currently commanding the center, which was instructed to only move forward slowly, allowing the wings to take the greater risks, protecting the center of the line. Pembroke, on the other hand, remained impassive as always.

"The commander says he's extending his scouts around and beyond the village to be sure, but he wanted further orders before entering the village itself," the messenger continued.

"Very well. Get some food and rest before returning to your command," Pembroke said before waving one of the guards still standing in the open entrance forward. "Send messengers out to Sir Cedrick and Commander Baldwin, ordering them to probe the line ahead of them, and find out if the enemy has pulled back from those areas as well."

The guard bowed and took the messenger by the arm, pulling him along. Pembroke ignored both men, turning his attention back to William and Alistair.

"My Lord," the messenger said, escaping the guard's grip, reaching into a pouch at his side, and extending a sealed envelope. "I also have this. A man from the village came forward to the scout with this sealed message for the 'Sidorian Commander.' "

Pembroke raised an eyebrow. "A message?"

"Yes, My Lord. It has a seal."

Pembroke reached out and took the letter, turning it over in his hands, examining it closely.

"Thank you. You can go," he said after a moment, dismissing the messenger for good before turning to address William. "This has the seal of the House of Montborne."

William looked at the small, folded note in Pembroke's hands, confusion on his face. Why would someone from the Lynesian royal family send a message to them, and how did it end up in the hands of a villager?

William could see that Pembroke was right as soon as he took the letter. One of the topics his tutors loved to cover was the signets and seals of all of the major houses, not only in Sidor, but in Lynese and even to some lesser degree the island nations of Werna and Inos as well. The seal on this letter was unmistakable; it was the crest of the House of Montborne, the royal family of Lynese. Breaking the seal, he quickly read over the contents, his eyes widening in disbelief as he did.

"It's from Princess Isolde, one of the king's daughters," William announced.

"What does it say?" Alistair asked.

"My Lord Commander," William said, reading the note. "I implore you to withdraw your forces immediately from the village of Molinad and send Disciples into the village instead. There are people suffering from the Elder Curse in the village, placed there by my father's command, in hopes of infecting your soldiers. I fear for my own people if an outbreak of the plague happens, that will be all the more likely if your soldiers get sick and infect villagers and other Lynesian citizens in your area of control. I beg you, help me prevent this calamity."

Alistair gasped in horror, his hand flying to his mouth. "The Elder Curse?"

"This is the same princess whose name was used with that fake Disciple supply train, isn't it?" Pembroke scoffed, taking the letter from William's hands and crumpling it up in his fist. "It's another Lynesian trick, hoping we drop our guard and fall to a planned attack. We won't fall for it this time."

That made sense, and it was likely that Pembroke was right, but what if he were wrong? Could they accept that risk? The thought of the Elder Curse spreading through his ranks filled William with dread.

"Shouldn't we at least pull the men back and send in a few scouts to explore, talk to the locals, and make sure that the curse isn't real?" William asked. "It will cost a few days, at best."

"That is exactly what the Lynesians want, William. They want us exposed so they can destroy a part of our army. There hasn't been an outbreak of the Elder Curse in decades. They want us scared, running from the bogeyman."

"But what if it's true?" William pressed. "We should be as concerned for our men as she is for innocent civilians."

"You're too soft, Whitton," Pembroke said dismissively. "This is war. There are no innocents."

William was annoyed at Pembroke treating him like a child, but he let it pass. He was young, after all, and nothing would prove that more than starting to bicker with his subordinates.

"What danger is there, though?" William asked. "Our lines are solid. If they were trying to get us to rush forward then, maybe, I could see how that could turn it into an ambush, but to keep our lines intact? How could that threaten us?"

"War is chaotic. You can't always see the enemy's moves. Sometimes you just have to feel them and understand the enemy is trying to get you to do something, move in some specific way. In those moments, the best thing you can do is do exactly the opposite of what they're trying to get from you."

It made sense, in a way, but maybe that was because he wanted to believe Pembroke.

"But are you sure?"

Pembroke returned William's gaze, his eyes hard as flint. "Positive. The army is yours, William. Aldric put you in command and we will do as you order, but I have not a doubt in my mind that what I am saying is right."

William didn't answer right away. Just looked back at Pembroke, thinking. When Aldric had left him in command, he had made it seem so simple. Listen to Pembroke and Sir Alistair and follow his own intuition. Aldric had never mentioned what to do if those came in direct conflict.

He knew that if he followed Pembroke's advice and the village was indeed infected, the consequences would be disastrous. But if he held his men and it was a trap, he could lose the army. Even if it turned out to be a false alarm, he would be seen as weak and indecisive, losing the faith of the soldiers. Which was the entire reason he'd been left in command in the first place.

"Very well, My Lord," he said finally with a resolute nod. "We will do as you say."

"Good choice," Pembroke said. "I will pass the order for the men in the center to move forward."

As Pembroke left, William turned his attention again to the map, trying to see what Pembroke saw. What if he was right and Pembroke was wrong?

What would happen to his army?

Starhaven, Duchy of Kingsheart, Sidor

Captain Taran Bramwell walked down the hallways of the Royal Palace, toward the king's private study. Strangely, he was not going there today, however. The duke had recently appropriated a new office, a spacious chamber near the king's study, but not exactly adjacent to it. What made it strange was that he was rarely ever called before the duke in his own chambers, since the duke was almost always with the king. Or at least, he used to be.

Lately, according to the guard schedule, the duke had become a much less frequent visitor in the king's private study, which had facilitated his picking an office of his own. Bramwell couldn't help but wonder about the shift, especially coupled with rumors that had been circulating around the palace, but he knew better than to ever put those thoughts into words.

"Enter," the duke's voice called out when he knocked.

Bramwell pushed open the door, stepped inside, and received his second surprise. Although the duke's being less in the king's presence had been something of a topic of gossip around the palace, Bramwell knew that was often because the duke was with Colm, who until very recently would never have been accepted in the king's presence. Which is why Bramwell had expected the brigand to be in the office with the duke, and was surprised when he wasn't. Instead, the duke sat behind his desk, in the office by himself, a sour expression on his face.

"Would you care to explain the increase of incidents of unrest in the city?"

"My lord, there has been widespread unr..."

"No," the duke said, interrupting Bramwell. "There was widespread unrest, until Colm ... sorry, *Sir* Colm, defeated the rebels several weeks ago. Since then, we have had no more large-scale attacks against either the king's men or those of his vassals. And yet, the number of incidents inside the city, the Capital and heart of the kingdom, I might add, have increased."

"Yes, Your Excellency, incidents of direct attacks have decreased, but I believe smaller incidents of disobedience have increased. If the latest reports to the king are to be believed."

Edmund's lips pulled into a tight line, his nostrils flaring. Bramwell knew he was on dangerous ground. Beyond not being in the king's office as regularly, the duke had also been "away" during several audiences in front of the king, and those he'd been at had involved more than one incident of the king putting the blame for bad reports on the baron. Bramwell was almost certain the duke was looking for someone to take some of that blame, and the last thing the captain wanted was to be the one the duke decided to pin it on.

"Not like they have here, Captain. If you want to talk about reports, I have some here in front of me," Edmund said, picking up a piece of parchment from his desk. "In just the past ten days, there have been multiple confrontations with your guards, some of which turned violent. I see several injuries to your men and even one death. I also see an injured tax collector and one warehouse burned to the ground by a small mob. Sounds a lot like direct attacks on the king's men to me. Would you like to try again? How do you explain yourself, allowing the rebels to infiltrate our own capital?"

"My Lord Duke, I don't believe these incidents are connected to the rebels. Our reports indicate that the last of their forces were spotted near the Shatterstone Mountains, on the other side of the duchy."

"And yet, here we are, with guards and officials getting attacked. Seems like rebellious activity to me."

Bramwell hesitated. There was an obvious answer to the duke's statement, but it was one he knew the duke wouldn't want to hear, let alone believe. It was also the only thing he could say in response.

"I'm not sure … I believe these incidents are isolated, Your Excellency. Each one seems to involve a commoner becoming angry over some perceived slight, usually the travel edicts, but also taxes and the recent requirement to quarter soldiers in their homes. As you know, these edicts and laws are unpopular, and as the king brings more and more men into the capital to quell the insurrection, requiring more to be quartered in homes here in the city, the tensions are rising."

"Isolated incidents, you say?" Edmund scoffed. "I see a pattern here, Captain. A pattern of disobedience and disrespect for the Crown. And a pattern of failure on your end. It seems to me that you are failing in your duty to maintain order in the city."

Bramwell choked down his anger. It was amazingly unfair, and not something he could respond to in any way. The duke was angry, lashing out, and had all of the power here. Anything he would say in his defense would be seen as a challenge by the duke, one that he would likely respond to.

"My Lord Duke, if you are unhappy with my performance, I will, of course, step down. I have handled each situation exactly as I've been instructed to, aggressively and instantly. We have arrested anyone in violation of the king's laws, several of whom have already been executed. But with each arrest, unrest increases. I believe that our hardline stance is only exacerbating the problem, not solving it."

His response was borderline, at best. Yes, he hadn't disagreed with the duke directly, but it could also be taken as a challenge to the duke's standing orders.

Edmund darkened as he said, "So, you would suggest we take a softer approach? Allow these rebels to run rampant in our own capital? Is that it, Captain?"

"Not at all, My Lord. I am only suggesting that, perhaps, we should consider trying a different strategy, one that addresses the root causes of the unrest, rather than simply …"

Bramwell was cut off as Edmund shot out of his seat, slamming both fists on his desk.

His nostrils flaring and face turning deep red, a cord of veins standing out on his neck, Edmund shouted, "The only strategy I'm interested in is reminding these peasants who their king is! They will learn obedience and respect, or they will face the headsman's axe. I'll not have rabble stirring dissent in my kingdom!"

Bramwell forced his face into a non-expression, "I understand, Your Excellency."

"You better. You are to hire as many men into the guard as you need to, and I want you to increase the patrols. I want no incidents of dissent or resistance to stand. By order of the Crown, anyone involved in violating the king's laws, no matter how small, will be subject to execution. Their property and homes will be confiscated by the Crown as repayment for their treason. Any families that resist or inhibit the seizure of this property will also be found in violation and added to the list of executions."

Bramwell clamped his jaws shut for a moment, forcing the words in his throat back. This was going to come back on them ten-fold and create a mass uprising. There was no way this ended without it being an unmitigated disaster. And he knew without a doubt, that the duke would find a way to turn it around on him and make it somehow his fault.

He also couldn't say any of that.

"As you order, Your Excellency," he finally managed to vocalize. What else could he say?

Chapter 19

Aldric stepped off the ship's gangplank onto the bustling docks of Starhaven, taking a moment to appreciate the soaring spires of the palace and Grand Hall high above him, on the city's third level, towering above the rest of the city below. Though he had seen the sight countless times, its beauty and grandeur never failed to impress.

He was just about to start toward the market road that led up from the docks to the city center and the palace, when a messenger in the king's livery came running down the street, straight toward him.

"Your Excellency, I've been sent by the duke to escort you directly to the palace. He insists on speaking with you most urgently."

Aldric frowned. He hadn't sent word ahead that he was coming. Of course, Edmund had enough people in the city that he would know that the Pride was sailing back to the capital, but he didn't know why Aldric had come. Perhaps he could guess, based on the timing, but Edmund wouldn't welcome confrontations against his orders, even from Aldric. He wouldn't have wanted to hasten the confrontation, which meant this was about something else, and after a long voyage, the last thing Aldric wanted was to deal with being thrust into more of his brother's machinations.

"Has the Duchess Alyssa arrived in the city?" Aldric asked instead.

The messenger hesitated for a moment before stammering, "I ... I believe so, My Lord, but the duke was quite adamant ..."

"I'm sure he was," Aldric said, interrupting the man. "Show me to the quarters she's been assigned, after which, you can run off and tell my brother that I will be with him as soon as I've had some rest."

The messenger took an anxious half-step up the road toward the palace, and then back to Aldric, and then back again, clearly trying to work out how to obey two dukes giving conflicting orders, before bowing slightly and starting up the street toward the palace.

As they made their way into the heart of the city, Aldric could feel a change in the air. The usual vibrant energy of Starhaven seemed muted, the laughter and raucous nature of the lower city was palpably absent. People went about their business, heads down, avoiding looking at anyone.

There were also many more guards than Aldric ever remembered seeing in the city before. Aldric watched as people gave the guards a wide berth, refusing to look up at any of them. This wasn't the city Aldric remembered, but there was nothing he could do about it. Not yet.

Arriving at the palace, he was led to the ambassador's wing, where dignitaries and visiting nobles were housed. Aldric felt it an odd choice, since normally he and his family would be given rooms near the king's quarters. The rooms here might be luxurious, but he couldn't help but see the message his brother was sending by putting his wife here instead.

He gave a nod to the messenger, who looked anxious and worried as he turned to rush toward the royal wing of the palace. Sparing the man one last glance, Aldric opened the door, walked in, and then stopped as his eyes fell on his wife, who was standing by the window, looking radiant in the sunlight that spilled into the room, staring out toward the palace gardens.

She turned as the door opened, and sucked in a breath, freezing for a moment. And then she was across the room, throwing her arms around him and hugging him tight, standing up on her tiptoes.

"My Darling," she said in his ear.

"You got my wyvern."

"I did, and I came as soon as I got your message. I've missed you so much. You've been gone far too long."

He held her back at arm's length to look her over, "I know, and I'm so sorry about that. I'm also sorry I won't be able to spend the time with you I wish, there's still so much to be done.

Alyssa reached up and gently caressed his cheek, and, looking into his eyes said, "You look tired, My Love."

"I am. I saw the city as I made my way here from the docks. How have things gotten so bad?"

"It's the new laws that Serwyn has been passing. They've thrown the entire kingdom into chaos."

"Yes, I've heard about the new decrees. They sound more like Edmund than Serwyn. This smells like him."

"I know. He always complained about the barons, saying they have too much power. What's worse, is it's working. The baronies are in chaos. They even hired new bailiffs, who work directly for the crown, and sent them to those holdings that have delayed enforcing the new edicts, and the people are blaming their barons for these ... thugs. I tried to get in to see Serwyn, but Edmund told me he was too busy to see me. I didn't press him, wanting to talk to you first."

"Probably for the best."

"How bad have things been back home?"

"Bad. The people are angry. I know they still trust and love you, but there have been incidents. People dragged from their homes at night, the barons forced to hold them in jail under the king's warrant. It's worse in Kingsheart, where some of the people have turned to open revolt, and there have been several very bloody clashes. Executions are at an all-time high, and the jails are overflowing. The barons won't put up with this too much longer. Some will cow but others, I don't know what they'll do. I'm very worried, Aldric. If this keeps up, we could have civil war on our hands."

"Edmund won't believe it until the day it happens. He's almost certainly convinced himself that the barons will bow down and allow the crown to reassert its dominance."

"But why? I know he has a hold on Serwyn, for now, but he can't think that will last forever, and his duchy is the one hurting the worst. What could he hope to accomplish for himself?"

"I don't know, and that's what worries me. He never goes into something like this without a plan, and you and I both know he doesn't particularly care if Serwyn remains on the throne or not. He always thought he'd be a better king that Gavric, and I doubt he's changed his mind now."

"You don't think he's planning on ..."

"I don't know," Aldric said, interrupting her.

They were in private rooms, but the palace walls had ears, and it was best not to discuss things like that too openly. Already, they were walking a fine line.

"He has a plan," Aldric continued. "Of that, I have no doubt. As to what it is, only he knows."

"And what do we do? What do our people do?"

"For now, the best we can. I have some plans, but ... they will take time."

Alyssa gave him a look. He knew she wanted to ask him for specifics, but she'd spent enough time in court to understand why she couldn't.

"Good, that's what I wanted to hear," she said instead, before changing the subject. "And how is our other nephew faring?"

"He's doing wonderfully, actually. You would be so proud of how he has grown and come into his own these past months. I've seen him show real leadership. He's got a lot of Gavric in him."

"Probably a lot of you, too," Alyssa commented.

Aldric waved her comment away and said, "At first, I was hesitant to place too much responsibility on his young shoulders, but he has proven himself ready for more. He's quick-minded and steadfast. I honestly believe William may possess the potential for great things, if given the opportunity. He has the makings of a fine strategist and commander."

"I always knew he had potential, regardless of how Edmund treated him. He just needed a chance to show what he could do. Edmund sending him away from the palace, and his meddling, was the biggest favor he could have done for the boy. Of course, had he known that, he would have kept him at home, under his thumb."

"No doubt. I'm glad he sent young William away. This is the most time I've spent with him since his mother married Edmund, and it makes me realize the mistake I made by waiting so long. Even Pembroke says William has potential."

"That's rare praise indeed, coming from Rowan. I didn't think that curmudgeon liked anyone."

"He's not that bad."

"He is, and you know it."

"Anyway, Edmund sent someone down at the docks to fetch me, all in a bother, so I suppose I should go see him before he sends guards next."

"Not before I get some real food in you. You've been living off of camp food, then fish and hard-bread on the ship. If you have to go do battle with your brother, I'll see you fattened up first."

"You're too good to me," he said, putting his arms around his wife and pulling her close to him.

"And don't you forget it," she said, smiling.

Aldric eventually pulled himself away from his wife's warm embrace to see what his brother wanted. Never one for the capital, he found the place even colder and less inviting than it had been when Gavric was here. Everyone he passed looked either strained or worried. Gone was any sense of joy in the people running the kingdom.

After getting directions, Aldric made his way to the office his brother had set himself up in, not failing to notice how close it was to the king's quarters. Edmund certainly was keeping everything in very close reach. Turning a corner, he was surprised to find he recognized one of the guards standing outside his brother's door. Having not spent much time in the capital, Aldric wasn't familiar with most of the guards. He knew Edmund would switch some out, as all kings, or semi-regents, as Edmund had set himself up to be, tended to do, but he hadn't expected to see Bramwell.

One of his brother's functionaries, the last he had heard, the man was still in charge of the duchy guard, stationed in Edmund's capital city. Now, if Aldric was not mistaken, he wore the insignia of the royal palace guard. Clearly, Edmund had gone well past tradition in asserting his dominance and control over the royal household.

Aldric gave the man a nod and reached for the door, the captain managed to knock quickly, a beat before Aldric let himself into the study. It was a petty move, to be sure, barging into Edmund's study, more like the things Edmund himself was always doing, but Aldric wanted to remind Edmund he wasn't some lackey to be ordered around.

His brother's voice called out just as Aldric opened the door and stepped inside.

His brother, sitting behind a large desk with quill in hand, surrounded by stacks of parchment, looked up as the door opened.

"It's about time you got here. Your ship docked two hours ago. Did my man not find you?"

"He did, but I've been on that ship for a month, Edmund. I wanted to see Alyssa first," Aldric said, stopping in front of Edmund's desk, noting the absence of a place for a guest to sit, and folding his arms. "Now, what did you want?"

"I want to know what you're doing here instead of off winning the war like you're supposed to be doing," Edmund said, setting down his quill. "Who's in charge of the army if you're here?"

"I left William in charge, with Pembroke and Alistair as his advisors,"

"What?" Edmund said loudly, suddenly sitting up straight. "Have you lost your mind? He's a child? You're going to cost us the entire war, leaving that idiot boy in charge."

"He's not an idiot, and we agreed I was the best fit for commanding the armies, remember? Unless you've picked up a lot of experience in the last six months, I'm going to assume that remains true and appoint whoever I damn well please to command. As to winning the war, that's precisely why I'm here, because without proper supply, it's an impossible task. Since you ignored my wyverns, I came to ask you directly about the dramatic drop in supplies being sent to arm and feed my men."

"You don't understand what the situation is like here at home, Aldric. Things are too difficult at the moment for us to send more.

You aren't the only one in need of supplies, and unlike others, you have the option of taking the supplies you need from the enemy. Perhaps if you were more concerned with attacking the enemy, you'd have managed to capture enough supplies to feed and arm your men."

"And why are things so dire here? What's going on that you can't spare supplies for the war effort?"

"It's the barons, Aldric. They're stirring up trouble, seeing Gavric's death as an opportunity to gain more power for themselves. Serwyn had to put edicts in place to limit the movement of their paid agitators."

Aldric rolled his eyes and said, "Don't treat me like an idiot, Edmund. We both know Serwyn neither thought up nor crafted those edicts. I can recognize your hand in them from a mile away."

"Of course I helped, as is my right and duty in guiding Serwyn to his destiny as king. But give the boy some credit, Aldric. He was smart enough to see the need for change on his own, once the barons started causing unrest."

"Unrest that conveniently aligns with your agenda. Come on, Edmund. What's your play here? You're not just trying to consolidate power for Serwyn's sake."

"My play, Dear Brother, is to ensure the stability of this kingdom. Something you're supposed to be doing by bringing the war in Lynese to a quick end, remember?"

"Which barons, precisely, are causing unrest? The first word I heard of problems was commoners reacting to the edicts. What happened before that to warrant their creation? Which barons were stirring up trouble?"

"Now who's playing the fool, Aldric? You know precisely which barons I'm referring to, considering most of them reside within your own duchy."

"You have to be joking."

"Am I?" Edmund said, standing. "We all know that your vassals have always had more loyalty to you than the kingdom, something you've never had trouble exploiting before. Unless you wish to become suspect in aiding these traitorous nobles, I suggest you spend less time questioning the measures taken to protect the kingdom and more time focusing on the task at hand."

"My barons have always been loyal, Edmund. They've supported the crown without question, even in the face of your ludicrous demands. Besides, from what I've heard, most of the open revolt has been in Kingsheart, not River Mark."

"I think you might have missed that the baronies on the Thunderhorn were the first to have large-scale problems. Curious, isn't it, how that happened just across the river from your own duchy? I also find curious the number of wyverns flying back and forth between your barons and the army. One might think there was more to it than mere coincidence."

"What are you implying, Edmund?"

"I would never question your allegiances, Dear Brother. But your capability? That's another matter entirely. If you can't keep your own duchy in order, well ..."

"You'd do well to choose your next words carefully," Aldric warned.

Edmund spread his hands in a placating gesture. "I only relay the words of the crown. You know, it would break Serwyn's heart to have to attaint his own uncle. But if you can't keep your house in order, it might be the only choice."

"If you're worried about unrest now, imagine how much worse it would be if you ever tried such a thing. The people of River Mark are loyal to me, Edmund. They would not take kindly to any move against their duke."

"Then I suggest you fix your barons and get them back under control," Edmund retorted, sitting back down. "Now, as to your request, the kingdom has no additional supplies to send the army. But if you feel that strongly about it, you're welcome to fund it from your own coffers."

"If that's what I have to do."

"Since you've arrived so late in the season, I assume you plan on taking charge of the forces in Shadowhold over Maw season?"

"Yes," Aldric bit out.

"Good," Edmund said with a dismissive wave of his hand. "At least you'll have managed to do one thing for the benefit of the kingdom. That will be all, then."

Aldric stared at him for another moment, but Edmund had made a point of picking up his quill and going back to his writing. Aldric turned on his heel and strode from the room, his blood boiling.

Sidorian Army Camp, Lysmir Woods, Northern Lynese

"... grows dire. More soldiers are being quarantined by the Disciples, showing early signs of the Elder Curse."

The messenger seemed nervous, standing in front of Pembroke and William, whose expression for once matched the sour countenance of the much older baron.

"How thin is our line?" William asked, trying not to let his annoyance fall too hard on the messenger.

"The center is stretched dangerously thin, my lord. Sir Alistair has already ordered a pullback to our previous positions, but there are significant gaps in our patrols due to the lack of men. The time between our patrols grows longer each day."

Pembroke cursed under his breath before saying, "Lynese will exploit this weakness given the chance. We cannot afford to lose any more ground."

William nodded but didn't respond to him directly. "What are the Disciples saying?"

"That this is the largest outbreak any of them has heard of, let alone seen. A senior Disciple has requested to quarantine the entire section of the line that went near the village."

The messenger's voice fell off as he got near the end of the sentence, Pembroke glaring at him for even suggesting such a thing.

"Absolutely not. We cannot afford to weaken our line any further. Those men are needed to hold the center."

"No, what we cannot afford is to allow more of our men to fall to this. We can always reclaim lost territory, but only if we still have the men to do it."

"William," Pembroke said, dropping into his lecturer voice that, at times William found helpful, but now sounded only patronizing. "You need to remember that ..."

"No, you need to remember who was left in charge," William said, a little more harshly than he intended. "While I appreciate your counsel, now and forever, the decision is mine to make."

Pembroke's jaw clenched, but he remained silent.

William turned back to the messenger and said, "Return to the front line and inform Sir Alistair that he is to pull back to our previous positions immediately. Any soldiers showing signs of illness are to be withdrawn from duty and sent to the Disciples for treatment without delay."

The messenger nodded, relief evident on his face. "Yes, My Lord. And what of reinforcements?"

"No units or reinforcements are to join the center line until further notice. Anyone that entered the village and any soldiers quartered near or working closely with those men is to be pulled back entirely and sent to the Disciples for evaluation and treatment. We cannot risk further spread of the Curse."

"Understood, My Lord," the messenger said, bowing and, after casting one last worried glance at Pembroke, rushing away.

"You don't understand what you're doing," Pembroke said as the messenger walked away. "By pulling back our forces, you're going to kill our momentum. The enemy will bring in reinforcements and stabilize their line after the losses they suffered on the retreat from the Chisholm."

William turned on Pembroke, meeting his glare head on, and not flinching. "That's almost certainly why these Curse victims were put there. We fell directly into their trap in spite of the warning we were given."

"You know that warning could have as easily been a trick as not."

"And yet, clearly, it wasn't, and the fact remains that our men are falling ill. Now that we know it isn't a trick, we can't again pretend like this threat isn't real."

"No more that we can pretend that the cost of hesitation in war isn't real."

"I seem to remember one of the first lectures I received from you after arriving, was to be wary of rushing in headlong. There was something about using my brain and thinking before I acted. That command was about the decisions we made before any actions were taken. Clearly, I have done a poor job of listening to your advice. Next time, I will be more cognizant of my actions instead of barreling recklessly into a situation, as you advised. I apologize for my error."

Pembroke's eyes flashed and his nostrils flared, but William didn't back down. This time he was right, and Pembroke had been wrong. If the man was too stubborn or prideful to admit it, then he needed to fix his attitude, and fast.

The baron seemed on the verge of a retort when he glanced around and noticed all of the soldiers and laborers nearby, watching their exchange. Some tried to appear busy with tasks, but their furtive glances betrayed them. William didn't blame them. If he'd had two of his superiors fighting next to him, he would have listened to.

The baron looked back at William. He was no less furious, but a flicker of understanding passed between them. In spite of their disagreement, they needed to maintain a united front and, even if Pembroke hadn't been so much older and experienced, William wasn't about to cut the legs of someone he needed to work with out from under him. Especially not in front of witnesses. It was one of the things he'd noticed in his uncle's dealings and admired about him.

If Pembroke wanted to continue this conversation in a more frank way, they could do it later, in private. Pembroke seemed to understand all of that and gave a barely perceptible nod.

"It was a clever trap," he ground out, his tone a bit too loud to be entirely natural. "One that any commander could have fallen for, given the circumstances."

"Thank you for saying so."

"If you'll excuse me, My Lord, I have matters to attend to," Pembroke said, casting a last, hard look at William before turning on his heel.

Chapter 20

Village of Quenby, Barony of Ambleton, Duchy of Kingsheart, Sidor

The late afternoon lull that had settled over the village of Quenby, as the workday neared its end and the day's end meals started to be prepared, was broken by the sound of hoofbeats and a large cloud of dust coming down the single road that led into the village.

Ambleton, generally not near anything exciting, had for a long time been a quiet barony, and Quenby was a quiet village in that quiet barony, which meant that large groups of visitors were more an occurrence of interest than one of fear. Not a particularly rich place, but well patrolled by the Baron's men, banditry was exceedingly rare, so the people here didn't often worry about much.

Of course, that had been changing. They'd felt the pinch of the Edicts of Travel and had heard of the unrest in other villages, so the men started to make their way in from the fields at the sight of the dust plume. The riders, when they arrived, would not normally have been a cause for alarm. Bailiffs, determined by their armor and insignia, wearing the symbol of the Baron of Ambleton, a large tree on a hill, would have been a welcome sight in other times.

Now, it put everyone on edge.

As the bailiffs rode into the center of the village, the villagers gathered around uneasily, talking to each other in hushed tones as the armed men dismounted. Their leader, a grizzled man with a bushy beard, stepped forward.

"By order of Baron Falkirk, we are here to collect taxes and penalties. Bring out your grain, your livestock, and any other provisions."

The people of the village exchanged uneasy glances. This was the third such visit this year, and it was still only summer. In previous years, the baron's men would only come for taxes once, but each visit this year the taxes were higher than they were for the single annual visit in previous years.

Padarn, one of the older farmers, who'd lived here the longest, stepped forward when none of his neighbors dared to, and said, "But sir, we are down to our last cow and three hogs, the rest being taken by the baron two months ago. We've barely enough to feed ourselves."

"The kingdom is at war and every citizen must do their duty. Now step aside, old man," the bailiff said.

Padarn reluctantly moved aside, his head bowed in resignation. The other villagers followed suit, allowing the bailiffs to enter their homes and barns. They watched helplessly as the armed men took what meager provisions remained, leaving them with even less than before.

As the bailiffs loaded their ill-gotten gains onto their horses, a young man named Ethan couldn't contain his frustration any longer.

Stepping forward, he said, "This isn't right! We've given all we can, and now you're taking what little we have left!"

"Ethan," the young man's mother hissed at him, pulling at his shirt sleeve.

"Watch your tongue, boy. The baron's word is law," the bearded man said, turning on the boy.

Ethan pulled his sleeve free from his mother, clenched his fist and yelled, "How can his law starve us to death? You're nothing but brigands!"

The bailiff's face twisted with rage. Reeling back, he backhanded the boy, sending him crashing to the ground.

"Another word, and taxes won't be the only thing we take from here!"

Suddenly, an arrow plunged into the man's chest, seemingly out of nowhere, surprising everyone, but no one more than the bailiff himself, who looked astonished, his hands going up to the shaft protruding from his leather jerkin. He stumbled back a few steps, mouth working uselessly, before his knees buckled and he crashed to the ground.

For a moment, no one, not the villagers nor the other bailiffs, moved, everyone just staring at the dead man in shock. From the edges of the village, a group of men emerged, armed with an assortment of swords, axes, and bows. They wore no armor, but their weapons looked dangerous nonetheless, sharp and gleaming as they charged. Then chaos erupted. Shouts of alarm were shouted from the other bailiffs as they drew their swords.

"Raiders," the bailiffs screamed, but none of the villagers reacted the same way.

These didn't look like raiders. In fact, they were dressed much like the people who lived there. News didn't travel to Quenby much, but even here, many of the villagers already suspected who these men were.

Not that these men responded. They simply yelled and charged in, sending the villagers scattering for hiding places, not wanting to be caught in the middle. There was a clash of steel and screams as arrows and blades found their targets.

Ethan, the young man who had been struck, scrambled to his feet. For a moment, he almost rushed off to join the others in hiding, until he saw the blade dropped by the dead bailiff. Reaching down and snatching it up, he leaped into the fray, swinging the blade with more enthusiasm than skill.

The fight was brutal and quick, the rebels pressing their advantage against the surprised and outnumbered bailiffs. A burly rebel wielding a massive two-handed axe swept his weapon in a wide arc, cleaving through the shaft of a bailiff's spear before burying the blade in the man's shoulder. The bailiff went down with a shriek, his arm hanging useless at his side.

Ethan found himself face to face with one of the bailiffs who, seeing his fallen leader's sword in Ethan's hand, charged. Ethan barely managed to get his blade up in time, the shock of the impact sending numbness shooting up his arm.

The bailiff pressed his attack, raining down blows that Ethan struggled to parry, giving ground continually. Just as it seemed the bailiff would overcome him, a sword exploded from his attacker's chest. Behind him stood the man who had been at the head of the men who'd attacked the bailiffs, coming in from the woods. A tall man with wavy brown hair and what would have been a kind face if it wasn't for the streak of blood that had spurted from the bailiff as the man impaled him.

The bailiff gurgled, his sword falling from nerveless fingers, and collapsed, sliding off the man's sword. Ethan stood over the fallen man, his chest heaving as he wrestled with what had just happened. Around him, the battle was winding down as the last of the bailiffs were cut down.

None were given the chance to surrender.

"Are you alright?" the man asked.

"I ... uhh ... I ..." Ethan stammered.

"It's okay," the man said, clapping him on the shoulder. "You fought well. I'm Tom."

"Ethan," Ethan got out after a moment.

"Thank you," Padarn said, coming over and saving Ethan from any more embarrassment.

Fletcher smiled at Ethan before reaching out and shaking Padarn's hand. "We're happy to help. These men have been devastating villages like yours across half the duchy. We just came from another settlement that they'd stripped bare yesterday and followed them to you. We weren't going to let them strip anyone else."

Padarn nodded, and then looked to the bodies of the fallen bailiffs. "But what about repercussions? When the baron finds out ..."

"My men will take care of the bodies, leave them somewhere on the road and make it look as if we ambushed them before they reached your village. If anyone comes asking, just feign ignorance of what happened and say they never made it here. Make sure all of your people are on the same page, though. If they handle this like other fights, they'll already have made up their minds that we were involved and attacked them where they fell, and they won't ask you too many questions."

"I will. Again, we owe you a great debt. Without your intervention, I fear we would have been left with nothing to sustain ourselves."

"No need," Tom said, turning to his men who were already starting to gather up weapons and valuables from the fallen bailiffs. "Give everything to the villagers. Keep the armor and weapons, but the food, the money, everything else goes to the village."

Padarn looked at Fletcher with shock.

"You're going to want to hide these things, use them for your village, but don't let any other bailiffs know about them. If they try and take taxes again, and we aren't here, it will go a long way to buying replacement goods for the winter."

"We will. Forgive me; I should go speak with the others," Padarn said, seeing the growing crowd watching the rebels stripping the bailiffs' bodies. "But truly, thank you. For everything."

Fletcher gave the farmer a nod, watching as he walked to join the growing crowd.

"Who are you people?" Ethan asked as Padarn left.

"We're just normal folk, like you. Farmers, craftsmen, people who are tired of seeing our livelihoods stripped away by the king and his nobles' tyranny."

"You're the rebels? The ones the king said were killed in Lindenwood?"

"I guess you can call us rebels, although I'd prefer to think of us as people who love Sidor and are fighting for what's just and fair. As for Lindenwood, that was a tragedy, no doubt. But no, we weren't all killed. Some of our friends, the best of us, sacrificed themselves to ensure our escape. That doesn't fit well with what the king wants people to know, so he says we were all killed. We're here to prove that wrong."

As Ethan thought about that, a lanky man with a bow slung over his shoulder joined them. He had a weathered face that looked tanned from long hours spent outdoors.

"Good job," Fletcher said, slapping the man on the back.

"I'm just happy we're back to it, taking the fight to those bastards."

"I told you we wouldn't stand aside for long. We just had to be patient."

"Yeah, I'm sorry for doubting you. Your friend certainly came through, and not just the money. The weapons and supplies ... they made a world of difference for the boys. Just knowing we have support."

"I know, Fulk. I wish it was more, but he has to be careful how much he sends, lest the king find out."

"I still wish you'd tell us who he is. It doesn't seem right, owing a man we'll never know."

"I know, and if I could tell any of you I would. It's how it has to be. We still have a long way to go. Small victories like this are good, and help the people, but they're not going to put an end to these insane laws and oppression until we get strong enough to take the fight to the king himself. All the way to Starhaven."

The man named Fulk's eyes widened at the mention of the capital.

"Wait, what? I thought we were just trying to help the people here, protect them from the bailiffs and the baron's men. You're talking about marching on the capital."

"That's how it started, but ... that can't be where it ends. These small victories, they're important. They show the people that there's hope, that they're not alone. But if we want to truly succeed, to bring about real change, that will never happen until we show the king and everyone else that this is serious. That they can either change the rules for the people, or the people will change who their ruler is."

"That ..."

"Rebellion," Fletcher said. "That's what this is, even out here, so far from the capital. We're in rebellion. We've killed the king's soldiers. Our necks are no less on the line here or at the capital. There, at least, we can effect real change."

"But the capital ... that's a whole different scale. The king's army, the royal guard, they'll outnumber us ten to one."

"I know it seems daunting, but it's not impossible. It's almost winter, and with so many men in Lynese, the barons and dukes will have to scrape their holdings dry to get enough men to send to Shadowhold. That'll give us a window of opportunity. In the meantime, we focus on building our strength, gathering supplies, and rallying more people to our cause."

"I want to come with you," Ethan blurted out, not able to hold his voice any longer."

"Do you?" Fletcher said, raising an eyebrow. "I know you're brave, but this isn't a decision to be made lightly. The path we're on, it's dangerous. There's no guarantee of safety, or even success. You'd be standing up to the king and all his nobles."

"I don't care," Ethan said, shaking his head. "I can't just stand by while they bleed us dry. I want to fight, to make a difference, just like you."

"Ethan, no!" a woman who was standing not far away said, pushing past the few people between them. "You can't go with them. It's too dangerous."

"Mother, I have to do this," Ethan said, turning to face her. "You saw what happened today. If it wasn't for these men, we'd have nothing left. I can't just sit here and wait for the next time the bailiffs come."

"But you could be killed," his mother said, tears welling in her eyes.

"I could have been killed here, today, if they hadn't come to help us. I could be killed the next time the baron's men come to take everything from us. They don't care about us. They think we're dirt."

Ethan looked to Fletcher, who held up his hands defensively. "I can't make this decision for you, Ethan. We'll be here for a few more hours. Take some time; talk it over with your family. If you still feel the same way when it's time for us to leave, we'll welcome you. But make sure it's what you truly want."

"I will. Thank you," Ethan said, grabbing his mother by the arm and pulling her away.

He was going to convince her that this was the right thing to do. He had to.

Sidorian Army Camp, Lysmir Woods, Northern Lynese

William stomped his way through the camp, trying very hard not to snap at any of the soldiers who stopped to salute or speak with him on the way. He respected his men and wasn't one to take his anger out on them unfairly.

It was a close thing, however.

Another unproductive conversation with Baron Pembroke had left him feeling drained and disheartened. They'd managed to halt the spread of the Elder Curse by large-scale quarantining of entire units, but it had ground the army's progress to a dead halt, and the enemy had begun to build up enough men to make breaking out of this forest and into the plains of Lynese much more challenging, giving up everything they'd earned with their breakthrough, months earlier, across the Chansol River.

Pembroke continued to be furious with William, blaming him for the army stalling. Worse, William wasn't sure he was wrong, at least about it being his fault. William was certain that he'd made the right call, since a stalled army was preferable to a dead one, which is what it would be if the curse had continued to spread. But his Uncle Gavric had always said that the blame for an army's failures always stopped with its commander, and not his men. William was left in command of an army on the advance, which meant it was his fault now that it sat still.

If his Uncle Aldric was here, William would have gone to him seeking advice, but Aldric not being there was the source of the problem in the first place. The other men left for William to turn to, Pembroke and Alistair, both blamed William for their current situation, which left William only one person to turn to.

William approached Eskild's tent, situated slightly apart from the others. The Sidorian soldiers had made it clear that they were uncomfortable sharing quarters with someone from Thay, a sentiment that William found both disappointing and short-sighted. Eskild's loyalty and dedication to their cause should have been enough to earn him a place among them, but old prejudices died hard.

Stopping outside the sergeant's tent, William called out, "Eskild, do you have a moment?"

"Come on," the sergeant said from inside.

William ducked under the flap of Eskild's tent, finding the man stretched out on his bedroll, reading a tattered little book.

"What can I do for you, My Lord?"

William suppressed a smile. Eskild provided none of the pleasantries or formalities that he would get from a Sidorian, be it someone as high as Baron Pembroke or a common soldier. It's what he liked about Eskild. He treated everyone exactly as he found them, without accounting for their station.

"I need your advice, Eskild," William said, settling onto a stool across from the sergeant. "It's about Baron Pembroke. He's furious, ever since I made the call to quarantine the units affected by the Elder Curse. I know it was the right decision, but he's been increasingly hostile and stubborn, even though time has proven me right. I listened to him, in spite of the warning we had, and it cost us dearly. I would have thought he would have taken that failure personally, but he seems to consider it little more than an inconvenience."

"Some men don't like being wrong."

"I know, and if it was just that, I could deal with it," William said, thinking of several instances with his adoptive father, who was very much that type of man. "It isn't, though. When we meet, he can't help but make petty comments, usually about my youth and inexperience, and suggesting that I'm not being aggressive enough with the army. It's like he thinks I should just ignore the curse and keep pushing forward, no matter the cost."

"And what do you think you should do about that?" Eskild asked, doing the same thing his uncle did, instead of just answering his question directly.

"I don't know. I'm at my wit's end. Part of me just wants to send him home, get him out of my hair."

"That would be a mistake. Baron Pembroke is like every powerful man I've ever met, easily offended and sure of his own infallibility. It's a common trait among those who are used to having their way."

"I've noticed."

"I'm not saying that he is somehow a bad man or leader. He's an excellent field commander and, at least in your uncle's estimation, a good leader of his people. It's just that men like this, they take a certain finessing. I had similar issues with your Uncle Aldric when I first entered his service. He was stubborn, set in his ways, and not particularly fond of an outsider questioning his decisions."

"How did you change that?"

"Patience, mostly. That, and a willingness to prove my worth through my actions rather than my words. Your uncle came to trust my judgment, but it took time."

William sighed. "I don't know if I have that kind of time with Pembroke."

"Perhaps not, but sending him home would only make things worse. Pembroke's retainers are loyal to him. If he leaves, they'll either follow him or become disgruntled. Either way, it weakens your position and creates unnecessary tension."

"Which we can't afford. We're already short on men everywhere."

"I know. And even if you could spare them, it would only strain your future relations with the baron. He's a proud man and being dismissed would be a blow to his ego that he wouldn't soon forget."

"So what do I do?" William asked, frustrated. "I can't just let him undermine my authority."

"As I said, Pembroke isn't a bad man. He's just used to being in charge. You need to find a way to convince him of your value, to show him that you're not just some green boy playing at being a commander."

"And how do I do that?" William asked, spreading his hands. "I've tried reasoning with him, but he dismisses my arguments out of hand."

"You stand up to him. You show him that you're right."

"But I've tried that. It only seems to make him angrier."

"Of course it does. Like I said, he's not used to being challenged. Men like him expect everyone to fall in line, to agree with their every whim. When someone stands up to them, it rattles them. It makes them uncomfortable."

"So you're saying I should just keep arguing with him? Even if it makes things worse?"

Eskild shook his head. "Not arguing. Asserting. There's a difference. You're not trying to prove him wrong, that will only make him defensive. You've got to simply state what is. You're not looking for his approval or agreement. You're telling him how it is."

William considered this. It made sense, in a way. He'd been trying to convince Pembroke, to get him to see reason. He hadn't considered just telling the baron to shut up and follow orders. Mostly because it seemed insane.

"And you think that will work? That he'll just accept it?"

Eskild chuckled. "Oh, he'll get angry. He'll probably throw a fit. But deep down, he'll respect you for it. More than he would if you seemed hesitant or scared. He respects strength, even if he doesn't like it. It's the second part that's more important, though. And harder."

William thought back to his decision to hold the army back, to listen to the warning from the Disciples. Pembroke had been furious, but he hadn't actually done anything about it. He'd grumbled and complained, but he hadn't openly defied William's orders.

"The second part?"

"Showing victories. Pembroke ... he values people for their achievements and hates those who try to take credit for things they didn't earn. If you want to truly win his respect, you need to show him that you can lead this army to victory."

"Great. Now I just have to figure out how to do that."

"Welcome to command, Lord Whitton. Heavy is the head ... and so on, and so on," Eskild said with a laugh, picking up his book again.

Chapter 21

Valemonde, Lynese

Isolde Montborne walked into her father's office, her head held high despite the tension she could feel from the guards outside the lavishly carved doors, who were always a good barometer of how her father was feeling at that moment.

As was often the case when she was called before him, her father sat behind his ornate desk, his rotund frame sinking into the plush velvet of his chair. He was angry at her. She could plainly see that from the way his eyes followed her as she made her way across the wide expanse of floor to stop in front of him, his near-permanent scowl somehow etched even deeper than normal.

"You summoned me, Father?" Isolde asked, keeping her voice steady and clear, to make sure he knew she wasn't afraid of him.

She took it a step further, clasping her hands before her, the picture of composed elegance in her flowing gown of emerald silk.

"I certainly did," her father said, fixing her with a piercing stare. "You've been busy, haven't you? Warning the Sidorians about our plans. Do you have any idea the damage you could have caused? Do you deny your treachery?"

"I deny nothing. I know exactly what I did. I put a stop to your monstrous scheme."

"Monstrous?" Baudric scoffed. "This is war, you idiot child. Infecting the enemy with the Elder Curse would have crippled their army, brought them to their knees. And you nearly ruined it all with your meddling."

"It was an act of pure evil. Spreading a plague, using our own people as carriers? Have you no conscience? What if there was a true outbreak, here on our soil? How many thousands would you condemn to death?"

Baudric slammed his fist on the desk, causing Isolde to flinch despite herself.

"As many as I have to, damn you. I am trying to win a war! Sometimes sacrifices must be made for the greater good."

"The greater good? Tell that to the soldiers lying in the hospital, their bodies ravaged by the curse. Tell that to their families who have to watch them wither away."

"Soldiers die in war, Isolde. It is an unfortunate reality. I would think you, of all people, would understand that, given your penchant for playing nursemaid in the infirmary.

"You insolent girl! I am the emperor and I will not be lectured by my own daughter. Especially one who commits treason by sending warnings to our enemy! People occupying our land!"

"It's not treason to stop an atrocity. I did what I believed was right. What was necessary."

"It's treason to spy for Sidorian scum. To snoop around like the little mouse you are, looking for secrets you can reveal. How did you even learn what was happening?"

"I'm not spying for anyone. You yourself said I spend too much time in the hospitals, helping the Disciples administer to the sick. I learned about it from the victims themselves. From our own loyal soldiers. They told me how you had them take the infected; transport them all the way from Varencia, and leave them in one of our own villages, to spread the sickness to everyone there."

"I should have you hanged for this."

"Then do it, Father. Hang me for the crime of defending our people from your cruelty. See how well that plays out for you."

"You dare threaten me?" Baudric growled, rising from his chair.

It's not a threat, it's a warning," Isolde replied evenly. "The people are already tired of this endless war, the lives lost, the suffering inflicted. There has been talk of unrest in the countryside. If I've heard of it, so have you. How do you think they will react when they learn their beloved princess was executed for trying to protect them?"

"What?"

You underestimate my standing among the people, Father. They know me; they trust me. I've spent countless hours among them, caring for the sick, comforting the grieving, listening to their fears and hopes. All they know of you is that you send men to take their sons for the armies, sons who far too often never return home. If you were to execute me, your own daughter, for trying to protect our people, how would they react? Would they see a just king upholding the law, or a tyrant lashing out at those who dare to question him?"

"You delude yourself."

"Do I? Send your thugs around; have them listen to what the people are really saying. I think they are tired, Father. Tired of war, of suffering, of loss. They are desperate for a leader who cares for their well-being, who values their lives over political gains. If you're so certain that the people will back you, no matter what, then sacrifice me. See what happens to your empire then!"

Baudric jabbed a meaty finger at his daughter and said, "You forget yourself, Daughter. I am the Emperor of Lynese. My word is law. You dare threaten me?"

"I threaten you with nothing. I only tell you the truth, unlike the yes men you surround yourself with. Is the mighty emperor afraid to hear what his people really think of him?"

"Enough!" Baudric roared, slamming his hand on the desk again. "I will not stand here and be lectured by an insolent child. I have tolerated your defiance thus far because you are my daughter, but even my patience has limits."

"Then do what you must, Father," she said, glaring back at him with equal intensity.

"Get out," Baudric seethed, his voice trembling with fury. "Get out of my sight before I do something we will both regret. Go back to your hospital and let this be the last time I hear your name from my ministers. If you interfere again, you will regret it."

Isolde curtsied, giving him a small, defiant smile.

"As you wish, Your Majesty. But remember my words. The people are watching."

With that, she turned and left the room, her head held high and her pace even. The guards stepped aside hastily as she passed, trying hard not to look at her or her father.

As the doors closed behind her, Isolde let out a shaky breath, her legs going suddenly wobbly as the adrenaline from the confrontation wore off. She knew she had just crossed a dangerous line. Her father's temper was legendary, and she had openly defied him, threatened him even.

But she could not bring herself to regret what she did. The lives of her people were at stake. She could not stand by and watch as they were sacrificed for her father's ambition.

Starhaven, Sidor

King Serwyn glared at Edmund from behind his massive carved desk, his pale blue eyes blazing with anger. The young king's jaw clenched as he slammed his fist on the polished surface.

"You told me the rebels had been nearly decimated! That they were pushed back to the Shatterstone Mountains!" Serwyn shouted. "And now I hear reports of a whole series of new attacks in the heart of your duchy!"

Edmund stood rigidly before his nephew, his face an impassive mask hiding his frustration. He had worked tirelessly these past weeks to repair their relationship and regain his influence over the boy. The idea that all his careful maneuvering could be undone by a handful of rebels killing a few bailiffs, which wasn't exactly what he'd call a 'series of attacks,' was galling.

"Your Grace, I assure you I had reliable information that--" Edmund began, but Serwyn cut him off with a sharp gesture.

"Reliable? Ha! Your 'reliable' information has proven to be nothing but horse shit! I have lords and ladies demanding protection at court. Demanding justice. What am I to tell them? That my own uncle, the mighty Duke of Kingsheart, had 'reliable reports'?"

"No, you tell them that the kingdom won't stand for rebellion and is taking the matter seriously. That's what we face here, Serwyn. Rebellion. Not upheaval or unrest. That is what we should be concerned about ... not the fears of a few court nobles. These rebels were nothing more than a ragtag band of peasants a few months ago. Poorly armed, poorly trained, and with no real leadership to speak of. Suddenly, they have recovered the losses they suffered in Lindenwood and rearmed themselves. Someone is supporting them, someone with resources and a vested interest in seeing your rule challenged. This is what concerns me. Not the rebels, but the people who must be behind them."

"And who exactly do you suspect, Uncle? Surely not the Lynese; they have their hands full with our armies at their doorstep."

"No, not the Lynese," Edmund agreed. "I believe we must look closer to home. To the very lords and ladies now crying out for protection and justice."

"The barons? I thought that the goal of the edicts was to undermine their power, bleed them of gold and wealth, and sap their influence. I believe that is how you put it to me. Now you're telling me that, somehow, instead of struggling with their angered subjects, they have the resources to fund a rebellion against the crown in secret?"

"My King, as I counseled you when we first discussed these measures, the process of consolidating power is not a simple or swift one. The barons have long enjoyed their privileges and influence. Did you truly believe they would surrender them without a fight?"

"Then perhaps it's time we stopped playing games and simply arrested the lot of them. Or are you going to once again tell me 'that's not an option.'"

"If only politics were so simple, Your Grace," Edmund said, splaying his hands out in an apologetic gesture. "The barons are not a monolith. Some may indeed be working against you, but others remain loyal. To move against them all would be to risk alienating even those who support you."

"Then what do you suggest, Uncle? That we do nothing while these rebels eat away at my kingdom, piece by piece?"

"Of course not. I simply suggest that we must be strategic. We need to identify the specific individuals responsible for supporting the rebellion. Once we have proof of their treachery, we can move against them without risking the ire of the entire nobility."

"And how, exactly, do you propose we gather this proof?"

"I think we should target their leaders. If Sir Colm could manage to take his force and capture one or two, we could bring them in for questioning."

"And hope they just hand you the names of the nobles assisting them?"

"Our interrogators are quite ... thorough. We will find out everything they know about who's been supporting them, supplying them. Once we have names, once we have proof, we can move against the barons involved without fear of political repercussions. We make their treachery public, attaint them for treason, take their lands and put their families to the block or in bondage. Not only will it end the support of this rebellion, killing it in the cradle, but it will serve as a lesson to the other barons about the cost of standing up to the crown. Perhaps we add the names of a few more barons. Ones less popular with their fellows who've proven less amenable to working with the crown than we'd like. We could then give their lands to men more loyal to you, strengthening your rule and putting their coffers in your treasury. It is a win-win scenario."

"Assuming you manage to capture the rebel leaders," Serwyn said, although much of the anger had seeped from his voice. "Fine. Send out Sir Colm, and make sure he knows how critical this is. I do not want this to drag out through the winter, when we will lose much of the guard we still have. Make sure he knows I am placing my faith in him, and the cost if he should fail me."

Edmund had him. He could see the scene playing out in front of his nephew's eyes, imagining who he'd be able to remove from their holdings and who he would put in their place. His concerns were much different. While it would be nice to get rid of barons who'd proven difficult to control, the key really was to deal with whoever was funding these people. Until that was cut off, there was no way they'd be able to stop this. Not with so many of their forces still in Lynese and winter on its way.

"Of course, Your Grace," Edmund said, bowing.

Central Kingsheart, Sidor

The noise level in the barn was louder than anyone there should have been comfortable with. They were in an abandoned village that had been left to rot for several years, but Tom still worried about the groups of king's men scouring the countryside looking for them.

It was one of the reasons why he called this meeting. Their numbers were growing, which was good, but they were now becoming a large enough target that they couldn't hide easily. It was one of the numerous things they needed to deal with, and having the men assembled here caught would end the rebellion here and now.

Not that he begrudged them their excitement. They all thought it was over after the calamity in Lindenwood, and it almost had been. The fact that they'd not only rebounded, but now had more men than ever, was a miracle. And spoke to how bad things were in the kingdom as a whole.

Tom raised his hands, calling for quiet. Slowly, the din subsided as all eyes turned to him. He cleared his throat before speaking, his voice carrying through the barn.

"My friends, you have all done excellent work. Our group has grown beyond what any of us could have imagined when we first set out on this path. But with this growth comes new challenges. We now find ourselves at a dangerous crossroads. We are too large to remain hidden, striking when we wish, yet too small to take on the king's forces directly."

"What are you suggesting, Tom? That we give up?"

"No, not at all," Tom replied, shaking his head. "What I'm suggesting is that we adapt. We need to break apart, operate in smaller groups as we continue to grow."

"But won't that just make us more vulnerable? Easier for them to pick us off one by one?" another man asked.

"Yes, it's a risk," Tom said. "But a risk that's no different than the one we were all taking when we started this, or even after the losses we suffered in Lindenwood. More importantly, it's a necessary risk. What we need is more people. To get them, we need to spread our message further, and to do that effectively, we need to split up."

"We can't pull back now, Tom. Not after all we've achieved. The king has increased his attacks on the villages, many being accused of helping us. If we decrease the pressure, split up our forces, we'll lose the momentum we've gained," Fulk said.

The rest of the men murmured their agreement. They'd all seen the last few villages they'd passed through, where the people had tried to stand up for themselves, only to have their homes burned and families killed. It was heartbreaking and made each of them want revenge badly enough to taste it.

"I agree, which is all the more reason we need to split up. Right now, we can only help villages one at a time, while the rest go unassisted. In smaller groups, we'll be able to get more help to the people and cover a wider area. Maybe even get further north, away from the lowlands, up past Twin Lakes and the northern forests. The king is taking from them as much as he is from the people here. And they have no one coming to their aid. Splitting up will change that and allow us to do what we really need to do. Which is grow into an actual army, and the king's playing right into our hands."

"How?" someone asked.

"With every village he ravages, with every family he steals from, he creates more people like us. People left with nothing else to lose. If we are there, if we show these people another way, they will join our cause."

"And then what?" another man asked. "We'll still be outnumbered, outmatched."

"For now, yes. But as our numbers grow, so will our strength. When we're big enough, we can take the fight directly to the king. If we play this right, we can do it right when his armies are the smallest and most vulnerable."

There was a ripple of uneasiness in the gathering, the men looking to one another, but none wanting to say what was bothering them directly.

"I know what you're all thinking. You want to know if it's true, the rumors you've heard," Tom said, looking at each of the men, one at a time. "It is. Our ultimate goal is to march on Starhaven itself."

He could almost hear the news hit the men, some looking determined by the confirmation, while others looked almost afraid.

"A kingdom cannot exist on rotten foundations. If these policies, these edicts stay in place, the base that holds Sidor aloft, its people, will be no more," Tom continued. "The king must remove these laws before our very way of life ends, and we all know there is only one way to get him to end them - we have to *force* him to do so. We have to show him that he can't keep taking from the people without consequences."

"But how?" a man near the back called out, his voice tinged with doubt. "How can we possibly take on the king's army?"

"We have a window. Most of the sworn men in the kingdom are in Lynese, and more will have to travel south during Maw season. Yes, it will still be a challenge, which is why, right now, we need to focus on growing our numbers and helping the villages that are being robbed by the crown. We need to show them that they're not alone, that there are those willing to fight for them. The king has made a mistake, tightening his grip with each loss. It's going to force more people into our ranks. There are more of us than them, and it's time we show them that."

Tom could see that struck home. Every man here had a tale of some wrong committed in the name of the crown and had all seen the more recent atrocities committed in the new king's name.

"I've been in talks with our benefactors. They've agreed to start delivering food and goods to replace what has been lost. It's not much, but it's a start. It will help us gain the trust and support of the people."

"So, what's the plan?" Fulk asked, looking at his fellows to make sure they were all as committed.

Tom smiled, clapping Fulk on the shoulder. "We split our force and start recruiting. We let the people of the kingdom know they're not alone. We show them that there's hope, that there's a chance for a better future. It won't be easy, but with every village we help, with every person we bring to our cause, we grow stronger. And when the time is right, when our numbers are great enough, we will march on Starhaven and we will *make* the king listen."

A cheer went up from the assembled rebels.

"Now, start figuring out who wants to go where. Who has contacts where. What each of you might need."

The men began talking excitedly to each other as they fanned out. Tom was proud of them. They'd all come so far in the last several months. He was also a little sad, knowing that not all of them would make it through this.

"Can you get the food to help them?" Tom asked, seemingly to no one.

A man stepped out of the deep shadows behind him, pulling the hood that had concealed his face down, revealing his distinctive blond hair and blue eyes.

"I'll talk to the barons and see what I can do ... but yes. Probably," Aldric Whitton said.

"Good. I know you've already given a lot, but we're still a long way from finishing this."

"I know, but we're nearing the end. Just a little longer."

"I hope you're right," Tom said, looking back at the duke. "I really do."

Chapter 22

Sidorian Army Camp, Lysmire Woods, Northern Lynese

The commander's tent bustled with activity as William's officers filed in, all looking concerned. The last month had been difficult for the entire army, as their men lay dying, forced to watch the enemy that had been fleeing, on the verge of destruction, pull itself back together and reinforce, establishing new lines, extending the war even further.

Even Pembroke, who normally looked as if he was immune from self-reflection and rebuke, seemed somewhat diminished. On top of his worry, however, was something else, something between concern and annoyance. Pembroke kept eyeing the other commanders as they took their places around the large table with the map of the front drawn out in detail, updated with all the information their scouts had been able to obtain.

William had a guess about what was bothering Pembroke specifically. Since Aldric returned home, leaving William in charge, he'd allowed Baron Pembroke to take the forefront in their conferences, calling the commanders together, leading the meetings, and directing the strategy. This was the first time William had called one himself, without speaking to Pembroke directly, and clearly, the word had spread to the other commanders, as they returned the looks Pembroke was giving them.

William didn't take offense to it. There was bound to be some friction when he made his first independent command, and he imagined Pembroke was less concerned that he was showing independence, and more concerned that William might try to pass blame to him for the losses they had suffered to the curse. Something that William had never addressed directly, either publicly or in private. William didn't plan on changing that today.

William cleared his throat as everyone found their places, "Gentlemen, thank you for coming. Before we begin, I want to take a moment to welcome back Sir Drummond. It's good to see you recovered and back with us."

Sir Drummond, his face still bearing the scars of the Battle of Dead Man's Hill, nodded in appreciation. "Thank you, My Prince. It's good to be back, though I must admit I'm not yet fit for the front lines."

William clasped the knight's shoulder, his grip firm and reassuring, "While I appreciate your sword arm, I'm just as much in need of your experience and wisdom, and glad to have you with us today."

Sir Cedrick, Commander Haverhill, and Commander Baldwin all nodded their agreement, smiling at the comment.

Pembroke did not share in the moment of levity. "With all due respect, Prince, I'm sure everyone is needed back at their commands, what with the Lynesians bolstering their forces by the day."

"You're right, they are," William said, meeting Pembroke's gaze, not letting the older man shake him. "Gentlemen, I understand your concerns. We face a dire situation. Our enemy believes us routed, weakened by the Elder Curse ravaging our ranks. They perceive our sickness as an opportunity, a chance to press their advantage. While this is concerning, I think it also contains a chance for us to put things back in our favor."

William had spent the past several days in deep conversation with Eskild, running what he wanted to say, what the barons and others might counter with, and the feasibility of his plan. This was his first chance at real command, not as a figurehead for Pembroke, and he had to make sure everything, from its proposal to execution, came off just right.

"What do you propose, My Prince?" Sir Cedrick asked.

"That we attack their lines directly. My plan is an immediate frontal assault. We catch them off guard, strike while they believe us crippled."

That got their attention, with each of the commanders looking to his comrades, clearly concerned the boy left in charge had lost his senses.

"With all due respect, Prince," Commander Haverhill said. "Our men are already on half rations. And the sickness ... it spreads daily. Mounting an attack under such conditions will be ... challenging, to say the least."

"I understand your reservations, Commander, which is one of the reasons I want to attack. Now. We all know that one of our challenges, aside from the sickness spreading through our ranks, is our supply situation. It's why the duke chose to return home when he did, to correct the problem. The enemy has been building up in front of us for weeks, and our scouts report that buildup includes a large amount of supplies, probably in preparation for an attack of their own. By moving swiftly, we can capture their stores and resupply our forces while weakening theirs. It's a risk, I grant you, but one we must take."

"And what of the sick?" Pembroke said. "We can hardly bring them into battle and we are undermanned without them."

"Undermanned from our initial force, but not as much in comparison to the Lynesian forces. Right now they have the advantage on us, but only by a small amount. If we wait and they continue to bring in reinforcements, their force advantage could grow even greater before the quarantined men are released by the Disciples. While I know it has been suggested that we release those men from quarantine now, and take the risk that the sickness spreads further, I cannot take *that* risk. The quarantined forces will remain in the rear with the Disciples. Our attack will commence with the forces we have at our disposal."

"You expect to win an all-out attack with a smaller force?" Commander Haverhill said, the words escaping before he could stop them. "I apologize, My Prince. I simply am ... concerned with such a plan."

"Normally, yes, your concern would be well-placed," William said. "But our scouts have reported that the enemy, fearing the plague, has weakened their center and instead reinforced their flanks, probably expecting us to remain on the defensive and, if we were to attack, to do so from the flanks as well."

"Which is why the center is exactly where we will strike," William said, leaning over the map and putting his finger on the midpoint of their line. "We will strip our own flanks to the bare minimum and concentrate every available man in the center, far enough back to remain unseen. They are expecting the sickness to spread and, hopefully, will write off a reduction in our forces to exactly that. When the time for the attack comes, we will make one decisive push to break their lines."

"And if they attack our flanks? They'll collapse like a house of cards."

"A risk, to be sure. Commander Haverhill and Commander Baldwin, I want each of you to dig in on your respective flanks and hold your ground. Do your best to fortify your position. Based on all of our recent scouting reports, the enemy isn't currently in place for an attack and has brought up mostly line infantry, and very few knights. They will likely increase their deployments once they see our lines thin, but it will take them some time. It will be a race to see who gets their forces in place first, except we will know when the race starts, and they will not. Giving us an advantage."

"What about the village between our force and theirs, the one where the sickness originated?" Sir Drummond asked. "Both armies have avoided it, putting it almost in the center of our two armies, creating an almost no man's land. Any attack would end up being split by the village, weakening it."

"Which is why we do not split our attack but go through the village instead, directly to the point of the enemy's line that is the weakest, concentrated, punching through the Lynesians like an arrow through chainmail."

"Through the village?" Pembroke said, almost aghast.

"I've spoken to the Disciples who've recently come through the village, purely in terms of concern over the spread of the disease. I know they are normally neutral, and refuse to discuss anything military or secular they might see; perhaps because I've been so focused on our own afflicted, they told me that the sickness in the village has been contained and all those infected moved into the same quarantine tents as our men. What's more, they were adamant that the sickness only transfers from person to person and never from items. The village is safe to travel through."

"The men won't like it," Pembroke countered.

"The men will do their duty. I have complete confidence in your ability to convince them of the safety of this plan, Your Excellency."

William met Pembroke's gaze, not blinking or looking away. This was the moment his plan could turn south if the baron balked or challenged his leadership. Of course, that would mean admitting he was not, in fact, capable of convincing his men to attack in spite of their fears. Something William knew Pembroke would never admit to.

After a moment, Pembroke nodded and said, "And once we break through?"

"We'll be in the heart of their army. They'll have no choice but to retreat before our central force can wheel around, get behind either flank, and roll them up like a carpet."

The commanders all looked to the blocks on the map representing the respective lines and units, playing out the scene William set for them. One by one, their expressions changed as they came to the same conclusion he had.

Commander Baldwin leaned forward and said, "It's a gamble, My Lord. If our center fails to break through ..."

"It won't fail," William said firmly. "Not if we commit everything to it."

"It's bold, I'll give you that," Sir Cedrick said, smiling for the first time since entering the tent.

"We've been on the back foot long enough. It's time we seize the initiative, catch them off guard."

"It's a good plan," Pembroke said, grudgingly, but still with respect.

"I hope so," William said. "Gentlemen, those are your orders. Sir Cedrick, Commander Haverhill, Commander Baldwin, Sir Alistair - I want you to begin repositioning your forces immediately. Strip your forces as best you can, keeping the minimal forces you need to hold your wings. It's imperative that you send every man you can to the center, to better the chance we break through. Baron

Pembroke, as the senior commander and most experienced in the field, you will, of course, lead the attack itself."

Pembroke nodded, accepting his due. William hoped giving him the proper amount of respect would be enough to smooth over his earlier ruffled feathers.

"How long do we have before we launch the attack?" Pembroke asked. "I assume soon, if you want to go before they build up enough forces to overwhelm our flanks and defend the center."

"You're correct. I'm setting the attack for the twenty-second. That gives you four days to move your men and prepare."

"The 22nd? But that's Lion's Day, My Prince," Sir Drummond said.

"I am very much aware of that," William said.

He should be. Lion's Day celebrated the day his ancestor, Charles Whitton, was first crowned in the great hall of Starhaven, beginning the Whitton family rule over Sidor.

"A fitting day to honor your ancestor's victories with one of your own," Sir Alistair said. "It will give the men something truly worth celebrating."

"Only if we win," William said. "You have your orders, gentlemen. See to your men, make the necessary preparations. We'll reconvene tomorrow to finalize the details. Dismissed."

Starhaven, Sidor

Aldric made his way through the finely gilded palace corridor, its opulent surroundings a stark contrast to the villages he'd spent the last week touring. He should have come to see his nephew sooner, right when he arrived back in the capital, but the reports he'd been getting from the cutouts between himself and Fletcher had been concerning enough that seeing the situation for himself had seemed like a priority at the time.

Part of him was glad he did. He knew about Serwyn's, or more likely Edmund's, new policies, but knowing about them and seeing the results were two different things. Witnessing the results of these policies in person had been startling. While there hadn't been much he could do in Lynese, beyond agreeing to support the barons who'd contacted him and ultimately Fletcher himself, as a member of House Whitton, he had to at least try and settle this the right way. If Edmund had been in charge, this would have been a lost cause, but Serwyn was still young. Aldric had to give him a chance to do the right thing.

A pair of guards stood outside the king's personal study. Not the normal city guards who served as palace guards, but men in different armor, who looked much less formal and polished than the men who should have been there.

Again, almost certainly Edmund's doing, another step in a long line to control access to the boy. Not that it worried Aldric. That might work to keep away the courtiers of the palace, but Aldric was a duke, a peer of Edmund himself, answerable only to the king.

The two men looked at each other, clearly conflicted.

"Announce me," Aldric said in his duke's voice.

It had its desired effect as one of the men knocked on the door and said loudly, "His Royal Highness, Prince Aldric Whitton, The Duke of River Mark, Knight of the Realm."

"Come," came Serwyn's voice from inside the room.

Aldric entered the study, noticing the changes from when Gavric had occupied the space. Swords, axes, and armor lined the walls and many of the bookcases. Definitely Serwyn's work and not Edmund's.

"Uncle, this is a surprise. I heard you returned to your duchy," Serwyn said, smiling.

A good sign.

"Only briefly, Your Majesty. Summer is almost at an end and the kingdom runs short on manpower. I wanted to come back and have words with Bramwell and some of the barons here at court, getting a sense for the number of men able to go to Shadowhold come winter."

"Ohh ... I hadn't even considered," Serwyn replied, looking thoughtful.

That was a surprise. The annual maw season was one of the major events in their kingdom, one that required all of the nobility to rally together every year. This year would be even more important, what with the army at war as it was. If Edmund had been preparing him for anything, it should have been for that.

"Not to worry. It is traditionally handled between myself and Duke Blackwood. I will, of course, be submitting our plan to you and the noble's council, once it is in prepared, for approval, along with a request for the men we need, but that won't be for another month at least."

"Good. Thank you for keeping me informed."

"I am simply fulfilling my duty as one of your loyal dukes," Aldric said with a slight bow. "I will say, the months have been good to you. You've grown since I last saw you at your coronation."

"You think?" Serwyn said, swelling a bit with pride. "I have been working diligently with the weapons master, honing my skills. A king must be strong to lead his people."

"Indeed, he must. You learned from your father well. I've heard you've grown in more ways than one. Word is you've really come into your own as king since I last saw you. Your father would be proud."

"Thank you, Uncle. I will admit, it's been difficult, but I'm determined to be a strong king. So, if it isn't to inform me about your duties come winter, what can I help you with?"

"On my way to my duchy, I spent some time touring through the villages between here and there, trying to get a sense of things since my last trip home. What I saw made me somewhat ... troubled."

"Troubled?" Serwyn asked, a hint of defensiveness in his voice. "In what way?"

"It's these new laws and restrictions, Your Majesty. I understand the need for order and control, especially in times of war. But the people are suffering. The increased taxes, the limits on travel and trade ... it's taking a heavy toll. For many villages, it is weighing them down to the point of starvation."

"These measures are necessary, Uncle. We must ensure the loyalty of our subjects and the strength of our kingdom."

"You are very right, of course, but the kingdom cannot exist without its people. I'm certain there were pressing reasons for these rules to be put in place, but every rule should be reevaluated after it is enacted, to determine the exact cost it places on our subjects. Perhaps it is time to ease up on some of these restrictions. To show the people that their king cares for their well-being, even in difficult times."

"Uncle," Serwyn said, the smile from earlier fully gone, replaced by thinly controlled annoyance. "During your tour of the villages, did you happen to notice that parts of the kingdom are in open rebellion against my rule? These very people you speak of are rising up against their rightful king. Do you suggest we simply give in to the demands of the rabble?"

"I, of course, do not think we should give in to the demands of *any* hostile force, and I believe that every man in arms against the crown should be dealt with. At the same time, I believe the people are not reacting without reason. I know you want to be a strong king, one who commands respect and loyalty. But true strength lies in compassion and understanding. By removing some of these burdens, you show your love for your people. They will no longer be distracted by their basic needs and will be able to see the wisdom that I see in you. The rebels will lose their support and their uprising will wither and fade."

"No, Uncle," Serwyn said, standing up from his chair and thrusting a finger at him. "This has nothing to do with the rabble and their demands. This rebellion is a sign that the barons have their hooks in too deep. They are willing to burn the kingdom to the ground rather than let me lead it as I see fit. Mark my words; this defiance will not stand. I am the king, and my word is law. If the barons think they can undermine my authority, they are sorely mistaken."

Aldric did not reply. What could he say? Serwyn might be speaking, but he could hear his brother's voice coming from him.

"If you truly wish to see the burden eased on the people, then I suggest you speak to your friends, the barons. Convince them to end their sowing of unrest and discord. And while you're at it, Dear Uncle, I suggest you warn the barons that if this rebellion continues, I may have no choice but to respond with a more direct approach. One that will leave no doubt as to who holds the power in this kingdom."

"I see," Aldric said, keeping his expression carefully neutral.

What else could he say? Serwyn had made his position, and the position of the kingdom, painfully clear.

"If there is nothing else, Uncle?" Serwyn asked, returning to his seat and picking up a sheet of paper Aldric was all but certain he had no use for.

The message his nephew was sending was crystal clear.

"No, Your Majesty," Aldric replied, bowing his head. "I see you are very busy. Thank you for your time."

Serwyn waved a dismissive hand. "Safe travels, Uncle. Remember what I said about the barons."

Aldric inclined his head once more before turning and leaving the room. All of his worst fears had been confirmed. Edmund had done his work well, twisting Serwyn's already aggressive tendencies into something his brother could use.

The barons had long been a thorn in his brother's side, and he'd found the vehicle through which he was going to get them under his thumb. It was clear now that if Serwyn was going to change his mind and ease his insane laws, it would not be done willingly.

He had to be careful, though. Rebellions like this could easily spiral out of control. People, when pushed too far, could become unreasonable. Fletcher was a good man and Aldric trusted him to keep things moving in the right direction, but this still had to be managed. Serwyn was the king. All Aldric wanted to do was nudge him, albeit forcefully, into doing the right thing.

Chapter 23

Sidorian Lines, Lysmire Woods, Northern Lynese

The Sidorian cavalry rode through the tightly packed streets of the village, infantry following behind. They had to move quickly, since this level of movement would be impossible for the Lynesians to miss, but they needed to keep their men together, ready to fight when they got through to the other side.

William wasn't overly concerned that they'd manage the task. They were good men, battle-hardened, and understood the need to maintain a good formation. The only moment that worried William was as they turned a corner, bringing into sight a row of houses marked with a grim symbol, a black handprint, put there by the Order of Healing to tell anyone that ventured near that the Elder Curse lay inside.

He'd warned the men to expect it, told them it was harmless and that the Disciples had confirmed that as long as no one went inside, they were safe. But telling men that was a far thing from them believing it, and part of William worried about the reaction he would encounter when the men actually saw the warnings for the first time.

Thankfully, his worry was for naught. The men definitely looked askance at it and even his line seemed to edge away from it as they passed, but his men didn't slow or falter. They were set to their duty, and hopefully, trusted his leadership.

William spurred his horse onward, leading the way through the winding streets. The village seemed eerily quiet, with villagers who hadn't fled hiding as the enemy army pushed through their streets.

Passing the last of the plagued houses, William pulled down his visor, a move copied by the other knights leading the charge.

"Here we go," William muttered to himself before commanding, "Pick up the pace. At the double time. For Sidor."

Kicking his horse as he turned the corner, launching the beast into a gallop, William could see enemy soldiers ahead of him. The terror on their faces was clear. They might have heard the commotion, the sound of men and horses, but they'd ignored their own senses, doubting anyone would ride through the cursed village. They hadn't believed it possible until they saw the first Sidorians.

The men with him and behind him echoed his yell as the knights all charged at a gallop, the infantry behind them running flat out, screaming like the specters of ghost stories.

The Lynesian soldiers scrambled to form a defensive line, shields locking together as they braced for the Sidorian charge. Spears thrust forward, a bristling wall of steel points aimed at the oncoming cavalry. They were slow, however. Slow to react. Slow to move.

William led the charge, his sword raised high as he urged his mount forward. The distance closed rapidly, the ground shaking beneath the combined might of the Sidorian cavalry.

The Sidorians collided with the Lynesians with a resounding clash of steel and flesh. Horses slammed into the Lynesian line, their armored bulk shattering spears and sending men tumbling. William swung hard with his sword as they rode through the line, cleaving through a Lynesian shield and biting deep into the soldier behind it.

The rest of the Sidorian knights and cavalry followed after him, hacking and slashing from atop their mounts, while the Lynesian infantry desperately tried to drag them down. Men screamed in pain and fury, the sound mingling with the ring of steel on steel and the whinnying of wounded horses.

"Hold the line!" a Lynesian captain near William bellowed. "Drive them back!"

And then the Sidorian infantry hit, smashing into the gaps created by the cavalry. An entire section of the Lynesian line stumbled back as the Sidorians attacked, trying to defend the infantry in front and the knights in their midst.

Inch by bloody inch, the Lynesian line began to buckle. Men fell, trampled beneath the hooves of the cavalry or cut down by the onslaught of Sidorian spears. William spurred his horse forward, not allowing his men to stop or slow down, where the enemy could pull them from their horses. He led a wedge of knights into the heart of the Lynesian formation. His sword rose and fell, each blow claiming another life.

"Push forward!" William yelled. "Break their line!"

The Lynesians had been caught on the back foot, and his men had the momentum. Slowly at first, with one man here or there running for their lives, the enemy's line began to crumble, until the slow loss became a torrent. Once enough began to run, the rest followed as the enemy soldiers scattered, their formations breaking.

Only in one section, but that was all William needed. The Sidorian knights and infantry poured through the breach, spreading out to engage the disoriented Lynesians, the wedge growing with each moment.

"Well done," William shouted. "Their line is broken! Push forward! Roll them up!"

William pulled back on his reins, his horse prancing as he looked up and down the line, as a pocket began to open in the heart of the Lynesian line. Reorienting himself, he could see that the Lynesian line had begun to break apart where the Sidorian wedge had cut into it. More and more infantry poured into that breach, pushing either side of the Lynesians further apart with each moment that passed.

"We have them on the run!" Baron Pembroke said, pulling his horse next to William's and lifting his visor.

"We're not done yet. Follow the plan. Take half our force and roll up their right flank. I'll take the other half and do the same on the left. Push them back between yourself and the men holding our flanks. Smash them.

With a firm nod, Pembroke snapped his visor back in place and began shouting orders. William left him to it, focused on his own side of the battle.

"With me, men of Sidor!" William cried, raising his sword high. "Let's finish this!"

A roar of approval went up from the Sidorian ranks as they fell in behind their young commander. William spurred his horse forward, leading the charge into the left half of the Lynesian army.

William's cavalry smashed into the Lynesian left flank. The Lynesians, already reeling from the Sidorian breakthrough, scrambled. Swords clashed against spears, shields splintered, and men cried out in pain and defiance as the two forces collided.

William led the charge, his sword a blur of steel as he hacked and slashed at the enemy. His knights followed close behind, their lances finding gaps in the Lynesian armor and sending men tumbling from their saddles.

The Lynesians weren't beaten, however. Not yet. They rallied around their own commanders, forming tight clusters of shields and spears to fend off the Sidorian assault. They fought with the desperate courage of men who knew they were all that stood between their comrades and annihilation.

William gritted his teeth as a Lynesian spear glanced off his shield, the impact jarring his arm. He knew he had to keep the pressure on, to drive the Lynesians back towards the waiting Sidorian right flank. But the enemy was making him pay for every inch of ground.

The Sidorians redoubled their efforts, the infantry surging forward to support the cavalry. Slowly, painfully, they forced the Lynesians to give ground, the enemy soldiers fighting tooth and nail every step of the way.

Sweat streamed down William's face beneath his helm, mingling with the blood and grime of battle. His sword arm ached from the constant exertion, but he pushed the pain aside. There would be time to rest later.

More Sidorian infantry joined the fight, increasing the odds against the enemy, who were being pressed into their own reinforcements, giving William a wider front to fight on and compressing the enemy together, limiting how many swords they could get into the fray at any one time.

Slowly but surely, the Lynesian left flank began to buckle under the assault. The Lynesian line bent, then broke, the enemy soldiers falling back in increasing disorder. Seeing the enemy try to flee, pushing back into their own lines, not yet realizing they were trapped, the Sidorians surged forward. They crashed into the wavering Lynesian ranks like a tidal wave, scattering the enemy soldiers.

The Lynesian left flank crumbled, trapped between the hammer of William's force and the anvil of the Sidorian right flank under Sir Alistair and Commander Haverhill. It was only then that the enemy realized they were surrounded.

The reaction was mixed. A large group of the trapped men threw down their weapons and raised their hands in surrender, realizing the situation was hopeless and having no desire to throw their lives away on a lost battle.

A few officers tried to rally their men. William saw a Lynesian captain trying to get his men to fight on and spurred his horse forward, closing the distance between them. The captain turned to face him, sword raised in defiance.

"Yield, Sir," William called out, his voice firm but not unkind. "There's no need for more bloodshed. Your men are beaten."

The Lynesian captain hesitated, his sword wavering. For a moment, it seemed he might surrender. But then his face hardened, and he lunged at William with a cry of rage. William parried the blow easily, trading blows with the man as their two horses circled around each other. The man was already tired and beaten, however. With a final, desperate lunge, the captain overextended himself. William saw his chance and took it, his sword sliding past the captain's guard and plunging into his chest. The captain's eyes widened in shock and pain. His sword fell from nerveless fingers as he slumped forward in his saddle.

William felt little satisfaction as he pulled his sword free, letting the man topple from his horse. But, this was war. Men died.

A cheer went up from the Sidorian ranks as they redoubled their efforts. The Lynesian left had shattered, becoming more of a mob than anything resembling an army. With the Lynesians unable to bring their numbers to bear and divided into small pockets, it became a series of small melees instead of a battle. In each one, the Sidorians had the advantage of numbers and momentum.

Not all surrendered, and William lost more than a few men, forced to fight already defeated soldiers who had no chance of escape. A waste on all sides.

Still, the battle was done. The enemy line had completely collapsed, with hundreds of soldiers being gathered up to be marched away while their comrades ran for the hills.

William only hoped Pembroke was doing as well with his half of the army.

Barony of Penleigh, Duchy of Kingsheart, Sidor

Aldric made his way down the tradesway from Westborough back toward Havensport and the docks to Starhaven, having taken a very long about route for the last two days to circle his ultimate destination, part of multiple steps to ensure that he wasn't followed and that his identity remained obscured.

A lot of trouble had been taken early that morning, after going through Westborough, to ensure no one saw him leave, even if they'd been following him, and gave him an opportunity to enter a wooded area unobserved, where he changed into simple woodsman clothing, covering his face and hair in the tradition of the hunters of the region, another reason he'd chosen this as his meeting point.

It might have been overkill, but after his confrontation with both Edmund and Serwyn, he did not trust either of them not to have him under some sort of surveillance. It's why he'd scheduled meetings in the region with barons and knights to start working out what forces were available for Shadowhold that winter. While important, and something he did need to do, it afforded him reasons to be in baronies outside of his duchy and traveling in effectively a large circle.

Arriving near the pre-arranged point on a small cart trail, he dismounted and led the animal deep into the thicket, again on a circuitous route, listening for the sounds of armor or men. As he neared his destination, he heard the latter, but not the former. A positive sign. Tethering his horse, he made his way through the thick undergrowth, slowly, ensuring he didn't disturb things enough to sound an alert, in order to get a clear view of the meeting point.

A group of men and four mules stood to one side of a small clearing where the trail opened up, used mostly for carts to turn around when they couldn't in the tight confines of the path itself. The men were a nervous-looking bunch, clad in simple peasant garb, their faces weathered by hard labor and harder times. This was the problem with working through cutouts. He didn't know them and they didn't know him. They looked right, but Edmund was smart enough not to blow the game by picking obvious plants.

Still, there was nothing for it. If he'd had more time, he could have arranged for one of his more trusted men to make the drop, but the urgent note from Fletcher hadn't given him enough warning to take proper precautions.

"Gentlemen," Aldric said, stepping out of the brush, hand on the hilt of his sword, just in case.

"You the one sent by Fletcher?" one of the men, a tall, broad-shouldered fellow with a thick beard, asked.

The group of them stepped back, hands going to knives on their belts. Aldric relaxed somewhat. That was a giveaway. Commoners didn't often go around with swords, at least not where bailiffs might see them. While not strictly outlawed, it was the first sign someone was a bandit. Besides, good steel was expensive, and not something most farmers would spend their money on.

He'd spent too much time at the front, around soldiers.

Aldric inclined his head. "I am. I believe I'm supposed to tell you Nightingale."

The men relaxed at the code word set up by Fletcher. Foolish of them. If he was an agent of the king, it would mean that someone along the chain had been captured and talked, which would have also meant the code word had been given up as well.

Oddly, that did bring Aldric a measure of comfort. They were a combination of overly trusting and jumpy that suggested they weren't plants.

"Okay," the guy said. "We brought the mules."

"I see that. If you look about fifteen paces that way," Aldric said, pointing into the trees opposite from where he'd come. "You'll see two wagons. The supplies are in them, along with a chest of more portable funds to distribute."

Aldric walked toward the wagons that his agents had left a few hours before, lest someone stumble upon them, and pulled the tarp off one of them. Filling the inside of the wagon to the brim were sacks of grain, barrels of salted meat, and crates of vegetables. It was simple fare, the quality much lower than Aldric would have found in the kitchens of his own keep, let alone in the palace in Starhaven, but compared to what most villages had been living on these past seven months, it was a veritable cornucopia.

"The ancients be praised," the bearded man breathed. "I ain't seen this much food in months."

"I know, and yet so much was available to purchase in the capital that much rotted before it sold and it had to be fed to strays."

"Damn the king and his taxes," one of the men said. "Lords feast while people out here starve."

"Which is why this shipment is so important. It isn't much, but it's what we could get on short notice. I will contact Fletcher when I have more, although I can't promise it will be delivered here. People are starving across the kingdom, and we have to be careful. Too much at one time will not go unnoticed."

"We understand," the bearded man said, all traces of suspicion and hostility now fully gone. "We know the risk Fletcher and the rest of you take, and we appreciate it. You're doing the Disciples' own work, and we won't forget it. Let Fletcher know that when he needs us, we'll be there."

"I know he'll appreciate it. You need to be careful with this. If a bailiff sees you, he will be suspicious and confiscate it, assuming it's looted or withheld goods. Either could end you in a noose. For the same reason, try not to give too much to any one village.

Spread it out. You know the people in the area who've been hit the hardest. The money isn't much, but keep it secreted away, use it a little at a time when the winter comes and stores run low. Focus on those suffering the worst, where the need is greatest."

"We'll make sure it goes where it's needed. You can count on us," the bearded man said.

"But to bring all this ... You must be someone important. Who are you?" one of the younger men in the group, a lean, wiry fellow, said.

"I'm no one important. Just a middleman willing to help out when asked. There are people out there willing to help the common man and willing to do what they can. I'm just someone who could get all of it from there to here."

"Well, thank you. And please, convey our deepest gratitude to your masters. Tell them their kindness will not be forgotten. When the time comes, they'll have our support."

"I will pass along your gratitude," Aldric said, stepping back as the men set about yoking the mules to the wagons.

Not the best draft animals, but quite likely all they could afford. Horses were much more expensive, both to purchase and in upkeep. The men bid their final farewells and pulled onto the track, making their way wherever they planned to stash the food until it was distributed.

Aldric hoped they had luck. More and more men roamed the kingdom these days, looking to take from people just like these men, either in the name of the king or just for themselves. They were stout men, but it was obvious how ill-prepared for real fighting they were.

As Aldric watched them, a sense of unease settled in his gut. He wished there had been any other way to do this. He'd known Edmund would not listen, but he'd truly held out hope that Serwyn would. They'd left him little choice.

And so he'd done what he had to do. He knew that his actions here, in aiding the rebels, would only escalate things. They would have more food, the bailiffs would see less suffering and come to the right conclusion and take more from them. Round and round the cycle of suffering and injustice would go, generating an ever-expanding amount of unrest, until things couldn't stay contained any longer.

But what choice did he have? To stand by and do nothing while the people starved and the land bled?

Sadly, it was to the point that things boiling over was the only way change would come, that Edmund and the barons happily assisting him would be forced to confront the consequences of their decisions.

Aldric shook the thought off. He'd made his decision months ago, with the first monies he'd sent to Fletcher's supporters, and dug himself deeper each time he became more and more involved.

There was no turning back now.

Chapter 24

Sidorian Lines, Lysmire Woods, Northern Lynese

A day after the battle, the field still lay strewn with the dead and the dying. The Disciples of Healing picked their way through, trying to sort the two, but in many cases, it was difficult to tell. Friends of the fallen men did the same, trying to find a comrade who never returned to the line after the battle or who they had seen fall during the chaos.

This was William's third major clash, not even considering the dozen smaller ones he'd experienced since coming to this cursed continent, and he still hadn't gotten used to it. The smell, the cries of the injured who'd spent the evening sleeping in mud and blood, the carnage that blanketed the once peaceful fields and forests.

He'd heard that, over time, soldiers became inured to such sights. William still couldn't imagine how that was possible.

He paused beside a fallen soldier, a young man barely older than himself. A Lynesian, who'd only be able to rely on the overworked Disciples for help, otherwise he'd be left to rot in the field. The soldier's eyes fluttered open as William knelt beside him. For a moment, the boy's face filled with terror, seeing the lion crest, probably thinking he was about to be butchered, pieces of him taken for a trophy. A small, terrified sound escaped his cracked lips.

"No," William said, laying a hand gently on his shoulder. "You'll be fine. The Disciples are coming to help you."

William didn't know if that was true. The boy's left arm was mangled, smashed with a heavy weapon, maybe a mace favored by some of the knights when on horseback. The ground under him was soaked with blood, a chunk of his hair was missing and one leg was turned at an unnatural angle, a piece of bone sticking through the boy's simple trousers.

William looked around and waved a hand, getting a Disciple's attention, pointing to the boy. The Disciple nodded and dashed off, hopefully to get another to put the boy on a stretcher, to be carried back to an aide station.

"W... Water," the boy croaked out.

William unhooked the canteen from his belt and tilted it slowly into the boy's mouth. His first drink came back in a choke, the water mixed with blood sliding out the sides of his mouth and down his jaw. William tried again. Thankfully, this time, the boy began to swallow.

"Thank you," the boy said when he finished.

"They're here," William said, seeing two Disciples running over with a stretcher of canvas and wood carried between them. "Let them do their work and rest well. I'm sure you have a mother at home worried for you. You have to get strong to go back to see her."

The boy nodded, a tear slipping out of the side of his eye as William stepped back, making room for the Disciples. William had no hatred for the boy. Probably a conscript, he had little choice in the conflicts of nobles and kings. He was simply a cost of war; one marked down on a paper somewhere, but otherwise considered an 'acceptable loss.' William had heard his own commanders say that, after a battle. Another thing William hoped he never adjusted to. Seeing men, boys, like that, begging for water and crying over their mothers, as an acceptable loss.

Necessary, yes. But never acceptable ... never acceptable.

A third Disciple made his way over as the other two loaded the boy up. A weary, gray-haired man with robes soaked in mud and blood.

"How are the wounded, Caretaker?" William asked the man as he passed.

"The same as men after any battle. Some will make it, others will die. Some fast, some unfortunately not as fast. It is up to the Ancestors to decide which."

"Do you have enough supplies to tend to them?"

"No. We are short of bandages, salves, poultices, and mandrake for pain tinctures."

"I know our own stores are running low, but I will see what we have and send whatever I can to the aide tent."

"The Ancients will smile upon your service," the man said, with a slight bow of his head as he excused himself to check on more of the injured.

William continued on his trek across the field. There were not a lot like the boy left, alive enough to be saved. He'd been lucky. Most of those left on the field overnight were already doomed, skipped by the healers to allow them to tend to the injured more likely to be saved.

He found a group of thirty or so Sidorian footmen clumped together near an opening in the tree line where it expanded into a wide clearing that had been the site of the same particularly grueling combat. He noticed several of their pockets bulged and knew they had been scavenging the dead for valuables. A time-honored but completely dishonorable activity that every commander before him had been forced to ignore. It was hard to tell them no after they'd risked life and limb in your service.

They saw him at about the same time and let out a cheer, "Lord William! Huzzah to the Warrior Cub!"

William had heard that nickname several times now. He knew they meant well, but he didn't particularly love the affectation. The cheer was taken up by several other groups across the field. William approached the group, raising a hand to calm the cheering.

"Not for me, boys. You're the ones who won that battle. We should be cheering yourselves."

"I'd rather a draught," one of the men said, setting off a laugh across the group.

"I'll see what we have in the stores. If not, once we're back to Sidor, I promise a round to every man who served."

That sent up another round of cheers, louder this time. William couldn't help but smile. The only thing that cheered the men more than a hard-won victory was the chance for free booze.

"Seriously. You should commend yourselves. You all fought brilliantly, a true testament to Sidor. I'm proud to have commanded you. Well, except you Tellmon," William said, picking out one of the men who'd served a few days as an aide at headquarters, doing manual tasks, whose name he remembered. "I've been in the privy after you. That should never be commended."

That got raucous laughs out of them as they began to joke and tease one another, offering William a chance to escape. It was strange, being in a position of leadership to men who, some of them at least, were twice his age. It was a fine line to walk. He knew Pembroke would have frowned at seeing him interact with the troops. Men like that believed the nobles should never consort with the lower class, but William had spent enough time with Gavric, and seen him with his men, to know which role model he preferred.

Speaking of which, he could see the older baron making his way across the clearing towards him. William altered his path, assuming the baron had been looking for him.

"You shouldn't encourage them," Pembroke said as they reached one another.

"Just giving some praise after a hard fight. Your messenger found me. Your men did very well."

"Thank you," Pembroke said. "I've put out enough men to ensure we aren't caught unawares. It will be a few days before we're ready to march again, so it's better to be careful. Yesterday's battle took its toll."

William had to refrain from shaking his head. The baron had many good qualities, but at times, it seemed as if he was incapable of enjoying anything, even a great victory.

"How long do you think it will take for the Lynesians to recover?"

A grim smile tugged at Pembroke's lips. "Longer."

"We have some breathing room, then?"

"For now, yes. The enemy was well and truly shattered. It will take them time to lick their wounds and gather their courage for another go at us. They've mostly retreated to the city of Cestralion to the east, just south of Lysmir Lake. We've well and truly held the field. Although, there are still issues. Our own stockpile of supplies is lower than I'd hoped. We'll need to be careful with our resources moving forward."

"I know. I haven't heard anything from Aldric since he sailed. I'd hope to at least get a wyvern-delivered message by now."

"I know he's doing everything he can. I'm hoping we see some supplies soon."

William wasn't so sure. Regardless of his uncle's intentions, what mattered was what his cousin and stepfather were willing to do, and they were much less reasonable.

Pembroke looked around a moment before putting a hand on William's shoulder and leading him away from the soldiers milling about to a more isolated section of the field.

"William," he began, his voice uncharacteristically soft. "I owe you an apology."

"An apology?" William asked, a little surprised by the sudden change in the older man's demeanor.

"For my behavior and attitude towards you, especially after you overruled me on the decision to quarantine the men who came in contact with the Elder Curse warning. I was angry, and I let that cloud my judgment. I was wrong about the warning we received and you were right, and when that was proven, I was angry at myself, but I took it out on you. I blamed you for making me look bad, when I'd done it all by myself. It was wrong."

"I could have very easily been wrong, and you right. Getting a letter like that, from the emperor's daughter no less ... it's unprecedented. We were both guessing at that moment. It was a difficult situation for everyone."

"Maybe, but that's no excuse for how I treated you after we knew which one of us was right. Your actions since then have shown me that you are a competent and capable leader. You've demonstrated wisdom beyond your years, and I've been remiss in not acknowledging that sooner. You are the son of a duke, in the line of succession, and my own duke put you in command. I should have given you the respect and deference your station demands, and I let my own ego get in the way."

"You have nothing to be apologetic about, but I appreciate it nonetheless. I know I'm young and inexperienced, and you were, and still are, right to judge my decisions. My uncle gave explicit instructions that you were to guide me while he was gone, and offering advice, even aggressively, is what you were supposed to do and, in my eyes, you fully performed your duty.

"Well, thank you, My Lord. Your uncle would be very proud to see how far you've come."

"I hope so," William said. "I also hope you'll continue to challenge me if you believe I'm making a mistake. I value your experience and expertise, and I promise to always take your input seriously."

The baron raised an eyebrow. "Even if you don't agree with me?"

"Especially then. I know you want the best for this army and our people, which means I also know you wouldn't argue so patiently if you didn't feel it was the best decision for them. I may not always follow your advice, but I will never disregard it without careful consideration. Your counsel is invaluable to me, Baron Pembroke."

"Well, then I guess I'll continue being difficult," Pembroke said, offering a rare smile.

"I have no doubt you will, My Lord," William said.

William had won a battle and gained much-needed supplies, but the greatest victory he'd felt in some time was getting the eternally grumpy Pembroke to smile.

William left the baron and headed from the field to the aide tents. He'd had enough of seeing the bodies and gore caused by his orders. He didn't regret giving them, and their victory had been great, but it was still difficult to see. Besides, most of his men who weren't already dead had already been pulled off the field. The only living people there now were either the uninjured or Lynesians.

He owed it to his injured men to see them, to hear their complaints, and visit with them. He'd started making a habit of it after the fight by the Dead Man's Hills and he'd decided then that it was one he would continue as long as he led men into combat. If they could follow him, he could be there for them.

William ducked into the aide tent, squinting as his eyes adjusted from the bright sun to the dim interior. As always, the scent of blood, sweat, and medicinal herbs hung heavy in the air. Cots lined the tent walls, each occupied by a wounded soldier in various states of consciousness.

A man here or there called out or said hellos. Some tried to congratulate him on the victory, but he always turned it to them. Praising them for their fighting, their courage, their strength. He promised them more victories to come and that they would heal. He told them their families would be proud of them.

Continuing down the row, he paused by an older man with a grizzled beard, his leg wrapped in bloodstained linen. The man struggled to sit up straighter as William approached.

"Easy," William said, placing a gentle hand on the man's shoulder. "No need for formalities here."

"Begging your pardon, M'lord, but I was hoping you might have word from home. My wife and little ones are there, you see."

"Where are you from?"

"Aldersey, M'lord. It's in Gallows March. Near the Thunderhorn."

"Ohh, you're one of those," William said, smiling. "My uncle's warned me about you people."

"Only when he doesn't do us right," the man answered, choking a bit as he laughed.

"I'll make sure to remind him of that," William said before turning serious. "I'm sorry to say I haven't heard much from home since I came out in the early fall, although I've spoken to Lord Marlowe a few times. I assume you're with his forces?"

"I am, M'lord. I ask because I got a letter in the last batch of mail that came on the supply ships. Reading it, well, it seems things aren't going well back home. Our village, sitting right where the bay estuary and the Thunderhorn meet, does a lot of fishing, plus selling lumber down the river. They say the taxes just keep going up. She tells me half of this year's dried stores have been taken in taxes, as well as more than half the money from lumber sales. Something about extra taxes for selling goods outside the barony. It's how the people in my village have always lived, and now we get penalties for it?"

The man was getting agitated as he spoke, wincing slightly as his movements jostled his injured leg.

"Folks are struggling to get by, and my wife, she's worried we might not have enough food now to feed her and my son through the winter."

"I'm so sorry they're going through this," William said. "I've been hearing some similar stories."

"That's not the worst of it, M'lord. The king's men, they've been coming around more often. Causing trouble. Anyone who complains or can't pay, they rough them up. Drag them off sometimes. Some of the women ... my wife tells me they never came back. Their families are worried. Most of the baron's men are here, so there's no one to go to. They said they sent word to Lady Marlowe, but they haven't heard anything yet."

A chill ran down William's spine. He'd been hearing more and more about this, about what his stepfather and cousin were doing. They might not be sending men to kidnap people, but he'd heard some of the people they employed to bleed the country dry weren't the type you'd want to have any sort of power. Worse, they were being left unchecked, with no one to control them.

The man wasn't done, either.

"Some of these new boys, the ones they brought in fetters, they've been saying things. About what's happening back home. About the king's new decrees, the way folks are being treated. People rounded up for complaining about conditions and conscripted. Or just executed. Is it true, M'lord? What they're saying?"

"I won't lie to you," William said, his voice heavy. "I've heard similar stories. Too many to dismiss as mere rumor. I fear there may be truth to what you've been told."

"But why? Why would the king treat his own people this way? We're loyal; we've fought and bled for him. I'm lying here now because I followed orders, because I believed in my duty. I've always been loyal to House Whitton. And this is how he repays us?"

"I wish I had a better answer for you. The truth is, I don't fully understand the king's motives myself. He's my cousin, but we've never been close, the king and I. What I can tell you is that you aren't alone. Whittons stay true to their word and their people, and the situation is being addressed at the highest levels. While the official reason Duke Aldric left was to secure more supplies for the army, it wasn't the only reason. He went back to investigate these very rumors we've been hearing. To see the truth of what's happening with his own eyes and attempt to set things right."

"Truly?" the man said hopefully. "You think the duke can make a difference?"

"I have every confidence in him. The dukes wield significant influence, and my uncle is a good man. He'll do his utmost to rectify these problems. To ease the burden on our people and ensure they're treated justly."

"Good. I hope he's successful."

"I do, too. I also know this won't help your situation directly. I'll speak to Baron Marlowe today and see that he has someone go and check on your village. I will be checking up on him and if they don't help your people, I will send word to my aunt that she needs to send some of the duke's men to check on them. But I know the Marlowes. He's a good man and his wife loves all of her people. She'll come through for your family."

The man sagged in relief. "I knew it couldn't all be true. The things they said about the Whittons. Maybe the king, but not you and the duke. You two have been good to us. I told my wife, I told her in my letters. I said you were both good men. Told them about our victories, about how you led us. Everyone knows you always come to see the injured men. Make sure we have enough to eat even with supplies being low. They were angry, but I told them they'd see. Duke Aldric and the Warrior Cub, they'd never fail us."

William resisted a frown at the name again. He'd thought after the battle on the Chisholm it would fade, but it had started coming up again, more and more. Still, he knew it was a term of endearment, and he couldn't exactly scold the man after hearing about the horrors his own family was committing on the man's family.

"Fear can do that to people. Make them lash out, even at those who are trying to help," William said instead. "But I give you my word as a Whitton, I will not allow our people to suffer needlessly. Not you, not your family, not anyone under my protection."

The soldier grasped William's hand, his grip strong despite his injuries. "Thank you, M'lord. Truly. It means the world to hear that from you."

"And I mean every word of it. We're in this together, all of us. We'll see it through to the end. Now, get some rest. Heal. I'll make sure your family is taken care of."

As William moved on to the next cot, he couldn't stop thinking about what the soldier had said. He knew things were bad. More taxes, more suffering, but he hadn't known they were this bad. He needed to speak not only with Marlowe, but with Pembroke. The man had been a baron since before William was born, and his family was one of the oldest in the kingdom.

If anyone knew what they could do, or if they could do anything from this far away, it would be Pembroke.

Chapter 25

Starhaven, Sidor

Serwyn paced behind his desk, a scowl etched into his face. While scowling was not unusual for Serwyn, this time, it wasn't in annoyance or petulance. This was a new version that Edmund hadn't seen before, at least not at this level. Serwyn was in a full rage.

The desk, normally completely empty, due to Serwyn's disinterest in the more 'boring' parts of ruling, was covered in pages. Each was a report, with details of assaults and incidents that had occurred across the kingdom as peasant backlash to the higher taxes and new laws, thrown there by the king as he built up to his current tirade.

All he, Colm, and Bramwell could do was stand there and listen as the king listed off every wrong they had ever committed, and many that existed only in the king's mind.

"... with complete impunity. I'm told they are defeated, and yet here are reports of them killing my men and hiding what they owe," Serwyn said, waving a hand at the pages on his desk. "That doesn't sound very defeated to me. When I knighted you, it was because of that victory. I can't help but wonder if you killed any of the rebels at all."

Before Colm could say anything, Serwyn whirled and thrust a finger at Bramwell. "And you! You call yourself Captain of the Guard? My own capital is out of control! My guards can't even walk the streets without being jumped by ... by ... peasants."

Picking up an inkwell, he hurled it across the room, missing Bramwell by inches before it smashed against the wall, splattering ink across a tapestry.

"Your Majesty," Bramwell said. "I have men scouring the city as we speak, searching for the perpetrators. They will be found and brought to justice, I assure you."

"You've shown me how you care about my justice!" Serwyn shouted, moving around the desk and closing the distance between the two of them in two long strides. "Protests still happen in the streets of my capital, and your guards stand and watch. If justice was being carried out, these ... vermin would be terrified to show their faces, let alone attack your own guards. They should be hanging in the central square. Their heads should be staked along the pier as a warning to any others who might disrupt my city. Instead, you're searching for peasants in a sea of peasants. You make a mockery of my justice! You make a mockery of me!"

Before Bramwell could respond, Serwyn lashed out, striking the captain across the face with a backhand blow. Bramwell's head snapped to the side, a trickle of blood appearing at the corner of his mouth where one of the king's rings had cut him. Bramwell's lack of response threw Serwyn into an even greater rage. Grabbing the captain by the front of his tunic, the king slammed him against the wall and pressed his forearm against Bramwell's throat, pinning him in place.

Bramwell didn't fight back, and in fact looked to be allowing the king to manhandle him. While Serwyn might have been working with the weapons masters, and he certainly was filling out with muscle as he grew, he still wasn't particularly large. It seemed doubtful that the king could have thrown Bramwell around like he did if the guard captain didn't allow it to happen. And yet, how could he stop it? Knocking the king down, even in self-defense, was a good way to get executed.

"I am the king!" Serwyn snarled, his face inches from Bramwell's. "When I give an order, I expect it to be followed! I expect results, not excuses!"

Bramwell gasped for air, his hands grasping at Serwyn's arm, but he made no move to remove it or defend himself. His eyes darted to Edmund, pleading silently for intervention.

Edmund looked to Colm, who seemed completely uninterested in what was happening, and back to Serwyn and Bramwell. Things were getting out of hand. Stepping forward, Edmund grabbed his nephew's forearm and pulled the young king back, breaking his hold on Bramwell.

"Your Majesty. This isn't helping."

Serwyn whirled on him and shouted, "Do not presume to tell me what is helping, Uncle. I am the king!"

Edmund held up his hands in a placating gesture. "I know you are, Serwyn. I know you want to be a good king, as good and wise as our ancestors were. I know you're angry. Rightfully so. But attacking your own men, the very ones who defend you and this kingdom, will not solve the problems we face."

Serwyn's chest heaved with barely contained rage, but thankfully he didn't lash out or escalate things. A good sign, at least.

"The people are scared and angry. They don't understand why their lives are getting harder. Lashing out in violence will only breed more resentment and resistance. We must be smart about this."

Serwyn paced away, hands clenched into fists at his sides. "Smart? Like passing these laws in the first place? I question if any of our choices have been smart."

"I know this isn't easy and I understand your frustration, Your Majesty. Things are always difficult when you try to make changes. But we must not let anger cloud our judgment. The rebels are a symptom, not the disease. We must root out the source of this unrest. That was one of the reasons we started this plan in the first place, to find these elements and start your rule off on the right path."

While that was a bit of rewriting history, Edmund hoped Serwyn was too angry to question it.

For a moment, his nephew just glared at him before whirling on Bramwell, who'd pulled himself away from the wall and was gingerly touching his throat.

"You heard the duke. Root out the source. I want you personally leading the effort to crush this rebellion. I want them found and dealt with, swiftly and brutally. Make an example of them. Leave no doubt in anyone's mind what happens to those who defy their king."

Bramwell bowed, wincing as the movement pulled at his injured throat. "As you command, Your Grace. I will not fail you again."

"Your Majesty, if I may," Edmund said. "Captain Bramwell's expertise lies in maintaining order within the city. Sending him against the rebels in the countryside may not be the most effective use of his skills."

"And what would you suggest, Uncle? More diplomacy and restraint? That's worked so well thus far."

"No, not restraint. I believe Colm ... I'm sorry, Sir Colm, has shown he can get results. If, perhaps, we gave him more resources ..."

"Results? Like 'destroying' the rebels that somehow miraculously reappeared just a month later, attacking officials again. The kingdom can scarcely survive more results like that. No, I've made my decision. Clearly, Captain Bramwell isn't doing any good here, so maybe, since you and Colm have been incapable of stopping these attacks, he might do better in the field. And if he fails ... well, then it gives me a good enough reason to remove him from my service. Permanently."

"I will not fail, Your Majesty," Bramwell said.

"See that you don't." Serwyn waved a dismissive hand. "Now get out of my sight. All of you."

Bramwell bowed and hurried out of the room, probably happy to be given the chance to escape, followed by Colm, who watched the more stiff-necked man with amusement. Edmund didn't immediately follow them out.

He wasn't particularly worried about the captain himself, but rather the safety of the city, which was, indeed, unraveling. Most of the officers of the city guard had come with Bramwell and had a degree of loyalty to him. While that was useful when Bramwell was under their thumb, giving them a more indirect level of control, with the captain gone and possibly someone else chosen by Serwyn in his place, that control weakened.

Something Edmund was worried about.

"Your Grace, if I may," Edmund said carefully. "While I understand your frustration, I fear this course of action may be unwise."

267

"Unwise? What would you know of wisdom, Uncle? Your counsel has led us to this point. The people openly defy me, and you would have me show weakness?"

"Not weakness, Your Majesty. Strategy. Sending Captain Bramwell away from the capital at this time could be seen as a sign of instability. The people need to see strength and order within Starhaven itself."

"The people need to see the consequences of defiance. They need to fear their king."

"Fear can be a powerful tool, yes. But it can also breed resentment and further rebellion if wielded too heavily. The capital is the seat of your power; we cannot afford to have it in chaos."

"If there is any resentment, we will stamp it out. I already told you that I've made my decision. Captain Bramwell will lead the efforts against the rebels in the countryside. He will crush this uprising or he will face the consequences of his failure. I am growing very tired of being second-guessed."

"I would never second-guess you, Serwyn. I simply want to offer my fullest counsel, to ensure you have all the facts that you might need."

"Consider me informed. Now leave me."

Edmund bowed again and backed out of the room, closing the door softly behind him. In the corridor, he paused, rubbing a hand over his face. Serwyn's behavior was becoming increasingly problematic. The boy was so consumed with asserting his authority that he failed to see the larger picture. All of his father's stubbornness wrapped in a child's petulance.

Although it wasn't a lost cause yet, if Edmund couldn't rein him in he would have to start considering other options to keep the kingdom together.

Lysmir Woods, Northern Lynese

"Baron Pembroke, do you have a moment?" William asked, intercepting the baron.

"For our glorious Lord Commander, of course," Pembroke said, giving William a smile to let him know he was teasing him.

"I've spent the afternoon with the quartermasters, and I'm concerned about our supply situation. What we got from the stores the Lynesians had built up is helping, but we're essentially living off of that now. Winter is approaching and I'm not sure we will be able to continue taking what we need from the Lynesians, as it is likely they will pull back to divert forces to the southeast to deal with Maw season, we might find that our army withers and dies for want of food."

"We still have the treasure we took. For a time, we can buy from Wernese merchants, who seem more than happy to sell to anyone they find."

"Which is fine until the shipping lanes close. And we haven't taken enough money to buy our way out of this."

"You're right, it's a concern," Pembroke said. "And if Duke Aldric doesn't come through, which is looking more likely considering how much time has passed since he sailed, we'll have to find other means to relieve the problem."

"What do you suggest?"

"Well, we control all of the Rendalia province now and can take what the Lynesians would have normally taken as tax on the harvests. Things have calmed to our rear, so doing more than that or outright stripping the region could force us to divert men to control unrest. Most of the peasants who stayed don't care who is in charge, as long as they're allowed to live their lives. That, however, doesn't completely solve the problem. This isn't a food-producing region in general, so that will have minimal impact."

"What about Cestralion?" William said after a moment. "It's the largest city north of Valemonde on this side of the Lysmir River. With their forces on this side of the Lynesian plains pulled back or destroyed, there can't be that much holding it."

"I had the same thought, since it also has control of the southern end of Lysmir Lake and it sits at the edge of the Lysmir plains, which is a large food growing area. But we're spread pretty thin. I'm not sure if we have the manpower for a prolonged siege or to take the city directly."

"They don't know that, though. We could handle a shorter siege, as long as we played it right. It's a wealthy city. Taking it would both give us a foothold in the region and significantly more resources to resupply with, at least enough to carry us through to the winter. We could also shut down traffic from the north traveling down to Valemonde. It would cut off at least some of their supply lines, especially to the larger markets of Werna across the Merchant Sea. They'd have to take supplies and goods by land to ports like Talabot well to the west."

"True, but practically, that won't do much more than inconvenience and cost the Lynesians a little money. They still have the rivers that extend south out of Dawnstar Lake. From there, they can sail around the continent and up to Werna."

"Sure, but every piece of gold they can't spend on the war helps us, right?"

"You don't have to sell me on the idea, Your Royal Highness. Besides agreeing with you, you are in command of the army. If you say we take Cestralion, we take it. I'll get the commanders together, and we can meet this afternoon to begin talking strategy."

"Good," William said, but then reached out and grabbed the Pembroke's elbow, stopping the baron as he turned to walk away. "Have you had word from home?"

"Some, mostly from my wife," Pembroke said, looking at William's hand as the younger man took it away. "Why do you ask?"

"I've been making trips to visit the injured men and check on some of the rank and file since the battle, and a lot of them are concerned about news they're hearing from their families back home. It isn't a major issue yet, but this could become a problem."

Something in Pembroke's posture changed. Not dramatically, but enough that William noticed it. The man became stiffer than normal, which for him, was saying something.

"Baron Pembroke," William added, taking a guess at what he was concerned about. "You can speak openly with me. I'm not my father or my cousin. I want to know the truth, even if it's unpleasant."

Pembroke studied him for a long moment before nodding. "The reports I've received from my wife are ... concerning, to say the least. The situation in Sidor is dire and deteriorating rapidly. Increased taxes, restrictions on movement, shortages of food and other necessities. The people are growing desperate enough that there have been open attacks on the bailiffs trying to collect taxes and on the royal guards sent to deal with those attacks. Things are escalating."

"That's what I've been hearing, and it worries me."

"Because you're smart. If things continue as they are, we may face a full-scale rebellion."

"I'll send a wyvern to my uncle. I'm not sure what he can do, but having the kingdom fall apart while the bulk of its fighting men are across the sea seems ... counterproductive."

"I'm not sure what choice we have. We're so close to breaking the Lynesian forces. If we pull back now, it will embolden them, confirm to their emperor that we do not have the fortitude to make him pay the price for interfering with our people.

"I get that, and I am far from being the first one to turn my back on what Gavric started, but if Sidor falls apart while we're gone, what's the point of winning the war? It will teach him much the same lesson. I feel like I'm being pulled in two directions. My duty is to my men, to this campaign. But my responsibility is also to the people of Sidor as a whole, or at least the people of Kingsheart, who I'm supposed to rule one day."

"It's not an easy decision," Pembroke said, placing a hand on William's shoulder. "But sometimes, your only options are between two terrible choices, and you have to go with the one that is the least bad."

"What would you do?"

"Just what you're doing. Stay focused on the war, doing what you can for the men in your direct care, while prompting people back home to see what can be done there. We both know Aldric went back as much to find out what was going on at home as to deal with our supply situation. He's the right person to talk to about this."

"Okay," William said, not able to hide the disappointment in his voice.

He'd been hoping for something a little more directly helpful.

"Don't doubt yourself. You've proven to be a capable leader. Your men believe in you. As do I."

Port Linnet, Barony of Daunton Isle, Duchy of Iron Keep, Sidor

Aldric pushed his way into the Buzzard's Lament, a dingy tavern nestled on Port Linnet's western wharf. The tavern was busy, packed with sailors, dockworkers, and men who looked like the sort better left alone than approached. A few patrons glanced at the newcomer, but most paid him no mind. In a place like this anonymity was the norm.

Although it was cooler here, so much further north than his home, it was still warm enough that the heavy cloak he wore would have been out of place had he been in a more reputable establishment, especially with the hood pulled up and so far forward as to obscure most of his face. Here, he wasn't the only one wearing something to help obscure their identity, including a man in a far corner, away from other tables, whose face was likewise obscured.

Even with that, Aldric recognized the man he'd come to see and made his way over to him.

Sliding into the opposite seat, Aldric said, "Baron Sinclair. Thank you for coming."

"I must admit, I was surprised by your message, Your Grace. This is an unusual place for a meeting."

"Which is why I chose it, although I believe this isn't the first time you've met someone in an establishment along these docks."

272

"Maybe not," Sinclair said. "And what, pray tell, does an esteemed duke of the realm need that requires such a clandestine location?"

"I've heard that you've been facing difficulties dealing with some of the new laws coming out of Starhaven."

"You should know. Your brother is behind them, is he not?"

"You know as well as anyone that Edmund and I have never seen eye to eye," Aldric said. "I don't support these laws any more than you do."

"Fine. You're an upstanding hero. That doesn't explain what you want or why you're here so far from the River Mark."

"I've heard that you've not only been defying the new laws, limiting what your bailiffs take from your people, even covering many of the fines they would otherwise be required to pay. I've also heard you've been doing the same for your neighbors."

"I don't know what you're talking about."

"I think you do. I'm not here to scold you or get you to tell on yourself so I can run to my brother. In fact, I have been doing something very similar in my own duchy and encouraging my barons to do the same. That, and more."

"What do you mean, 'and more?'" Sinclair said. "Why are you telling me this?"

"I'm telling you this because our people are not the only ones hurting, Garris. What is happening in our lands is happening across the kingdom, except not all of the barons have the means or the will to counter the king's orders for the good of their people. I'm here because if this continues, many of those baronies will fall, and when enough collapse, the kingdom will collapse with them, and take our own people with it, no matter what we do to protect them."

"Do you think I don't realize that? I'm aware of the danger my people are in, but there's nothing I can do about it beyond what I'm doing. I'm just one man, one baron. I don't have the power to change the laws or the king's mind. Edmund has been looking to take power back for the crown since he was elevated to replace your uncle. If I push too far, he'll use it as a reason to strip me of my lands and give them to some crony who won't push back."

"Maybe alone, there isn't much any of us can do, but what if I told you that you're not alone? That there are others, other barons, who feel the same way we do? Who want to do something to alleviate the pressure on their people?"

"What are you suggesting?"

"You're not the only one my brother is targeting. True, he hates you the most, but he has a long list of lands he'd like to get his hands on, all run by men who think like we do, who care about our people. I'm suggesting that we work together. I have people, loyal people, who are willing to distribute aid, even into baronies where the barons are staying true not only to the new laws but to the intent behind them. People who are willing to risk themselves to help those in need."

"Fools, you mean."

"Perhaps. I know Edmund would agree with you that anyone who put their people first, above their own wellbeing, is a fool."

Aldric could see the remark strike home. Garris hated his brother every bit as much as his brother hated Garris, and the thought of being compared to him was one of the few things that could break the baron's famously unreadable exterior.

"You strike low," Sinclair said. "What you're proposing, it's dangerous. The king has made it clear that any attempt to intervene with his new policies will be counted as treason, and my duke has publicly supported the measures. I can't defy my king or my duke."

"You already are, Garris, by feeding your people. By covering their fines. You're smart enough to know what this is really about."

"That doesn't change the danger in this. If anything, it makes it more perilous."

"It doesn't. Playing into his hands is where the danger is. He's trying to cause so much unrest that you have no choice but to agree to whatever new restrictions he wants to put upon the barons. Or worse, your titles are stripped because of your inability to manage your realm. Either way, it's the same result."

Sinclair drummed his fingers on the table, staring across at Aldric, frowning. Aldric held his silence. What he was asking was dangerous, but he knew Sinclair. The man wanted to do something about it. He was practically itching to stand up to Edmund. He was just afraid.

"And what's your solution? How do we stop this?"

"The only way around this is for the barons to stand together," Aldric said. "Not publicly. Not in the open. But we ensure that his measures fail. That the people remain safe and have no reason for unrest or violence."

"And what happens if the people do rise up?" Sinclair asked. "If they decide that even with the aid, they can't abide by these new laws? If things break down, the barons will have no choice but to take a stand against the crown."

"I don't want it to come to that. But if it does, such things would be easier if a network of cooperating barons already existed."

"You're talking about treason."

"No, I'm only talking about feeding our people, keeping them from starving over the winter. Nothing more."

"And what of the unrest in Kingsheart?" Sinclair asked, his eyes narrowing. "They've been remarkably successful. And, from what I've heard, well equipped. I've wondered how those men have been supplied in the heart of Edmund's duchy."

"I couldn't tell you. It's a mystery, and a serious problem for Edmund and the king."

"I see. And what happens if some of the supplies this network of barons sends ends up in the hands of these rebels?" Sinclair asked, staring hard at Aldric.

"I doubt it will, but once given to the people, it's impossible to tell what they will do with what they have been given," Aldric said, meeting his gaze unblinkingly. "The mob is a fickle and untamable beast, as my brother says."

The two men stared at each other for a long moment, each trying to glean some kind of tell from the other without giving anything away themselves. They both understood that this was about more than just distributing aid. This was the first step in something much larger, much more dangerous.

Sinclair blinked first. "If I decide to participate, with either goods or money, it would have to be handled carefully."

"It would be. From here on out, everything will be handled by cutouts. No one will be directly involved."

"What's the next step?"

"I'm headed to Shadowhold, to prepare our forces for the winter defense, but a messenger will come to you with information on the next step."

Again, Sinclair fell silent. Aldric could see his internal struggle and said nothing. With what he was asking, he couldn't influence the man's decision. He needed him to come to it on his own, to ensure his commitment.

"Send your man. I'll be waiting for him."

"Good. Thank you, Garris. The Ancients will smile on you for this."

"I hope so," Sinclair said. "I really do."

Chapter 26

East of Cestralion, Lynese

William rode at the head of a long column with the rest of his commanders, his army finally on the move again after being stalled for months in the Lysmir woods. The spread of the Elder Curse had been stopped, and almost all of the quarantined soldiers had been released by the Disciples. Thankfully, with the widespread quarantining and halting of the men, allowing the Disciples to do their work more efficiently, they'd managed to halt most of the spread of the disease, losing only a few dozen to its ravages.

Most of the army was with him, leaving only a small force to block any Lynesian troops who had retreated into the Lysmir Woods from entering into Rendalia. It was a risk, but one he deemed necessary.

It had been a long three-day ride from their previous lines, but they were close enough to Cestralion that signs of civilization had reappeared. Farms, large roads, and the like showed they were almost to their destination. Their progress slowed as a group of scouts rode towards him, bringing their horses to a halt and saluting.

"Report," William ordered.

"Your Royal Highness," the lead scout said. "The Lynesians have reinforced the city. Their walls look to be strong and well-manned. From the standards I could see, I believe some of the forces who fled our battles to the east came here. The city looks to be fully manned, maybe more so."

"Not a surprise," Pembroke said. "This is the largest settlement for them to return to, keeping them near the front, as opposed to running all the way back to Valemonde. It's the dregs of broken armies, but still a significant force behind stone walls."

"Taking those walls will be a costly affair," Sir Alistair added.

"Which is why I don't think we should take them," William said.

Sir Alistair raised an eyebrow. "Then what are we doing here?"

"We're going to surround the city," William said. "Cut them off from their supplies and starve them out. Commander Haverhill, Commander Baldwin, assemble your squads. I want you to start pulling in supplies from the countryside immediately."

"The locals may not take kindly to that, My Prince," Commander Baldwin said. "Unrest in the surrounding countryside will make things more difficult for us, and possibly cause issues with our supply lines back through Rendalia."

"Try to be as diplomatic as you can. Use the money we confiscated from Port Belmar and the Lynesian build-up in Lysmir Woods. Pay a fair price for what you take. But make it clear they don't have the option to refuse to sell to us."

Haverhill frowned. "And if they don't have surplus to sell?"

"Leave enough for the villages to get by," William said. "But anything extra, we take. Inform them the markets they usually sell to in Cestralion are closed. We'll be their only buyers now. They won't like it, but I'm hoping the fact that we leave them enough to not starve and pay them fairly will offset that."

"Even paying them, a lot of people won't want to sell," Sir Drummond said. "They'll hoard what they can or try to sneak it south to Valemonde."

"I know. I'm trying to soften the blow, but we can be more forceful as needed. We'll have to send out regular sweeps to confiscate harvests as they come in, but they will sell to us. This will also be costly, so any manors, noble residences, or keeps are to be stripped bare, as long as it doesn't draw us into prolonged fights. Treating the peasantry fairly will make our lives easier, but I see no reason to offer the same consolations to their nobles."

"What about the nobility themselves?"

"Put them in chains. If the emperor wants them back, he can ransom them back from us. If not ... well, we can always use some forced labor in the works. Send a detachment to secure the roads leading south. I want checkpoints on every route. Nothing gets through without our say-so."

"It will be done," Haverhill said.

"If a keep or other defensive work is fortified heavily enough skip it and inform us, and we will make the determination if it should be taken or bypassed. Do not let yourselves get bogged down in protracted fights."

"Understood," Baldwin said.

"Sir Cedrick," William said, turning to the grizzled knight as the two men-at-arms rode off. "Once the perimeter lines are established, I want you to position siege equipment and archers along the shoreline on both sides of the city."

"Not around the city itself?"

"No. I'm not looking to storm the walls unless we have to, and would prefer to take it intact if at all possible. These actions are to further limit their supply. I want you to target any ships attempting to resupply Cestralion. We cannot allow them to bring in fresh provisions or reinforcements. Every vessel that reaches the docks lengthens this siege."

"It will be done," Cedrick said. "I'll see to it personally."

William hadn't interacted with Sir Cedrick much, but the times he had, he'd been impressed with the man's willingness to get his hands dirty carrying out orders, instead of standing back and letting others do it.

"We should also send word to our fleet in Rendalia Bay," Pembroke suggested. "Have them redeploy to the mouth of the Lysmir River. They can intercept any ships trying to aid the city from the north."

"Agreed," William said. "That will allow us to concentrate our efforts on vessels coming up from Valemonde and Dawnstar Lake to the south. Cestralion's position on the river gives them too many avenues for resupply. We need to cut off as many as we can. They also have a port up there that I'd like to deal with. We can't siege it, since they're on the wrong side of the river, but we can choke it off from the river once we have Cestralion. I'd like to take both this city and that one before winter. Together, they'll give us a jumping-off point for the march to Valemonde and allow our army to supply via the river instead of a long overland route."

"One thing at a time, however," Pembroke warned.

"Yes. Just thinking ahead. Send a messenger under a flag of truce to Cestralion. Offer them terms for surrender. If they yield the city peacefully, we'll spare them a sacking."

"They won't agree to that," Pembroke said. "Not now, at least. Those walls are strong, and they've got plenty of soldiers to man them."

"True, but they also have a lot of mouths to feed," William pointed out. "Every refugee and soldier that fled into the city is another drain on their food stores. The downside of our foes in the city being so strong is they all have to be fed, and you can't keep soldiers you want to be able to fight on half rations. It's why I want to cut off their access to the river and strip the countryside. Anything we do to make their ability to bring in more supplies weakens them and feeds our men. Give them a few weeks, maybe a month or two. When the granaries start running low and the belts start tightening, they'll start thinking differently."

William had never run a siege himself, or been present at one, but he'd heard stories from his Uncle Gavric and some of the weapons masters in Starhaven, all of whom did time in the armies before mastering their craft enough to be allowed to teach the prince ... and William.

In the beginning, the defenders would be defiant, confident in their walls and their stores. But as the days dragged on and the food dwindled, their resolve would start to crack. First would come the rationing, the cutting of meals to stretch the supplies. Then the first pangs of real hunger would set in, the gnawing ache that never quite went away. Tempers would fray, and fights would break out over scraps and crumbs.

When they looked out over their walls, they would see the besiegers, well-fed and waiting, the promise of plenty dangling just out of reach. Few cities could withstand that kind of pressure for long. Sooner or later, someone would decide that a quick surrender was preferable to a slow death by starvation. They would either convince their commander or replace him with someone who was willing to end their suffering.

It was just a matter of time.

Grand Hall, Starhaven, Sidor

The ancient grandeur of the Grand Hall was on full display, with long tables laid out across the central chambers, and the massive columns decorated with banners bearing the sigils of Sidor's noble houses and tapestries showing scenes from Sidor's history, long before the unification.

The hall was packed with guests from across the kingdom, all gathered to celebrate Redwald's Day, the commemoration of Sidor's triumph over Thayan invaders in the sixth century. Nobles from as far away as the Duchy of Icelands in the north to the far southern Duchy of Shadowhold filled the space, each dressed in their best finery, making an impressive showcase of the breadth of styles to be found across the kingdom. Servants wove through the crowd bearing trays laden with delicacies and flagons of rich wine.

Edmund lived for these sorts of affairs. It allowed him to dress in his finest, which today included a magnificent doublet of deep blue lake silk and a thin, magnificently elaborate duke's crown to remind everyone of his station. In addition, this was the second biggest event in the kingdom, after Lion's Day, and was one of the few times so many of the kingdom's nobility would all be in one place, making for an excellent opportunity to feel out Sidor's current political undercurrents and begin planning his moves for the next year.

Of course, that was a downside too, especially in difficult times, such as the one the kingdom found itself in at the moment, since it gave those same nobles a chance to waylay their betters and complain about things above their station.

"I admit things are not as advantageous as they should be, Arden," Edmund said to Baron Stonehill, who'd pulled him aside to complain about more unrest in his region, as if he was the only one facing difficulties. "But you've been given more than adequate resources to deal with it. In fact, from the reports I have been getting, the troubles in your barony are worse than in any of the others in the region. How is it that your neighbors have managed to maintain a hold on their people while you have not?"

"Your Grace, I was not saying the situation was out of control or that I cannot contain the issue. I simply wanted to bring the problem to your attention. While I will acknowledge that some of my fellow barons had suffered fewer indignities from the rabble, I would argue that is perhaps a side-effect of their shirking their responsibility to the crown and refusing to uphold the law as vigorously as I have. If you are suggesting that I should lessen my efforts ..."

"If you have specific charges against any of your fellows, Arden, lay them out. The king has made it clear he wants to root out any of the nobility unwilling to uphold the king's law."

Edmund, of course, knew that he would do no such thing. The one thing he could always count on the perfidious baron for was his willingness to do whatever he had to do to socially climb higher. In that way he was much like his father, Tolan Harald, the previous Baron Stonehill, ready to put a knife in anyone's back he could if it meant bettering himself.

He also wasn't an idiot and knew he couldn't outright accuse any of his fellows of direct misdeeds. Edmund had read the reports, and knew that, while it was true some were shirking on their duties, the problem had more to do with being spread too thin, with most of their men headed south or in Lynese, and not some avarice. Harald knew this as well as he did and also knew most of those men had as much dirt on him as he had on them.

"I'm not laying specific charges ..." Harald said, holding up his hands defensively.

"Good. Then I hope I can expect improvements in your barony."

Stonehill opened his mouth to respond, most likely to dodge more responsibility, when the sight of the king, looking furious, pushing his way through the crowd, halted him. The man might have willed up enough courage to complain to Edmund, but most of the barons had learned the dangers of doing so in front of their new king.

"Have you seen this?" Serwyn demanded, thrusting a crumpled set of wyvern messages in Edmund's face.

"If you'll excuse us, Baron Stonehill," Edmund said, looking past Serwyn.

The baron, smart enough not to want to be involved in whatever this was, bowed and disappeared into the crowd.

"I'm afraid I don't know what 'this' is, Your Grace," Edmund said, turning his attention back to Serwyn and taking the strips of paper from him, smoothing them out.

"The latest dispatches from the front," Serwyn said through gritted teeth. "All praising William's exploits while leading the army and defeating some insignificant Lynesian force. Of course it doesn't mention he *still* hasn't made it to the plains or anywhere near their capital."

Edmund scanned the messages from Baron Pembroke, Sir Alistair, and others, updating the king on the progress of the war. They did indeed speak highly of William's recent victories against the Lynesians. One even went so far as to call his stepson the "Warrior Cub," a clear reference to his deceased brother's epithet, the Golden Lion. High praise from men who'd served with his brother for years. Edmund was honestly surprised, more than anything.

When he'd sent William with the army, it was partially to get the boy out from underfoot and hopefully to man him up some. He hadn't actually expected him to succeed and certainly not for Aldric to leave him in command. Edmund had been highly skeptical of that move, except that every message since had proven his brother right.

"It's becoming infectious. Did you know that over the past month, I've overheard courtiers and nobles alike comparing him to my father. Saying he has the makings of a new Golden Lion. It's an outrage. An **outrage**!" Serwyn spat, loud enough that several guests turned to look at the pair. "He isn't even a Whitton. Not really. To compare him to my father sullies his name and memory."

While Edmund did see some issues with the level of praise William was getting, he wasn't so concerned about Gavric's memory as he was any time a noble began building fame. Although in this case, he was less concerned than he would have been had it been someone like Pembroke or Sinclair, who could have turned that fame into a hammer against the crown. Or maybe even a sword.

"I understand your frustration, Your Majesty, but ..."

Before Edmund could finish the sentence, Quentin Blout, the Baron of Langmere, approached them, looking concerned, bowing deeply as he reached them.

"Your Majesty, forgive the interruption, but I must speak with you about the dire situation in my barony."

Edmund sighed inwardly. It seemed everyone had a complaint today.

"Go on," he ordered.

"Your Grace, the losses we've sustained at the hands of the rebels are devastating. With so many of my household guard sent to bolster the army in Shadowhold for the winter defense, I fear we are vulnerable. The rebels grow bolder by the day, and I do not have the men to keep them in check."

Edmund had suspected as much. Aside from the fact that all anyone wanted to talk about was the rebel activity in the kingdom, Langmere and the other baronies along the border with River Mark were seeing the bulk of the attacks. A pattern Edmund had taken note of and was concerned about, which pointed to much more dangerous trends that he preferred not to bring up with anyone else until he was sure how to deal with them.

"I recognize the difficulty of your position, Baron Langmere. Truly, I do. But we all must make sacrifices for the greater good of the kingdom. Would you rather endure temporary hardships now or see monsters from the Maw ravaging your lands and homes come this winter?"

"If you had done your duty and crushed the rebels when they were weak, we would not be having this conversation," Serwyn cut in. "Your failure has brought this upon yourself."

"Your Majesty, I assure you, I have done all I can with the resources available to me. The rebels are like vermin, multiplying faster than we can exterminate them."

"Perhaps," Serwyn said coldly, "it is time for a new Baron Langmere. One who can handle the responsibilities of the position."

The color drained from Langmere's face at the thinly veiled threat. Edmund stepped in quickly, placing a hand on Serwyn's shoulder.

"Now, now, Your Majesty. We are all allies here, working towards the same goal. Baron Langmere, rest assured that the crown is deeply concerned about the growing rebel activity. We will review our resources and see what aid we can spare to assist in your barony's defense."

Relief washed over Langmere's features. He bowed again, this time to Edmund.

"Thank you, Your Grace. Your support means a great deal in these trying times."

"If you'll excuse us, Quentin," Edmund said, taking Serwyn by the elbow and, as gently as possible, leading him away from Blout to a more secluded side of the Grand Hall, on the other side of its massive pillars.

"Your Majesty, I must advise caution," Edmund said, keeping his voice low. "Relations with all of the barons are strained right now, and Baron Langmere is one of our most steadfast supporters. With other barons likely plotting against us, we cannot risk alienating any more allies."

"For someone so loyal, he complains about doing his duty to the crown quite a bit," Serwyn said, but apparently accepted the correction as he shifted back to his original topic. "You know my father; he led men into battle. Led armies and the people loved him for it. He didn't cower behind castle walls while his kingdom fell into chaos. Maybe that's what I should do. Leave the peasants to you and show these rebels the true might of their king."

Edmund placed a firm hand on Serwyn's shoulder. "Your Majesty, your place is here, in the capital. Your father was a great warrior, yes, but his prolonged absence may have contributed to the peasants forgetting their place. They need to see you, to feel your presence and the weight of your authority."

Serwyn frowned but didn't say anything to dispute Edmund's statement.

"While you're right, the rebels have to be reminded who the true king is, the barons, too, must be reminded of who sits upon the throne. Until we can identify who is behind these attacks and remove them, it is crucial that you maintain a strong presence here. To keep them in line."

Serwyn's jaw clenched as he worked over Edmund's reasoning. Edmund knew he didn't like it, but he had to see how poor an idea it was for him to join the armies now.

"And what of William? The people sing his praises while I sit here, doing nothing."

"William is doing his duty, as you commanded him to do. His victories reflect well upon you, Your Majesty. The people see a king who can lead his armies to triumph, even from afar. Perhaps we haven't communicated that strongly enough. I will start drafting a proclamation to be read across the kingdom to recognize the victories your armies have achieved and the glory you are bringing to your people. If worded right, and if we continue to be proactive, claiming each victory for its rightful bearer, I think we can make the people remember who's really behind our successes."

Serwyn was silent for a long moment, looking past Edmund at the milling crowd of nobles and sycophants.

Finally, he nodded and said, "Fine. See to it."

With that, Serwyn turned and left. Edmund watched Serwyn join a group of barons, their faces lighting up with practiced smiles as they bowed and greeted the young king. No doubt they were already singing the king's praises, stroking Serwyn's ego.

He sighed, turning away from the spectacle. Serwyn's actions had already become untenable, with his outbursts and threats were becoming more frequent, more public. It was only a matter of time before he said or did something that couldn't be taken back, something that would turn even more of the barons against him. Against them.

Edmund rubbed his temples, feeling a headache coming on. He'd worked so hard to keep the kingdom together through his brother's foolish war and inevitable death. He'd gotten Serwyn on the throne and begun the reforms needed to right the monarchy and repair the damage his brother had done to the kingdom. And for what? To watch the boy tear it apart with his own hands.

If Serwyn continued down this path, something would have to be done. Edmund had no illusions about his own position. If Serwyn fell, he would fall with him. The barons already blamed him for the new laws, for the chaos that had resulted. They would not hesitate to turn on him if given the chance.

But what could he do? Even if Serwyn were to be removed, there was no guarantee the throne would fall to him. In fact, it was more likely the barons would rise up in revolt, each vying for power in the vacuum left behind. They would tear each other and the kingdom apart.

He'd fallen into a trap, and for the first time in his life, he couldn't see a way out of it.

Chapter 27

Kenna, Duchy of River Mark, Sidor

As Aldric slid off his horse in the courtyard of the keep that sat at the center of the city, a feeling of warmth filled him. He hadn't been back to his capital in almost a year, and he'd missed it.

It was good to be home.

Handing his reins to a stable boy who came running out, Aldric climbed the steps of the keep and stepped through its large central doors. These were as they always had been, a reminder that life at home did not stop just because the armies were away.

"Your Grace, it is good to have you home," Thurston Whitby, his majordomo, said, intercepting him only a few steps into the doorway.

"It's good to be home."

"Will you be staying long? Is there anything I can do for you?"

"A few days at the most before I have to ride south. And yes, I would kill for a warm bath and fresh clothes. I've been in the saddle for weeks and nothing sounds better than a nice, clean bed. Is the Duchess home?"

"Yes, Your Grace. She arrived three weeks ago, and not a moment too soon. The duchy withers without guidance."

"I'm sure the duchy carried on just fine without us," Aldric said, stifling a grin.

It was an old game he and Thurston played. The majordomo knew how much Aldric hated fawning and played it up to the hilt as a way to tweak his master's nose.

"If only that were true. I will have the servants prepare you a bath and fresh clothing," Thurston said, bowing. "I believe the mistress is in the study."

"Thank you, my friend," Aldric said, patting him on the shoulder as he passed.

Making his way up the stairs, Aldric entered his large study where most of the business of the Duchy passed through, although in all honesty it was more his wife's study. She was the heart and brains of River Mark and did the necessary work to keep it running.

She was seated in a large, comfortable chair, her feet tucked under her, poring over sheets of parchment when he entered. She gave a mildly annoyed look at the interruption that shifted into a giant grin as soon as she recognized him.

"Aldric!" she exclaimed, jumping out of the chair and rushing forward to embrace him. "I didn't expect you so soon."

"I decided to stop for a night and visit before continuing on to Shadowhold," he said, pulling her into a deep hug, breathing in the scent of her hair. "I've missed you, my love."

"What of the men you have gathering on the other side of the Kingshold? They've been marching through for weeks."

Pulling out of the embrace, Aldric tucked a stray lock of hair behind her ear and said, "The army can wait a few days. This is my first chance to be home in almost a year. I wanted to take it."

"Your timing is impeccable," she said, pulling out of his arms and picking up a pair of rolled wyvern messages from the desk. "I received wyvern messages for you from Baron Pembroke and William. They seem urgent."

Aldric took the two pages and unrolled the first one, noting the wax had already been broken on it.

Uncle,

I hope this message finds you well. Our supply situation continues to be difficult, and the men grow restless. We have managed to capture enough supplies to sustain us for a time and we are in the process of making a plan to secure more that should keep us going through the winter. Without additional supplies from home, however, the advance will grind to a halt.

More troubling are the rumors from home. Word of unrest has reached the men from their families back home, mostly about the laws passed earlier this year. They fear for their families and question the purpose of our fight. I've done what I can to reassure them, but I fear it's not enough.

I implore you, Uncle, to speak with my stepfather. Convince him to change course before it's too late. The kingdom cannot sustain this path.

I eagerly await your guidance.

Your nephew, William

Aldric sighed heavily and looked to Alyssa, "You read these?"

He was already fairly certain of the answer, considering the broken seal, not that it was a problem. He kept no secrets from his wife. If anything, he valued her opinion almost more than his own, and often asked her to weigh in on decisions.

"I have, and he is right to be worried."

"He's a smart boy, and the new 'recruits' made it pretty clear what was happening here, although if men are starting to get complaints from home, it could significantly endanger morale. I'm not sure what to tell him about Edmund. Their relationship is already so troubled, telling him there's no chance Edmund or Serwyn will change their minds will only make it worse."

"I doubt there's anything you could tell him that will do more damage to their relationship than your brother has done willingly all by himself. He's never been subtle about how he feels about William."

"I know," Aldric said, switching to the other letter.

Your Grace,

I write to update you on the progress of our campaign and the development of your nephew, Prince William. The boy has shown remarkable growth in the months since you left him in my charge. He has a keen mind for strategy and a natural ability to inspire loyalty in the men. In many ways, he reminds me of your late brother.

However, William has been asking pointed questions about the actions of Duke Edmund and King Serwyn back in Sidor. It is my belief that the time has come to have a more open conversation with the Prince. The boy has proven himself trustworthy and capable, and his influence with the men grows by the day. Important qualities.

There may be some haste needed in the matter. As the Prince's status rises, I believe there may be attempts to sway his loyalty. While it seems unlikely, from what I have heard, that such attempts will work, should he change his priorities, it could make future work difficult.

As always, I remain your faithful servant.

Baron Rowan Pembroke

"Rowan is walking a fine line," Alyssa warned as Aldric lowered the letter. "Should someone intercept his wyvern and read that ..."

"It would be fine. It might clue my brother in to the idea that there is more going on, but Edmund has never trusted me anyway. We've already assumed he knows I'm doing something, and this tells him no more than that."

"Maybe," Alyssa said. "You have a bad habit of underestimating him, though. He has many faults, but lack of intelligence was never one of them. He's very capable of working out what is happening here."

"I will keep that in mind," Aldric said, not dismissing her, but not wanting to continue an argument they'd been having since he'd first begun his work against his brother's efforts with Serwyn.

"Is he really suggesting that Edmund might convince William to back him and Serwyn? While I get why Edmund might want that, if what Rowan says about William's status with the men is true, it's absurd to think William would ever consider such a thing. Anyone who's spent more than a few minutes with the two of them can see the tension there."

"Which Rowan never has done, and William's very good about not talking about his issues with his stepfather to anyone outside of the family. It's admirable restraint for someone so young, but it would leave others with a skewed view of their relationship. From his perspective, it's a reasonable assumption."

"He should still see that William is too smart for that."

"Maybe, but he's also only fifteen, or rather almost sixteen. Remember what we were like at that age?"

"Barely," Alyssa said with a soft chuckle. "So, will you do it?"

"I don't know. Like you said, there is almost no chance that William will back Edmund or Serwyn, meaning there isn't the kind of time pressure Pembroke assumes, and the last thing I want is to put William in danger by involving him in this."

Alyssa placed a hand on Aldric's arm, her expression softening, "He's already in danger, my love. Edmund has never trusted him, and their relationship has always been strained. If Edmund discovers what's happening, he will almost certainly blame William. Especially considering how poorly he thinks of the boy and the proximity he has had to you, Rowan, and some of the others. Put that with your brother's conspiratorial way of thinking, and it's a foregone conclusion. At least by telling William, you give him a chance, should things go badly."

Aldric scrubbed his face with his hands letting out a guttural noise. She was right, of course. Edmund thought everyone was part of the game, and couldn't conceive of anyone not vying for power. The depths only knew that, even if he didn't suspect William, he might use the opportunity to rid himself of an annoyance or use the boy as some kind of scapegoat.

"You're right," he said finally. "I'll send a message to Pembroke to let him know to proceed with caution. But we need to be careful about the timing of involving William. Not everyone in the army's command structure is aware of our plans."

"Rowan is a smart man. He'll know when the time is right to bring William into the fold. And he's always been loyal to you. I trust his judgment."

"As do I," Aldric agreed. "I'll send the message first thing in the morning before I leave."

"I wish you didn't have to go so soon. I know they need you in Shadowhold, but I miss you terribly when you're away."

Aldric pulled her close, resting his chin on the top of her head, and said, "I miss you too, my love. If I could stop the seasons or close the maw for good, I would do it for you. In a heartbeat."

"I know, I'm not blaming you, but that doesn't make it any easier to watch you ride away, knowing I won't see you again until spring."

Pulling back, he tilted her chin up, smiling down at her. "Then let's not waste the time we have together talking about politics and war. We'll have plenty of time for that come morning."

Cestralion, Aurorin Province, Lynese

A delegation of Lynesian nobles and commanders sat on fine white horses in front of the high stone walls of Cestralion, a large white banner signaling safe passage of parley was held by a retainer near the rear of the group.

William could see hundreds of faces peering over the battlements, watching the commanders of the two armies facing off. William didn't blame them for their curiosity, since they would be the ones to feel the effect of whatever he and the other nobles below decided. Not for the first time, William was aware of the position he'd been born into, a life where he was the one to decide his fate, rather than have others decide it for him.

Baron Pembroke and Sir Alistair rode with William, along with a contingent of guards that were more of a formality than for actual protection. While these types of negotiations did sometimes turn into violence, that normally happened in more secluded meetings and not on the field between two armies, at least not when both leaders were on the field. If something did happen, the viceroy knew as well as William did how unlikely it would be for either of them to make it back to their own lines intact.

It wasn't hard to pick out which man the viceroy, Raemond Valiterre, was. In resplendent attire, his finely embroidered doublet a rich burgundy, a fur-trimmed cloak about his shoulders, and enough jewelry and other finery to be effective as a kind of armor all on its own, he practically announced his station. While William had met pretentious barons and knew how well his own stepfather liked to put on an impression, no one did pomp like a Lynesian. Especially someone as high as a provincial viceroy, only one step removed from the emperor himself and essentially the same standing as his stepfather and Uncle Aldric held in Sidor.

They halted a dozen paces from the Lynesians. William's destrier snorted, pawing the ground. He patted its neck, more to calm himself than the horse. For him commanding men in the field was simple, straightforward, and he'd been at it for months, growing more comfortable with it each day. Negotiations of this sort, however, were new to him. He'd gone over it repeatedly with Pembroke, after the Lynesians signaled their offer of negotiation, but the baron had been insistent that this had to be done by William himself.

Valiterre urged his mount forward, alone, and William matched him, riding forward so that the two sat between their respective parties. Up close, William saw that the man was older than he'd first thought, his dark hair shot through with gray at the temples.

"What is this? I will not treat with a green officer barely out of swaddling clothes. I demand to speak with the commander of your forces of whom I have been hearing so much," the man said, looking William up and down as he spoke.

It was clear this man was not fluent in Sidorian and spoke with a thick Lynesian accent. William was almost certain that his Lynesian was better than this man's Sidorian, but Pembroke had suggested that William stick to his native tongue, pointing out one of the many power plays that can happen in a negotiation between opponents, where anything that made the other person off balance only helped their position.

"I am William Whitton, son of Duke Edmund Whitton and nephew to the late King Gavric Whitton, the Golden Lion. I command the Sidorian army," trying for as confident and steady of a tone as he could muster without sounding like he was playing at soldier.

"You?" Valiterre said in disbelief.

"Yes. Me. If you doubt my word, you're welcome to return to your city and await starvation alongside your men. The choice is yours."

Valiterre's face reddened and his jaw clenched. For a moment, William thought the man might turn his horse around and do just that.

But after a long pause, he said in almost a pained tone, "Very well, let us cut to the hunt, then."

"Chase," William corrected.

Waving a hand dismissively, Valiterre said, "I am willing to surrender the city, but only on the giving of promise for good conduct marching of my men south, taking with us what supplies are to be needed."

"Those are not my terms. If your men wish to return, your emperor will have to be willing to ransom you and any others he wants freed. I will agree to send a single messenger down the river with word of the ransom request, but only after my army is inside the walls and your soldiers are held under guard," William said, before pausing for dramatic effect. "Any ships sent south before then will be sunk or boarded, just like the ones you've already tried to send."

Valiterre's eyes narrowed. "You think to hold me hostage?"

"You already are held hostage, behind your walls. You wouldn't be here, speaking to me, otherwise. I think if your emperor values you, he will pay the ransom. If not ..." William let the implication hang in the air between them.

"This is an outrage," Valiterre bellowed, causing some of the men behind him to stir, the mounts stamping nervously. "You dare to be threatening me? I have months of food storing within these walls. We can outlive your siege through winter and into spring if be needed."

"I think not. While it's true you have stores, they were for the city and its guard, not all of the additional soldiers you've taken in. By my count, what you have is not enough to feed your men and the city's population through the winter, let alone the spring. Not without the supplies being harvested across your province as we speak. Supplies that my army is collecting instead."

"My emperor will send reinforcements. He will not be abandoning his loyal subjects."

"Are you certain of that?" William asked, raising an eyebrow. "Your emperor has lost several armies already, with thousands of men dead or wounded ... and winter approaches. Even now, he's sending men southeast to prepare for the opening of the maw. It is unlikely that, even if he wanted to, there are enough soldiers left in the empire to send here until spring. By which point your men will all be dead and I will still gain control of the city."

He could see his words land. The man was full of bluster, but even with how entrenched the Lynesian nobility was, anyone who made it to such a high position as viceroy would understand just how bad his position was.

Valiterre's knuckles whitened as he gripped the reins tighter. "And what of my men? What assuring do you have for their safety if we are to be surrendered?"

"You have my word as a Whitton. Any man ransomed will be sent south and those not ransomed will be held under guard until the war ends and they can be released. It will not be comfortable, but we will not let them starve. Those who do get ransomed, however, shall leave with only the clothes on their backs. Everything else—money, supplies, weapons—is forfeit. Those are my terms."

"You ask too much! To leave my men defenseless, at the mercy of their enemies? It is an insult to their honor and mine."

"This is war. You will return home intact and alive, which is far better than honor-bound and dead. Besides, you have little choice. Your men are already defenseless, trapped within those walls. Which is more important, your honor or your life?"

The viceroy's mouth worked silently for a moment before saying, "Very well. We accept your conditions, but know this, the emperor will be hearing of this insult. You may be winning this battle, but the war is not over."

"Thank you for your cooperation. When you talk to your emperor, make sure he knows that come the spring, I intend to be at his gates, offering *him* insults," William said with a smirk.

Valiterre's lips pressed tight as he jerked his horse around, riding back to his lines.

'Negotiations were easy when you have all the leverage,' William thought as he headed back to his own lines.

Of course, he would probably feel very different if the boot was on the other foot.

Chapter 28

Kingshold River, Duchy of Shadowhold, Sidor

Aldric pushed open the weathered wooden door, stepping into the dimly lit interior of the farmhouse, not for the first time wondering where Fletcher managed to find these out-of-the-way places. They always looked unkempt and lived in, meaning this was someone's home, and yet the occupant always managed to find somewhere else to be when these meetings happened.

It spoke to how far-reaching Fletcher's network had become and what kind of loyalty he received from the people in it, willing to give their homes to him without question, upending lives that were almost certainly already difficult.

The man in question was sitting in a chair in the middle of the room, looking at his hands and deep in thought as Aldric entered.

"Your Grace. I wasn't sure you'd come," Fletcher said, jumping up from his seat.

"I said I would come, and I always keep my word. I'm sorry I'm late. This far into the country, it was hard to ditch my household guard and find a way out without being noticed. I should warn you that this will probably be the last time we can meet like this for a while."

"I assumed as much. I've seen the men marching south and the building is all most folks can talk about. You've about stripped the country bare of guards and soldiers, although how you convinced the king to part with his precious cutthroats I'll never know."

"I wouldn't call them all cutthroats, but he had little choice. Your protests may be difficult for him to manage, but they would pale in comparison to what would happen if we didn't stand in the way of what the maw will be spewing onto our shores. Faced with a choice between unrest and total destruction, even the king has to make the obvious choice."

"Well, I appreciate you taking the time to meet with me with all that going on. You've already done more for us than we could've hoped. Those supplies you sent, they've been a godsend. With you being gone through the winter, shouldn't you put us in contact with some of the others you're working with?"

"No. I'm sorry, and I know it seems that it would be better if you had access to more of the network, but these are delicate negotiations. Not everyone providing supplies is thrilled with the more aggressive tactics you are using. I'm not judging you, and I agree they are needed, but it requires finesse to convince some of our backers, and the more access they have to information, the less likely they are to give. I know it's difficult, in the scenario we find ourselves, to ask you to trust me, but it is, unfortunately, all I have to offer."

"Of course I trust you, Your Grace. I'm not trying to sound ungrateful or asking for more than you're willing to provide, I'm just worried that, with you gone, the support might dry up just when we're getting close."

"I won't let that happen, Tom. I've already set up cutouts and associates to facilitate getting everything you need when I'm not around. The supplies will keep flowing. I promise."

"I'm glad of it. We've been pushing toward the capital from every direction, faster now that you've pulled most of the king's retainers away. We're squeezing in on Starhaven Bay. If things continue, we'll have the city isolated within the month, then we can finally take the fight to the king himself."

"Remember what this is all about, Tom," Aldric warned. "You're not here to fight the king."

"What do you mean? Isn't that the whole point of this? To make the king bow to reason and change his ways?"

"Yes, that is the point, but it's a difficult one to make right. These things can easily get out of hand and go too far. Yes, we want to force change, but we do not want to overthrow the monarchy. The king's new laws have placed a heavy burden on the people, one I hope to remove, but there are worse outcomes for the people than living with the edicts on travel. If the monarchy were to fall, or be damaged to the point of true weakness, it could lead to even greater upheaval. There are many people outside our kingdom who would like nothing more than to see Sidor crumble so they could pick our bones, and many inside of it who would help them. If the crown becomes too weak to hold the kingdom together, they will swarm like vultures. The very people you're trying to help could end up suffering more than if you had done nothing at all."

"I see your point, Your Grace," Fletcher said, sitting back in his chair and contemplating. "We'll be careful. The people, they're upset, but they know what we're really doing this for. It's not about power, it's about justice."

"Good. Remember that and remember that real change takes time. Just getting the edicts reversed won't solve everyone's problems. Patience is the key to victory."

"I won't let you down, Your Grace. I won't let the people down," Fletcher said solemnly.

Aldric was about to respond when a noise outside the farmhouse caught his attention. The sounds of men on horses and men in armor.

Fletcher shot out of his seat, a hand going to his sword, until Aldric stopped him, placing a hand over Fletcher's and keeping the weapon in its sheath. Pressing a finger to his lips, Aldric moved to the shuttered window, peeking through a small opening.

Outside were a dozen men in the livery of the Starhaven city watch. An unusual sight this far from the capital, and well outside of their normal purview.

"Start searching the houses," a man wearing the insignia of a captain of the guard commanded, sending his men sliding off their horses to carry out his orders.

"Let me handle this," Aldric whispered to Fletcher. "Stay here and stay quiet."

Fletcher looked like he wanted to argue, but only nodded, stepping further back into the room, away from the windows and sources of light. Checking to make sure Fletcher couldn't be seen, Aldric pulled the door open and walked out of the house, head held high and shoulders back.

"Captain. What is happening here?"

"Your Grace," the very startled guardsman said, his jaw dropping slightly at the sudden appearance of one of the highest members of the Sidorian peerage. "What are you doing here?"

Aldric raised an eyebrow. "Are you seriously asking a duke to explain himself?"

"No, Your Grace. Apologies. I was just … surprised to see you outside of the capital or your duchy."

"I am on my way south to oversee preparations for the maw season. It's been a long ride, and I needed to rest for the night. These people were kind enough to take me in. Speaking of being in unexpected places, you are very far from Starhaven. What is the city guard doing in Shadowhold?"

"The king dispatched us to track down the leaders of the rebellion. We have reports that one of their leaders is in the area."

"Good. The sooner this foolish rebellion is quashed, and the kingdom can regain some peace, the better."

"Agreed, Your Grace," the captain said. "I am very sorry to have disturbed you. We will search these buildings quickly and be away."

Aldric looked at the building behind him and then back to the captain, "Do you really think I am hiding the leader of a rebellion that is trying to overthrow my own nephew and House Whitton?"

The captain paled. "No, Your Grace! Of course not!"

"Then you can assume I am the only one here," Aldric said firmly. "Now, go do your duty elsewhere. I need my rest, and I'd rather not be disturbed further."

The captain bowed hastily. "Yes, Your Grace. Apologies again for the intrusion. Men! Mount up!"

Aldric watched as the guards swung back into their saddles and rode off, waiting until the sound of hoofbeats had faded before turning back to the farmhouse.

That was too close.

Starhaven, Sidor

Edmund passed in front of the window to his chambers as his servants prepared the room for the evening, lighting a fire in the hearth and padding the bedding for that night's rest. He ignored them, keeping his eyes locked on the high window as he cut a line back and forth across the thick rug, his impatience in full view.

A light came on in the courtyard below. It was small, a lantern uncovered near one of the far sections of the wall, and only for a moment before being hooded again. Then it reappeared, finishing the pattern two more times before darkening for good.

"Leave me. All of you," Edmund said, turning from the window finally.

His servants, who were used to him and his foibles, bowed and filed out, the last one closing the door softly. Edmund crossed the room and locked the door, to ensure his privacy, before resuming his pacing across a new stretch of the room. Each step became more agitated as he crossed back and forth in front of the large bed.

Finally, he heard it. A click of a latch being worked, but not from the door. This came from a bare section of wall between a large bookcase and a tapestry. The section swung inward without a sound, showing only a dark void inside. A moment later, his scribe, Orlan, and a man in a dark cloak that covered his face came through the doorway, Orlan looking around to ensure the coast was clear.

Of course, if it wasn't, both the man and the door would have been revealed, but his scribe was needed more for his loyalty than his brains.

"Were you seen?" Edmund asked.

"No, Your Grace," Orlan said.

301

"Good. Wait below and keep watch to ensure we are not disturbed. When he returns to you, see that you aren't seen as he leaves the city."

"Of course, Your Grace," Orlan said, bowing deeply before melting back into the darkness.

"I trust you have good news for me," Edmund said as Orlan left.

The messenger reached into his cloak and withdrew a small pouch, tossing it to Edmund, who caught it and then looked at it as if the pouch were a dead rat instead.

"What is this? He promised shiploads, not … this. How am I to hire Werna or Inos mercenaries with this?"

"That is equal to what you have provided. No more. My master's demands have not been met. Until the Sidorian armies are withdrawn, that is all there is."

"Tell your master I'm working on it. It's not as simple as waving my hand and making it so. Anything too overt will raise suspicions and make things more difficult," Edmund said angrily, beginning to pace again. "It doesn't help that your master has been pushing his allies to increase harassment and raiding on the borders. It's distracting me from the task at hand."

"From what I hear, border raids are the least of Sidor's problems," the messenger said, his head slowly turning to follow the path of Edmund's travel, but otherwise unmoved. "Regardless, the agreement you have with my master hinges on removing the armies and bringing them home. Any difficulties in doing so are yours to solve, not ours."

Edmund stopped pacing and turned to glare at the man. "I'm working on it. Tell your master that I will soon have an excuse to recall the men. As it is, I've already been choking their supplies, slowing their advance. That should count for something."

"Then your efforts are insufficient. Our men continue to die and our cities continue to fall. Now your armies are stripping our farmland in the middle of harvest season. They grow fat on stolen grain and livestock. They eat well while our people starve."

"That isn't my problem. I can only promise what is within my control. If your lord cannot protect his own supplies, then perhaps he is unfit to keep his lands."

"Then perhaps I should tell my master there is no need for this partnership at all," the messenger said, finally showing some sign of emotion in his voice.

"I only point out the reality of the situation. I can't order my people to just stand aside and not fight. Not and remain in a position to offer any help. All I can do is limit what is available to them. I will see what I can do to further limit them. That is the best I can do."

"And what of your promise to bring them home?"

"Again, it isn't that simple. The people hold my late brother in high regard and see this war as his legacy. If I bring them home, especially on the heels of victory, it will raise suspicions. I must have a pretext. If your men could counter them, even cause them to suffer some defeats, then I would have a pretext. Otherwise," Edmund said, and then held his hands up in a 'there's nothing I can do' gesture.

"We will do what we can, but once our armies begin achieving victories in the field, there would seem to be no need for this partnership anymore. It is on you to find a pretext in spite of their victories. And quickly. My master's patience grows thin. Our agreement was clear. Remove the Sidorian threat, and you will have our support."

"And I will have it done, but I need more time. And more importantly, I need more resources. The funds you've provided thus far are a pittance compared to what I require."

The messenger regarded Edmund for a long moment, his face unreadable beneath the shadows of his hood. "I will pass your message to my master, but I must warn you, if things do not show marked improvement soon, he may be forced to seek out other allies who are also looking to gain advantage in Sidor now that your brother is gone."

Edmund's eyes narrowed. "What are you talking about? What other allies?"

"There are always those who see opportunity in times of up-heaval. With a young, untested king on the throne, some may see this as a chance to … negotiate a better arrangement for them-selves."

"Anyone else would have no access to the king," Edmund scoffed. "They would have to rebel openly, and then where would they be? If word got out that your master was supporting them, it would only fuel more public support for the war to continue. The people would demand retribution."

"Perhaps," the messenger said, his voice maddeningly calm. "But desperation can drive men to take risks they normally wouldn't. And if those men happen to be powerful barons with armies of their own ... well, let's just say the future is often hard to see clearly, even for those with the gift of foresight."

Edmund clenched his fists at his side, fighting with all his might to control himself. Throttling this man for his insolence would feel good, but it would not help him. He needed to be smart, to play this carefully.

"I understand your master's concerns," he said, his voice barely controlled. "But I assure you, I am the only one in a position to give him what he wants. Anyone else would just be blowing smoke. I have the king's ear. I can make this happen. I just need a little more time."

"I will convey your assurances to my master. But I would advise you not to take too much more time. Patience, like loyalty, has its limits."

With that, the messenger turned and slipped back through the hidden door, disappearing into the darkness beyond, Edmund staring after him.

Was it a bluff? A ploy to try to force his hand? Were they already dealing with some of the barons to double-play him? A civil war would serve their purposes better than even just having the armies withdrawn, since they couldn't stay in the event of outright war at home, and the end result would be a weaker Sidor. They had to know that was foolish, though.

It was also exactly how their emperor operated.

Havensport, Barony of Penleigh, Duchy of Kingsheart, Sidor

The bitter chill off the bay cut through Taran Bramwell's cloak as he led his men up the tradesway, away from the docks and into the heart of Havensport. Even for the final day of fall, it was unusually cold; a portent of a particularly violent maw season, if one was to believe the superstitious types. Bramwell wasn't one of those, but he had still sent out orders to the Gates, the two forts protecting the mouth of Starhaven Bay, to make sure they had already put up the chains and netting to block anything from entering the bay from the straits. It was standard procedure, but it was better than to assume it was done.

It had been on his mind anyway, as those preparations were the source of his current problem.

With the connection to Leviathan Straits and the greater seas now cut off, the bay that supplied the capital was now reliant on the ports that dotted Starhaven Bay for its supplies, all of which were now in the hands of the rebels, with the exception of Havensport. He'd moved his flag to the port a week ago, after the last of the remaining large ports fell, partially to ensure it stayed open and partially to avoid finally being stabbed during one of the king's rages, which had been growing in intensity the closer the rebels got.

He'd promised the duke and the king that he would hold Havensport at all costs. He had little choice. Although some of the smaller villages on the bay could still supply goods, none could send enough to keep the massive city at the heart of the bay fed. As it was, Havensport was straining to bear the weight of what was needed, with ships continuously sailing the short distance to the capital and back every day.

Bramwell also wasn't sure how he was going to keep his promise. They had stripped half his guards, sending them out into the kingdom to track down and fight the rebels. That had been bad enough when he'd only needed to keep control of the city, but another large contingent was sent to the Gates for the season, and even more were pulled and sent to the army Duke Aldric was building in Shadowhold. He'd had to abandon all of Starhaven save the port, the main thoroughfare, and the palace tier in order to properly defend those three. The nobles had been forced to hire toughs from the city to protect their homes and the lower peasants tier had fallen into complete chaos.

That left just under one hundred guardsmen to hold all of Havensport from what he'd heard was thousands of well-armed peasants. Bramwell was determined to do his duty, but the odds were not good. The people of Havensport knew it as well as he did and the streets were all but deserted except for the traders heading to and from the docks.

Or maybe it was just because of what day it was. Tonight was Sorrow's Night, the last evening before the beginning of the season, where families gathered for quiet celebration. A last time together before the long winter. Of course, ever since Sidor unified, its armies had deployed to protect the homeland from the horrors unleashed by the maw, so it was unlikely many this far north would lose people to the creatures. But people clung to tradition, and this was one of the oldest dating back to the first years after the fall, and one of the few celebrated across all countries, even in heretical Thay.

All of which meant, it was traditionally a night when everyone stayed home. So maybe that was why it was quiet, and not the fear of an upcoming attack.

As he thought that, he realized it had suddenly grown even quieter. For weeks, the merchants and drovers had come down the tradesway night and day, dropping off loads at the docks, and yet as they pushed closer to the center of town, he realized he hadn't seen a wagon or anything else in almost ten minutes.

Even for Sorrow's Night, that was unusual. He opened his mouth to order his men to heighten their vigilance when the first arrow whizzed past his ear, embedding itself in the neck of the man to his right.

Chaos erupted as a swarm of figures burst from the alleyways and around the corners of the surrounding buildings, all well-armed and some even in simple armor. Bramwell barely had time to draw his blade before they were on him and his men.

"Form up!" he ordered. "Defensive circle, now!"

His men were well-armored and on armored horses, but if they were swarmed individually, without support, it would take short work to pull them all from their saddles and kill them. Already he could see the men on the edges of his force suffering just that fate, the tide of attackers so overwhelming they couldn't swing their weapons fast enough to prevent being unhorsed.

As city guards, his men were well-trained for specifically this situation and reacted instantly, pulling their horses into a tight formation, each man covering the one next to him. But the rebels fought ferociously and continued to swarm out of the darkened lanes between the buildings, their numbers seemingly unending. His men were pressed from all sides.

Bramwell's men did well, cutting their attackers down again and again, piling up the bodies. It was not enough.

One by one his men fell, pulled from their horses and slaughtered. Bramwell pushed into the battle with his guardsmen, fighting like a man possessed, hacking and slashing as fast as he could swing his sword, each stroke killing another attacker. But for each one he struck down, two more rushed forward to take their place.

"Stand fast!" he roared. "For Sidor and the king!"

Suddenly, a spear took Bramwell's horse in the throat, sending him and the animal crashing to the ground. Bramwell rolled clear and came up swinging, his blade taking the spearman in the gut.

He whirled to face the next attacker, a burly man wielding a heavy axe. Their weapons clashed, the impact sending shockwaves up Bramwell's arm. He gritted his teeth and shoved the man back, then followed up with a riposte that caught his opponent under the chin.

There wasn't a moment to breathe. Even as that man fell, another rebel slipped past Bramwell's guard, their blade scoring a deep gash along his ribs. Bramwell grunted in pain but kept fighting.

His men had been forced back against the walls of the surrounding buildings, almost all of them off their horses, either pulled down or the beasts killed. They were fighting desperately to hold their ground. His ninety-eight men were now only a handful as, one by one, they fell.

"To me!" he yelled, seeing the men getting separated and made easier targets. "Rally to me!"

The survivors tried to fight their way to his side, but the rebels cut them off, surrounding them in smaller and smaller circles until they were completely overwhelmed.

He killed two more men, but not before paying the price of another injury. Blood poured from a dozen wounds, and his vision was starting to blur. He knew he couldn't last much longer, but he refused to go down easily.

He stabbed out, skewering another man, bellowing with rage when a heavy blow caught him on the side of the head, sending him reeling. Another slammed into his sword arm, numbing it to the elbow.

Bramwell staggered back, his weapon falling from nerveless fingers. A sword found him, stabbing into his side. Then another, into his stomach. And then a third. The captain's legs went weak, his knees buckling, sending him to the ground, his head banging off the hard stone.

Bramwell lay on his back, the cold stone leaching the remaining warmth from his broken body. Blood bubbled at his lips with each labored breath. He watched, vision blurred, as the rebels stripped his men of their weapons and armor, not even sparing a glance at the dying man at their feet.

Feet stopped near his head. Bramwell's vision was fading, blackness creeping in along the edges. He had to focus hard to make out the face of the person standing over him. There was something about the man that struck Bramwell as familiar. He'd seen, not the man, but his likeness before. His brain was growing foggy, making it harder to remember.

And then it struck him. He had seen the man before, or at least drawings of him based on rough descriptions given by captured rebels and injured king's men. This was, supposedly, the leader of the rebels. It struck Bramwell as odd, in that moment. They had his picture, but no one had his name.

Why hadn't they found his name?

"Secure the docks! I want every ship searched and every warehouse locked down. This is their last port. Nothing else goes to the city without our say-so. They'll have to either negotiate ... or starve."

The man only stopped there for a moment, barking orders, sending men running this way and that, before he was off, heading toward the town center with a large group of men.

As the sounds of the rebels faded, Bramwell felt a strange sense of peace settle over him. He had failed in his duty, yes, but he had fought to the end. He had given everything for his king and his kingdom.

At least the king couldn't yell at him anymore.

Chapter 29

Cestralion, Aurorin Province, Lynese

William stood on the balcony of the viceroy's keep, looking out over the city of Cestralion. Although snow hadn't started to fall yet, there was a notable chill in the air, helpfully marking the first day of winter. The city bustled with activity, people going about their daily lives despite the cold and the occupation by Sidorian forces.

That part, at least, had gone well. William's biggest concern over the negotiated surrender was that the people would still have defiance left in them and push back against their occupiers. Amazingly, they'd adjusted relatively well. There had been a few contentious spots, and he'd maintained pretty rigorous patrols, but he'd also made sure all of his officers knew to come down hard on anyone who abused or took advantage of the locals, which would be the surest way to turn this into a problem.

Cestralion would be their home for the foreseeable future, and the last thing they needed was civil unrest all winter.

"My Prince, if we could continue," Pembroke called from inside.

William gave one last look at the city, his biggest achievement to date, a real, tangible trophy, before going back inside, where Pembroke was still seated at the long table the viceroy had used for entertaining.

"As I was saying, with winter here and the first snows most likely to start within the next few weeks, I recommend we hold our position here. We've managed to secure enough of the harvest and ransom payments from the Lynese that our supply situation is good; we have strong fortifications to operate from, and complete control of the entire Rendalia province. If we handle things correctly, we will have enough resources to last through the winter and cover at least half of next year's campaign, solving most of our problems from this campaign season. I am concerned that if we continue to operate aggressively, we will burn through our resources now, leaving us unable to hold onto any new gains we do make and giving the Lynesians an advantage when they do bring their forces back from the coast once winter ends."

"We'll stop soon," William said. "I'm concerned we aren't as secure as we'd like to think we are."

"How so?"

"Our supply lines are still too long. I know we're mostly relying on captured supplies at this point, but Aldric is trying to get that fixed, and I have hope that he will do so by the spring, when it's time to begin the campaign again. When he does, I want us to be prepared for it, and the smaller ports we've captured, like Port Belmar, are just too small to do the job."

"True, but we can work on expanding their capacity over the winter. It's not ideal, but it's manageable."

"I'm not so certain we can get the capacity where it needs to be, and that is only one concern," William said, shaking his head. "We are still open to attack by river from the north and south, which will make us weak during next year's campaigning season."

"While it could be better, I would argue our stance right now is still fairly good. We have patrols along the Dead Man's Hills, and they already saw how easily we defeated the last group that tried to attack through there, and the Lysmir Woods are well within reach of here. Between Cestralion and Rendalia City, we have both ends of the province, giving us a strong position for defense."

"It could be better and the Lynesians will not sit still come the spring. I want to get us prepared for that by controlling at least from here north through Lake Lysmir to the sea. Which is why I want Barentez, the port at the mouth of the Lysmir River. It would give us control of most of the northern coast, with the exception of Uvengati Bay."

"Crossing the river there would be no easy task," Pembroke said, pointing to the map spread on the table in front of them and tracing a line from Cestralion to Barentez. "The Lynesians could easily contest our landing on the other side. We would need to cross south of Lysmir Lake and march north, exposed to attack the entire way. They have an army in Talabot to the west that could march in time to either intercept us or break any siege of the city we set up. They've been limited by our partial control of the river so far, but if we attack Barentez, we will be the ones in the weaker position on the wrong side."

"That is all true. There are, however, considerations in favor of this," William pointed out. "Barentez itself is lightly defended at the moment, having sent most of its garrison to bolster the forces in the Lysmir Woods in anticipation of our advance. Men who we either just ransomed or are sitting in our prison camps. With everything that's going on in the southeast, I don't think they will reinforce until spring. From the reports I've seen, other than keeping a garrison on hand and the walls lightly manned, they aren't doing much, and no one from Talabot has shifted to Barentez in preparation for an attack. I don't think they expect us to do anything before spring either."

"But you want to do something? How do you plan on taking the city without losing a large number of our men? Men that, I should remind you, will probably not be replaced from home anytime soon."

"I'm not planning on taking a big risk. In fact, I have a plan that might work. It's risky, but if we pull it off, we could take Barentez with a relatively small force and secure the city before Talabot even realizes what's happening."

"Really?" Pembroke said, leaning forward. "Tell me more?"

Starhaven, Sidor

Edmund stood next to the king on the balcony of his personal study, watching the crowds below. Hundreds of people, maybe thousands, swarmed the gates, pushing them with enough force to cause the thick metal to shake and bend. Edmund couldn't see the faces of the few guards still in the closed courtyard below, but he could imagine the fear they felt.

Even looking down on them from above, everything about the guards looked anxious, worried. And they were right to be. Before he got the remaining guard in the city pulled back to the palace, several had been literally ripped apart by the angry mobs as the peasant tier rose up in a giant, violent force, storming the merchant tier and the docks, taking anything that wasn't nailed down.

Those merchants and nobles smart enough and with a few guards had managed to seal themselves up in their homes, like small islands in a violent sea. The rest had become chum for the starving masses.

It had been fifteen days since the last shipment of food to the city, after three weeks of reduced shipments as ports fell to the rebels, which had left the city in incredibly short supply when the food stopped coming at all. By day three, people were hungry and angry, with fights and violent conflicts over stolen food on the rise. By day five, most of the smartest had taken the last ships out, choosing to take the chance of being captured by the rebels surrounding Starhaven Bay or hoping to swim across it into the wilderness, running for their lives.

The riot itself started on day ten, when a group of protesters ran into some of the last guards trying to hold the market square. Things had gotten out of hand and a few peasants were killed, sending the rest of the city into a bloodthirsty rage. Half the guards in the market quarter had died, swarmed by men and women ready to lash out at anything they could over their current state. For the last five days, they had been trapped in the palace, eating through the stores in the sub-basements, waiting to see which would go first, their food or the gates to the palace.

It was only a matter of time.

"It's time to negotiate with the rebels," Edmund said, turning to Serwyn, who was busy glaring at the crowd, silently trying to will them all to drop dead.

"Absolutely not!" Serwyn slammed his fist on the balcony railing, his face twisted in rage. "I want the guard sent out to slaughter every last person daring to attack the palace."

"You know that's not possible. We barely have enough guards left to keep the palace from being overrun."

Serwyn whirled on him, red in the face and nostrils flaring. "Then bring back the army that Aldric put together and marched to Shadowhold. He has thirty thousand men. They could easily crush the rebels holding the port and end this damnable revolt."

"That isn't possible either, Serwyn. The Maw has already opened, and the assault on our southern shores has started again. If we were to pull the army there back, the creatures would ravage the south, maybe even through River Mark and into Kingshold itself. We would lose a full duchy for a generation, and maybe half the kingdom, which would be the end for us. Even if they didn't, to give away Shadowhold would make the rebellion exponentially worse. Right now, the rebels are just peasants, but if we allow the Chaosborn to ravage the country, the rest of the people, including knights and barons, will rise up. The result would be the same as if we just wait to starve here."

"This is unacceptable! I am the king, and they dare defy me? I'll have their heads on spikes!"

Serwyn was working himself into a fit of rage that threatened to overwhelm even what little reason he had. Edmund needed him to get it together, or they were doomed. Grabbing him by the shoulders, Edmund spun him around and held him tight, meeting his furious eyes with anger of his own. It was a gamble, but only a minor one. Most of the guards who'd made it back to the palace were more loyal to Edmund than they were to the king, who had terrorized them since he was little. It was still a risk, but Edmund needed the boy to snap out of it.

"Serwyn," he said, shaking the boy hard. "Get a grip. You need to listen to reason, and you need to do it now, or we're all dead. You are the king, and it's time to act like it. I know how infuriating this is, but being a ruler means making difficult decisions, even if it means accepting a temporary setback."

Serwyn tried to jerk away, but Edmund held him in place. "I will not bow to the demands of rebels and traitors!"

"Do you want to die? Do you want these people, this mob, to rip the gates down and tear you limb from limb? I love you, boy, but you need to get it together right now, before it's too late. Are you ready to give up your crown to these people?"

Edmund wasn't sure which part of that got through to him, but Serwyn stopped fighting, almost sagging as he weakly said, "No. I want to be king."

"Good. That's good. Now, it's time to understand that a wise king does what needs to be done for the greater good of the kingdom. Sometimes, you must take a step back before you can move forward. I know you are a wise king, Serwyn. You have the potential to be one of the greatest rulers Sidor has ever known, but only if you learn to make the hard choices."

"What would you have me do, Uncle?" a defeated Serwyn said.

"Negotiate. Even the rebels have yet to call for your head or crown, so there is room to make this work. We will have to repeal the Edicts of Travel. It will strengthen the barons, who will see this as a victory, but we have no other choice. There are other ways to deal with the barons and the peasants who defied us, but we must do so from a position of strength. Offer to put things back to how they were."

"They'll see that as a victory. It will open the door to more demands. To thinking they can stand up to us every time things go wrong."

"Some will, it's true. Others will just be happy it's over and want to go back to their lives. It will buy us time. Time to bring the armies back from Lynese, fortify our position, and we can deal with the traitors then. It's our only real option. We have only three paths before us: Negotiate, giving the rebels the minimum of what they want, recall the army in Shadowhold and allow the kingdom to fall to the Chaosborn, or do nothing and die from starvation or the mob. The choice is yours, Serwyn. I know you'll choose wisely."

Serwyn pulled out of Edmund's grip and turned, leaning against the railing, watching the crowds screaming and pushing the fences below.

"Fine," he said in almost a whisper. "We'll negotiate."

"A wise choice, Your Majesty. Unpleasant, but wise."

"Send word to whoever is leading the rebels holding the ports. Express our willingness to negotiate if they resume food shipments and assist in quelling unrest in the city. We will guarantee safe passage."

"I'll see to it, Your Majesty," Edmund said, bowing and backing away.

He left quickly to carry out the orders, before the boy could work himself up again and change his mind. There would be far-reaching repercussions to this. The only question was if they could end up on the right side of them.

Port of Barentez, Desmonte Province, Lynese

Juelle Villant, standing in the center of the docks he had called home for twenty years, watched his domain proudly. It was very slow, with only two ships in the harbor at the moment, but that was to be expected. A life on the wharves meant he didn't need the puff of misty breath that came out each time he breathed to tell him what season it was.

Even for winter, though, it was slow. Aside from the small amount of traffic from the south, most years, they would have ships that would brave skimming the coast from Rendalia City or one of the ports on Uvegati Bay, braving the horrors of the Maw to try and eke out a little more profit. Not that it was so dangerous. The Merchants Sea got much less of the creatures than the Sea of Kings or the straights between Sidor and Lynese. Still enough to make sailing the sea itself unwise, but they usually only lost a handful of the ships that tried to hug the coast.

That was before they lost Rendalia and Sidorian ships began to sit near the mouth of the Lysmir River, all but drying up their traffic just as winter set in. He would be glad to have this war done with, so his docks could get back to work.

Still, it afforded him something he hadn't taken in almost five years. A vacation.

"Looks like we'll have a long winter ahead of us, Marien," Juelle said, glancing at his assistant. "With the port all but shut down, I'm thinking of heading to Talabot for a while, get some time away from watching this sad excuse for a wharf."

Marien Delar, a wiry young man with a shock of red hair, shrugged.

"Might not be a bad idea, sir. Even the north-bound traffic is all but done, what with the Sidorians in Cestralion. We only had two ships make it through yesterday," Delar said, pointing at the two Lynesian-flagged ships currently sitting in harbor. "I suppose I can handle things here while you're gone. Not much for a dockmaster to do when the ships are few and far between."

"Oh, so you think you can manage without me? Are those four ships that just came out of Lake Lysmir going to unload themselves?" Juelle asked, holding back a smile and trying for a peeved look instead.

Marien saw through him. The boy had worked for him for ten years, making his way up through the ranks, and knew his boss's teasing well.

"I didn't mean it like that, sir," the assistant said, holding up his hands in mock surrender.

Juelle clapped the younger man on the shoulder, chuckling. "Relax, lad. I know what you meant. And I appreciate you holding down the fort in my absence."

"Of course, sir. You can count on me."

"I know I can," Juelle said, his tone turning serious. "These are troubled times, Marien. War, winter, and who knows what else lurking on the horizon. We've got to stick together, watch out for each other. Let's get those ships docked and unloaded. The sooner we're done, the sooner I can be on my way."

"Right away, sir," Marien said, hurrying off to rally the dock-workers and get them to where the four ships were pulling into port.

'He's a good lad,' Juelle thought, watching him work. 'He'll make a fine dockmaster one day, once the powers that be decide to let me retire for good.'

The four ships were the classic river transports. Sitting much higher in the water with a much smaller sail plan, they would swamp easily if ever allowed out on the seas, but did a good job making it up and down the river that started at this end, went through Dawnstar Lake, and all the way out the southern end of the continent at Gray Harbor.

He was just starting to join Marien and the others, to look over the boys' shoulders and make sure they had no problems, when a shout pulled him up short. It took a moment for his brain to recognize what was happening. The sailors who'd been manning the ship had disappeared and suddenly, without warning, a swarm of Sidorians came spilling over the side of the ships, tearing their way through everything in their path.

In horror, he watched young Marien get cut down, a sword slashing through him, sending the red-haired boy tumbling over the side of the dock. On and on the Sidorians poured from the ships, a seemingly endless supply of them. The few guards on the docks, there mostly to deal with the occasional brawl and scuffle between rowdy dockhands, fell quickly, most not even putting up a fight.

"Run," he yelled to the men still far enough back. "Into the city. Run!"

He didn't wait to see if they did. The Sidorians were charging forward and would be on him in moments. Villant was unarmed and wouldn't have survived even if he had been. He was no warrior, and he knew it. He turned and ran as fast as his legs could carry him, pushing through the mostly quiet city, still waking up and starting the day.

Behind him, he could hear screams and shouts as people who didn't realize what was happening were set upon by the Sidorian monsters. Villant couldn't spend a moment looking back at them. The best he could do was to shout to run as he passed by, but most were so surprised they stood there in horror trying to understand what was happening until the moment they were struck down.

Not all ignored him. Rounding a corner, he nearly collided with a woman carrying a basket of bread. She yelped in surprise, the loaves tumbling to the ground.

"Run," Villant gasped, not stopping to help her. "The Sidorians are coming."

The woman's eyes widened in terror, and she abandoned her fallen goods, fleeing in the opposite direction.

Villant continued his desperate sprint, weaving through the narrow streets. He could see Sir Santil's keep ahead, towering above the nearby houses. He and his knights had been given sovereignty over the city in exchange for their protection, and Villant understood the need for that now, more than ever. Other than the men on the city walls and the handful of city guards, they were the only people in Barentez capable of dealing with the horde swarming their city.

The shouts and screams were starting to pick up as more and more people encountered the enemy. Enough that it must have been audible even in the keep, as the gates to the compound surrounding the building swung open just as Villant arrived, and Sir Esmond Santil and a handful of his retainers stepped out.

"My lord," Villant cried, stumbling to a halt before the knight. "We're under attack. The Sidorians, they've breached the city."

"What?" the shocked knight asked. "How did they get past the wall? Why was an alarm not sounded?"

"They came on ships, disguised as merchants. They slaughtered the dockworkers and guards before anyone realized what was happening."

The knight cursed under his breath. "How many?"

Before Villant could answer, screams and the thundering of dozens of boots pounding against stone came from behind him. Spinning around, Villant saw the Sidorians, who had been on his heels, flooding the open plaza in front of the keep's gates, a sea of steel and grim faces charging at them.

Grabbing him, Sir Santil pushed Villant hard behind him, sending the dockmaster crashing into the stone wall surrounding the keep, as he pulled his sword.

The Sidorians overwhelmed the knight's retainers, outnumbering them three to one. Sir Santil showed how he achieved such a high position, fighting valiantly, cutting down two of the Sidorians with fluid strikes.

Villant slid to the ground, wrapping his arms around his legs, terrified. The Sidorians were everywhere, cutting down anyone that ran within range of their blades. Villant felt completely paralyzed.

In the middle of the Sidorians was a young man with short brown hair, no more than sixteen or seventeen, and wearing fancy armor, shouting orders to the men around him. Even Villant could see the boy was some kind of lordling in charge of this attack, and Sir Santil wasted no time, ignoring the other Sidorians he charged right for him.

The young man brought up his sword, deflecting Santil's attack, parrying it and counterattacking so fast that Villant was surprised the knight stopped the blow. Both were incredibly fast, and Villant was having trouble following the movement of their blades as metal met metal again and again. For a moment, it seemed like they might be at a stalemate, and then Santil took a high swing that would have taken off the young man's head, had he not ducked under it. In a lightning-fast counter, the young man's sword came up, inside Santil's guard, his blade finding a gap between helm and breastplate.

Sir Santil stiffened, his eyes going wide as the young man's sword punched through his throat. He staggered back, blood fountaining from the wound, and collapsed to the ground.

The young man didn't pause, already moving to engage the next foe. His men swarmed over the remaining retainers like ants over a carcass, until all of the armed men around the keep were dead. A few Sidorians lay with them, but not nearly enough as the enemy continued to flow past the keep and further into the city.

In the middle of the chaos, only a few feet from where Villant sat on the ground, stood the brown-haired noble, his sword and armor streaked with blood.

A group of older men came running up to him. They spoke in Sidorian, a language Villant understood well enough from his years dealing with merchants, many of whom had been Sidorian before the war.

"My Prince, we've secured the docks and the southern half of the city."

"Excellent," the young lordling said, before turning to the larger of the men. "Sir Drummond, move your knights forward quickly. Get to the walls while the enemy is still surprised. It's imperative that you take the guard houses and barracks before they can rally. Don't slow for anything, including taking prisoners. Do what you have to do."

"Understood, My Prince," the large man said, sprinting off without another word, waving a large group of men to follow him west, toward the city walls.

The boy didn't stop. As soon as the large man left, he turned to one of the other men with him and said, "Commander Baldwin, check the keep. Make sure there are no more soldiers hiding within."

Orders given, the boy paused, looking over the courtyard scattered with bodies. For a moment, his eyes met Villant's, and the dockmaster's body froze up, fearful of what might happen. He was the only uninjured Lynesian in the square, and feared what might become of him.

But the moment passed as quickly as it had come. The young man looked away, seemingly dismissing Villant as unimportant.

Instead, he said to the other men standing with him, "Come with me."

Without another word, the boy turned and ran deeper into the city, his chosen men following close behind. Villant remained where he was, listening to the fading shouts and screams as the Sidorians tore through his city, hearing the moans and cries of the injured and dying around him. His legs refused to obey him, to take him away from here.

He could only listen as his city fell.

Chapter 30

Starhaven, Sidor

The grounds outside the palace were covered in people, more than even the largest celebrations the capital had ever seen. People had held their place for ten long hours, no one wanting to leave lest they miss what was happening. The leaders of the rebellion had gone inside to negotiate with the king to finally end the conflict.

The very city itself was holding its breath. Although the rebels had allowed a trickle of food shipments to resume, Starhaven was no more than a day from starvation again and would be until the rebels gave up their captured ports and went home. The people's tier had finally ended its rioting and settled down after ten days of mayhem, but the city was a wreck and would bear the scars of this time for years to come. The merchants' tier, the docks, and even some of the nobles' tier had significant damage to buildings, and the loss of life had not been limited to any one of them.

Which is why so many were willing to wait, hour after hour, to find out if the rebellion had really ended. When Fletcher and the handful of men with him finally emerged, the crowd exploded with cheers.

Fletcher waved them down, finding a cart to pull himself up onto so the people could see him. Guards, some still bearing injuries from the riots, ringed the palace, in case this crowd became violent like so many had recently, but the people ignored them.

The peasants had identified the limits of the guard and had taken much of the fear they generated away from them. The people knew that, if the tyranny grew too be too much to bear, they could rise up again and defeat them.

Tom raised his hands, calling for silence. Slowly, the cheers and shouts died down.

"Friends, I bring you good news. Our wise and just king has heard our pleas. He has agreed to our demands!"

The crowd erupted in cheers, a thunderous roar that echoed off the stone walls. Tom let them have their moment of elation before gesturing for quiet once more.

"The Edicts of Travel have officially been ended. We can now travel freely to sell our goods wherever we see fit, as free people of Sidor. The fines and onerous taxes that accompanied the edicts have likewise been repealed! Furthermore, His Majesty has graciously consented to reduce the additional taxes burdening the common folk, with taxes going back to what they were on the final day of his father's rule. Not only have the taxes been reduced, but the king has also pledged not to raise our taxes so unjustly in the future and has agreed to limit the rate of tax increases for the next ten years."

Another wave of jubilation swept through the throng of people. Men embraced, and women wept tears of joy.

"I know many of you who stood up for your rights have been worried, because to defend the rights given to you by the Ancients, you had to stand up to the laws made by men here in Sidor, sometimes aggressively. It would not do for those who only defended themselves and their families to be punished for doing so, especially after the king himself acknowledged the position these now-canceled laws put us all in. Because of that, the king has agreed to a blanket pardon of anyone who acted in open rebellion against the crown during this period of unrest. That includes those here in the city who demanded food during the shortages and your family members held in the dungeons for protesting the changes, who will be released. I know some of your men were sent to the armies in Lynese, and that will take more time to unravel, but the king has promised to see that justice is done for them as well.

Fletcher could see the relief on the faces of the people around him. The rebellion against the crown had led to violence unseen in

Sidor since the unification under Charles Whitton. Had the crown wanted to, a large number of those involved could have been hung for treason. This agreement hadn't been easy and was one of the parts of the peace agreement that took the longest to debate. The young king had made it clear he thought anyone involved in the rebellion, including Fletcher himself, should be handed over to the crown for punishment. It wasn't until Duke Edmund stepped in that cooler heads prevailed and the king agreed to their demands for amnesty.

"While those are the things we fought for, neither is our biggest accomplishment. I and the other leaders didn't speak about this openly, because it seemed an impossible achievement. Which is why I am so happy to announce it now. His Majesty has agreed to the formation of a council of commoners to sit alongside the council of nobles. Two representatives, chosen by the people, shall be sent from every barony to give voice to the common man in the governance of our great kingdom."

Instead of cheers, a shocked silence fell over the crowd. Never in all of Sidor's history had the common man had a say in his fate. The very idea that commoners would get a voice in how they were governed was so unthinkable that he could see each person having trouble even processing what he'd said.

"The council will be allowed to weigh in on the king's laws, offer advice and counsel, and ... most importantly, have some limiting factor on taxation of the people and how those taxes may be used by the crown. This will, however, take time. We are venturing into uncharted territory. But I am told that the people of Gnestig have a similar system, which may serve as a model for our own. Rest assured, the king is committed to ensuring the people have a say in the fate of the realm."

Tom paused, letting all of that sink in. The idea of using Gnestig, the island nation to the west of Lynese, as a model for their system of government, even in part, hadn't occurred to Fletcher. He hadn't even known that they had a way for people to participate, at least not until Duke Aldric had told him about it and made suggestions when they'd discussed what he should ask the king for in the negotiations. Fletcher had actually been skeptical, at first, that it would even work, which is probably what all of these people were feeling. He trusted the duke, however, and if he thought it a good idea, who was Fletcher to argue?

"Now, let us give thanks to our king for his wisdom, his compassion, and his willingness to listen to the needs of his subjects. Long may he reign!"

"Long may he reign," the people echoed, almost reflexively.

Most probably wouldn't have had the same sentiment just a day ago, even with the long-bred habit of repeating the phrase in honor of their monarch, which showed just how stunned they all were by the sheer scope of what they'd gotten the crown to agree to.

Of course, it went without saying that they had achieved this only because they gave the king no choice in agreeing to their demands.

"And now, my friends, it is time to return to your homes and your lives. Go in peace, knowing that a new era has dawned in Sidor. An era of justice, of equality, and of hope."

Tom hopped down and gathered the men who'd traveled with him. Together they would hand out their last orders. He'd told the king that they wouldn't relinquish the ports, returning to their homes, until he signed the orders and word went out on wyverns to all of the barons.

Already, some had flown, and a decree from the king, stating these changes, had begun going up on the walls around the palace courtyard. It would probably take a week to get the word out across the city and the kingdom, but seeing the first ones go up was what Fletcher had been waiting for.

The rebellion was over.

Edmund watched the rebel leader finish his speech, getting swarmed by the rest of the mob like he was some kind of hero. It was pathetic. They pretended to be on some kind of noble quest for the common man while telling none of their supporters that they were essentially puppets for the very nobles they claimed to stand against. Edmund was sure that was never mentioned to the others.

As the people began to celebrate below, the door to Edmund's quarters burst open and the king stormed in. As angry as Edmund was at how this had turned out, he was a far cry from the level of rage of the king, who was practically fuming, pacing from one side of the room to the other as he vented.

"I can't believe these ... these peasants. I'm supposed to not only sit with them, but they really expect me to listen to their demands? The very idea that this council of commoners would have the right to tell me what to do ..."

"We talked about this, Your Majesty. The council is a shell, nothing more. A bone to throw them to make them happy, let them think they can claim a long-term victory, and to allow us to push the blame for our future decisions to them, insulating you from this kind of reaction in the future. We made no guarantee of how the representatives to this council would be chosen. By the time it goes into effect, most of these people will be back to work and focused on their lives, and we can simply have the barons choose their representatives, ensuring the vast majority are people who unequivocally support you."

"I shouldn't have to take anything to the people, or anyone else, for support. I am the king. THE KING. My people listen to and obey me, not the other way around. I can't believe I let you talk me into this. You and your sycophant barons. You failed me, Uncle."

"Things did not end ideally, I will admit. But ..."

"Ideally? Ideally?" Serwyn interrupted, his voice rising. "This wasn't some minor setback, Uncle. I was forced to sit with those filthy peasants and listen to their demands. To even bend to them, even if just as a gesture, weakens me and strengthens them. This entire situation is how kingdoms fall. I have to ask myself, is this what it felt like when the Ancients fell? Their world turning upside down, everything they knew crumbling around them?"

"Your Majesty, you're being dramatic. The situation is not nearly as dire as ..."

Serwyn rounded on Edmund, jabbing a finger at his chest. "You promised me control, Uncle. You swore that under your guidance, my reign would be unquestioned. Yet look at us now, bowing to the whims of the rabble. Give me one good reason why I shouldn't have you thrown in the dungeons for your failures."

Edmund didn't flinch or step back. "You are the king, Your Majesty. You can do as you wish. But if you had followed your original instinct, to arrest the barons and take their land, we wouldn't have faced a peasant army, we would have faced the barons and their retainers. An army of peasants, even a well-supplied one, is a far cry from that. We both know the real danger lies with the barons. They are the ones behind this rebellion, pulling the strings from the shadows. If you choose to take them on in the open, then you must be willing to accept the consequences of that decision."

"And what would you have me do? Roll over and show my belly like a beaten dog?"

"A good leader understands that in this kind of war reverses sometimes happen. Even your father faced setbacks during his reign. The key is to adapt, to bide our time and play the role of benevolent rulers until we are strong enough to strike back."

"So we let their treason go unpunished?"

"Of course not, Your Majesty. When the time is right, when our position is secure, you can take your revenge. Crush our enemies beneath your heel and remind them of the true power of the crown."

"I want them all to pay, Uncle. Everyone who had a hand in this. The nobles, the rebels, every last one of them. They will learn the price of defying their king."

"And they will, Your Majesty. I promise you that."

"I will hold you to that promise, Uncle," Serwyn said, before turning and storming out with only a little less anger than he'd come in with, probably to go to his room and brood.

Edmund just shook his head and returned to the balcony. Let his nephew rage. Edmund would be patient, waiting for the right opportunity. And that opportunity would come, he thought as he looked down at the peasants once more, eyes falling on their now-unmasked leaders. While he was certain that the barons, or at least some of them, were behind this uprising, he found himself agreeing with Serwyn on one thing.

Those people would pay.

Cestralion, Aurorin Province, Lynese

It had only been a week since William left Cestralion for the assault on Barentez, but the city seemed to have transformed in that time. While it was still an occupied city, more people had come out of their homes, maybe accepting that this was the new normal, making the city feel less abandoned than it had just after it had been taken. Sidorian patrols still wandered the streets, but the people were giving them less of a wide berth.

While the city hadn't taken any damage, since it had surrendered, a lot of public projects had stopped when the Sidorians had put it under siege, which had added to the abandoned, run-down feel. In his absence, those projects had been started again, probably by Pembroke's command. It was a clever way of getting the city operating once more, showing the people there could be a peaceful occupation. And it seemed to be working.

The central keep was still the hub of the Sidorian activity, with most of the city patrols operating out of the bottom floor of the building. William made his way up to the higher levels of the keep, where they had set up a war room just before he'd left for the port assault. Pembroke had expanded it since he was last there, with a large map someone had created of the area, marked with symbols of all of the known Lynesian forces.

This was William's first chance at a more permanent, or at least a long-term, base of operations, instead of working out of command tents that had to be constantly ready to move, and he could see the value of it. It wouldn't be practical to haul something like this around, but being able to so clearly picture the entire area of operation like this would really help in planning the spring campaign.

One of Pembroke's knights, whose name William couldn't remember off the top of his head, was in the room with the baron when William entered, the two in deep conversation.

"Prince William! Welcome back, Your Highness," Pembroke said when he noticed him, and then turned back to the knight. "Take care of it. I want each of them interviewed by tomorrow."

"Problems?" William asked, watching the knight leave quickly.

"No, Your Highness. The city is doing well, but some of the outlying settlements are being ... difficult. We're still trying to honor your promises to the Lynesians, that we wouldn't be unduly burdensome, but it is becoming an issue. I'm hoping that if we can identify the few actual troublemakers, the rest will fall in line. I should offer you congratulations, though. All of the reports from Barentez say that your victory was stunning, with very minimal casualties."

"It went well."

"You took a heavily defended town completely by surprise, securing it before their wintering army could even get news of the attack, let alone do anything to stop you. I'd say that went more than well."

"Thank you," William said. "With it secured, I believe we're in a good position to hold for the winter. With the supplies we do get from home and what we can pull from the provinces we control here, and what can now be delivered to our line by ship from Rendalia City and further up the province, eliminating the need for a long supply line, once the waters open again, giving us a new jump-off point. We should be in a good position, come spring."

"Although we should be careful about that. Barentez gives us complete control of the river, but it is separated from the rest of our line if attacked, meaning reinforcing it will be slower."

"Agreed. While I don't expect that they will try to retake it over the winter, we should keep the river well patrolled and reinforce the garrison there. I left Sir Alistair in command for the time being. We need to use our time well. I'd like to start the campaign just *before* spring, to get the jump on the Lynesians. If we can take Talabot quickly, we will have more of a line to operate from on that side of the river and will be able to make the final push to their capital."

"I'll see it done," Pembroke promised, and then changed the subject. "While you were gone, I received a wyvern from Duke Aldric."

"He responded? Any news on supplies?"

"Only bad news," Pembroke said. "The duke indicated in his letter that he does not believe the king will be sending any more supplies, even come next year when the campaign season begins again. With very little exception, we cannot expect any additional supplies or men from the crown."

"Nothing? How do they expect us to win this war, or even end it short of a full retreat, without supplies?"

"I'm not sure that they do. My only hope is that they are simply distracted by the commoners currently rebelling, although what information I have gotten from other barons over the last few days suggests that is about over."

"It is? How did they defeat a mass uprising like that? It's not like there was one army to defeat or a city to conquer to end it."

"It went the other way. The rebels managed to surround Starhaven Bay itself once Aldric took the bulk of the remaining retainers south for maw season. The king was forced to hold talks with them and reverse some of his policies."

"Really?" William said, pacing in a small circle as he absorbed the news. "That must have been quite a blow to my cousin."

"I imagine it was."

"How did they manage that? While I know people of all types are capable of great things, the rebellion lasted almost six months. That's a long time for people without resources beyond a single farm or workshop to sustain themselves. How did they manage to not only do that but stand up against armored knights? I wouldn't have thought they'd have had the supplies for that."

"Normally, you would be right, but they were not doing it alone. The commoners weren't the only ones upset by the king's policies. A group of nobles has been supplying them for some time, which is what allowed their remarkable success."

"What?" William's voice rose in disbelief. "Sidorian nobles were trying to overthrow the king?"

"No, Your Highness," Pembroke clarified. "The nobles were not trying to overthrow the king. They only wanted him to reverse the wave of new taxes and policies put in place since his rule began. They were given no choice. The king refused to listen to reason, and this was the only way to keep the kingdom from falling into complete chaos. You've seen those results yourself. Do you think, with what you've heard from the 'conscripts' we were sent and the news from home, that the decisions being made for the kingdom were the right ones?"

"I don't," William admitted. "But there is a large gap between disagreeing with the king and outright rebellion."

William stopped for a moment. Something was bothering him, picking at the back of his brain.

"Baron, how do you know what the nobles supporting the rebels were doing? I'd assume any such activity would be secret, to keep the king from retaliating against them. Even if they weren't attempting to overthrow the crown, that kind of activity would be enough to get them thrown in the dungeons and their lands taken from them."

Pembroke met his eyes evenly and said, "Because I am a member of the group of nobles supporting the rebels."

William stared at Pembroke, involuntarily taking a step back. "You ... what?"

"It's just as I said. I am one of the nobles supporting the rebels to force your cousin to end his disastrous policies. What's more, so is your uncle."

"Aldric? No, I can't believe that. He's loyal to the crown, to Sidor. He wouldn't ..."

"Your uncle is loyal to his people, William. He knows what needs to be done to protect them, even if it means defying the king. Neither King Serwyn nor your stepfather would listen to reason. They refused to see the suffering their policies were causing. Aldric had no choice but to take matters into his own hands."

William started to respond, and then stopped. He had so many questions, but a single realization put them all on hold.

"He told you to tell me this, didn't he?"

"Yes," Pembroke confirmed.

Pieces began to fall into place. Things his uncle had done and said began making more sense.

"He's in charge of it, isn't he?"

"He is."

"Why now? Why does he want me to know now?"

"He believes it's time for you to know what's really happening in Sidor. Things could go one of two ways now. The king could honor his word, work with the peasants to ease tensions, and bring peace to the kingdom. Or ..."

"Or he could go the other way," William finished.

"Yes. Aldric wants to be prepared for that possibility. We haven't decided on a specific course of action yet, but we need to be ready to protect the people if the worst comes to pass."

William didn't answer right away. Again, he thought it through. Considered. He knew his stepfather and his cousin. Knew what kind of people they were.

"They won't honor it. They might, at first, but this is a holding action. A way to buy time. Serwyn will take being forced to do even this much personally and will want to take it out on anyone he can."

"That is the duke's conclusion as well."

"What can I do?"

"For now, nothing. Focus on your duties here, on making sure our men aren't wasted by the crown's refusal to supply them. The men have come to respect you, and are loyal to you, My Prince. They believe in you. You need to return that loyalty, to be the leader they deserve. We just wanted you to be aware of what is happening, and to know that you're with us."

He still wasn't sure about this. Everything he'd ever been told reinforced that his duty was to the Ancients and the crown, in that order. But everything inside of him said his true duty was to the people. He knew which way he wanted to go, and if he had to choose between his stepfather and his uncle, he knew who he'd follow.

"I'm with you."

To Be Continued ...

About the author

Travis writes science fiction, fantasy, and thriller novels (and the occasional coming-of-age story), with the hope of transporting and enthralling readers. Publishing novels since 2015, Travis's passion is creating worlds and characters that live and breathe, and experiencing the joy of those stories with his readers.

When not writing, Travis enjoys connecting with readers and other writers, managing the popular Complete Marvel Reading Order website, where he works on his other passion for comics and graphic novels, and spending time with his family.

If you have enjoyed this book, please consider taking a moment to rate or review it wherever you found your copy, as it helps new readers find my works and ensures I can continue writing book into the future.

Find out more at:
amazon.com/TravisStarnes/e/B072YBDC3S/

Or visit
https://tstarnes.com

Maps available at

https://tstarnes.com/book-series/imperium/

Signup to get free previews and notifications of upcoming books at

http://tstarnes.com/preview-notification-newsletter/

Other Books

John Taylor Stories

Rebirth
False Signs
The Wrong Girl
Burying the Past
Family Ties
Election Day
Danger Close
Extraction
Designated Target
Border Crossed
Desperate Rendition

Country Roads Series

Playing by Ear
Fanfare
Dissonance
Elegy
From the Top
Center Stage

Imperium Series

Volume 1
The Sword of Jupiter
The Trumpets of Mars
The Sands of Saturn
The Depths of Neptune
The Fires of Vulcan
The Triumph of Venus
Volume 2
The Wings of Mercury
The Plains of Pluto

Shattered Lands Series

In the Shadow of Lions
An Ending of Oaths

False Start Series

Second Down

The Veilguard Saga

Threads of Destiny

Stand Alone

Going Home